Fables Unbound

Brooklyn Bain

Table of Contents

The 100 Year Song..1

Visions of the Sand Serpents..17

The Hanged Man and the King..49

When the Huntsman Killed the Wolf....................................74

Baba Yaga's Daughter 95

Amphibious Totalus 114

The Baku and the Lost Dreams of a Storyteller.................133

The Funnel of the Universe 169

The Rise and Fall of the Monkey King.............................208

The Seven Eyes of Wonder...238

This book is dedicated to my mother, Jane, my father, Jerry, and everyone at Blevins Elementary School. Without you and your constant support, this book wouldn't exist.

Thank you for everything.

-Bain

THE 100 YEAR SONG

Many people have speculated that deep within the snowy mountains of the Himalayas lived the Yeti. A giant, ape-like creature with stone-cold eyes and skin as blue as frostbite. However, not many people know that it was the Yeti that taught the Tibetan people its unique singing voice. The deep and gravelly sound that can be heard within the ancient songs came from the Yeti itself. Their language is the longest and most time-consuming in the world. Depending on who you are talking to, a simple "hello" can take an hour, and if you wish to have an entire conversation, then it might even take a few days. The Yeti's voice can travel over hundreds of miles, and the echoes of the wind carry their voices to endless lengths and depths. Yet, no records or rumors of this forgotten language could surpass the 100-year song.

Long before man had created the sled or domesticated the mighty wolf to run and hunt along with him, the Yeti lived in the deep caves of the Himalayas. Like the tigers in the deepest jungles, the Yetis were solitary creatures. They soon forgot the names of their mothers and fathers, slowly venturing and traversing the mountains and valleys alone until they died in their caves.

As he was sleeping, one Yeti named High-Cliff felt a rumble from the earth. It was so faint, to us, it would have been the equivalent of a fly passing by our ears, but to the Yeti, with its excellent hearing, the earth's grumble caught his attention. High-Cliff paid it no mind and was about to fall asleep. Suddenly, the earth gave a louder and fiercer rumble.

High-Cliff jumped and decided this time to pay attention. He thought that maybe there was someone trapped under the earth that was trying to speak to him and so he responded.

"Hello. Who is he that speaks?" said High-Cliff.

"Hmmmmmm IIIIIIIIIIIIII aaaaaaaaammmmm heeeeeeee," said the voice within the earth. The voice sounded like an avalanche and the swift crash of snow. It sounded like thunder from a distance after a great storm, the crashing of a fierce wave hitting the side of a large cliff face.

High-Cliff's breath stopped, and his eyes grew wide. He had never known that anyone could dwell under the very bowels of the earth and live. All those that were under the earth had died thousands of years before and even they did not wish to speak.

Cautiously, High-Cliff whispered in his dark cave, "w-who are you? Why do you speak?"

The voice yawned and grumbled, "I am the one your grandfathers and their grandfathers have called home for centuries. I am the sleeping giant blanketed in snow. The wind cannot carry me. The waters cannot crush me. I cannot grow, but I can never fall. I am the MOUNTAIN." As the mountain told High-Cliff its name, it shook and howled as if proud of his mightiness.

High-Cliff's massive size became timid and small in the midst of such power. He scrambled on his calloused feet and bowed. His hands shook, and his heart pounded, but still, he bowed his forehead to the cold, wet cavern floor.

"What do you seek, great mountain?"

"I seek to teach you to sing in my voice and to tell all I have experienced. Sing of the tales of your people. Tell of their lives before they perish."

His head jerked, and he growled under his breath, saying, "My people will *never* die."

"You are mistaken, Yeti. Your people will not last for more than 100 years. You must sing my song before they fade."

And so, for days, High-Cliff did not eat, did not sleep, did not dream sweet dreams, but he learned to sing like the avalanche and the rumble of thunder, like the waves of the ocean as it crashes against a cliff face. He continued his training and listened. With every vibration within the mountain, he perfected his voice. Then there was the matter of telling the stories of old. Soon after the Yeti are born they are left to be independent.

The mother teaches them all she knows and prepares them for the most treacherous winters. Their children know how to dig deep into the tunnels. They know how to climb and run up the face of the mountain. They know how to expand their lungs beyond their breaking point and make one gulp of air last for three hours. They know how to create rocks into shapes of sharp teeth and slice the flesh of bison and mammoths. Yet, no Yeti stayed with each other. Sometimes they would forget even their own names. Some become like rock and wither away into the snowstorms. Despite all that High-Cliff knew, he set out to meet his own kind. He began to learn of their stories so that he may sing them on the wind.

It had been many long days since High-Cliff had seen the sun, and as he stepped out of his cave, the sun burned his eyes and prickled his skin. For the first time, he understood the voice of the wind and listened the same way as he listened to the mountain. The wind sounded like the hum of a hummingbird, a ghost's prayer to pass to the other side, and the buzzing of cicadas before the sunset.

"Leave quickly. Your kind are not far from here. Down the mountain, you will find one just like you. Ask him his name; ask him his story," said the wind as it cradled his ear.

Soon, High-Cliff gathered his wits and went down the mountain. Yetis perfected their footing and felt every crag and crevice as they walked. Their feet were calloused and worn but always sensitive to where they were going, even during the most dangerous blizzards. The sun was shining brightly. The snow glistened under the light. Small sparkles glitter and shine like diamonds. High-Cliff slowly walked, slid, and walked again. He then came upon a small ledge and found a small opening no bigger than a rabbit could fit. Gently, he moved his body into a crouching position, being careful not to make any sudden moves so as to not wake the Yeti that was inside. Although Yeti is large and could never fit within small spaces, the smell of a Yeti was unforgettable, and all other Yeti could tell of each other's presence by the musk and the ice that lingered in their fur.

High-Cliff whispered to his brother. "Awake and know my tale. Our world does not have much time, and I must know your story." Any strange request would awaken a Yeti so it was no surprise when two startling blue eyes stared astonished into High Cliff's face.

"Why have you awoken me, stranger? Go back to where your home is and sleep like the rest of us." The Yeti placed a rock over the hole. High-Cliff looked up at his home. The walls of his cave were tempting, but his conviction dragged him to his fate, and thus, he began again. This time, he decided to use the voice that the mountain taught him.

Low and demanding, High-Cliff said, "Awake and know my tale. Our world does not have much time, and *I must know your story.*"

This time, the Yeti took the rock away and peered again at High-Cliff's face. He bared his teeth, snarled and growled. He disappeared from his hole and reappeared, seemingly out of nowhere, right in front of High-Cliff. He slashed his mighty claws, reared his ugly head and howled, but High-Cliff did not move. He thought more and more about the endless sleeping days and nights learning from the mountain. He felt the mountains grip his feet. Eventually, his brother saw High-Cliff's resolve. The Yeti's shoulders slumped, and his eyes grew dull. Eventually, he began to speak.

"My name is Blue-Eyes. I was named after the sky because my mother saw that my eyes and the sky were the same color. She told me that my father was the sun and that he blessed me with a beautiful sight. Before she left, she told me to look for what was beautiful and to remember all that I saw."

"What did you see?" Asked High-Cliff

Blue-Eyes took in a deep breath, slumped down into a seated position, and began his tale:

"One day, many years after my mother had left, I saw the brightest color one could ever see. It wasn't the color of the sky, the sun, the moon, the rock, or the snow. It was the color of blood.

It cried a sharp cry, one that I had never heard. I covered my ears, but the beast's call went past the thick flesh of my hands. Instead of the cold, I felt the heat from its mouth come crashing down upon me. I fled and ran down the mountain. The slithering creature came ever faster. I crawled into a cave. The beast could not follow me, but I saw its face. It had the snout of a goat but teeth like ours. Sharp. But it was much larger than us. Its skin was red, and its body was covered in golden scales. Around its snout, two long tendrils flowed as if in the wind.

'Give me, give me back my eyes! You disgusting wretch! You should not have my eyes!' it screeched. He dug his claws into the mountain. The opening of the cave became larger, and his body was able to slither in. The rest of his body coiled endlessly around and in and out of itself. I looked, and his eyes were gone. Only hollow spaces remained.

"You will never have my eyes. My father, the sun, gave them to me," I roared.

"I will have your ears, your hand, your foot, and your blood as well." in that instant, he lunged at me, and I ran through the winding tunnels of the mountain. I dug frantically, but his long, winding body uncoiled and followed me wherever I went. I threw huge rocks at him, but they fell away like dust. I scratched, bit, and gnawed his miserable face, but his skin was too thick. Eventually, we both fell into the depths of the mountain, into a vast cavern filled with water. As I sank deeper into the water, I noticed the beast struggled to breathe, and the vibrancy of his scales began to fade. I grabbed a large rock and shoved it down the beast's throat. It choked on the rock and eventually died. Blind and snuffed out like the light of a dying star."

"When I finally was able to leave the cavern, I saw the sun setting. It was the color red. Then I knew I had killed the true offspring of the sun and had stolen his eyes."

High-Cliff was silent. He lowered his head and breathed deep through his nostrils. He then lifted his dark eyes to match the bright eyes before him. Blue-Eyes was covered in deep scars and had lost the first finger on his right hand.

"I believe that the sun chose you to hold onto those blue eyes. Even so, the beast was beautiful."

Blue-Eyes pondered on this thought, "Yes, it was beautiful. Even unto death."

High-Cliff left, and Blue-Eyes went back into his cave. However, he never covered up his rabbit hole again.

• • •

High-Cliff continued his search, looking into every nook and cranny he could find. Eventually, he decided to venture deeper into the mountain in hopes that there would be more of his kind sleeping. He found an entrance and began the long walk down, down, down into the mountain. As he walked, the mountain whispered to him, helping him know which way to turn. Eventually, he came upon something he had never seen before. Giant crystals that jutted out of the ground and grew out of the ceiling. They shined in hundreds of arrays of colors. Even in darkness, they emanated a glow that was enticing.

Tempted, he began to peer deeply into the recesses of the crystal. Suddenly, the earth shook violently. High-Cliff lost his balance and fell at the feet of another Yeti, lost in the light of the crystal. High-Cliff shook his head, coming back to his senses, and said, "Awake and know my tale. Our world does not have much time, and I must know your story."

Slowly, the figure turned its head toward High-Cliff. The figure was gaunt, his fingers elongated. All of his fur had left his body except for a strip of white fur that went along his spine. The face of the figure had elongated, and its mouth was constantly agape. There were no teeth. Not the strong, meat-tearing teeth of the Yeti. His mouth was almost like a vacant abyss. Never consuming, but all-encompassing. Where its eyes were, only two small sparks of light were left.

High-Cliff's hands shook. He crawled away from the figure, growling and hissing. He was not defending himself like prey from a predator but was cursing and wishing for the figure to vanish from the face of the earth.

The figure began to speak, but his mouth never moved, "Why have you come here? What do you want with me? All I am is what the gem has told me."

It took every bit of ferocity and strength within High-Cliff to stay where he was and to continue his quest. The figure's entire body shook as it gasped for air. Its ribs had sunken, and his skin was sagging from his bones. "I say again: Awake and know my tale. Our world does not have much time, and I must know your story."

Finally, he spoke, "My name is Gem-Finder. Like you, I also dwelled in the open air. Sleeping and wandering as Yeti do. But then I found the crystal. I forgot the taste of flesh; I forgot the taste of the snow and the biting cold. I forgot everything."

"Why are you here?" asked High-Cliff, shivering for the first time in his life.

The figure moved closer, leaning its body and then freezing in that exact position, "when I was young, I used to like to dig deep into the mountain. I was endowed with the gift of being able to find shiny stones. I could feel it as if it called to me. I have found gems of every color. Blue, red, green, purple, white. I have found gems that were brighter than the sun and harder than bone."

"One day as I was roaming the mountains and valleys, when I found the gaping mouth of the mountain itself. I made a torch of fire and slowly made my way into the tunnels. Suddenly, while in the depths of a canyon, I saw a blinding flash of blue and white. A fabulous array of sparkling rocks appeared before me, and I was in awe. I never knew that something like this could live within the cold, black mountain. My friend, this is the heart and the secret of the mountain. My secret that I kept safe. The heart of the mountain would be protected and loved by I and I alone. I discovered more within the mountain the deeper I dug. I forgot that air and the wind. I did not need them." He stroked the crystal with the back of his hand- as if it were his great love.

"My greatest treasure I did not find, but it found me," his head painfully turned back toward the stone. "I have found nothing that could surpass her. The Seeing One. I have knowledge of the mountain- knowledge that none could dare imagine." His body bent over in aches and pains. He grabbed his stomach, and blood spurted from his mouth. He gasped and coughed. His entire being was scrapped for life- his ribs expanded as his lungs took in the air slowly. He was no longer strong. He could no longer beat his chest and scream to the moon. His teeth withered. Any beast desperate enough could eat him. But his mind was forever connected to the Crystal.

"I will tell you my secret, young one." Gem-Finder's voice sounded like a low growl. It echoed and vibrated against the crystal which seemed to sing a melodious song. High-Cliff could hear it. It was sweet and gentle. Nothing that he had heard before. Not like the deep earth or the hissing wind. It was a flow of energy, lulling.

High-Cliff saw the figure again. The music of the crystal turned stale… and evil.

Gem-finder started again, "I will tell you a secret: what I saw within the crystal. I saw a race of beasts rise like a falcon in the wind. The fire burned, and trees collapsed under their might. Blood, rivers of blood, stood in their wake. One man stood above them all, and the Yeti feared them beyond measure. The Yeti will die! Yes! They will be no more! Our lives are as meaningless as ash and dust!" His voice turned into a high screech of laughter. Tears poured down his face.

"They will come with spears; they will come with axes. They will come with fire and ride faster than the wind. They will clasp our severed heads in their hands and scream like eagles. One will lead them. Their leader will slaughter the Yetis, take our pelts and our voices, and run the world in the palm of his hand. Those deep within the mountains, stirred by the smell of the blood of our brothers, sisters, fathers, and mothers, will be killed.

"I see this leader. Black eyes- wearing the hides and skins of other animals. Our strength will fall to his bloodline, and his children will spread like the snow on the mountain. Upon his stead, he rides towards us. On the mountain, we will roar and pound our chests. We will sharpen rocks. With our bare hands, we will tear their limbs from their bodies. But even with all of that. Even with our strength, we are no match for their intelligence. I saw him! Heard him! I could feel his breath as he raged and slashed through our bones with a single swipe. He ran towards us with his army.

Many fell by our hands, but our numbers, though mighty, were nothing compared to his kingdom. His men were crushed underneath our hands. He were smeared in blood, and the heat from our kill melted the ice. However, with so many all around us it was not long until we were consumed by them.

"I saw you. You… *were singing*. The deep rumble in your throat rang out into the battle. You spoke of things of old… They will die. WE will die soon." His voice trailed off.

High-Cliff starred in fear and wonder, wanting Gem-Finder to continue but begging the mountain to consume the creature into its deep bowls. Gem-Finder looked at High-Cliff. His eyes were full of life. Strength had come into his muscles; breath filled his lungs as he breathed deeply. The same deep breath the Yeti took when they traveled to the highest points of the mountain. His arms quivered, and he began to crawl.

"You must know this. In my soul, I can sense you have heard of this. Someone has told you of what is to come. Stay here. Stay with me.

Please. Stay here and pray with me to the crystal. Let us see the cosmos. The moon, the sun, the earth, the stars. Jupiter, Saturn. Let us escape within the worlds beyond us and not see death ever again!"

Gem-finder dragged his body toward High-Cliff. His legs had shrunken into lifeless twigs. His calves and feet shriveled into his body. His long arms stretched out and latched onto the mountain floor, and his eyes peered hungrily at High-Cliff. High-Cliff slowly backed away. He did not show his fear. He would never show his fear to a creature who could not kill him. But what scared him most was what was killing Gem-finder. What had killed him a long time ago?

"Come with me. Let me share this existence with one soul. Let me share with you the wonders of what I have seen. The new beast and his army will kill us! THEY WILL TORTURE US! COME WITH ME AND NEVER DIE!"

In a leap, Gem-finder had somehow latched onto High-cliff's body, trying to gnaw and bite him. High-Cliff grabbed Gem-finder's throat and attempted to throw him across the room when High-Cliff saw Gem-finder's face. High-Cliff had the poor creature's throat in his hand. His claws barely scratched High-Cliff's skin, but black blood poured out from his mouth. Gem-Finder's hands were scratching and pulling at High-Cliff. He was pleading. He did not want to die. Gem-finder looked longingly at the crystal. The one he called "she."

High-Cliff spoke in a low voice, "This… this is poison. You are a coward for drinking it." High-cliff let Gem-finder go. Gem-finder scampered over to his crystal. Once he settled into its light, it was as if High-Cliff were never there and their conversation never happened.

"Mountain that speaks to me. Hear *my* call. Take this life into your own hands. Let him fade into dust and snow."

• • •

High-Cliff found his way back into the mountain air. He breathed deeply. The moon was high in the sky.

"Mountain. Did you create the crystals?" said High-Cliff.

The rumble was low… solemn, "Yes."

"Is what Gem-Finder said correct? We will die by the hands of this new creature that shall rise to meet us?"

The mountain was silent. The wind stopped. The air was thick and heavy.

"ANSWER ME. YOU HAVE BROUGHT ME HERE FOR A REASON! ANSWER ME!" High-Cliff roared and smashed his great fists into the ground.

"All these things will come to pass… And more," spoke the mountain.

High-Cliff's brow furrowed. His teeth gnashed together. His fists clenched, and his heart grew hot with hate. He kneeled on the ground, and for the first time in his life, he looked back into his memories. He looked and saw nothing but cold and sleep. His dreams were nothing. Life and death and sun and moon. Nothing. He never thought such things. Never knew such ideas were possible. He was confused and frightened, but he did not stop. He moaned like a sick animal as he tried to comprehend the things running through his mind. They were too much. They were too much to cope with. He wished them to fade away, to never return. He collapsed to the ground.

"The future is too much," High-Cliff finally said, "there is too much to grasp." His voice cracked. The moan and ache swelled within his body.

"Yes," whispered the mountain, "but it is all we have. The past is gone. The future is our solitude and our burden."

After a long pause, High-Cliff whispered, "I will sleep. I will rest and dream."

"Sleep High-Cliff. Son of my caverns. Sleep."

The wind picked up again. This time, it blasted and blared. Whipping the snow and carrying it on its back. The clouds covered the sun, and a blizzard raged. But High-Cliff slept and wept for the very first time.

• • •

High-Cliff was buried under feet of snow, but to him, this was his blanket and his peace. He opened his eyes. The snow fell from his back like water as he shook his body to get rid of any frost or ice. He stretched and looked ahead. The entire mountain was consumed in its own white blanket. The previous Yeti he had talked to still screamed and plagued his mind.

"The Yeti do not consume or waste. We do not rage or burn. We are the sleepers. Sons and daughters of the mountain. We walk and climb. Dig and dream. We do not know… regret." The word bloomed like a flower in his mind's eye. Its thorns were sharp, and its stench was pungent.

High on the wind came a mourning voice. Deep and slow. The air swirled it around like small snowflakes and draped it around High-Cliff's ears. He listened closely and closed his eyes. To humans, it would sound very much like a deep horn or a growl that came from the deep parts of the stomach. The voice, however, was female.

High-Cliff raced up the mountain, bounding from ledges and digging his claws into the stone. Once he finally reached the voice, he stopped and breathed hard. Looking around, he saw a figure crouching in the snow, looking down at something. The same fear of Gem-Finder came upon him. He came forward cautiously. As he got closer, the figure became more apparent. It was a female who was leaning over her dead child, stroking the little one's head as it lay in the snow. She was still prodding its body and weeping. She then raised her head and howled a clear, deep howl. Her face was drenched in tears.

Instead of addressing this female in the way he had with his other encounters, he gently said, "Oh weeping one, why do you cry?"

In a bound, the female had pushed High-Cliff to the ground and started to bite and rip at his skin. She sunk her teeth into his left shoulder and held on to him as he writhed, growled, and hissed in pain. He attempted to get up, but she was too strong. High-Cliff put his right hand into her mouth and grabbed the nape of her neck with his left hand. He opened her jaw, and she was flown across the cliffside. His head dangled over the edge. Both of them were stunned. Neither one moved for a very long time. Finally, High-Cliff, holding onto his left shoulder, gently came forward and dragged the female away from the edge. She looked up at him with pain and hatred. He looked at her with pity- another emotion that blossomed and took root.

"Do you have a name?" High-Cliff was still calming his senses as he spoke.

"What do you want to be called?"

"Want?"

"Yes, what do you want to be called?"

She was perplexed. She did not know how to react and was more stunned than when she was thrown back from her attack. *'Want,'* she thought, *'want.'* For all of her life, she never thought of what that meant to her. If she "wanted" something it was more of an instinct and not a thought. Looking back she remembered a word she heard, something her mother taught her before she was to roam the mountains alone.

"Star. I want to be called Star."

"Then you shall be Star," proclaimed High-Cliff. After he said that, he sat down. The body of the baby lay between them. Star grabbed at her child and nestled it into her arms. Its head was bleeding.

"What happened?" asked High-Cliff.

Star swallowed and closed her eyes. She clenched her fists and held back tears.

"I was walking along with my child when the blizzard came crashing upon us. It was so wild and thick that I could not find the entrance to our cave. My baby clung to my back as I dug my way into the mountain. The wind then picked him up from me. He was not strong enough. He flew into the air. I grabbed after him, and when I could not see him. I ran into the blizzard, calling his name. I searched and searched and searched. My voice could not bear to call his name any longer. I believed that maybe he was carried away by the wind to be protected. So I waited until the blizzard was over. When the sun rose, I searched again, pushing the heavy blankets from cliffs and edges until I found my baby."

"When I did find him, he was gone."

She stopped. High-Cliff stared at her and then looked at the small baby in her arms. Its eyes were blank. High-Cliff wondered to himself, *'The mountain enslaves us, and the wind snatches our children. Why do they do this? Why?!'*

High-Cliff looked back at Star. He felt a twinge in his chest, and tears were in his eyes. He gently came toward her. He took her hand away from his wound and placed his handprint into the snow. The blood made a startling contrast in the midst of the white. Star nodded. She knew what his actions meant.

"What is your name?" she asked.

"I am High-Cliff."

"Would you climb down the mountain with me? I wish to let my child go."

So together, they tentatively went down the mountain and into the valley below. Into a clearing, they dug into the icy earth and buried the child. Both sat beside the grave, saying nothing.

• • •

Star and High-Cliff departed. He did not know what she would do next. He worried for her and asked if she could join him on his quest.

She did not want to leave her home. So she buried herself into her cave and began dreaming of her child.

The world was watching and waiting for him. He began to climb again. Only this time, it would be at the top of the mountain. The very peak where the world could watch and listen.

"I speak to the wind. Why did you carry Star's child? Was his life so worthless that you saw to take him from her?"

The wind rustled. It curled around him cautiously. It whispered, "I travel and flow with the current of this earth. There is no predestination in my life. I do not judge. I do not stand. I am only the wind."

High-Cliff nodded. He was numb to the things he could not understand and let go of the things he could not control.

To the wind, he replied, "*I* will remember him. *I* will be his stand, his judge. He was pure. He will be remembered."

• • •

For ages, he traveled and met his people, gathering hundreds upon hundreds of stories. By the time he had finally reached old age, he had accumulated every story he could find from every Yeti that was willing or alive to be able to tell him their tales. Some of them were found dead as he arrived. Their hide was stripped from them. They were only a mass of flesh on a white mound. However, High-Cliff would still tell their stories, even if he had to make them up.

One day, as the sun rose, after reflecting on the stories he heard, he strode up the mountain once more. Star and her child had long passed away, but he stood in the place where they met and looked towards the east. The sun reached its golden arms towards the snow. The warmth cascaded over High-Cliff and he bathed in the light, the air, the cruel cold. He felt everything all at once. His heart swelled in pain and pride. He was the first Yeti to smile.

There was no time to bask in the day. The future was too close to wait any longer. Sitting in his spot, he bowed his head and closed his eyes. From his throat and stomach came a rumbling that shook the small pebbles balancing on the cliff edge. He opened his mouth, and the first deep and resonant note poured out. Birds from trees far, far below the mountain rose with the note. The first story fell from his heart. Then another and another. As night fell, the first story had ended. High-Cliff once again bowed his head and closed his eyes. When the next sun rose, he would sing the next story and would continue this way until the one-hundredth year passed without a trace.

VISIONS
OF THE SAND SERPENTS

The sands of the Sahara swirl and dance as the wind travels in the heat, and the illusive Alirami, the Sand Serpent, travels below. Taller than the mountains and large enough to block the sun, the Sand Serpent rules beneath the Sahara. Or they once did.

The Alirami were aloof, solitary, and intelligent. Some say that the Sand Serpent opened the minds of humanity to speak and think; unlocking a small piece that was not considered. They speak in visions and dreams, coaxing all within the desert in order to fit their own needs. Without words, they can conjure entire cities in the mind's eye of their victims. Sometimes, the Alirami would make their victim forget their own name as they meandered the desert until they starved.

No one ever worshiped or loved the Alirami. They were too scornful to be gods, more like demons in the flesh. To say the Alirami were mischievous would be an understatement- sadistic is a more fitting term for their schemes. Yet, even then, some say they enacted the justice many were not brave enough to enforce.

Ironically, the Serpents (also called the Alirami) are the biggest source of food and shelter. Without the aid of science to explain, wherever an Alirami died, an eternal oasis would appear. Water that never evaporated appeared crystal clear. Fruit trees produce new kinds of fruit every year. No two would ever be alike. The humans during these times were overjoyed and content, thus establishing their camp near the oasis. As families grew bigger, tribes began. The Alirami observed small skirmishes being fought and won. The humans eventually appointed a sultan as ruler and established a sense of order for humanity. But the Alirami still watched and waited, waiting for humanity to kill each other.

However, this story is not about the history of the Alirami or their eventual death at the hands of a witch on her deathbed, but about a humble man.

• • •

Mohamed was part of a small community of tribal people who lived on the furthest outskirts of the Sultan's kingdom. He was a craftsman and would often travel for many weeks between his tribe and the kingdom. There was no particular thing he created and traded. He was a craftsman in the sense that he could make anything and sometimes with almost nothing. The people of the desert were cunning and resourceful. They wasted nothing and wanted nothing as long as they drank the waters of the oasis. Nobody could find the bottom of the Oasis. No matter how long the rope or how heavy the stone. The trees near the oasis were plentiful. They lived and died in the same place. But Mohamed's aspirations for more grew each time he visited the city.

Al-karam, the city of the great sultan, was an expanse of riches. A feast of delights for every human sense. The eyes are delighted by the vibrant color of the fabrics. Soft silks and satin hung in long sheaths-their sparkling thread cast like starlight as they danced in the dry winds. The smells lured all. From thousands of miles away, people would travel just to taste the unique spices. Their perfume filled the air, and some swear on either their lives, ancestors, or gods that they catch whiffs of the aromas on some special days. Musicians hummed and thrummed. Voices rang out seductive and mournful, telling tales of the past. Some even warned of the Alirami's power. Al-Karam was a gem in a barren land. A welcoming paradise that simultaneously soothed and damned.

Life was a luxury within the Sultan's kingdom, and the Sultan made sure of that. Sultan Elian Mohamed Indala, the lion of the Sahara, was strong, charismatic, and craved sumptuous things. Lust was his bedfellow, and he would partake in his desires for anything and everything with unbreakable zeal. If he wanted a castle for each wife, he would make it so. If he wanted to kill an entire nation, he would make it so. If he wanted the secrets of the universe, he would make it so. No man challenged him, and until his death at the age of three hundred and six, no one *ever* would. As Mohamed saw and tasted and touched and smelled the splendor of the kingdom, his own desires grew. Leaving the kingdom caused a knot to grow in his stomach every time, but he promptly rectified it when he could come back again.

Unlike the beautiful women who bathed their skin in oil and lined their eyes in gold, His wife was nothing like the lovely women of the city. In Mohamed's eyes, she was far from a flower. Her hands were rough, her hair was a wiry black. Her body was round but not covered in fine oils. She was always busy. Cleaning the hut, cooking, mending clothes, tending to her two sons. She would often not sleep as she worried about the tasks she had to do for the next day. She was kind, but she was angry.

Mohamed came back from his latest trip, the knot twisting in his stomach, and he could not eat the food Balim had prepared.

"My love, eat! You are skin and bones! I worked all day for this food, so I expect you to enjoy it!" exclaimed Balim.

"How can I when all I can think about is work? I am constantly at work, and you have the nerve to talk to me like that?" Mohamed scowled and played with his food.

"*You work?* I am doing the work of two women for your sake and for our children. You leave and do nothing and come back with nothing."

"I am the only source of money within this family, and you will respect me as such! From now on, learn to cook decent food! Did I not marry you for your words or your cooking?!"

"NO! You married me for my father's goats!" Balim left the hut to do the laundry, and Mohammed, stunned and insulted, marched towards the desert, past the snooping eyes of his neighbors, and sat within the sand. Pouting like a small child.

"Why must whoever created me hate me? They cursed me to this life just to suffer and die."

He tussled the sand and got so angry that he got up and threw his shoe into the distance. The shoe flew and thudded against something solid. The mound of sand shifted slightly in front of him, and lazily, a giant Alirami appeared out from a mass of darkness. Mohammed, not knowing what to do, falls prostrate to the ground and begins praising the snake in every way he can think of. The snake snickers and sneers as it watches Mohammed attempt to save himself from being eaten- or worse.

Mohammed, in his panic, hears a deep laughter within his ears, a rumbling and tumbling deep sound that mocks him. He lifts his head and stares into the emerald eye of the snake. The snake relaxes its body but does not greet Mohammed as a peer but as a toy.

With unmoving lips, the snake speaks, "So, do you wish to revere me as a god? With unmoving lips, the snake speaks, "So, do you wish to revere me as a god? You are unique compared to the rest of your kind." Mohammed hesitantly nods his head, not knowing what else to do, and the laughter begins again, only louder and more vicious.

"I can tell *many* things. My mind is sharper than my teeth and more lethal than my venom. I am higher than the clouds but still silent. You must tell me why you are here- human. So far away from home!"

Mohammed could smell the acidic breath of the snake. Tiny scars cover its face, and many scales gently reveal raw bits of flesh. Mohammed, in this moment attempted to grab at a hundred and one reasons other than the truth why he was in the desert. Anything except that he was furious with his wife and threw his shoe into the sand.

Looking into the eye of the snake, he decided to speak at least a half-truth, "I am… I was just… coming home from a journey. I do not need to be here!" Mohammed attempts to run away, but the snake slithers and circles Mohammed until the only thing Mohammed can see is a wall of golden scales. The snake's head towers over Mohammed with two emerald eyes peering down in the dark.

"You seek something. Is that not true?"

"Yes… I do… I suppose"

"What do you wish? What is within your heart?"

Thinking now, Mohammed wishes this snake ate him. He remembers the stories he was told by almost every member of his family about the Alirami and their wicked ways. How they can tempt you with the world in the palm of your hand, but truly you are wandering the sands- soulless. However, something within Mohammed believed in this Alirami. Like a moth to a flame, Mohammed gave in to his greed and his lust for life, fully accepting a death that at least he would be happy dying for.

Mohammed's mouth watered as he recounted his deepest secrets. "I wish to be rich. I wish for a house with fine tapestries, silk, and gold. I wish to have servants who will do the work for me. I wish for my wife to not complain but to be beautiful and sensual, my children to be out from under my feet, and for me to be respected by lords and ladies… I need these things. *I weep in these rags!*" Mohammed tears at his clothing and his hair. "I wish to be away from these stupid people with their stupid thoughts! What can you do? I give my life to you."

The snake drank in every word and felt its cooling embrace at the recesses of its mind. They had reached a deal, and now they were ready to carry out the first transaction.

"Give me your oath. If I were to give you these things and reward you with all that your heart desires, you must serve me. You must also fulfill my desires."

"Yes! Yes, I will do this! I will do whatever you wish!"

The snake lowered its head. "When you go back home, you must not tell a soul of this. You must tell no one. Go home, eat, and make love to your wife. But, when the moon rises directly over the desert, bring your camel to me."

Mohammed did as the snake had told him to, and later that night, when the moon shone directly over the sand, he awoke his camel and dragged it to the middle of the desert, directly under the moon. The earth was completely still. There was no wind. No noise. The sand sparkled. It was serene. In the distance, dunes began to shift and rustle. The movement waxed and waned, bobbed and weaved wildly until finally, the Alirami shot its head out of the sand, extending its long body, and came crashing down upon the camel.

In an instant, mouth wide and hungry, the snake swallowed the camel and sunk back into the sand. The crash and wave of the Alirami shook Mohammed to the core, flinging him back. His head ached, and his body shivered from the fear. Mohammed leaped back onto his feet. There was nothing… Absolutely nothing. He wondered if any of it was real. Suddenly, the snake reared its head from the sand. Mohammed cautiously walked toward the Alirami, "Tomorrow, you must go to the capital. I will provide you with a new stead. Tell no one."

The snake sunk back into the sand, and the desert was still once again.

The next day, Balim almost killed Mohammed for not tying his camel properly, and it somehow got eaten by an Alirami. Mohammed felt somewhat validated that his story was partly true, but Balim's wrath became unhinged. He scurried out of the hut, his two sons staring at him as Mohammed walked away with his tail between his legs.

Slowly moving out from the oasis and deeper into the desert, Mohammed takes his knapsack of tools and walks, hoping the Alirami keeps his word. In the distance, a white flash heads towards him. At first, Mohammed believed it was the snake coming to eat him again, but as the flash moved toward him, he noticed a pure white horse. Strong and tall, racing toward him. The bridle had intricate embroidery; the stead's mane shone like silver in the sun, and the strength of the beast was unlike anything that Mohammed had ever seen.

As it caught up to him, it stood at attention like a soldier waiting for orders. Mohammed paced around and inspected every glorious detail, marveling and drooling at the richness of it all. He jumped onto the horse, clicked his heels and the stead let out a great neigh, leaning on his hind legs, and darted faster than the wind toward the capital. Mohammed saw the sand lifting off of the stead's hooves. He could feel the wind as the stead glided across sand dunes with ease. Mohammed let out a wild yelp of exultation and glee! Nothing could compare with this!

The glowing metropolis, Al-Kareem, rose like the sun in the east. The glowing domes and spires were heavenly to his eyes. Many other merchants on their camels were trudging through the sand. Some were struggling to make their camels move as the beasts decided that rest was more important than selling fake medicines and potions. As Mohammed's horse (which he named Farrah) raced past them, the sand foamed up into clouds, and every merchant cursed and coughed, shaking their fists and spitting at the ground in pure jealousy.

As Farrah came to the gates of the capital, it slowed and happily trotted past the guards and into the bustling city streets. Thousands of people were pushing past one another as they were buying from *every* vendor. Mothers dragged their crying children to examine fruits and vegetables that would spoil by the end of the week. A group of men were arguing over the age of a donkey and whether it could still carry heavy loads for days at a time. A woman was selling fine satins and linens, boasting that her fabrics could make *any* woman married within a week just by her handiwork. Two older men were treating Alirami skin, which had been soaked in chemicals, causing their hands to be bleached white. The stout, feverish man sold his spices with an excited grin, flying back and forth to weigh and sell his wares, which were piled high in small baskets.

Mohammed never felt more alive and more frightened in his entire life. The vigor and the energy of the place set fire to his senses. It overwhelmed and confused him so much that sometimes he would forget the experience entirely. At home, during menial chores, he would remember riotous glimpses, sometimes laughing to himself how lucky he was to be part of a parade of life for such a short amount of time every day.

He found a vacant spot and decided that he would set up his shop there. He got off his horse, guided it by the reins, and left the horse near a stable close to his post. He laid down a small woven mat, laid out his tools and called out to the passing crowds, "I am a mender of everything! Come and let me sew patches back to your clothes, repair your shoes, shine your armor. My vast knowledge is at your command!." Variations of this same call chimed through the crowd, competing with the rest of the vendors that were also calling and advertising their various delights.

Four tall and strong men carrying a large palanquin, veiled by a green sheer curtain, strode through the market. Inside, a squat man, amply dressed, fanned himself. From the green haze of the curtain, the man looked out and spotted Mohammed in his humble spot, which intrigued him. Calling out to Mohammed, the man said, "Why don't you have a proper stand like everyone else? You stick out like a sore thumb!"

Mohammed looked up at the man and said his trademark call, "I am a mender of everything! Come and let me sew patches back to your clothes, repair your shoes, shine your armor. My vast knowledge is at your command!" However, this time, Mohammed was more enthusiastic and irreverent, giving a slight bow.

The man looked at Mohammed from his palanquin and said, "Come! I have a job for you." And the palanquin moved towards the heart of the city, closer to the home of the Sultan himself. Mohammed couldn't breathe but forced himself to pack all of his things and retrieve his horse. Quickly, he followed the palanquin on Farrah, gaining confused stares from vendors and customers alike.

Inside the house of the rich man, there were soft cushions and incense. Rich ruby-red curtains and tapestries made the room daunting but sensual. From the ceiling, there hung several intricate chandeliers, varying in shape and size. Flickering lights danced, painting colors across the room. In a corner, a group of musicians were playing a lullaby as a gorgeous woman lounged among the cushions and sheets, sleeping peacefully. The woman Mohammed saw was the most beautiful he had ever seen. Her skin was a deep caramel color, covered in fine lotions and oils that made her shine. Her lips were crimson, and her face had a rosy hew. Her hair was raven black and silky. She was sweetly dreaming of the melody of the minstrels.

The rich man motioned Mohammed towards a corridor away from the red room and led Mohammed up a flight of stairs. Both he and the rich man were practically nose to nose as they stopped in front of a small wooden door.

"If you are as able as you say you are, then I wish for all of this to be taken care of by tomorrow morning." The man opened the door. Mohammed peered into the room and found piles upon piles of shoes, discarded for various reasons, filling the room to the brim. Every color and type imaginable toppled onto the floor as the door opened. The rich man shoved them back in or threw them towards the back of the room in frustration.

"These are all mine. I have sensitive feet and a particular size no one can replicate. They break, or I grow tired of them. I had no other choice but to place them here."

Mohammed's jaw dropped, and his knees shook. He scanned the room from left to right. The toes of some shoes were emerald green with a curly tip. Among them were slippers with jewels that were yellow. There were pink, dainty slippers that were lined with silver silk on the inside. Some shoes were riding boots with ornate spurs that rusted (mainly for ceremonial purposes rather than actual riding). The copious variety shocked Mohammed. He was confused about how a man should concern himself with shoes if he relies on others to carry him around.

"I will pay you handsomely if you fix these shoes. If you cannot fix them properly, then I will make sure that you never step foot in the capital ever again. And I will also confiscate your handsome stead. Do you understand?" the man glared at Mohammed. His eyes were heavy with bags, and the jowls on his face sagged like an old dog's.

Mohammed nodded and forced a smile, "I will not fail you, my liege." And bowed deeply to where his nose touched the ground.

"Yes, yes, very good. We will provide you with candles for light and a small amount of food. Do not forget what I said."

The rich man waddled down the stairs. Mohammed kept watching the man, hoping that he would fall, simply to see what would happen. Looking back, he stepped into the dimly lit room, surrounded by shoes.

• • •

Hours passed, and three candles had already melted into puddles of wax on the floor. Mohammed's hands were getting numb, but he worked vigorously and did not stop until he fixed every shoe he could grab. The pile of fixed shoes, however, could not match the ones that were discarded or broken. At last, Mohammed glanced up from his work and surveyed the room. His heart sank as he saw the multitude of shoes. He threw down his tools and stomped on the shoes until they were dirty and squashed. He kicked the wall and bruised his toe. He plopped back onto his spot, holding his foot and regretting his rage.

From the corner of his eye, Mohammed saw something move. Mohammed noticed a shiny, golden object wriggling out of a small crack in the floor. Mohammed took the candle, not minding the burning wax dripping onto his hand, and moved closer. A smooth lump was breaking apart the concrete between the bricks. Mohammed poked the thing and up popped a shiny golden hand. It was not a human hand (although it had five fingers), and its arm was thin as a reed. The hand was holding a pair of tools identical to Mohammed's. Another one right beside it popped up and blossomed like a flower with needle and thread.

Mohammed backed away from the hands, wide-eyed. He believed that because of his lack of rest, his mind was playing tricks on him. However, from right under him, he could feel even more hands wanting to break free. He rushed to a pile for safety, and another pair of hands with the same tools sprang loose from their confines. Mohammed raised the candle above his head, ready to throw it down to burn himself inside the room if need be. More pairs of hands with spindly arms popped up all over the room. Shoes toppled over in piles, some emerging from the walls and the ceiling. The entire room was a garden of whatever freakish creature had emerged.

Each hand was ready with its tools. The first hands emerged, sat, and quickly grabbed a pair of shoes. Like Lightning, it worked on the shoes and tossed them aside. Mohammed picked up the first discarded pair and examined it. The shoes appeared undamaged. He scratched his head and sat down, placing the candle to his right. The hands were methodical and mechanical, like a well-oiled machine. At some points, some pairs of hands would fight over a pair of shoes until Mohammed would introduce a new pair to settle the horrible squabble.

"This must be some kind of twisted joke from hell or the gods," he laughed nervously and observed as, within half an hour, all of the shoes were neatly stacked and perfectly repaired. The hands, utensils in their grasp, slumped back into the brick and mortar, never to be seen again. Mohammed fainted.

• • •

The next morning, the beautiful lady that Mohammed first saw opened the door to the room of shoes. Mohammed lay sprawled out on the floor, snoring like a lion. The lady looked, and as the sun shined, it illuminated. She felt amazed! Every shoe was fixed. She had seen nothing like this happen in her life, and she had been a consort of the Sultan's court for quite some time. The lady walked over to Mohammed and leaned down closer to wake him. She tousled his shoulder, and gradually, Mohammed rose from his slumber. The last tethers of a strange dream were slipping away from him now. He looked into the beautiful face of the woman as she congratulated him on his stunning feat.

"Well done, humble cobbler. Few have been able to achieve as much as you have for my lord. You surely will be greatly rewarded." Her voice cooed and purred like a cat playing with a mouse, but there was no hostility.

"You are mistaken, my lady…" he stopped and looked at the array before him. *'Then it wasn't a dream. What a horrible sight, but… what luck!'* he thought.

He got up to his feet and faced the lady, "Tell your Lord that the work is done. I now seek compensation." He stormed out of the room and dashed down the stairs, leaving the Lady amused with the whole affair.

The lord was relaxing upon his sheets and cushions, smoking from a hookah pipe. The contraption, which was larger than him and inlaid with mother of pearl, caught the lord's attention.

"So!" said the rich man, looking lazily at Mohammed, "you tell me you have failed?"

"No, my lord," the lady spoke behind Mohammed before he could open his mouth, "he surprised us all with a victory." In her hand was the pair of emerald shoes that curled at the toe. She gave it to her Lord, and he examined it with scrutiny. He sighed and slipped the shoe on. He moved his foot and wiggled his toes. To his surprise, it was a perfect fit.

He scowled at Mohammed and barked, "Did you receive ANY help for this task, wretch?!"

"No, sire. I did all that you asked alone," Mohammed bowed.

The Lord looked at his lady, who nodded in approval and back at the suppliant Mohammed. The lord never enjoyed sniveling commoners, but to his astonishment, he took a liking to this man.

"I will offer this deal. You will not need to travel or leave the capital ever again. If you have a family, you can bring them as well. But, you must be my head cobbler for the rest of your days. What do you say to this offer?"

"I accept wholeheartedly. Merciful Lord," Mohammed held back his excitement with all of his strength. It was bubbling at the top and boiling over within him. The sweat dripped onto the rich carpet as he was still bowing.

"Yes, well. A deal's a deal. Make whatever preparations you need to and come straight here. You will be my head cobbler, and that is all." The rich man sucked in a long drag of pink smoke that filled the room and sunk deeper into his cushions.

Mohammed mounted his horse and raced back to his home. He told Balim the news and, for the first time, he kissed and hugged his rowdy children. Balim cried with joy and danced around the hut. She grabbed both of her sons and pored over words of affection. All of them left immediately, leaving the hut to Balim's family and trekking the long journey to the capital.

• • •

After arriving at the Lord's house, Mohammed and his family were established with rooms and jobs. Balim would become the official cook, preparing meals for the entire household. Mohammed would be the cobbler. The lady, later identified as Alani, mainly took care of the children while also helping their father with his work. Lady Alani bought toys and clothes for the children, and instead of helping their father, they would run around the house playing with swords and dreaming of becoming great conquerors.

The Lord was away most of the time, working within the inner sanctums of the palace, so the lady Alani was head of the home. Balim consumed herself with her work as the captain of the kitchen. The servants respected her abilities and her strength but feared her temper. She could not tend to her children like she wanted and often would call the servants who helped her by her sons' names.

Mohammed, however, could hardly keep his mind on his work. He dreamed of the lady Alani. He secretly coveted his insidious visions of lust for himself as he worked in the small room up the stairs. Often, he would be in such a state that he would cut his finger or tear a thread, and so the entire process had to begin again. The lord of the house loved shoes. They were his favorite element of fashion, but he never wore the same pair twice and always destroyed each. It was easy for Mohammed to have work.

One day the lady Alani took the boys out into the market on a fabulous palanquin. Balim was so sick with not being able to be with her children that, for the first time in months, she could not manage the kitchen. She lay in her comfortable bed with all its amenities. Smelling the sweet scent of flowers but ignoring it all. Eventually, she went to confide in her husband.

Mohammed heard a knock at the door of the room and hoped beyond hope it would be the lady, but in fact, it was simply his wife. He pretended not to be disappointed and opened the door for her, "Come in, my love. How are you feeling?"

"I am in agony most days, my husband," she stifled her tears and continued, "I miss my children. You are the closest to the Lord. Would you be willing to have him give me days to be with my children as well as discover the city?"

Mohammed did not care for her words or for the request and brushed her off, saying, "Yes, of course, of course," and went back to his work.

Balim looked at Mohammed for a while. She saw something in him she hadn't seen for a very long time. She remembered when she was younger and softer, how she used to sing sweet songs by the oasis and look deeply within the waters. She played with her sisters as they prepared the fruit and the rinds for teas and tarts. She met Mohammed when she was 17. He was tall and relatively handsome, but most of all, he was kind. She believed, maybe he would be someone to confide in. She knew now that she was wrong and had been for a long time.

Balim closed the door and knew that she would have to ask the lord herself.

Balim served yet another exquisite meal. Roasted meats, sweet flowery pastries, spicy foods that lined the middle of the table and an entire stuffed bird that Balim had never seen before. She personally witnessed the array of foods being escorted from the kitchen. She took a tray of tarts covered in petals for garnish to the lord and sat it down gently in front of him. Balim instructed the servants to ensure the entire kitchen was clean after the meal and granted them permission to have all the leftovers. She would not eat as much as they did when all the work was done. The same thing she would do for her sons.

Balim excused herself and entered the red room of the lord. Again, he was lounging and smoking his hookah pipe, staring into the chandeliers as they hypnotized him. She bowed low and spoke, "My lord, I request an audience with you."

He looked at her as if she had appeared from a dream, "what do you want, woman? Speak clearly," he barked.

She looked up at him now, a glint of fire in her eyes as she was prepared to fight for her family. "My family and I have been loyal to you for a long time now. Yes, we are not like the servants who came before us, but we all have worked hard for your house. I ask you if I may have one day to be with my sons. I am grateful to the gods and the lady Alani that my sons have not faced abandonment or forced labor, but as their mother, I long to be with them. Please, I beg for this request," and again she bowed, this time not as low.

He choked on the smoke he initiated. He coughed until his eyes bulged, and a servant had to be called to give him a drink. Finally, he straightened himself (or tried to) in the voluminous cushions. He knew of her existence in his house, but until she placed the plate in front of him, he never truly remembered her. According to her request, he was not overly concerned with a fresh meal every day, and sometimes he did not eat. So, in a casual manner, he responded, "Yes, my dear lady, you will have your day. I give you each day at the end of the week as a day to rest from your troubles and to be with your children.

In the corner of the room, a small door cracked ever so slightly. Two small pairs of eyes poked through the door and watched as Balim was speaking to the lord. The boys saw their mother for the first time in months. The servants often prevented them from entering the kitchen, or they were too small to navigate through the hustle and bustle. While they liked Alani, they yearned for the rowdy embrace of their mother and how she smothered them when they hurt. They missed her stories and the smell of her humble cooking at home. They watched breathlessly, not able to hear but waiting for the chance to see her again.

"Thank you, my lord. I cannot tell you how you have healed my heart. I thank you for every opportunity that you have awarded my family and for your kindness. We will always be indebted to you." She bowed and walked backwards away from him. Suddenly, her sons ran after her, tears in their eyes and tumbled her to the ground. At first, she was furious, but upon seeing her sons, she snatched them up in her arms and cradled them tightly. It was a pile of tears and kisses between all of them. The Lord saw the scene and was embarrassed but thought to himself: *am I also in need of sons myself?*

The next day, someone treated Balim and her children to a day out in the capital while the Lord, once again, went to the Sultan's palace. Alani and Mohammed were alone in the house. Alani was bored. She had had many lords who were obsessed with her beauty and would make every effort to drown her in every trinket and bit of entertainment they could muster. After a while, she would grow tired of them and set her sights on another wealthy lord of her choosing. She was already planning to leave her lord and enter again into the game of love, but this time she stayed only because of the new occurrences that invaded her plans. And the new man that came with them. As a young girl, she received schooling in such ways as to prepare her to become a royal consort. She wanted to play a little game with this cobbler as she had done to greater men than he.

Mohammed twirled a small slipper at the end of his finger, procrastinating, fixing the last pair of the day as he daydreamed of Alani. The door opened, and there she was, dressed in jewels that highlighted her hair and eyes. Purple silk caressed her body, hugging her curves. Mohammed got up from his spot, bowed, and, trying not to make his voice crack, he asked, "How can I be of service, my lady?"

She moved closer into the room, "I was wondering what you really do all day. It must be tiring having to fix shoe after shoe for hours on end? Why not come with me, and I can give you ease for a short while." She smiled a welcoming, innocent smile.

She took him by the hand and led him to her quarters. The room was warm with the smell of cinnamon and cloves. The bed was a round basin of pillows and blankets that sank into a deep jasmine shade. The window looking out into the capital framed the castle of the Sultan perfectly. It was like a serene vision of power and pleasure that made Mohammed gasp in awe.

"You know, I was born in the palace," said Alani. She had prepared a sweet drink for Mohammed and small sweets. On the other side of her bed was a small table with cushions on either side. A place where she can entertain guests.

"Really? But of course. It would be the only place fit enough for a woman," Mohammed was still staring at the palace and forgot himself. For a moment, his face was flushed, she apologized to Alani for his comment.

She laughed and motioned him to sit by her. The drink was warm and smooth as it went down his throat. A mixture of chocolate and orange. She watched. Like a spider waiting for a fly to trap itself in her web.

"My dear Mohammed, I must confess something to you," began Alani, "my lord and I have been together for a long time. He has taken care of me and has gifted me with every pleasure one can imagine. I have never wanted for nothing, but I am afraid his heart has grown cold to me." She looked at Mohammed with the slightest bit of tear at the edges of her eyelashes.

Mohammed quickly swallowed, trying not to choke on his food, and responded, "Any man that would grow cold to you would be a shame to our sex. You are a gem, my lady. There is nothing that can compare with your beauty." The drink had loosened his lips and so his desire ran away with his mind.

"Mohammed, you are too kind. I knew I could confide in you." she acted relieved and knew that she had found the edge to push him off of.

• • •

Balim and her children were ecstatic with glee as they walked the streets. Balim ran with her children to every delight that enticed them and even bought a few things that she could call her own. She bought some extra spices for the kitchen and a nice sash to wear on outings. There were acrobats that came to the capital from a far-off country, delighting their audiences with contortionists and those that ate fire and swords. Balim and her children found the acrobats from a far-off country captivating. There was also a man who claimed to be a magician. He invented fireworks that burst into the air in radiant colors and solid water that was cold to the touch.

Balim haggled with more vendors, bought a few more things, gave treats to her sons, and decided that it was time to go back to the lord's house. Coincidentally, the lord was heading back as well since the court proceedings had finished. He spotted them from his palanquin Balim and her children and called for the men carrying him to halt. Balim quickly bowed and motioned for her children to do the same.

Alani was brushing the tangled curls of Mohammed's hair as he lay on her breast. Alani felt surprised by Mohammed's passion and believed that he would be "useful" after all. The lord came to the entrance of his house, opened the beautiful brass door with a large doorknob and started towards Alani's chambers. Mohammed and Alani looked at each other in fear and scurried, grabbing at the clothes on the floor. Mohammed ran back to his cobbler's room, and Alani went downstairs and to the right of the red room to a large bath. She wanted to make sure the smell of Mohammed left her entirely before her lord could detect anything. Yet, her lord suspected nothing. In fact, he did not even enter the bath but relaxed again, thinking deeply of where his riches would fall after he was gone.

Balim entered through the kitchen entrance with her children and began making plans for dinner later that evening. She remembered the joy of the market but suspected the lord. She knew well not to trust men like him so easily and could see in his eyes how he was testing her. It did not matter what he thought of her, but what scared her most was that her husband was not there to protect her.

• • •

The lord, Alani, Balim, and Mohammed endured the same games for months. The lord, Alani, Balim, and Mohammed danced circles around each other, either deliberately ignoring each other or catching glimpses they suspected to only be spirits or visions. One night, as Mohammed and Alani were together again, he thought to himself, *what would I do to have all of this? This woman, this house, these riches.* And his heart sank as he remembered *Alirami.* He slipped out into the night and, with Farrah, headed into the desert. The moon again was full and shined brightly, aiding Mohammed's journey into the sands.

Mohammed found himself completely alone. A familiar silence surrounded him. He got off of his horse. It was cold. There was a chill on Mohammed's skin as he warily walked into the desert. His knees were shaky, and his breath was shallow as he waited for what seemed like hours. Then, without warning, the giant head of the Alirami emerged from the sand and peered down at Mohammed. Its eyes glowed with expectation and malice.

"You have forgotten me, Mohammed," it whispered into Mohammed's mind.

"No! No, my dear master. I have not forgotten you. I have been busy as of late. But I have another request for you."

"Ah, but Mohammed. Even the gods gain praise during good times. Mankind is so willing to forget the things that work for their good. Lying to me is not a wise decision." The giant head of the snake now lowered and snarled at Mohammed, opening its mouth to display its venomous teeth and gaping maw.

"I know, I know," gasped Mohammed. He was kneeling in the sand in supplication to the snake. "I ask, humbly, for your forgiveness, oh great one. I have not been attentive to you." He lowered his head and bowed to the snake. He shivered.

"Come. Come, my human. You must not fear me so deeply. What do you seek? I am here to help, remember?"

Mohammed looked up at the snake. "I wish to inherit my lord's wealth. I wish to have his jewels, his wife, his servants. You can do this?"

A rumble of laughter quaked through the body of the snake. His ears rang, but the sands were silent. The snake spoke, "Of course I can! I am Alirami. My kind can do *many things!* But, in order for this to happen, I must have another sacrifice."

"I give you a gift, Mohammed. To obtain this sacrifice, you must have something to aid you." the Alirami opened its mouth and unfurled its fangs. From one fang came the smallest green drop of liquid. As the drop grew fat and formed into a bulb, it crystallized into a vial. Mohammed reached for the vial and broke it off of the fang.

"Give this to your prey, and then come to me."

The Alirami disappeared, and Mohammed raced back towards the lord's house.

• • •

Balim was sitting in her room with her children. She told them stories of her people's long past as they fought sleep to listen to every word. When sleep came over them, Balim blew out the candle beside their bed and headed to her quarters. Inside was Mohammed, staring out the window at the moon. It had been months since they had seen each other. She was no fool. She knew what he had been doing, and she no longer cared.

"What do you want, husband?" she said.

Mohammed turned around and saw her. She was short, stout, not dressed in fine clothes, but strong. Her hands were rough, she did not smell of flowers, and wrinkles formed around her eyes and mouth. Her eyes were tired.

"I wished to give you something to help you sleep, my dear wife. I bought it while out in the market. It will help you rest easy." He smiled and poured the green liquid into a cup of milk and honey, "I know how much you work. Drink this. You will feel better."

"No, I refuse to take anything you offer." she kept her hand on the door handle.

"My love. You are my wife. You must trust me."

"I do not trust snakes or vermin like you. You suck the life out of everything and leach your way into any ounce of joy. You are a beast that eats the dirt of the ground! Slug!"

She turned to open the door, but Mohammed caught her by her hair and threw her to the ground. She bit him twice. He screamed and reached to scratch out her eyes. She pinned him down, sweating and huffing. Her grip tightened around his arms. He riggled and kicked his feet under her legs. In a great leap, he opened her mouth and shoved the vial down her throat. She writhed and choked. He got off of her, and she moved to her hands and knees. She was gasping for air. She tried to scream, but the liquid had closed her throat, and she was dead.

Mohammed's heart was beating in his ears. He waited for her to move again. He knew that his wife's will was strong, and so was her stomach. After a long pause, he went over to her and turned her over. The veins around her throat were a deep green, and her eyes rolled into the back of her head. She was gone, and he had killed her.

"What have I done? What… What have I done?" he whispered to himself, backing away from his wife's corpse. Then, he remembered his second wish.

Although it took a herculean effort, he carried his wife's corpse out of the house, careful not to make noise as he walked down the stairs. Mohammed covered her in a cloak and placed her on the back of his stead, carefully walking them both back into the desert. Coming upon the same place where he previously visited the Alirami. He stopped. He took her down from the stead and laid her in the sand.

"I have done what you asked. Now fulfill your end of the bargain."

Silence. Nothing. Then the Alirami reared it head. It looked at Mohammed. He was exhausted and numb. His eyes were blank, and his body was pale. He swallowed the terror bubbling inside of him. Alirami looked deeply into Mohammed's heart and saw a change within him. Mohammed's heart twinged with a new strain of malice… or ambition? The Alirami then snatched Balim into his mouth and gobbled her down. It slithered back into the desert and sank into the sands. Mohammed stood there, staring out into the distance. Coldly, he walked to his stead, wiping Balim's name from his mind, vowing never to say her name again.

The next day, at the announcement of Balim's death, the entire household of the lord was in pure astonishment. She was not yet in her fifties, but she died on the spot. Mohammed said he had discovered her in the kitchen, dead at the table. The children were hysterical. Alani tried her best to comfort them. The lord stood from his cushions and was white with disbelief. He was close in age to her. *I could be next*, he said to himself.

Mohammed told the house that he brought her body back to their village and that her family would mourn her there. He also said that he would stay there in the house to provide for his children, at the will of the lord, of course.

"You have made the right decision. Stay. We will honor Balim," said the lord.

• • •

A week from the day of Balim's funeral, the lord died of a heart attack. The fear of his own death struck his heart like an arrow. Slipping deeper into his cushioned grave, he tried to get help, but he died before he could manage a way out. He had no children, and his inheritance, as well as the fate of his entire household, stood on the edge of a knife.

As the house was searched, they discovered the will of the lord. Scrawled out at the bottom of the will, it claimed that Mohammed would inherit the lord's entire wealth, servants, and wife. The royal court would give the children positions as squires to the Sultan, and the cobbler would become Alani's husband. Those who read the will were not surprised. Many things like this have happened. If a lord could not provide an heir, then a servant of high standing would gain the inheritance and would take on the lord's name in order to maintain the lineage. Regardless of social status, reputation was more important than blood. The person who would inherit it would then receive that reputation. The lowest peasants sometimes supplanted sons of lords because of their low reputation and the value of the name of their father.

Mohammed looked from his new window. He watched as the moon swelled high into the sky. His new wife was peacefully sleeping, and his sons were in the halls of the Sultan's castle, learning to be great scholars or warriors. He was proud. Exuberantly proud of his new inheritance! And yet, his new obligations as an advisor to the Sultan were something else entirely. He planned that as soon as he met the Sultan, he would fantasize about his journey as a poor and lower cobbler, humble and contrite, helping his lord day and night as he lay dying. He will inform the Sultan that he witnessed the lord writing on Mohammed's inheritance will and made a solemn promise to safeguard his Lord's reputation.

Mohammed beamed at the idea and laughed. He would become an advisor. He would be a worm within the Sultan's ear.

"Besides," he whispered to himself, "I was raised to be a jack of all trades, no?" As he grew sleepy, he went back into bed and dreamed sickly, sweet dreams.

• • •

The next day, Mohammed set out to his new vocation. His palms were sweaty. He could barely manage himself as Farrah rode through the marketplace. As he went towards the palace gates, he felt his vision grow blurry. Do *not be a coward! You sacrificed life and limb for this. Now go! Be a jack of all trades and do what you must do.*

As he thought more about the lie he would tell the Sultan, the more added on to it and the more he himself began to believe it. He believed he saw the Lord fall to his knees and scream a great cry before he died. He believed that as the Lord fell, Mohammed caught him and cried as he saw the Lord's lifeless body. At that moment, his own wife's soul was taken to heaven as she saw the great Lord perish in her husband's arms. Great spirits comforted her, and she was carried into paradise. The spirits also told Mohammed that, at the gods' orders, his sons be appointed as squires in the Sultan's castle, in order to carry on the memory of their Lord who loved them like they were his own. Mohammed believed that he and the Lord were lost relatives. The Lord fell in love with Mohammed's mother, but since he had obligations in the kingdom, he could not stay. Soon after, she gave birth to Mohammed, who was always destined to serve at the Sultan's side within the castle.

Mohammed finally entered the throne room of the Sultan. It was a grand room. The room was a beautiful dome cast in glass that reflected rainbows of light. There were people juggling, minstrels, soothsayers, storytellers, dancing girls, and the smell of fine food around an enormous table. As Mohammed walked through the myriad of sights and smells, he saw, like a glowing beacon, Sultan Elian Mohamed Indala in the flesh. Mohammed's heart beat out of his chest, and that sense of terror he felt when he made his second sacrifice resurfaced. He was ready to crumble and run back when he heard a deep and commanding voice from across the table call toward him.

"Young Mohammed. My new advisor. Come! Eat! You must be famished after such a long journey." The Sultan had a large black beard dashed with a bit of gray that was just peeking through. He was large, barrel-chested, imposing, with fiery eyes and a fiery appetite. His eyes, in fact, were almost a golden color, and they flashed voraciously. He was taller than the rest of the men surrounding him, all drinking from golden goblets covered in pearls.

Mohammed bowed slightly, took off his slippers and reclined at the table. Instantly, a servant filled his cup with a fragrant, sweet wine, and his plate was full of meats, breads, fruits, and sumptuous eats.

"I am deeply honored to be in the presence of the great Sultan Elian Mohamed Indala. You have given me and my family more than I can say, as we are foreigners to this land." Mohammed sipped from his cup. The liquid was delightful and danced in his mouth.

The Sultan looked at Mohammed carefully. He asked, "Tell me, Mohammed. Where did you come from? I hear you are not your Lord's blood relative but an outsider seeking a job. I believe you were his cobbler?" A light chuckle danced around the room.

Mohammed prepared his story. Like Alani's drink, this one had loosened his lips, and thus, his entire mythology poured out like a dam bursting from its confinement. Mohammed told of his Lord's death, how his wife followed soon after, his grief, his wailing, and the servants wishing to kill themselves after their Lord had perished. He told the Sultan of the spirits coming from heaven and taking the soul of his saintly wife in order to spare her from grief. His sons were devastated by such a ghastly event, but they soon grew into true men. Mohammed told of this with passion and fire. He believed in every word, and the more that he told this lie, the more the truth faded away from him. It was the only thing that could keep him alive, to forget.

The Sultan, unchanging, listened to it all. He watched the beads of sweat trickle down Mohammed's temples. The rest of the men, warriors, scholars, advisors, and rulers of other nations all wept in Mohammed's story.

The Sultan raised his goblet. "To your Lord, your saintly wife, and to your children. May they all find peace and prosperity for now and forever." The rest of the table raised their glasses. Mohammed, breathless, gulped down his drink and gained his strength once more. He felt that his own spirit would be taken into heaven. He put every last ounce of himself into convincing the Sultan of his spiraling lie. More and more of the truth was slipping away as the day continued, and Mohammed learned more of his new life.

The next morning, Mohammed stepped into the Sultan's personal study. Many diplomats and scholars waited on him as he made the decisions for this and decrees for that. He was rapidly reading and signing with his sealed stacks of papers. Mohammed gingerly walks in, bows, and asks, "I am your humble servant. What would you have me do?"

The Sultan looked up from his work and waved away the rest of the diplomats and scholars. They narrowed their eyes at Mohammed and briskly left. Some of them stayed behind and put their ears to the door. The Sultan beacon'd Mohammed to come closer and handed him three pieces of paper.

"What do you think about these men here? What do you think they deserve?" asked the Sultan.

Mohammed could not read. When he lived in the simple desert village, people communicated by drawing pictures on sheets of snakeskin and placing them on palm trees or stabbing them into the sand on tall flagpoles. Mohammed froze and searched in his mind for a valid excuse.

"I beg upon my soul for your forgiveness, your excellence. My people use a unique language to communicate, and my Lord did not teach me this script. You will have to read it to me."

The Sultan responded, "I will tell you then what these papers say. In time, you will learn to read or simply leave. Survival of the fittest is the first rule." The Sultan layed out the papers in front of Mohammed and pointed to each. He wanted to test Mohammed.

Three different men face charges of the same crime: murder. One man killed his master for his cruelty, one man killed another in defense of his wife, and another man killed his business partner for laundering money. Now, how should I punish these men?"

Mohammed thought carefully. Then he asked, "The man who was defending his wife, from whom or what was he defending her from?"

"There was a man who wanted to take advantage of the wife in the middle of the night. The husband came in, found a knife used to separate the snake hide from the meat and stabbed the intruder in the back."

Mohammed asked another question, "The one man who killed his master for his cruelty. What was the master doing that was cruel?"

"The master was punishing a slave who had served the house for most of his life by giving him one hundred lashes from the deadliest whip the master had. The master claimed the slave stole something from the master's chambers. However, there was nothing found among the slave's belongings."

"The last trial. Where did the money go?"

"The business partner was taking money for himself in order to drink and take prostitutes."

Mohammed thought deeply and carefully. Wisdom whispered in his mind. Wisdom that previously had never been before. He was no longer a humble cobbler. His understanding of diplomacy replaced his knowledge of leatherwork.

"The husband who killed the intruder should not be punished." It was self-defense when he killed the rapist. In fact, there needs to be better surveillance wherever the husband and wife live in order for such things to not happen again. The master deserves to lose his privileges for daring to treat a faithful servant with such contempt. Nobody provided evidence of any theft occurring. Honorable family members should receive the master's things, along with the servants and slaves of the house. In the last trial, however, soar the business partner should be, should have ended the partnership with his partner and reported his pattern's false dealings. Then there would have been no need for bloodshed."

The Sultan relaxed, "That is the most honest thing you have said since we have met. It is a dangerous thing to take me for a fool."

Mohammed said nothing

"Normally, I would have your tongue cut, and you would be hanging by the neck. Just to show what lying tongues in my kingdom deserve. Unfortunately, for me, you have chosen the right course for all three of the cases. It is unfortunate because I seldom give second chances. I am not a man to be disappointed twice and I take a risk giving you *any* chances.

"Then let me not disappoint with more dishonesty. The story I told was not true, but this is: my lord gave me his inheritance and has entrusted me to continue it." Mohammed kneeled, and his forehead touched the floor.

The Sultan did not move. Merely listened and watched. This time, the smell of fear was gone, *'Mohammed has balls, after all*, he thought.

"Prove to me your worth. Then I will believe you."

• • •

Many years passed. Mohammed kept his word, and his life was dedicated to learning and perfecting the craft of royal advisory, more specifically, on legal matters. At two hundred and fifty years old, the

Sultan is still strong in stature but does not spend his days in revelry as he once did. Mohammed, lavished in grand clothes and with a long white beard that reaches to his belt, looks upon the court of the Sultan with a calm scrutiny that analyzes each soul. Mohammed's sons were honorable men who served the Sultan. The oldest son is a soldier and war hero. He won dozens of wars for the Sultan and experimented with new strategies in order to subdue the enemy entirely. The youngest son is a scholar who looked towards the heavens, studying the planets and their influences on the earth.

Mohammed had almost forgotten the Alirami. The Alirami never forgot. Unlike men, the Alirami do not mind waiting. In fact, waiting for the right time was an art that the Alirami had perfected.

Mohammed had a dream one night. He dreamed that his oldest son planted a seed of bronze within the earth, and from it grew a sturdy tree with golden fruit. The fruit never ran out, and the people of the kingdom were prosperous. The second son planted a seed of words, and from it grew a tree more beautiful than anything in the world, but there was no fruit. But the roots of the tree grew deep and found water underneath the earth. Mohammed awoke from the dream.

He awoke with a start. Mohammed traveled far into the middle of the desert like he had done before. He hobbled carefully through the empty streets of the kingdom. With a staff and an adorned robe, he walked into the desert. Finally, Mohammed reaches the place of the Alirami. In an old voice, he calls out to the night.

"Alirami, you have given me my heart's greatest desires. I am old. I know my days will soon end. Please, fulfill my last wish before I die."

For a long time, there was nothing. Before Mohammed could leave, the earth stirred underneath him, and slowly, a familiar figure emerged from the sand and loomed over him. Mohammed crashes to the ground and guards himself with his staff. Emerald eyes stare blankly down and patiently wait for Mohammed's response.

"I... I wish you to interpret a dream I have had. Then whatever I choose next, you must fulfill," Mohammed shakily gets up to his feet. He leans upon his staff and takes in gulping breaths.

"Tell me your dream, human." The Alirami sneered.

"I dreamt that my two sons had seeds and planted them. One son planted a bronze seed that sprouted a tree that grew golden apples. The second son planted a tree, beautiful in every way, but there was no fruit. The roots reached deep and found water within the earth. What does this mean? What will become of my sons?"

Echoing within the mind of Mohammed, the Alirami's voice rang: "Your sons will bring two different futures. One will bring fortune and riches from the spoils of war. One will bring wisdom and knowledge from discovering more about the world."

Mohammed gazed into the eyes of the Alirami. For the first time in his life, he stared into death and felt nothing. He had seen death many times before and was unafraid and unalarmed.

Mohammed finally decided on the future of his sons. "I wish that my son of war would succeed. War guarantees my continuation in the Sultan's court more than wisdom." And even as he spoke, he knew what the cost would be.

The Alirami creeps its head so its eyes peer within Mohammed's soul. Its words scratch and gnaw at Mohammed's skull, "Give me your second son. The one who seeks wisdom. He will be your last sacrifice, and you will have your wish."

That night, Mohammed went back to his chambers. He was alone. A dagger drifted to him ages ago and sat peacefully on an ornamented stand on his desk. Carefully. He picked up the dagger. His motions became automatic. A force with him moved him forward as his mind sat heavy with the task in front of him.

Mohammed's youngest son was asleep. The boy inherited a softer and calmer spirit. He was the softer side of Balim. He even inherited her smile. Mohammed peered over the boy. He was twenty. He had finished an apprenticeship and would then be in charge of trade and industry. He had peculiar ideas about expanding trade relations as well as utilizing the Alirami more commercially. Mohammed Barely listened most times. His eldest was just like Mohammed: opportunistic.

Mohammed raised the dagger. The tip is aimed directly at the heart. He shook so violently he thought he might wake his son. Finally, the dagger found its place. The young man's heart stopped in an instant. His chest stilled. Mohammed wondered if he would ever weep, but there were no tears in his eyes. For the last sacrifice, he brought his son into the desert. The young man was dropped into the sand. Mohammed could feel his heart give way. His vision blurred. He fell to his knees and concentrated on breathing.

After several minutes, the Alirami arose.

"Why did you kill your son? In spite of loving him so much. You still willingly give him to me?" Asked the Alirami.

Mohammed said nothing.

The Alirami did not eat the young man. It simply shifted its body, and Mohammed's son sank languidly beneath the earth.

Your eldest will secure your place in the Sultan's castle forever. I hope you live to never regret your decision." Alirami's voice was filled with mirth and pity. Mohammed gave the Alirami another reason to hate all of humanity.

Mohammed made it back to his chambers. Just before the sun rose, Mohammed had made it back to his bed. When he closed his eyes, he let out his last breath and was dead with bloodied hands.

• • •

Over a small village, a sanguineous sun rises. The trees are ripe with green fruit and hang over a crystal oasis. Eternal as the night. Two children are sleeping soundly, and a woman comes out from her hut as she wakes for the new day. The woman, Balim, is drawn into the desert. She shields her face from the blazing sun and yet does not feel the heat. As she was walking through the desert, Balim discovered a shoe buried underneath the sand and felt an overwhelming sense of dread. Something evil had happened, and she was unaware and unprepared.

She had almost forgotten something, something important and ever-present. Her heart wanted desperately to forget. Yet stubbornly, she held onto the wisp of memory that clutched the edge of her mind and continued in the direction that the shoe pointed. She imagined that her life was once very different. Sleepless nights and hatred burned in her breast as she recalled something that she couldn't fully understand but knew once was there.

Walking, she found a huge mound of sand that blocked her way. In the distance, she thought she saw a tiny figure lying on the ground. She went towards it a little more hurriedly than before. As she got closer, the memories that haunted her became clear. Mohammed was dead. More than that, it seemed like someone had taken his very soul from him. His skin clung to his bones, and his eyes were gone. His teeth had rotted away. She remembered the last words she said to him as he stormed out of their hut. She remembered he was gone for some time.

Yet, a voice told her to stay in her hut and to not leave. She listened to that voice, remembering that even good spirits dwelled within the land and saved you from danger. The more that she looked upon her husband's body, the more she feared. Her heartbeat grew faster and faster. She looked back towards her hut. As soon as her eyes latched onto the thatch roof and the dome-like structure that kept her and her family warm in the cold nights, the image of her husband vanished. Slowly, the memory faded. Her history with her husband also left her. She was a lone mother. A mother still in his prime. She remembered her sons. Balim ran back towards her children and decided that maybe something sweet for breakfast would be nice.

As she left, the mound that blocked her way slinked into oblivion and it took the body of Mohammed with it.

THE HANGED MAN
AND THE KING

Ten years after the monks from Rome had come to England to spread the Gospel, they built a church on a hill somewhere in the heart of England in 1087. With the help of the recently converted local people, the monks finished constructing the church. However, soon after the church was built, strange things started happening within its halls. The books were knocked over, and the lit candles were snuffed out. Even though there was no wind. Visions of a skeleton hanging by a noose frequently appeared to the monks within the halls or in their dreams.

While Brother Charity was on a walk through the village, speaking to the people, praying with them, and taking note of all of their ailments and praises. Then, an ancient woman and her daughter-in-law approached him. Brother Charity remembered the woman. She was once a healer and a witch in the town. She kept her knowledge of the flora and fauna and the ways they healed but renounced the spirits that she once worshiped. The woman gave God credit for His pouring out healing within the earth for mankind, and Brother Charity shared her sentiments, for he was also studying herbal healing. She approached him, weary and deeply concerned, and begged Brother Charity if she could visit the dead tree that festered at the edge of the hill.

"Brother Charity, the Lord God has given me a vision. A restless soul needs healing and must be sent away. It is destroying your church and is deeply angry. Let me go to the Church. I will explain everything."

"Of course!" Brother Charity saw the sincerity and severe state of the woman, and thus, they all went to the hill. They approached the tree and immediately, the old woman doubled over. Brother Charity asked the monks to give her water and take her inside somewhere to rest. In an instant, someone attended to her, but the pain did not stop. Gasping for the words, she told Brother Charity to go to the tree with the strength of Christ in his chest. She warned him that the spirit there was furious and in pain.

He slowly left the church, praying the 23rd Psalm over and over. His faith was new, as he himself was a villager converted and sworn into the Church of Sussex Hill. He made it to the tree. A sense of uncertainty lingered. His being shook as he felt the spirit. It was not evil, but it was not good either. Its distress echoed within his mind. As he approached and looked at the black bark that was stained in soot, he noticed an ancient writing. The writing appeared hastily etched into the tree. Remembering the writing before his conversion, he read:

Here, the soul of a cursed man stayed, and here it shall remember him. Go to the oldest tree in the forest where there lay his bones.

Immediately, Brother Charity set out towards the forest that lay on the edge of the village. He carried nothing with him. He looked towards the sky, asked for strength and began walking through the thick brush.

• • •

A land a thousand miles away witnessed the crucifixion and subsequent resurrection of Christ after three days. Simultaneously, there was a baby born to a witch. She fell in love with a man who abandoned her and bore the child by herself in the same village where her ancestors lived and practiced witchcraft. She named the child Cian and brought him to the goddess Datelane of the Fae to bless him and give him gifts. Cian's mother wished for her son to dwell in the fae lands after his death, and the goddess granted that wish, hoping all mankind would dwell within her kingdom. As the child grew, his eyes beheld the fae. Goblins and ghouls whispered to him frightening tales as he slept. Faeries brought him sweet fruit and tricked him on the road. Giants that slept within the mountains told him tales of their birth and prophesied their death.

Cian grew with the spirits of the land like they were his siblings. They, along with his mother, taught him ancient ways. He knew secrets most fae would dare not tell, but because he was their brood, he knew them all and kept them close. When he became a man, he summoned the goddess at night. He burned the bones and fat of a boar as a sacrifice and instantly Datelane appeared. She was iridescent and fine. Her raven black hair cascaded down to her ankles while she shimmered in starlight.

Cian bowed in reverence and love with his goddess and asked for a small favor: "I wish to dwell within the land of your people. This land of mortals tires me, and thus I commit my allegiance to you."

"My dear boy!" she beamed, "I will take you to my home. You will be by my side to live forever and to love me forever." The bones and fat of the boar burned blue, revealing a door to a gleaming land. Eternally, in twilight, the fae world saw the sun and moon face each other without setting. The small light of pixies fluttered in the trees and sky like shooting stars falling to earth. Strange creatures, with the heads of birds and beasts, attended the goddess upon her return. The trees were tall, and the forest was thick with the scent of musk and flowers. Trolls played wild instruments, and furious fowl things danced around a blazing fire. The honey mead had the taste of tart berries and earthy herbs. Banshees howled, elves played games, changelings moved and twisted their faces, Leanan Sidhe told stories and sang. The whole forest was filled with strange and unimaginable delights and debauchery.

Cian joined the never-ending romp. He summoned glorious visions of dragons and war; fire and lightning came from his fingertips, and as he blanketed the sky. His hair grew wild and red; his body transformed into a wild boar as he danced and became mad with glee.

Cian came to live with the fae for one hundred years. Time stopped within his new home, and soon, he forgot the world of men. He did not age or feel the years as they passed. His spirit floated in a world without time, and he stood between life and death, unmoving. Soon, Datelane took Cian as her lover. He would tell her stories every night of the human world, each story becoming more fantastical than the last. Cian grew as wild as the other beasts, and where his legs were, the legs of a fawn took their place. He was king and cradled both humanity and fae within his body.

One night, as he lay with Datelane, he marveled once again at her circlet. It wasn't for its beauty but its promise of secrets and magic. Despite his rise in dominance, he was still lesser. Only a simple human graced by the goddess. Her concubine, her pet, her thing. He knew he would also be seen that way.

Finally, Cian dared to do what others couldn't. He gently lifted the circlet from her brow. As he attempted to place the circlet on his head, a cold, clawed hand grabbed the circlet and threw him back like he was a doll. He ran, his fawn legs bounding and leaping over the rocks and crags. Goblins and brownies laughed as he ran towards the tree, the door he stepped through one hundred years ago.

"HOW DARE YOU STEAL FROM THE GODDESS OF THE FAE! HOW DARE YOU TRICK THE BEHOLDER OF THE ANCIENT WORLD. MAY NO MAN BELIEVE YOUR WORDS AND MAY YOU NEVER DIE, SO YOU MAY LIVE FOREVER IN TORMENT AND RUIN!" she screamed and shoved him through the door. He fell to the ground unconscious.

After the sunset and the moon rose in the world of men, Cian woke up in the forest. In his attempt to find his mother and the village, he found them all dead. He was alone.

• • •

Five hundred years have passed. Noble knights and their king sit at a grand stone table. All the knights present, and the king laid their swords in front of them. Yet the tension between every man in that room made it difficult not to take up their swords and brandish them. Their vows, to themselves, God and King made that impossible.

"Sir Mordred," said the King, "you have brought forward serious allegations against this court and its King. What evidence do you have that proves them to be true?"

A young man stands outside of the ring of knights. He is almost the king's perfect replica, broad chin and serious brow. Only a learned smirk sets them apart.

"My testimony is this: the Queen of this court has been unfaithful. She has been lying with Sir Lancelot. Your closest friend. Additionally, and more damnably, this entire court that touts righteousness has been silent."

Sir Gawaine, fearsome with green eyes and red hair, studied the young man. Sir Tor and Sir Marhaus looked at their king. Sir Lancelot lowered his head. The King, Arthur Pendragon, King of Brittania, stared down the petulant man in front of him, "I ask again. What evidence do you have?"

"Honest and true Sir Lancelot should be able to tell you," Sir Mordred nodded towards Sir Lancelot.

"Do not play with me," The King growled deep in his throat. Sir Tor and Sir Marhaus leaned back, uncertain. Sir Gawaine whipped his head, looking at his King. His expression softened. He looked as if heartbroken.

"Arthur, my friend, I cannot hide any longer," Sir Lancelot almost crumbled as he spoke. All the knights stared at him with a mixture of surprise, rage, and betrayal. The King maintained eye contact with Mordred.

"What the boy says is true," said Sir Lancelot. The words poured out as he fought back tears.

"You cannot be telling the truth! Are you so simple-minded that you allow these boy's words to become your own!" cried Sir Gawaine.

"A better question is this. Who is this child that thinks he can cause chaos and falsely accuse this court?" said Sir Marhaus, pointing at Mordred with a finger like a talon.

"I do not lie!" Sir Lancelot's eyes were piercing. His teeth clenched, and his body shook.

"Ah! Finally, the truth. What do you say, King Arthur?" Mordred bowed low with a mocking flourish of arms and hands.

King Arthur slowly rose from his seat. He took his sword. It dangled from his grip. The rest of the knights stood at once. They knew the laws of Knighthood. They knew that no man was to lift his sword from the table. King Arthur made them. And now was about to break them.

Sir Lancelot rushed to King Arthur. The King's sword came over his head and was about to cut the neck of Mordred clean through. Sir Gawaine and Sir Lancelot both grabbed the King's arms and wrestled the sword out of his hand. It fell to the floor in a loud clang. Mordred grabbed the sword and ran out of the room screaming and howling, "YOUR KING IS A CUCKOLD AND A FRAUD! YOUR QUEEN IS A WHORE!."

Sir Tor and Sir Marhaus ran after Mordred but were assaulted by an angry mob of knights thrashing and killing each other. They, too, were sucked into the mob and killed. Sir Gawaine and Sir Lancelot used all of their strength as King Arthur foamed at the mouth, kicked and writhed.

Next came blood and flame.

• • •

Fire burns Camelot to the ground. Knights, once brethren, battle to the death. King Arthur, covered in blood, still searches for Mordred. He cuts through the flesh and rides on his horse through the burning battle. Gweneverse is dead. At the mention of her adultery, she flung herself out of her bedroom window. Mordred, waving the King's sword in his hand, rallies his knights. They seize the waning strength of those still loyal to their King. They pillage, burn and desecrate the castle. Every *inch* of it.

King Arthur spots Mordred burning a banner of a Pentangle. He rides hard toward him and, with a spear, pins down Mordred, piercing the man's heart. King Arthur gets off his horse, takes back his sword, and begins to plunge the sword over and over and over. It wasn't until he saw the flesh tear that King Arthur stopped. He looked around.

The world he created was gone. It was destroyed. He started this war in order to cleanse Camelot. Now, it is only ash. In the distance, men were dying. He hears them calling his name. King Arthur jumped back on his horse and escaped the fire. A sturdy rope somehow survived the flames (or was it destiny) laid not far from the rubble. He takes it and flees.

"God, I cannot take this! Take my soul." his words echo into the night as he reaches the top of the hill. A dead, black tree with mangled branches stretching to the sky welcomes him. A skeleton hangs on a branch on the left side of the tree. The King, coming to the top of the hill, gets off of his horse. He takes off the bridle of the horse and urges it onward. The poor creature did as it was told and mournfully trots out and away from the burning wreckage. King Arthur examines the skeleton. By the light of the moon, he notices the noose. An expert had woven the noose, but the strands glowed with a slight tinge of red as if they were dyed before the man hung himself. The wind makes the skeleton sway and for a moment, the King believes that the skeleton's head turns to look at him.

"I am ready to join you, friend," the King says to the skeleton. He quickly makes a noose and slings it over the right branch. He ties the rest of the slack around the truck of the tree. A rock was in position underneath him as if settled there for that moment, and the King stood on it. He stretches the noose around his neck and tightens it. The rope causes a slight halt to his breath. He closes his eyes, commits his soul to God and is ready to leap and die when suddenly he hears a voice.

"For five hundred years, I have hung here, and for all that time, I have never seen a man as foolish as you." The voice was scratchy. The King turns his head and sees the Skeleton's eyes glow with stunning white light. In fear, the King launches himself forward, and his feet give way underneath him. The noose tightens, and the King scrambles and swings as he attempts to shove his fingers to loosen the rope. Then, he drops to the ground, and the rope, uncut, tumbled in a pile beside him. He wretches and coughs on the ground, straining to breathe. Hesitantly, the King stood and looked at the skeleton. The skeleton swayed in the wind but looked at the King with crossed arms. Although the skeleton no longer had muscles or flesh, the King could feel the skeleton raising an eyebrow and smirking at him.

"If you are a demon, in the name of the Lord Jesus Christ, begone!" and the King unsheathed his bloody sword, pointing it at the skeleton.

The skeleton laughs, a cackling sound that bursts out of him, "You are a fool, born of a fool, lived a fool, and will die a fool. I am no demon, and that sword will do nothing to help you!" The skeleton kept laughing and flailed his arms around.

The King stared at the skeleton, looked down at his sword, felt a twinge of shame, and put it back into his sheath.

"Then, what are you?" asked the King. He walked closer to the skeleton.

"I am the son of a witch who asked an ancient goddess to bless me with sight, able to see the face of this world. That was more a curse than a blessing. If I could sink my teeth into that goddess, I would bleed her dry!" the skeleton's bones rattled with fury.

"What you speak of is Satan. That is evil," said the King. He spat on the ground.

"Oh yes, I agree. Evil indeed. But trust me, they existed. The one they call Christ conquered them all. They are nothing but memories now."

"Who cursed you then?""''"

"I was taken by Datelane as her lover, and to gain ultimate power, I stole her circle from her head. She cursed me to never die and for not a soul to believe what I saw."

"What did you see?" asked the King.

The skeleton stared at the King. He crossed his spindly arms.

"I-I. Nevermind. Well… would you at least let me take you down from your noose? You should be honored at least once in your life." The King took his sword and cut down the noose from the tree, careful to hold on to the skeleton so it would not crash to the ground.

"You are foolish but kind. Not a terrible combination. If you will, walk into the forest at the edge of this hill. Bury my bones at the foot of an ancient tree. I will let you know when we are there. What is your name, King of Fools?"

"I am Arthur, King of the Britains, son of Pendragon."

"Ah! You are the legendary king I have heard so much about. You vowed to create a world of peace and prosperity! How has that plan come to pass?"

King Arthur slung the skeleton over his back. The rope was now tied to the spine of the skeleton. "Please, do not speak of such things."

"I see. Not so good. I understand. All great things are destined to fail. This world is too twisted for change to be permanent."

"I understand your pessimism. But we were all on the cusp of finishing our task. Britain was at peace. Now we are at war." Arthur's voice almost turned into a growl at the mention of the war he left. He walked into the brush of the dark forest. The smell of damp earth and rotten leaves filled the air. Wild eyes of owls and wolves watched the strange duo as Arthur lumbered into the woods. His armor impeded his pace.

"My dear friend, I must take off this armor of mine. It will make the journey more painful for both of us."

"I don't see how, but do as you must," said the skeleton matter-of-factly, chuckling to himself.

King Arthur took off the armor. He also took off his crown and laid down his sword, seeing how they were of no use to him now. The king hoisted the skeleton on his back, and in only britches, boots, and a shirt, he began again.

"So, skeleton, what is your name?"

"My name is Cian."

"And how did you die, my friend."

"I succeeded where you failed," Cian tugged at the rope wrapped around his spine. "I believed it would solve my plight. Unfortunately, it made things worse. I hung on that tree for five hundred years, but who's counting? I watched my flesh rot from my body. I saw the creation and destruction of this grand country."

"I am sorry, Cian. No such curse should have been placed on you."

"I beg to differ. I made a mistake and now am bearing the consequences. The consequences are eternal," he shrugged. The nonchalant attitude of his companion startled Arthur.

"Did you not curse and rage?!"

"Oh yes!" laughed Cian, "for the first two hundred years, I cursed every god, demon, and beast that I could think of. For years, I would recite old curses and then create new ones. After another one hundred years, I prayed to any other god who could hear me. After that, I grew silent and simply watched the world turn without me."

"Cian, you break my heart."

"Do not fret. I cannot inflict any more pain upon you than I did to myself."

The trees of the forest grew taller and darker. Things lurked underneath Arthur's feet. Owls watched, and crows noted the scene as they flew past. The roots threatened Arthur's footing, but he had once trained in these woods before. He remembers every nook and cranny. Even now, the forest has not changed from when he was in his youth. Walking past, he recalled Merlin's lessons. He remembers being the swift rabbit running away from the fox. The memory of being a hawk, spiraling in the sky, and letting the wind carry him comes back to him. He remembers being the elk, strong and noble, as he led his herd to a fresh stream. How he wishes he were one of those beasts now.

Cian recalled the past as well. A more brutal time. When he awoke in the forest and ventured toward his village, the homes were larger. They were not the small tents and huts of his nomadic tribe. The homes were built of stone and wood. They tilled the clearing north of the village for farming. A fall crop was being harvested by the men. The women stayed behind, grinding wheat into bread. Cian, half naked and covered in ancient runes, ran towards the village. His hair was matted with blood and sweat, and his eyes were bloodshot. He looked like an apparition.

As he approached the village and came to a road, a small boy looked at Cian and screamed in terror. The boy ran, alerting the villagers, who looked on in Cian's direction.

"Please, someone. My life has been cursed. Datelane! Datelane has cursed me! She is here! She will destroy us all!"

Cian went through the village screaming and tearing at his hair. A burly man with a coarse beard stopped Cian in his tracks. The man's left eye was a naked socket under a rough leather patch. He narrowed his brow as he looked at the desperate creature before him.

"What is the meaning of this? You come into the village speaking of nonsense and scaring the children?! What do you mean by this?" his voice was deep and rough. He sounded like thunder. He was a man who took care of his village, and no task of protection was too great for his people.

Cian looked around. Unfamiliar eyes stared back at him. Men came back from the fields as word of an insane and naked man traveled fast. All the men looked at Cian with blood in their eyes.

Cian spoke again. It became harder and harder for him to draw breath as he spoke. "Datelane took me. She turned me into a monster and tempted me with the revelry of her subjects. The elves, the trolls, the goblins, the banshee. All of them were there. I escaped. I left with only my life." Tears welled in his eyes.

"No living person has even left the realm of the fae. Unless they were changeling destined to return, there is no man, woman, or child that can leave. You are a madman telling lies! GET OUT! GET OUT OF THIS PLACE!" The rough man with the eye patch grabbed Cian by the hair and dragged him through the town. The villagers followed closely behind and began throwing rocks at Cian. Children spat in his face. The rough man came to the edge of the town and flung Cian into the mud and manure. Stray rocks still tried to aim for his face, but he crouched and protected himself from their blows. Slowly, he got up, looked back at the place he once called home and entered once more into the forest.

Visions of terrible fae tormented Cian until death. Horrific faces and tormenting words filled his vision as he roamed the forest. Every few years, Cian would try to find at least one person who could believe him, but everyone he met only offered him hatred and scorn. Eventually, creating a noose and binding it in a spell with his own blood to make sure the rope would not snap, he killed himself. He remembers the moment he died, and he remembers how his spirit remained attached to his body.

• • •

Frogs and crickets were singing as the earth grew dank, and Arthur was walking through a bog. Cian looked up at the sky. His spirit could see the faint outline of the full moon through the trees. Then he spoke after much silence.

"Arthur, I have a bargain I wish to make with you."

"I will endeavor to do as you wish, but I already have you on my back and promised to bury your bones."

"I know, King of fools, but listen: you are helping me arrive at my last resting place. You are relieving my shame, and now I wish to relieve your plight as well."

Arthur paused for a moment, "you will help me? How."

"I will tell you three stories. Within these three stories, you will find your answers for redemption. You may save your court, but there is no guarantee. However, I promise wisdom to abound as we travel," Cian cocked his head towards Arthur's left shoulder. "Do we have a deal?"

"Yes. IF it means that this terrible war will end, then so be it."

"A war you left, by the way. Your men still wait for you."

"Let them wait. They will fare better without me."

Cian looked at Arthur. *How can there be so much piety and ignorance within such a man?'* he thought.

Arthur kept his head fixed on the road but continued the conversation (mostly to distract himself).

"Where were you born, Cian?"

"In these very woods that you are struggling to traverse, King of Fools. However, to find the very spot where I was born, we would have to travel even deeper than the tree you will bury me."

"Then why not take you to your birthplace?"

"There are too many painful memories. Besides, that tree is where the world of the Fae and of man are connected. What better place for me to rest eternally?"

"Yet, why to torture yourself, friend," asked Arthur, hoisting Cian further up onto his shoulders, "why place yourself with your most agonizing memories?"

"I… do not know," Cian's glowing eyes grew dim, "I believe that that is what I deserve."

"If I have learned anything from my God is that grace is a gift freely given. As we are called to forgive others, we must also learn to forgive ourselves. Give yourself grace, friend."

At that moment, Cian decided on a story. *"Forgiveness of others. A lesson you must learn as well, King of Fools,"* he thought. And began the first story:

"Once, there was a slave who served his master diligently every day. The slaves worked in the fields, milked cows, brought water, and slept on the hard floor. The slave once had his own money and housing but lost all of it. He was reduced to nothing and had to sell himself into servitude in order to live. The slave did not complain but worked. He was quiet and reserved. He always did as his master told him to. One night, the master asked the slave more about his life, curious why such a man would fall so quickly from a more comfortable existence.

'You work every day and do not complain. You used to own your own fishing boats and had a family. Why have you fallen so far?'

The slave looked at the master for the first time in all his time of serving. The slave had a worn and sullen face. His eyes were distant. He was not weak, but time had shaved down more of his humanity. While out in the fields, he reflected on his life and his past. He tilled the earth with his head down. He milked the cows with his eyes fixed on his task. Be brought water from the river without breaking a sweat. All the while, he maintained the same composure, consumed in thought.

The slave finally replies, "During the war, enemy forces raided my village and killed my people. I lost my wife and children that night."

The master looked at the slave in shock and remembered the night he had mentioned. The master was the commander of a legion of armies during that war. He fought against the fear of barbaric submission from a foreign power looming over their peace. He remembered his fury as he slit the throats of hundreds of people, never thinking of their names or how they lived.

The master replied to the slave, "You have been loyal to me for years on end. You have lost much. I am sorry that your family was taken from you."

'I think of my family every day. I used to curse and pray that those who killed my family would meet similar ends. Then I grew numb to them.' The slave looked the master dead in the eye, yet not a single ounce of rage.

The master nodded and ordered his slave to leave. The slave did not know his master's past. He never wanted to know, and thus, his life was consistent with only a few thoughts that kept him alive.

After a while, the master went to the village where his slave lived. The village was decimated and abandoned. Not a soul stayed except for the few stray dogs and vultures that roamed in search of scraps. He walked past mountains of funeral rights that were placed. He watched as the hounds yelped and hid from him. He knew this place well.

Soon, the commander found more secrets of the past. The war was merely to expand the borders of his country. This invasion grew by demonizing the enemy. He, along with the young men who fought alongside him, believed every word that was said of the enemy. They fought in the name of peace. As the enemy's casualties mounted, the commander felt certain his soul would be sanctified. Because of his valor, he would be seated next to his god in the highest place of honor.

Despite the death of the king who waged war all those years ago, his heir still maintained control over the nation that was taken over. He had very little to do with the inner machinations. He knew nothing of the truth.

The commander came back from his mission. He decided to speak to his slave.

The slave came in from the fields. It was a hot day, so he was sweaty, and dirt had caked his hands and feet. His hair became drenched in moisture. The master gave the slave something to drink and asked for the slave to sit at the table. The slave was careful as he sat, obeying his master but not losing eye contact.

"I have just come back after a long journey. I have discovered more of your village and of your life. I beg your forgiveness, my loyal servant."

The slave's expression did not change, but his heart began to race, "Forgive you for what, master?"

The master straightened himself in his chair and continued with his confession. His eyes dare not meet his slave's, "I was the one who killed your family and your village. The war destroyed your home, and all of those who were at fault lied about the dignity of your people in order to gain more land. Your people were killed in cold blood."

"Truth does not need to exist for people to be killed," growled the slave. He listened to his master but readied the knife within his canvas bag, "there is no reason in heaven or on earth that justifies the deaths of any persons."

The master saw the tension within the slave's right arm. He did not move.

"I have no words. Your people's death cannot be justified, and on behalf of my country, I apologize for the destruction of your world.

The slave breathed deeply and said, "I do not forgive you. I do not forgive your ignorance and hatred. I cannot and will not forgive you."

"I understand."

The slave tilled the field, digging into the earth along with the rest of the men who worked beside him, and imagined that his hoe was digging into the flesh of his master.

More years passed. The slave continued his work, and the master continued his life. Eventually, the slave could no longer work. His body withered away from exhaustion, and he died. The master, much older and infirm himself, buried the slave in a soft glade where he will forever be able to rest."

Cian had finished his story. Arthur furrowed his brow. He scratched his beard and whipped his face. The muck from the bog hung thick onto his body. He was silent for a long time and then finally spoke. "this story makes little sense to me. There is no point to it, it seems."

"How so?" questioned Cian.

The master should have at least given the slave the right to be released from his bondage upon hearing the truth of his plight.

"Maybe so, but he didn't."

Arthur sat perturbed and scratched his beard some more. "Maybe the slave should have killed the master in revenge, but then it would have been more bloodshed. Blood cannot heal blood."

Cian sat silently and listened to Arthur's musings. He crossed his arms. His eye sockets with the gleaming light flickered slightly.

"Speak, please. I do not have all the wisdom to understand this story," pleaded Arthur.

"Not all stories must have good endings. Majority of the real things in the world do not have good or bad endings. Some do not have endings at all. But I have a question: do you believe the slave could have died forgiving his master? Do you think it was possible?"

"Vengeance would have been justifiable. I would not blame the slave for slitting the throat of his master."

"Then you are no better than the master who killed innocent men and women under a false claim. What are you really, King? Are you a perfect man? Are you clean from every sin?

Arthur answered quickly, "No, I am not. I live in pursuit of purity. I aimed to set myself apart."

"You do not differ from this pagan bag of bones. You do not know purity anymore than I do," Cian chuckled, and his jaw clacked as he laughed. "Why do you believe you are above reproach? Do you know those who have hurt you? What was their reason?"

"Yes! Cian. I do!" Arthur dropped Cian from his shoulders, and Cian's body crashed pathetically the ground.

"I know them very well! The man who wormed his way into my court was my own son. A mistake. An abomination. Only because his mother, my sister, tricked me. She made me sleep with her so she could create the spawn of Satan in order to destroy me. She groomed that boy into my enemy. They are both to blame! I will never forgive that. I aim to hunt her down and kill *her* when this pointless war is over!" Arthur stared down at the bones underneath him. In his rage, he was close to crushing them.

He then heard the words 'Mordred' and 'son' in his ears. His only son. Gwenevere tried to have children, but her body could not hold them. That was the time he learned about the affair.

"My son. What a terrible twist of fate."

Cian twisted his head to meet Arthur's face, "you say you will never forgive that boy. But what price did he pay? How was his life? You could have saved him from his fate. But in the end, is he truly to blame for the things he could not control?"

Arthur closed his eyes. He replied, "The slave should have forgiven his master. Even if it would have taken his entire life, the slave should have granted that forgiveness. However, it will take more time for me to forgive my son... and myself. I gave him nothing when he was born, not even my name."

"That is the first step, King of Fools. There is more to humanity than we think, more to stories than we think. Come! We must walk further. The night is long, and so is our journey."

Arthur carefully picked up Cian and stepped into the swampy marsh, pressing forward. The swamp crept up to his knees and the sloshing of the thick water slowed down his progress, but Arthur kept forward, thinking more of his son and the life he might have led if all current things had not come to pass.

• • •

Further on, more stars decorated the night sky. Bats flitted overhead, catching tiny insects as the air grew thicker. The marsh dissipated, and briers took its place. Thorns and vines covered the trees so much that they almost completely swallowed the sky. Arthur was careful as he walked the path ahead. Everything became much darker.

Arthur sat into a small hovel and placed Cian beside him. He gathered wood, created a small fire, and took off his boots, "do not worry, friend. I will continue our journey, but I must rest for a while."

"I understand. I remember what it was to be fatigued." After a long pause, Cian asked the question he was most curious about, "what is it like being king?"

Arthur thought hard for a moment, "I feel you must know a little already. But in all honesty, you are tasked to be able to answer all questions with confidence and clarity. You are tasked to still hold authority while also listening to others. Your nation is at peace, but the politics that roam about within your court threaten otherwise. You are loved but not entirely known. It is not a fate I would choose again."

"You cannot be serious?!" If Cian could laugh he would expel all of the air from his lungs and end up in a coughing fit, "you are the most privileged and protected human being on the planet. Anyone in your position could make whatever radical decisions are necessary. Damn, the court! You are king!"

"And if I was smart enough to believe in your words, Cian, I would have done things differently."

"Ah. There is the Code of the Knight. Was that not enough?"

"Apparently not," Arthur sighed, "It was good for a while…Better than good. It was harmonious. Now, it's nothing." He smiled a rueful, half-smile

Another pause.

Arthur asked Cian a question he was curious about, "Why did you go to the world of fae? Even with what little I know, anyone who leaves is never the same."

"I thought that I could be king myself. I thought that I could rule a nation outside of pain and uncertainty. I played with fire and got burned," he chuckled.

"We both reached too high." Remarked Arthur dryly.

Cian looked at his friend. For the first time, he studied his friend's features. Arthur was noble in every regard. Clearest eyes of crystal. A broad chin. But in truth, there was a child still there who was never fully loved. Cian realized another detail of the famous King Arthur. Something precious. And so began the second story:

"There was once a man who died from excessive drinking. Before he became drunk, however, he was a rich man who had recently inherited a profitable business in his town. His father had passed the business onto him, but instead of the man tending to affairs as usual, he gave the business over to trusted co-owners and took what money he had to invest in debauchery and violence.

"Liquor was his favorite vice. One night as he was sleeping, Death visited the man. Death wore black robes, but no face was visible under the hood. Only a bony hand gripping the scythe was visible as death approached. Death said, 'If you are not careful, I will see you soon. Look, your skin is pallid and dull.'

'The young man said, 'I am healthy. This drink will not kill me!' and slept soundly.

"A second time, Death visited the man. He was a little older now, and his business grew over the years. He was very profitable, but this time his vice was women. The man had many wives and mistresses who had children with him. The man did not give most of the children recognition, and thus, they wandered as bastards throughout their lives.

"Death came upon the man and said, 'You must be careful. A snare like this will create havoc on you and others. You will certainly see me soon.'"

"The man looked at death and simply said, 'I am not hurting my body or my soul. Leave me alone and begone with your foolish talk'."

"Finally, as the man grew older and no longer invested in vices but counted the days until death would bring him, a young man came in the middle of the night and killed the man who wasted his days away. Death took his soul, and the soul screamed in terror as he realized Death was right all along."

Arthur tended to his wounds as he listened. There was a small opening of briers that allowed a small glimpse into the sky. The moon's glow cast light on the enormous briers, strangling and holding onto dying trees. Arthur sat with him and watched the bats as they flitted overhead. Arthur finally said, "I suppose another lesson lies within this one as well. I only see Death as the ultimate answer for all men- you being the exception."

"It was not death that took the man away," said Cian.

"Yes, again, it was the man's faults and sins that led him to ruin."

"Again, you are wrong, King of Fools."

Arthur looked over at Cian. He was determined to find the answer. However, between his aching feet and fatigue, he gave in, asking, "Then, my friend, what killed the man?"

Cian's glowing eyes became dimmer as he spoke, "denying the truth. Truth killed him."

Arthur's eyes were wide, and his brows furrowed, "you do not believe that I have grappled with the truth!?"

"No. There is still something that holds you back. Better yet, someone."

Arthur's face softened. Then his eyes looked wet with tears. He knew what Cian was talking about, and a knot grew in his throat. In his memories, he recalled the day of his wedding and his bride, Gwenevere. Her cunning was beyond something he had ever known, but she ultimately did not love him. They were companions, but love was always one-sided. When he found out about the affair, the will within him was already hanging on the edge- learning about such a betrayal pushed him over. There were also miscarriages. That grew distance between them. He attended court, but those around him secretly resented his call for righteousness when he himself denied his sins. They had disbanded even before Mordred could do that himself.

Cian stumbled over words to comfort Arthur, "Love is a- delicate thing, friend. I-."

"Please," interrupted Arthur, "I do not wish to think about her. Not right now. I know what lesson you are teaching me. Just please, not now."

Arthur got up and put Cian on his back. Cian said nothing as they walked deeper into the ancient forest.

• • •

The tree in the center of this forest was a gnarled, ancient, old tree that had died many years before. Despite everything, the roots stubbornly clung to the earth. The tree had a will to never leave. Cian and Arthur finally made it. Arthur slung Cian over and carried him up the hill in his arms. Cian saw the soft ground at the base waiting for him. He asked for Arthur to lay him at the base and for him to listen to one last story. Arthur did so and sat next to Cian.

"There was once a young boy born to a great king. Though the king died before he could claim the boy as his son, a great wizard raised the boy as his own. The wizard was a master of nature and sorcery, able to control and change the land at his will. He could see visions of the future and could visit the past. He opened doorways and traveled far and wide, inheriting knowledge in his wake. This wizard took the boy with him and helped him see the world as it truly was. King of fools, do you know this wizard?"

Arthur nodded grimly, "Yes, Cian, I know this wizard."

"He was a father to you, was he not?"

Arthur's head sank low as he admitted, "He was the only father I've ever known." His breathing became more labored.

"Do you remember when he turned you into the hawk? The fox? The water? The stone?"

Arthur nodded once more.

"What did you learn then? What did you see?"

Arthur closed his eyes, and he felt the wind rushing through the trees. A great torrent picked up and consumed the forest in a wave of frenzy. Arthur remembered the feeling of his wings spreading and catching the air. He remembered the rush as water, tumbling over rocks and insurmountable odds. Staring down at the fox, he remembered his prey. He remembered being indomitable as the rock, staring into eternity with assurance.

Arthur felt small droplets of water fall upon him. A storm, unlike any seen before, erupted from a rain cloud. Looking down, Arthur saw Cian's eyes were no longer glowing, and his skeleton lay limp on the ground. Arthur wept bitter tears that stung. He kept his promise and dug the earth with his hands. He ripped up old roots and threw away rocks. He placed Cian in the grave. The poor skeleton was curled like a cat asleep. Arthur covered the hole and stood back, letting the rain clean him.

Visions of the battle blazed, and he reached for his sword- it wasn't there. Behind him, a figure was standing only a few inches away from his face. Lightning struck with fury, and Arthur could see the face of

Merlin. The wild eyes, the bushy eyebrows, the wrinkles that curled like the knots on a tree. Merlin held his staff with both hands. Even though he was old and hunched, he was still much more dangerous than anything in the forest.

The vision of Merlin faded with the sound of thunder. Arthur could hear a voice on the wind, a whispering voice: "King Arthur, son of Pendragon, King of Britannia, Lord of these Isles. Why have you fallen this far?"

Lightning and thunder violently crashed. Trees burst into flames. Arthur did not move. He stood there, ready to face his punishment. He hoped once more for death to take him. The voice of his mentor echoed in his ears. Arthur's life flashed in front of him in time with the flashes of lightning.

"Do not let yourself go so easily, Pendragon! Do not let your past consume you." In a gleam of light, a vision of a man in blue and silver, standing tall in the heavy rain and furious wind, slammed his staff into the earth. Thunder rolled, and Arthur awoke on the battlefield clad in his armor. He raised himself to his feet, his ears ringing in his head. Arthur jumped on his horse and, with all of his being called out, "ALL TO ARMS, FIGHT TO THE LAST!" Swords clashed and sliced flesh. Fires burned, and buildings tumbled into ash. The court divided, stood face to face and fought till the bitter end.

At the very end of the battle, Arthur engraved into the trunk a last message for his friend and gave out his last breath.

• • •

Brother Charity stood at the base of the old tree where Cian's bones lay. His eyes adjusted to the light around him as he came back to his senses. Brother Charity stood back. He looked around. His brow furrowed, and he wondered, *'What does this spirit need from me?'*

Then Brother Charity' recalled what Arthur said: grace. His heart swelled. He walked towards the tree and placed his hand upon the writing.

He bowed his head and spoke to Cian, half in comfort and half like a prayer. "Cian. You have suffered much. Rest now. You are forgiven. You saved a man's life and gave him the truths you also learned and paid for. Go in peace." Nothing happened for a while. At last, Brother Charity got up and stood back to see the tree at its full height. Then, a small bird perched on the tree and stared at him. Brother Charity looked back, waiting for a miraculous voice from heaven or a trick from evil spirits. Then, the bird simply flew away.

Somehow, Brother Charity knew that that was Cian, finally able to leave this world. He crossed himself, said one last small prayer, and then headed back to the church.

WHEN THE HUNTSMAN KILLED THE WOLF

When the first crack of a rifle rippled through the forest, all the animals stared toward the sound. The rabbits' ears perked straight into the air, the frogs stopped their croaking, and the foxes and ravens stopped their sneering and their hunting. All were at attention, and all could smell the fresh smell of blood. It was not long after the rifle disturbed the morning air that a council of animals came together. The wolf was dead.

. . .

Many humans take advantage of the fact that the animal kingdom has a certain balance despite knowing that predator and prey animals exist and that a harmonious cycle ensures the prosperity of all living things. Humans overlook the effort and collaboration that all animals contribute to maintaining this balance. It isn't as sick as this rabbit is to be eaten on Sunday and this mole hunted on Wednesday. On no! It is a respect for boundaries and innate natures that coincide with a sense of direction from all parties, big and small. The rabbits must burrow and breed; the frogs must swim and sing; the foxes must hunt and run; the owls must sleep and fly; the snakes must tempt and slither. Each animal understands the nature, home, and way of life of other animals. It is only when an animal crosses those boundary lines do the more nastier pieces of nature come through.

The overseer of all living things, the ultimate predator, would be the guard and master of this cycle. None would overstep another under his watchful eye. Neither predator nor prey would be out of line, or else the balance would destroy all things within the vicinity. Something as delicate as this cycle would have to be maintained by the most rigorous and experienced creature in the entire area. This was the wolf's job. The wolf we know, the one who is currently dead, did this job for what seemed like centuries. Or, more so, the lineage of the wolf maintained this position. The sons and daughters of the wolf were masters and guardians of the forest and thus were the last word in most decisions. However, this wolf was truly the last. It was a hard winter, and unfortunately, this wolf's pups did not survive, and eventually, neither did his mate. In fact, all creatures were affected. It was a winter that not only made the earth cold but snapped out of some of the life that the earth would have gained during other winters. This one was stifling.

There were fewer trees with acorns or fruits. The fresh spring grasses were dry and without nourishment. Some of the prey animals, desperate for food, came out of their homes and died in the snow. The day that the wolf died was the first good spring day since that winter. The trees were blooming. Bushes of fresh fruit were becoming ripe. The birds sang a little more cheerfully. It was a spring day that all the animals awaited. Even as animals passed the boundary lines, the predators did not chase the stout or the mouse. It was a sacred event of freedom. But the peace was shattered when they discovered the wolf dead. A stray robin was passing by and saw a two-legged creature dragging the proud wolf onto its back. The wolf had a gaping wound in its right eye that passed through to his left, and the blood poured onto the ground as free as water from a spring. Mud matted the wolf's pelt, and its tongue hung limply.

The robin twittered and flew as fast as it could, spreading the news to every corner of the forest. Eventually, the news spread from one robin to several dozen. Then, the finches caught a whisper. The cardinals in the neighboring trees passed the message on until the squirrels and raccoons caught a whiff. Eventually, the message found its way, tumbling and mumbling about in every squawking, twittering, and yelping language. The wolf! The wolf? Good heavens! Great Stars above. The **Wolf?** Even the allusive brown bear heard of the news. However, his presence was not seen during the council. The brown owl, a puffed up, whirry, wild thing, heard the news and immediately asked for notices of a council meeting to be held just before dusk that evening.

All the usual representatives were present, including the mouse, the ferret, the hawk, the snake, the fox, the deer, and the raccoon. The toad and frog, representing the amphibians, allied together, while the turtle mainly listened. Despite their differing temperaments, the boar, representing the hooved animals, and the deer came together. A chorus of birds representing nearly every species sang in unison. The skunk, the raccoon, and the hare all worked together, although none were in official allyship, for their personalities were too anxious and antisocial for official conversations. The ferret and the mouse spoke under their breath as the council was coming together. The snake slithered into the clearing with the rest of the animals, and the hawk overhead came shortly after. The fox was late, as usual, but was ever careful to greet every creature with a cordial and fangy smile. One animal some half expected and others doubted was the bear. In the end, the badger took his place. Sadly, some lost bets that evening, which added a sour note to their temperaments. All the animals were in attendance, and the owl finally began the meeting.

The brown owl was not so much unorganized as it was brash and easily disturbed. He took careful consideration for every meeting and remembered every word spoken at each meeting by heart. There was nothing to use to record any of the meeting notes or decisions and thus, all owls were obligated to be secretaries of each meeting. Before the meeting, the owl in charge asked a barn owl to listen as a second ear so that every detail could be meticulously remembered for this important occasion.

With bated breath, an awkward silence hushed over the meeting of the woodland creatures. The woodland creatures hadn't held a meeting like this in a long time. The wolf, like his ancestors, understood better than most the ways of balance. It was unnecessary to think of the future when the wolf was around. Now, time had caught up to them and decisions would have to be made regardless of any hesitation.

The brown owl came from his hole in the tree and flew down to a gnarled and upended root. He fluffed his feathers, straightened his scrawny neck and said with a squeaky voice, "The meeting must begin! Before any discussion is to be had, a roll for all in attendance must be taken. Mole!?"

"Present!" said the mole, whose vision was too blurry to stand even the smallest bit of daylight, but thankfully, the hare with excellent eyesight helped him address the right animal.

"Rabbit!?"

"Present!" The Rabbit sprang all at once in an upright position as if it heard something from afar. Realizing he made a scene, the rabbit went back on all fours and lowered his ears.

"Stout?!"

"Present!"

"Frog and Toad?!"

"Present!" both the slimy creatures sat on a rock that was not too far from the small pond on the edge of the clearing. The frog was much smaller and perkier than the toad, but the toad had more experience. Their voices rang out with a hum of dragonflies and cicadas.

"Deer and Boar?"

The deer was about to speak up for them both, but the boar snorted loudly. The deer was lounging in the clearing. Its long neck and beautiful horns were slender, and its eyes were starry and dark. By contrast, the boar was the epitome of rough. It was lying on its belly with its legs tucked underneath it. However, compared to the deer, the boar looked more like a pile of red mud than a creature. Its snout was covered in scars; the tusks were long, and the eyes were small but fearsome. There truly was never a more unlikely duo, but both of their kind were of like mind, and thus, the alliance was natural.

"Racoon, Skunk, Squirrel, and Opossum?"

The squirrel spoke for the entire group as it scurried down the tree of the owl and met with the rest of his companions. He sat on top of the shoulder of the raccoon, who sat up. In its hands, the raccoon was opening and closing a small locket it had found near the edge of the woods. Rust covered the locket, and it had lost its gold chain, but there was a lock of hair inside.

Last, along with the squirrel, came the mouse. This mouse was the newest member of the council and the youngest out of all the animals. His father had been the representative of his kind for years until he was killed during the winter. A predator had snatched him from his own home. His son, the mouse at this current council, took up his father's place. This will be his very first council and his very first time seeing predator animals up close. Regardless, the business-like twitch in his whiskers told of his radical confidence.

The predators came at their own paces and in their own time. As mentioned before, the fox came dead last and was actually late. By the time the fox had arrived, a few stars speckled the sky. The sun was still narrowly present above the horizon. The snake arrived at the same time as the frog and the toad. You could barely see the snake, only because of the parting dry grass. The hawk came first. He had seen the entire murder of the wolf, along with the rest of the finches and cardinals in attendance that evening. Although, he would have loved for the first time to know what the wolf tasted.

In substitution for the bear, the badger came. He was a nervous, intelligent and even-headed animal, but could still bite harder than many of the burrowing animals he was kin to. The bear chose the badger as his representative for the larger omnivores because it was not yet time for the bear to leave his hibernation. Mostly, however, it was because the bear could hardly be bothered. Yet, despite his preferred solitude, the news of the death of the wolf surprised the bear enough to consider a puppet representative vital. Thus, the badger came in his place. The badger sat between the raccoon and the fox. The fox glared down at the badger and sniffed the air. The hawk overhead on a lower branch of the tree called out to the badger in a rough and raspy voice, "I have not seen you for many moons. It is good to see you, badger. How is the bear these days?" The hawk craned its neck to look the badger in the eye.

"Very good, thank you for asking. The bear wasn't ready to leave, so he chose me to take his place."

"I think we both know that that is a lie. The bear had never liked the council. He would not step from his hole even if the two-legged ones forced him out. Speaking of, have you seen the two-legged animals recently?"

"Oh no! No! I haven't. I have seen them in the past, but they were much quieter. I dare say they even respected the forest in the same way we do. Now it seems things have changed."

"Indeed- indeed." The hawk nodded gravely and squatted on his branch.

The snake slithered its way towards the badger before the beginning of the meeting. The snake straightened its body to have the height of the badger and smiled a raw grin.

"It hasss been a long time ssssince we have ssssseen each other, badger," said the snake. His voice was a little over a whisper. The fox also chimed in a cheeky and nonchalant voice, which was always his custom, " Oh Yes! I believe the last we saw you, you were cleaning your burrow or moving out of it, I don't really remember exactly. But I know it had something to do with a burrow. Yes, that's it."

"Yes, it was an old burrow that was abandoned by a family of rabbits not too long ago. I live closer to the bear, so I am not seen as regularly as the others", the badger smiled.

"What a shame it issss. We aren't able to be closseee to our comrades, the carnivoressss." The Snake nodded and slithered back towards his place next to the Frog and Toad. The Frog closed in on himself ever so slightly as the Snake came by, but the toad did not flinch. He merely looked at the snake passing and continued to squat slowly, letting one eye close and then the next.

"Yes, the carnivores only have each other. You must keep in contact more often, my friend," called the Hawk. His eyes widened, almost half-crazed.

"Yes, you're right. I shall try, I shall try!" and with that, the Badger pushed himself further out of the crowd, bumping into the raccoon and frightening the mole. He dared not speak until the brown owl called on him.

The brown owl gained the attendees' attention by flapping his wings furiously. He then settled into a comfortable position. "Animals! The kind of the wing, the scale, the paw, the hoof, and the fur. Thank you for attending this very important meeting. As some of you know, the master carnivore, the wolf, has recently been killed by the hands of the two-legged beast. This time, his methods of destruction are more dangerous than the hundreds of years that we have known this creature. This day, we shall decide three things: one, new boundary lines to be drawn between the prey and the predator. Two, the establishment of the two-legged beast in the balance's name, and three, a new master predator. Finches and cardinals, please relay the events you saw that fateful day!"

The brown owl called up to the canopy of the woods, and five songbirds danced and flew toward the clearing. Standing in the middle of the clearing, the birds recounted the death of the wolf in unison, "Three days ago, the wolf was making his regular rounds between the boundary lines of the hoof and of the scale when suddenly a great crash was heard, and the two-legged beast pierced the wolf's eyes." The birds stopped and flitted away again and stayed in the same tree as the hawk. The hawk sneered at the songbirds, who nervously stayed together on the same branch.

"Thank you," said the brown owl, "and so those are the events of that fateful day. My fellow animals of this wood, I implore you to consider the two-legged beast as part of the balance as we continue this meeting. But first, we must discuss new boundary lines. Would the burrowers please come forth?"

At this, the rabbit came forward. Hopping a little closer towards the center of the circle of animals, the rabbit, in his best voice, proposed new boundary lines for his burrowing brothers: "I suggest to the council that we give the burrowers a one-fourth extra of the forest and place greater restrictions on the fox's hunting." All must eat, but all must surely be able to live first."

"What does the fox say about this matter?" asked the owl.

"I shall give leave of half of that portion to the burrowers. Their population has grown this past spring, and they have been seen within the predator's circle many times."

The rabbit spoke up in haste, "Can you prove that the burrowers have been crossing the boundary lines? We may roam, but we are as careful as any prey animal. What proof do you have of your claim?"

The fox turned toward the grass behind him, and in his mouth was a small hare with spots on its ears. The burrowers stared and whispered to each other. They knew their fate, and they knew their lot, but seeing the predator with its sharp teeth never became easier.

The fox carefully laid down the dead hare at its feet, "I have a good claim, with witnesses, that this hare crossed the boundary line two days ago. He was with three others who could run away faster than this one. Previously, he would have been accompanied by maybe one or two others. Either the rabbits have become less careful than they claim, or their population has increased. I have also heard from others of my kind that the borrower population has increased as they have gone hunting in *their* areas."

The songbirds tweeted a reply, "We are witnesses, and we concur with the fox's claim."

"So then, one-eighth will be given to the burrowers," turning to the burrowers, the owl continued, "You must consider that the more mouths to feed, the harder to maintain safety within your numbers."

The rabbit twitches its nose. One hind leg was radically scratched behind an ear. "Very well, thank you for your generous gift." The rabbit hopped back to his companions, managing as best he could not to grunt furiously.

"The deer and the boar. Come forth."

The boar went towards the center of the clearing. He shook himself off and grunted from deep within his stomach. In a growling and low voice, the boar said, "Those of the hoof wish for more grazing fields. We also had a larger breed come this spring, and we need more areas to let them roam. Like the rabbits, we ask for more land, but we want it closer to the north end of the forest, where there is unclaimed territory. The deer also asks for this area as our allies will dwell together in that place."

"I am sorry to say, but that will be difficult," said the badger.

The boar slowly looked towards the badger and narrowed down his nose toward him. The boar's voice deepened even further, and he pointed his tusks directly at the badger's belly. "How so?"

The badger gulped slightly and took in a deep breath. "The bear wishes to claim those lands for himself. It is closer to the river, where he can hunt and drink. He also enjoys the honey that accumulates there. It would be dangerous for you." He averted his gaze and glanced downward.

The boar shifted his weight. All the animals became nervous at the mention of the bear. Even the hawk nervously flapped its wings and displaced its talons on the branch. The fox quieted himself, and the snake coiled tighter. The prey animals became still, and some even looked around to see if the bear himself would show. He was never officially the master predator; he was as mysterious as a ghost.

After a while, the badger spoke again with a forced sense of glee, "My deer friends of the hoof, I believe that there is still hope. The woods to the northwest are still vacant, and your children will live there in peace."

"But the berries and acorns are not as prevalent. In fact, there are many plants there that have died because of the frost," this time, it was the deer. He spoke in a fluid and soft manner, but his powerful muscles showed not only his grace but his dignity. His slender neck turned toward the badger and he looked down upon the creature, speaking.

"However, I have seen bushes come back to grow. Even some of the prey present have moved to the part of the woods and claim that it is very comfortable. Racoon, did you not say that those parts of the forest were well kept?" asked the badger.

The raccoon looked up from his locket and put it away., "Yes, it is a fine part of the forest. I will say that there are some parts of that area that are not as profitable. There are fewer acorn trees, but there are plenty of fruit-bearing trees. I believe you could make it!"

"That may be so, but how easy would it be to move two entire herds to the northwest of the forest? That would take almost three weeks. We have too many young that are not strong enough to make that long journey," urged the deer.

"I concur. Within our area of the forest, speaking for the burrowers, it has become crowded. Yes, we could all benefit from the extra room, but why move an entire kind to a remote part of the forest?" called the stout.

"Thank you, my friends," interrupted the boar, who gave a slight nod, "we will consider this amongst our kind."

The deer nodded, but his eyes shifted from the boar and the other prey animals.

"Very good!" said the brown owl, who fluffed his feathers, "next shall be the scale."

The Boar turned back to his place, scraping the dirt beneath his hooves. For any animal who would have seen his face, they would have seen a look of rage and hatred skillfully hidden behind a blank expression. The Opossum saw the glimpse from the corner of his eye.

Then he looked at the badger. The badger caught his gaze. The opposum bore his teeth from his wide mouth. The badger's fur began to stand on end. Before the claws were out, they were interrupted by the grave croak of a toad.

The toad hopped towards the center in one great leap, and the frog came shortly afterward. The toad, even with being smaller than some of the other animals, was still intimidating for the sheer fact that his expression was unreadable. Although the boar was gruff and stern at best, the toad was impenetrable. His eyes stared beyond those he spoke to and did not flinch from their indomitable gaze.

The toad spoke first in a low pitch that sounded like water splashing against the banks of the shore, "We require that you completely remove the snake from our pond," the toad said.

The owl, surprised, said, "Toad, more than anyone here, you must understand the ways of the balance. For this request to be granted, you must give serious evidence to support this."

The toad puffed its chest and turned its body towards the water. "look."

All the animals turned their attention to the water. The pond was as still as glass. Not a single thing interrupted the waters. The dragonflies danced in the air, but other than their slight touches to the water, nothing else disturbed the quiet.

"Years passed, frogs and toads filled this pond, singing their songs and maintaining the balance for its own sake. We have lived more with balance than anyone else, always respecting the boundaries of the land-kind. However, the snake had eaten our young and many other predators like him have disturbed the peace we once enjoyed."

"From what I understand, your kind wasssss overpopulating the area." The snake slithered its way toward the center. Although the snake could consume the toad whole, the toad did not move. The snake lingered over the face of the toad as it continued.

"I remember that thissss pond wasss filled to the brim with frogs and toadsss. They were on top of each other. There was not enough room, and the water began to recccede from the bankss. Tadpoles smothered the lily padss. I employed the fish and the gar to help me in balanccccing the pond as all must practice within their boundary linesss," and with that, the snake slithered back to its place.

"Snake, do you have evidence?" asked the owl.

"Look again to the pond, ssssee how the watersss have risen," the sun cast a soft light on the water, which made the pond glisten like crystal. The water was clear, and the lily pads flourished with giant pink lotuses. The aroma attracted large fluttering butterflies. The frogs and toads that were already populating the area were blissfully singing a low and droning tune.

"Toad, what do you have to say about this? What is your counterargument?" asked the owl.

"We responded to the need to manage the insect population. The insects ravaged our home. There were too many for so few of us."

"Be that as it may, the one population must be controlled by another. Such is the balance. Snake, your argument is valid," the owl nodded toward the snake, and the snake bowed its head slightly.

The toad blinked, paused and hopped back to its rock. The frog came shortly after, noticing the undulating throat of his companion. *'That isn't normal'*, he thought.

"Lastly, of the prey animals, we must hear from those who live in the trees. Raccoon, please come forth."

The raccoon adjusted the chain of the locket around its body and scurried forward to the center. "We, the tree dwellers, wish for the hawk to hunt south of our part of the forest. His hunting habits have been against the laws of balance, and our population, which has been regular even amid the winter, has depleted because of the hawk's overhunting. W-we have the evidence to prove our claim as well!"

The raccoon referred to the songbirds in the tree, "My dear friends, what have you found of the hawk's behavior?"

The songbirds, in unison, sang their response, 'We concur that the hawk has been hunting, along with his breed, in the areas of the tree-dwellers. We have seen many young tree-dwellers killed because of the hawk. Their population has dwindled because of it."

"What have you seen of their numbers?" asked the owl, who turned his great head almost entirely to face the songbirds in the tree. All of the rest of the animals looked up within the canopy to witness the testimony.

"We have seen many young that the hawk has killed without consuming them and with a piercing mark within their bodies. The hawk has been seen attacking victims, but only rarely consumes its kill, upsetting the natural balance.

"Lies!" cried the hawk, who opened his wings and screeched towards the canopy. He furiously flew to the canopy and grabbed the attention of all the animals present."

"My kind have strictly stayed in line with the balance! We have always obeyed the balance despite other predators who may greedily take what is not theirs. We live on the instincts that drive us, and such a claim is false in every manner!"

"What counterclaim would there then be, hawk?" asked the owl cautiously, bobbing his head.

The hawk was silent. His large yellow eyes glared, and his beak was open. He arched his wings and lowered his neck, searching for the words to speak. Then, the badger came forward.

"In keeping with the truth for the truth's sake, I bring evidence that may help the Hawk's claim." The badger once again called out, almost grimacing from the sound of his own voice.

All the animals moved closer toward the badger as he held something in his paw. The hawk swooped from the canopy and elbowed his way beside the owl who also was anxious to see what thing the badger was holding. The snake had woven itself around the legs of the fox and the fox nervously scratched his fur. When the badger had finally opened his paw, the object was clearly visible. A small, black, metal cylinder that came to a point. The object was cold and hard and slightly covered in blood. Instantly, as the rabbit saw the object, his eyes folded back, and his body slumped lower to the ground.

"The two-legged beast, the two-legged beast!" whispered the rabbit as he crept away from the ring. The left leg thumped wildly.

"My friend. You must tell them," the badger held back tears. The rabbit saw the badger's face, full of regret and gently shook his head as he backed away.

"Stay calm, friend! Tell us, what have you seen?" the brown owl hobbled his way to catch the rabbit before the rabbit would run back to his burrow.

The rabbit looked at the owl in a daze of fear. And then he scanned his fellow prey as they looked upon him. They were tired. They were skinnier than years past when he had seen them plump and without a care. He remembered when meetings like this were still under the watchful eye of the wolf, and even with the wolf's claws and teeth, at least the wolf upheld the truth. He looked at his brethren prey, and in his eyes, there was remorse and sorrow. The prey looking back at him knew exactly what he was going to do, and in their hearts, they both hated him and were sorry for him.

"Rabbit, we must know what you know. Anything you say is for the greater good," whispered the Brown owl.

The rabbit straightened its body. Its voke shook like autumn leaves in the wind, "I have seen the two-legged beast use this to kill prey and predator alike. I have seen this before… before the wolf was killed. The two-legged beast would kill my kind, big or small, young or old, with this, and sometimes he wouldn't consume his prey. Sometimes, they were left to rot."

The rabbit broke down now into tears. His body twitched and writhed unnaturally as he sobbed. His entire frame took in breaths and spilled aching tears. The raccoon went over to comfort the rabbit, nestling beside his friend.

The badger came over and hesitantly laid a hand on the rabbit, "I am sorry, friend. We do not understand why this creature is here. I am truly sorry." The badger's words were bitter, and a sour taste crept to the back of his throat.

The owl took a breath and waddled slowly back to his place. He was also tired and his body slumped a little as he nestled into the root that he was sitting on.

"Speaking of which," he took a deep breath and let it out slowly, "We should speak on this matter. I ask that-" but the owl stopped mid-sentence when he could see the fox making his way towards the center of the clearing and the rabbit being gently ushered back to his allies by the raccoon. The fox stood perfectly erect in the center and puffed its chest in a show of importance.

"I believe the agenda should be slightly changed, and before we speak about the two-legged beast, we should propose a new candidate for the new head-predator. The sooner we fill this position, the sooner we can bring ourselves to a sense of normality", said the fox.

The owl was noticeably irritated, "I see your point, fox. Do you have a candidate in mind?"

The fox raised its chin a little higher and replied, "I believe that I should be the head predator. I am the wolf's closest kin, and thus, the power should go to me."

There was an uproar of voices that burst the moment that the fox stopped talking. Screeches, barks, howls, and squeaks rose into the air and roared loudly. The birds chirped and chattered as they hopped from place to place in the tree. The boar pawed the ground and squealed wildly, flailing his tusks. The opposum growled. The rabbit fainted. The snake and the hawk, however, stayed silent as they listened. The snake's body tightened as he lifted his head, and the hawk stared intently at the fox while it spoke. The brown owl flapped its wings and screeched lowly and its assistant did the same in order to bring order back to the meeting.

"MY FRIENDS, MY FELLOW ANIMALS, CEASE THIS!" and the crowd slowly quieted. Furry and anger were barely kept behind their eyes. He regained his composure and, like the hawk, trained his eyes carefully on the fox. "No one here will deny your relation to the wolf, but this is a bold claim. A vote on this must be taken. Are there any others that would be willing to contest with the fox?"

"I would," cried the hawk who flew next to the fox.

"And ssssoo would I!" called the snake as it slithered its body towards the clearing.

The rest of the prey animals carefully scoffed under their breaths. The deer and the boar looked at each other with annoyed glances. The badger raised an eyebrow and looked towards his furry brethren.

The badger whispered to the mole, "What is going on?"

"Why on earth are you asking me? I can hardly see as it is and the sun has gone down. Why don't you ask someone else!"

"I'll tell you!" chirped the squirrel, "You aren't here as often, so you wouldn't know. Those three are always at each other's throats and once again are trying to one-up each other. Take your chances where you can, right?"

"Right, the candidates have been placed. Votes now will be taken." The brown owl looked towards the barn owl, who nodded in confirmation and took note of all the votes.

"All in favor of the fox as master predator, raise your votes." The animals cast their votes.

"For the snake." More votes.

"For the hawk." And more votes.

After the barn owl had carefully counted the votes, all the votes came to a tie. The owl's eyes grew wider. His breath grew heavy as he wracked his brain for a solution. He spoke in a private conference with the barn owl, who then flew away into the night. All the rest of the animals whispered among themselves what to do next. The candidates went back to their respective places, bristling with anger and avoiding eye contact. The owl came back to his position and gathered the attention of the animals once more with a swift flapping of wings.

"Because of the tie, the consideration for a new master-predator will be given to the bear. We will consult with the bear shortly, and hopefully, we will get an answer soon. Badger, I believe he is in the last days of hibernation?"

"Yes, He should awaken soon. Although, please be careful."

"I am well aware of the bear's habits, thank you." the brown owl rolled his eyes.

"My assistant will make quick work of waking him. Now, I believe that we all need a brief break. We will continue the meeting at sunrise. Even those who are more awake at night have agreed to stay alert during this hour. Everyone is dismissed."

The moon, full and bright white, was just peeking above the treeline. The sparkling pale glow was not yet touching the pond's still waters. All the animals left the clearing. All except one small creature who stood by and pondered the meeting's events: the mouse. The mouse looked towards the stars as it thought deeply. Last winter, his father had gone out to find what little food was left, but never returned. A day later, they found a small piece of his fur, leading them to assume his father was dead. The mouse's father was a representative of his kind, and thus, it was natural for his son to take his place. The mouse twitched its whiskers towards the dark woods and tentatively found its way to a hovel near the pond. The snake, however, saw the mouse and, in the night, whispered, "You have come a long way, little mousse."

The mouse raised his eyebrow. His right eye twitched, "I am a representative for my kind, snake and not your next meal. We have better things to do than to obey our most carnal natures. Would it not be best to have your fill of the scaled kind since you did such good work with them this spring?" He then left to his borrow.

The snake, for the first time in a long time, was speechless. Conversation between a mouse and him rarely lasted long, but this surprised him.

"Be careful, mousse, we mussst not bite too hard to draw blood in timesss like thessse." And he slithered away. Finally, all rested from the meeting, sleeping to the sound of the wind.

• • •

As the barn owl had come back from its journey, he panted as he rested on the tree branch where the songbirds were resting. The branch shook as he landed, waking many of the songbirds who promptly flew and sang for the attendants to wake from their slumber. Since most of the creatures were light sleepers, they all sprang into action and bound, leaped, scurried and ran as fast as they could back to the meeting circle. Despite any lingering exhaustion, the animals were not sparing a single second of the final vote from the bear.

The barn owl, still trying to catch its breath, had a noticeable scratch on one wing and the blood was trickling down from the tree onto the bare forest floor. It screeched a warning call, and the brown owl came swiftly into the air, flying gracefully among the trees. The hawk came flying faster and landed hastily on a branch. All the animals were present. The mouse squeezed its way toward the front of the prey representatives and locked eyes with the snake. The snake opened its mouth to show its fangs and then slithered to its spot with the predators.

The barn owl whispered something to the brown owl, and the brown owl dismissed him. The barn owl half flew, half fell as it made its way to a safer place to heal its wounds. The brown owl flew to its gnarled root and gathered the attention of all the animals.

"The bear has made the final decision as one of the most dangerous predators within the forest. He has decided that the fox, snake, and hawk should all be master predators of their respective regions and share the power equally since all are of equal talent and cunning." The brown owl slumped over a little, glad to have at least some type of answer.

The animals looked at each other. The hawk was livid; the snake was ready to strike the owl, and the fox's cool demeanor looked sharp and ragged.

"What do you mean we are to share the power equally?" asked the fox through gritted teeth.

"I mean what I said, or are you bold enough to go against the word of the bear?" asked the owl, who cocked his head slightly.

"No! I insist on a revote! Sharing power is not possible with predators and I would think that the bear would understand. I insist that only one predator be the master of the forest!"

"Unfortunately, your insistence is irrelevant to the bear's decisions, and if you did not realize we have a predator that has shown more aptitude for killing with a single pebble than all three of you could ever in your life, so shut up and get back in line!", the owl raised its wings, and its eyes were wild with rage and blood. The fox's ears folded back, and he bared his teeth. The snake reared its body back and opened its fangs. A loud hiss came from its mouth. The hawk swooped from the tree and picked up the snake. The two were in a battle as the hawk closed its beak around the neck of the snake, and the snake pierced the right leg of the hawk with its fangs. The fox leaped in the air and, in one swoop, caught the snake and the hawk in its mouth and, shook them around and threw their bodies to the ground.

"I WILL NOT SHARE POWER! I AM THE DIRECT LINEAGE OF THE WOLF!" cried the fox.

The hawk loosened its grasp on the snake and dropped it so it could scratch the eyes of the fox. The hawk's talons pierced the fox's left eye. The snake poisoned the hawk's leg. Blood poured from the wounds as the hawk destroyed the snake's throat. Eventually, the snake died from the loss of blood. The hawk, poisoned and weakened, thrashed and screeched wildly. The hawk's heart raced. The poison had taken effect, and before the hawk could take out the other eye of the fox, it fell to the ground, twitching; then it finally died.

The fox looked towards the brown owl, one eye caked in blood and dripping, "I will not share power, and I will not listen to a fat, groaning beast who cares nothing for this forest. A slithering imp and an empty-headed nuisance who eats small stupid creatures with no pride will not supplant me. I WILL BE MASTER OF THIS FOREST AND YOU OWL, I WILL EAT!" the fox leaped towards the owl, teeth and claws bounding in a flash of blood lust.

Then suddenly, a small voice cried out, "DEVIL!" with a tiny fist in the air and its back legs reaching as high as it could. The mouse had cried from the center of the clearing in a proud yelp.

The fox, with its mouth fully around the throat of the owl, watched the owl's body grow limp as it dragged the owl, wings scraping the ground, and looked back at the small creature. The fox threw away the owl, and the owl awoke again, breathing hard. He scampered towards the tree and stared at the fox who targeted another prey.

"Who are you to interrupt me?!" growled the fox.

The mouse stood proudly and stared the fox down as the fox's face grew closer to the mouse. The mouse's nose was overwhelmed by the smell of blood which made its eyes water, but it did not stand back from its place.

"In the name of the prey behind me. I propose a new vote in regard to the "master-predator." "I vote that we eliminate the predator from the forest, forever!" the mouse crept closer towards the fox and leveled its eyes to the fox's eyes, "All in favor, raise your votes."

There was nothing at first as the mouse declared his new vote. Nothing until the boar grunted. The rabbit stomped its feet. The deer scraped the ground. The squirrel made a guttural noise. The opossum, the raccoon, the songbirds, the stout, the toad, the frog, and the rest that were all in attendance confirmed their votes and locked eyes with the bloody fox.

The fox looked towards the large group of prey animals that looked at him. All at once, the fox felt a sharp pain in the back of his neck. The brown owl had dug its talons and started ripping the skin and fur away from the fox's neck. The owl was screeching and fluttering about while the fox leaped and soared. As the owl and fox grappled on the ground, the other animals attacked the fox. Bites, thumps, kicks, rams, and scratches. The only one who wasn't fighting was the deer, who sprang away as soon as the fighting began. He ran as fast as his legs could carry him into the forest. He wanted to be as far away from this chaos as possible. Dawn was breaking, but a raw, red sun peeked over the horizon.

Without warning, a familiar crack rang out from the forest, and dozens of birds sprang out from the trees. The bloodied band of animals stopped and listened as they felt the echo of the crack in their bones. The rabbit's ears perked up, and it listened intently. The smell of blood filled the air again as well as a strange smoky smell that triggered his memory. He turned towards the rest of the animals in a flash and said, "It is here! It has come!" as they all scurried and ran back into the forest.

As the boar ran into the trees, a shot pierced his side. As the rabbit sprained back into a hole, a trap grabbed him by his heels. As the frog and toad swam in the pond, a net scooped them like jaws of death. As the possum and the squirrel grappled the tree, more shots rang through the air. Every living creature sprang out and away. Those who lived left no trace. One two-legged beast, tall and mighty, grabbed the spoils of his hunt. He called his partner and left. The mangled body of the fox was left for the bear.

Baba Yaga's Daughter

In the heart of winter, in an old wood, Death traveled to attend a meeting with an old friend. No sound was heard except the cawing of crows and the malicious blowing of the wind. Cloaked in black and carrying his scythe, Death unfeelingly traversed the spiteful forest. Crows dashed and gathered in the bows of dead trees as they watched him, finally making it to his destination. In the middle of the cold and old forest was a house atop two chicken legs. The house was a wooden shack with cracked windows and a leaning door. Beaming a light like a lighthouse out to sea, The only light was a circular window shining out from the attic.

"I have come. Let me enter." Death approached the house and called out in a breathless whisper. The chicken legs kneeled, and Death entered Baba Yaga's house.

Upon entering, the shack seemed more like a small closet. The walls were covered in various collections of drying herbs, bottled roots and mushrooms. The skulls of every animal, as well as their furs, papers, books, and talismans, were scattered aimlessly. Hanging from every corner were bobbles crafted from shells and jewels. Others from bones and teeth. In the center was a large circular carpet heavily embroidered. Stories and tales of the old forest lined each stitch and all of it sat in the palm of Baba Yaga's hand.

Three doors led to the three other ram-shackle rooms of the house (which seemed to be hanging only by nails and rotting boards). In the center of the living room is a gnarled rocking chair. The seat of the chair looks as if it is worn to the bone. A stout table holds a stale crust of bread, half-eaten. Death entered through the center door, up a narrow flight of stairs. Baba Yaga's back faced Death. Her hands held onto the brim as her claw-like nails touched the swirling brew. Under her breath, she mumbled and spoke in tongues while her eyes darted from one end of the room to the other. Then, she stopped.

"You are late," she called.

"I beg your forgiveness. There were many things I needed to attend to before I came here. Men are always in search of blood these days."

"I know what men seek. You are still late!" she turned around. To any human who would have seen Baba Yaga, they would see the gnarled wrinkles of an old woman. However, looking into her eyes you would swear you saw the eyes of the devil himself. Her body was thin and straight, her left leg replaced by a wooden peg. Her left eye was covered with a patch, while her right eye was yellow. She wore a dress that came down to her ankles and a knitted shawl that flowed down her back. Her hair was kept under a handkerchief that was tied at the back. On every inch, small red runes tattooed her skin up until her neck. Baba Yaga's teeth scattered her black mouth, and at the tips of her fingers, her nails seemed more like claws.

She walked towards a dark corner and pulled out her pestle along with an old liquor bottle. She fully submerged the bottle into the cauldron. The whirlpool did not stop as Baba Yaga lifted the bottle into the air, took in the stench of the brew and walked towards her guest.

"I ask you to come to my house to attend an important ritual. You are Death. You cannot be late. You did not want to come, yes?" she scowled and stared down the void that was the cloaked figure of Death.

"I do not have to bend to your will, Baba Yaga. You have no hold on me. I am not trapped here like your pets," he hissed.

Baba Yaga spat on the floor and looked again at Death. "You are right, but have I not served you? Remember our bargain. You are at least bound to that." Then, Baba Yaga went outside of her house and walked towards the dead forest.

Death walked behind her, reluctantly compelled by the seal that connected them both. Both climbed over roots and ducked under branches until they came upon a tree in a clearing. It was a shriveled, dead tree that was once struck by lightning. The top half of the tree had long fallen, and what was left was a craggily and scrawny piece of wood with two skinny branches sticking out from either side. Baba Yaga bit off the stopper on the bottle and poured the liquid towards the roots. The mixture sizzled and fumed as it sank into the ground. Then, the roots began to fidget and move. The branches bent backward. The bark snapped. The truck of the tree split in two until the middle and branches grew longer, gaining spindly fingers at the ends. The tree sported a head with two hallowed eyes, and the roots swirled together until they made something that looked like legs and feet. Within the hallowed eyes, a small pin-point of light showed. The creature was born.

"Vesch. Vesch! I name you Vesch and thus give you life. You are to do my bidding without weariness, hunger, or thirst. You will be my slave, and I will be your master. Do you understand?" called Baba Yaga.

Vesch gave a stunted nod. The wood shrieked at its new demands of movement. Death watched as Vesch lumbered slowly and then looked at Baba Yaga. "Why did you need me for this endeavor?"

"I simply thought you would enjoy it. No! The spell needed a witness from a confidant. Do not flatter yourself. No, you may go and be late for some other sorry soul like you were for me!" Baba Yaga snapped. Then started towards her home. Death walked into the dark and vanished into shadow.

• • •

Vesch did just as she was told, whenever she was told, and however she was told. She found herbs from the forests, cleaned the house, organized the many items within Baba Yaga's collection, threw away slop, cleaned, caught game, and did this without complaint. When Baba Yaga no longer needed Vesch's services, Vesch was placed in a corner of the house and would stand or sit there unblinking. No sleep and no feeling. One day, on a brighter day than most days, Vesch was picking herbs and roots.

A figure could be seen walking between the trees. A thin figure, yet broad in the shoulders. He was often mistaken for a tree but then as a beast. In truth, the olive-skinned man grazed through the snow. His hooves left small, growing things that quickly disappeared. He smelled of flowers and the earth after rain. Covered in a moss robe, rams horns adorning his head, he approached Vesch curiously.

"Hello there. Who are you?" Vesch did not respond. The figure looked closer at Vesch and discovered her true nature.

"You poor thing. You are not even alive." With a smooth, chestnut hand, the figure touched Vesch. He essentially stopped Vesch from her work. In a commanding voice, "I give you the gift of mind, heart, and soul. You will breathe the air and feel it. You will drink from the stream and bathe in it. You will feel the sun and grow stronger from it. Daughter, awake."

With that, Vesch blinked for the first time. She staggered back as if waking from a dream. She looked around. The world overwhelmed her. She felt everything, everywhere, all at once and was frightened.

"I am sorry the world is so big. Let me help you." The figure came closer to her. She saw the man for the first time and gazed at the splendor of him. Yet, she was not afraid. She stared into his eyes and saw herself or who she used to be. He held her hand.

"What is your name?" asked the figure.

"V-ee-sch," struggled voice, who vaguely remembered the name.

"One day, you must earn your new name. I am bringing Spring soon. I will see you again."

Vesch watched as the figure walked away into the forest. She looked around her. She saw the basket of roots and herbs. She saw a wrinkled face that flashed and darted within her mind's eye. She remembered a howling, screaming voice. Walking south of the house, she tried to speak on her own. Her voice came out like a squawking sound. Her throat felt like she had swallowed ash. She continued, sounding like a wounded goose. She imitated words she heard. Some were simple, some more complicated with various loops and trills. She practiced this until dusk then, remembering her duties, ran clumsily through the forest, dropping half of the herbs from her basket.

By the time she finally made it to Baba Yaga's house, Baba Yaga was gone and had taken many papers with her. Vesch was completely alone for the first time. With new eyes, Vesch began to look around the small house. She fingered the hanging herbs and plants. She looked into each jar and smelled everything she encountered. She grabbed a few dried fruits and painfully chewed them until she gave up and spat them all onto the floor. Remembering when Baba Yaga did so, Vesch lit several candles within the small room and was astonished. She saw the grand collage of tinctures, potions, symbols, and trinkets. Everything contained an energy or life that drew her in. Vesch hobbled her way around to the doors. She clasped the handles and toggled them. The door leading to the attic toggled free, and Vesch climbed her way in.

She was overcome by the glowing, green light that rippled in the room. The mixture leisurely churned. She walked closer. Her chest grew heavy as her new-found heart took in the strain. But, Vesch did not stop. As she reached the rim of the cauldron, she looked into the mixture. Her face was almost touching the liquid. The energy ebbed and flowed like the tide. She took her hand from the rim and decided to dip one finger in.

Steadily, the mixture curled around her hand. The ooze curled back like a snake, and she flung her back. She fell onto the floor like a rag. She lay there, feeling a surge of power, light, sound, taste, touch, thought, memory, peace, and strength. Her body writhed as fresh vines curled around her. Amber jewels sparked in her sockets, and green things grew all over her body and breath; real air entered her lungs. She fumbled back towards her feet, trying to find balance in a new body. She looked at her strong hands, and she felt her body pulsing with fire. Quickly, she leaped again towards the cauldron and looked at her face.

Something like a nose pierced out from the center, and her eyes were wild and untamed. Vesch was like the first luxurious day of spring!

A familiar crash and boom of the house-finding ground knocked Vesch down, and she scurried like an animal back to the attic door when Baba Yaga stood at the entrance, glaring at her. Vesch, on her hands and knees, looked up at Baba Yaga. Baba Yaga grabbed Vesch by her locks and brought her inches from her nose.

Baba Yaga took in a deep smell of Vesch and laughed a deep laugh. "So, you have met your father, Life. I have been warding him for centuries, but he always finds a way back. You have been given many gifts. Should I snuff them out?" Baba Yaga pondered whether the slave would be valuable with life or without.

Versch couldn't speak. She curled within herself and desperately wanted to repel away from the woman who held her captive.

After a long pause, Baba Yaga made her decision, "I will allow you this way. But, you must only gather herbs at night. If I see you out when the sun is high, I will pluck every petal and burn every vine. I will snatch your mind, squeeze your heart, and snuff out your soul. Is that understood?"

Vesch was dropped to the floor and kicked through the door until she tumbled down the stairs and back into the main part of the house.

"I also will add one more precaution. You must wear this," said Baba Yaga with a sly grin. A small iron chain slinked like a snake around Vesch's neck and clamped into her flesh.

"That should hide you from anyone but me or anyone I want you to talk with. NOW GO! Fetch some firewood!" with that, Baba Yaga slammed the attic door closed. Vesch walked out of the house, feeling heavy from the iron chain.

Vesch found the axe wedged into a stump. There was a particular tree north of the house that was solely for the firewood. Carrying the ax, she trudged her way through the muddy ground, newly soaked with melting snow. For the first time, Vesch felt fatigue as well as fear. She did not know that this would be the lingering sensation for the majority of her days with Baba Yaga.

Going towards the tree, she could feel a beating heart like hers and roots that dug deep into the ground. A face is shown in the moonlight. It was like that of an old man. The arms of the tree forever raised to the sky, and the mounting head of branches was cut and shorn half-hazard. The tree was in pain.

Vesch came closer, and the eyes of the tree looked at her and then at the ax, "do what you must," it said. The voice was laced with sorrow.

Vesch looked closer at the tree. The bark of the Leishii had a cracked texture. The other parts of the great tree were of other types that spiraled around him. The warping prison of the Leishii was the grafting of other trees to produce fruit of every kind. He would never die, but he would never know relief.

"Who are you?" asked the Leishii, mustering strength to speak.

"I do not know," said Vesch. Her voice was hoarse and awkward. At night Vesch practiced speaking by reciting the spells that Baba Yaga had used the day before.

"What does she call you?"

"Vesch," she hissed.

"I do not know my name," the Leishii winced as more of his prison coiled around his body. "She took it away from me. I used to walk these forests and tend to the trees that grew here. I used to speak with Life often and drink the golden manna of the sun. She trapped me to grow firewood for her and to always produce fruit for her stores. She took my name. Without it, I am only a tree."

Vesch listened carefully. She saw more of the Leishii be absorbed into the wills of his prison. His spirit was fading.

"Will you help?" he asked. The golden spark in his eyes grew dim.

Vesch nodded.

"Take some of my branches. If she sees you come back with nothing, you will die or worse. My branches keep her cauldron flowing."

Vesch shook her head and began to back away.

"Do as I say!" he hissed. Reluctantly, Vesch took some of the branches. She ran towards the house, stumbling and kicking up mud while holding the fresh branches in a bundle. Vesch huffed as she ran. She was careless with her footing and tripped, falling into the snow and mud. The branches tumbled into a heap.

Vesch got up. She gathered the bundle of wood. Something in her chest burned. Vesch was filled with a desire to hurt, to burn, to kill. She imagined the ugly, wretched old woman hung by her hair from that poor tree, wailing in pain. She imagined Baba Yaga sinking into the cauldron and burning alive. Vesch stood for a long time, dwelling and concocting all kinds of terrible things.

'Not yet,' she thought, *'Soon, though. Or we all die.'*

After Baba Yaga went to sleep, Vesch carefully searched the immaculate journals and drawings of the witch: nothing. She found spells and curses for every possible reason but nothing about the name of the Leishii spirit. Finally, Vesch slumped into her corner and slept until the next night came upon her.

• • •

With her mortar and pestle flying through the air, Baba Yaga left the house in the forest in search of her ally, Death. He watched over a village on the outskirts of the forest, watching as a cloud raced towards them overhead. Baba Yaga walked beside him, ignoring the impending sign of doom.

"Death, you are wasting your time. The danger you see will not happen for another 400 years", called out Baba Yaga from behind him. She walked through the trees and stood beside him.

"I am tending to my task. What are you doing, old woman?"

"I need you to help me find a man. He has seen a creature that I want dearly, and I wish to know where to find it. Bring him to me."

"What creature and what man?" asked Death, looking down at her.

"A bird made of fire that flashed like the sun in the night. I wish for its heart. There was a man in this village who saw it. Where is he?"

"Ah, that man. He is dead, Baba Yaga. He did not live long in the face of the creature you seek."

"No matter, help me find him. Hopefully, you remember", she chuckled to herself, and Death headed towards the east where a cemetery stood.

Among the old gravestones, large and small, was one of the oldest gravestones that stood towards the back of the cemetery. The writing had withered away a long time ago, and thus, the man was forgotten- by all except Death, of course.

Baba Yaga spat on the ground and the dirt washed away, opening to the bones of the man. Leaning down, Baba Yaga extended a gangly arm and plucked out a skull. From the sleeves of her dress, she pulled out a candle, lit it, and placed it in the skull through the left eye. The skull glowed and sparked to life as the ghostly voice of the man filled the air. She put him on a staff and began to speak to his soul.

"Man of earth and bone, hear me. While breath was in your lungs, you saw a great sight: a firebird. Tell me where you saw the bird, and I will help you reach paradise." Her words soothed him.

In a howling voice, the soul spoke: "I saw the creature fly through the air and consume the world in light like the sun. The moon was high in the sky and so it seemed that the sun and the moon were finally together."

Baba Yaga nodded. "And where does this firebird call home?"

"It has no home. You will see it if you find the planet Venus in the night sky."

"Thank you, friend. Now meet paradise at last." She blew out the candle, and the soul was snuffed out.

"You sent the soul to a void, Baba Yaga. That was cruel of you," said Death casually.

"Are you surprised by me now after all these centuries?! I do not have to be honest, Death."

"Will you leave me finally?"

"Yes, I will leave you to do your duties. But I will not be far behind." She rode through the sky in her mortar and rowed with her pestle in the wind. Death continued his watch over the village.

The house of the Baba Yaga was deceptive. Although it was small and unassuming to the naked eye, Baba Yaga kept her secrets closer to the grain than most would believe. Upon entering the forest, Baba Yaga came to the door of her house and placed a key in the lock. The key was made from blood-red iron and as she turned the lock, the door opened into a different room. Instead of the room of potions and herbs, this room was decorated with the spoils of the hunt. Unicorn horns, dryad tails, and teeth of every dragon known to man, along with their heads stuffed and hanging on the walls. Baba Yaga selected a silver bow with glinting arrows. The arrows were ice-cold to the touch. Baba Yaga strapped the quiver to her back and placed the bow in her mortar. She hoisted herself into her vessel and locked the door behind her, this time with a green key. She soared into the night sky, reaching higher towards the stars and hunted for the firebird.

Meanwhile, Vesch continued with her chores in the first room. She cleaned, tended to the fires, and gathered vegetables from the garden along with herbs. Vesch was told to meet with Zhazhda and Golod, the wolves. Vesch heard their howling grow closer as they smelled her. The two wolves approached Vesch with hunger in their eyes.

"What are you? Tree?" asked Vesch.

"No," growled Zhazhda, "we are wolves, animals with red blood and flesh. We are the witch's hunters."

Vesch attempted to feed the wolf's rabbit from Baba Yaga's kitchen, but both wretched the food. The bile from their stomachs smelled putrid, and steam rose from the hot vomit.

Golod, gasping, finally explained: "We were cursed to be Baba Yaga's slaves. We must hunt until we finally kill the most dangerous animal. Until then, we are always searching and we are always hungry. We cannot eat or drink until the beast we speak of is killed."

"Yet, how did you come into Baba Yaga's hands?" Vesch asked. In meeting more creatures under Baba Yaga's power, her chest grew heavy, and her eyes brought tears. The iron chain around her neck dug deeper.

"We wished to gain power, like so many. Our pride brought this upon us. Now, my brother and I only seek peace." Golod panted.

"I will help you!" declared Vesch, and she soothed Golod. "I will free you and the Leshii."

"Do not speak falsely. Do you swear it?" snarled Zhazhda.

"Yes, I will. I wish for freedom, too."

With that, the wolves bolted for their hunt. Vesch stood there. A weight was added to her shoulders and she still could not find answers to her many questions.

· · ·

Baba Yaga sailed higher and higher, and the chill air covered her skin in frost. Her breath was like smoke from a chimney as she willed to sail further into the heavens. The night grew darker as the inky black sky enveloped Baba Yaga- all for except a brilliant flash of golden light cascading across the dark sea. The firebird appeared. The wide wings of the bird flashed and burned so brightly that the eye would be blinded from looking at it directly. However, Baba Yaga was not detoured by the cold, the dark, the light, or the flashing brilliance. With her bow in hand and an arrow ready to fly, she aimed for the heart of the bird. She pierced the blazing flesh, but the bird did not die.

The creature screeched a caw into the void. It sailed further into the night, heading towards the planet Venus as it flew. Baba Yaga brought back a second arrow. The arrow shot true to the heart, almost cutting the first. The bird continued to screech and wail, flailing and shedding burning feathers as it flew. It raced against the wind. The wings of the bird grew larger as it reached its destination. Then Baba Yaga shot a third arrow. The arrow streaked silver through the sky and tore the breast of the bird open, exposing the heart. Light a meteor in space, the bird finally fell.

Upon finding the bird in a wide patch of scorched earth, she saw the burnt body turn to ash. The only thing that remained was the heart. At the smallest fluttering movement, the flames grew hotter with the touch. Baba Yaga blew into the flame, and life sprang back into it, making it grow larger and yellower. She kept the heart inside a lantern that lit her way and fed it air to keep the heat fresh. Soon, Baba Yaga made it back to her chicken-legged house and opened the door, this time with a black skeleton key. Inside was a large bed, and on the bed lay a three-headed man.

Baba Yaga slowly approached the body with the glowing lantern and sat it beside him. She laid the burning heart at his feet and reverently bowed her head.

In a low voice, she said, "Triglav, the mightiest god of these lands, holding order over heaven, earth, and hell itself. I beseech you. I give you this gift in your honor, and I ask that you grant me knowledge of your brother."

Baba Yaga picked up the heart and layed it in the palm of her hand. She let the heart beat slower and slower until the light turned blue. She crushed it, and the heart burst into sparks. Brilliant colors danced around the room, which was cloaked in deep darkness. The ash was sprinkled upon the sleeping figure. The eyes and mouth of each head were firmly encased in gold bands, but the heart of the man was exposed by a gaping hole wrenched from the chest. The chest still heaved in a tranquil trance, taking in every breath and alleviating every breath through his great nostrils on each face.

Baba Yaga drew closer to the heart of the man Triglav and took out a ram's horn from a table. Listening carefully, she waited for his response.

Triglav, the god of the three realms, was tall and broad as a tree. His eyes and mouth were clasped in gold in order for justice to be blind and truth to be silent. His heart, however, couldn't help but let his weary voice slip through the cracks. A painful voice whispered into Baba Yaga's ear. Again, he replied like all the times before. "The soul of my brother is concealed forever, and even I will not tell where it lay. I am Triglav; the sins of even my kin are protected within me."

She took in a deep breath and let it go shakily. Without warning, Baba Yaga threw the ram's horn across the room. Like a furious beast, she screamed, tore out her hair, and sunk her claws into the walls. The talismans, offerings, candles, and shrines flew across the room as her screams echoed through the forest. Small fires from the candles consumed cobwebs and old curtains.

The room burned rapidly. Old curtains as thin as paper were swept up in flames. She plopped herself on the floor. Her heart raced, and the heat of her rage went into her ears. She took in the air while a throaty noise still echoed from her. She hung her head back against the bed as she watched the flames race. Just before the room was about to fall, she snapped her fingers, and the flame blew out instantly. The room went back as it was, cold and empty, except for the imprisoned Triglav. She had heard those words before- the ones that denied every sacrifice and offering. She would not find what she was looking for. At least not with Triglav's help, willingly or forcefully. She would not find Koschei's soul, not this way. Triglav was a lost cause.

Baba Yaga turned toward the sleeping giant. "You will not speak. You will not accept my offerings. You will do nothing. Then, I will simply feed you to my wolves. You will either satisfy them finally, or you will be vomited like the rest of their food. Either way, I don't care." Baba Yaga left the room, and the sleeping giant's heart beat faster.

• • •

Baba Yaga flew out of the door as Vesch was walking back to the house. She streaked across the night sky, soaring madly into the south. Vesch ran into the house, abandoning her basket. Upon entering she reeled around, unearthing everything that was within the small shack. She scavenged corners to the point of obsession and found nothing. The chains dug at the fresh sap that was seeping away and the pain was beginning to become unbearable. A creak from the door on the left opened. The soft glow of candlelight showed. Vesch carefully stepped through and closed the door behind her; any dangers within this room were more manageable than the witch that held her captive.

Vesch gaped at the giant Triglav. Her eyes grew wide in astonishment to see his full form. She then noticed the wrenched hole in his chest, revealing a massive heart.

Vesch sat next to the man and tried to whisper in his ear, "Who are you? Why are you here?"

Nothing. Vesch only saw the smooth rise and fall of his chest as he breathed, as well as the rhythmic pumping of the heart. Vesch tried again, and still nothing. In the corner of the room, the ram's horn still lay on the table. Vesch fondled the horn in her hands. Looking at the heart, she placed the larger end of the horn on the pumping muscle and the smaller end to her ear. She waited

Vesch heard an anxious voice gasping to speak, "I am Triglav. I have been imprisoned like you to serve only a purpose. If you free me, then I will be able to help you as well as those you have encountered. Release me from my bonds, seal my heart, and then I will help you to be reunited with your father."

108

Vesch shot back in surprise and disgust. She stopped for a moment to think. She asked, "How did you become trapped by Baba Yaga if you were so powerful? Why should I trust a caged animal?"

Triglav responded in earnest, "I was in search of my brother Koschei. I was searching for him in order to know the whereabouts of his soul and make it so that the secret would only lie with me. I would have the knowledge alone. Then, upon my journey, Baba Yaga took an arrow and shot me through my heart. I was paralyzed. She brought me here and has been trying to find the secret for herself."

"So you were successful in finding your brother's soul?" asked Vesch.

"Yes, but I have sworn upon my life to keep it secret until the earth falls into nothing," said Triglav, who took in a deep breath, "the spell that Baba Yaga used to capture me is used to paralyze me. Find it, and I will be free."

"Where can I find what traps you here?" Vesch kept listening closely, but also she kept one ear pricked towards the attic door.

"Look into my heart. The answer is there," and then Triglav grew quiet, falling deeply into weariness. Vesch drew back and put back the ram's horn. She peered over the heart. The heart had a visible scar that was not fully healed. A raised mark showed the fine work of an archer who had enslaved the giant. Vesch, in her curiosity, touched the scar and felt a small bump. Fear left her as she traced her leafy fingers over it. Then, as if upon impulse, she parted the scar and reached a finger down into the tissue. Her fingers touched a smooth, pointed stone, and she pulled it out carefully.

Triglav's body was wretched, and his muscles spasmed. When he finally relaxed, the great man rose slowly and looked at Vesch. The bands of gold around his eyes and mouth looked as if the metal had been poured and quickly sealed. The heads of the giant were perfectly still, but all were in unison when focused. Vesch receded into the walls of the room as she saw the god, Triglav, rise and listen for Vesch as she stepped. He healed the gaping hole.

Vesch huddled in the dark. Trying not to breathe. Triglav fumbled out of the bed and walked towards her. He crouched to meet her, hearing her heartbeat out of her chest. He touched Vesch's arm, and from him, she was granted strength to her arms and legs. She grew fuller and richer with muscles, fangs, claws, fur, and eyes that pierced through the vast darkness of night. She was both a plant and an animal. Vesch could feel hot blood rushing through her. She could feel a stronger heartbeat and hot breath turn into mist before her in the starkly cold room. Her ears could hear the slightest shift between the floorboards, and her mouth craved fresh kill.

Triglav then spoke to Vesch, "I will tell you how to free the creatures in Baba Yaga's possession, but this must be done tonight before she returns. She will try to kill me and eat me in order to gain my powers. You must do as I say to free your companions. Triglav gave Vesch the knowledge to free the Leshii trapped to grow in endless pain and to free the hunting wolves, Zhazhda and Kogot, who never stop their hunting. Vesch rushed out of the house, sprinting as the dawn came over the horizon. She swung from every tree and darted from every branch.

Finding the Leshii, she approached it and whispered the tree's name into his ear, "You are Rowan. You are the Rowan tree. Now be free." Darting into the wind, Vesch leaped away. The Rowan tree burst from its pressing vines and magic and burst into a budding tree that sprouted fruits and flowers. Higher and higher, the tree climbed, and the branches spread out wider. The fruits ripened and glittered in the sunlight.

Vzesch found Golod and Zhazhda and directed them towards the south. A fiery red bear three times their size would be raging across the lands and they must hunt it down and eat it entirely in order to be free. With all their might, Golod and Zhazhda ran through the forest with the sun at their side. They found the bear, tore it with their sharp teeth and ate every last bit of the bear. Then, for the first time, they slept under the sun.

Baba Yaga came back more furious than before. She looked more monstrous- her features sharpened and jaded. She rowed her way through the forest in her mortar with the severed head of a giant serpent hanging from the mortar; its teeth flared as its eyes rolled in the back of its head.

Baba Yaga flew into her attic window. She put the mouth of the serpent over the brim of the cauldron to collect the venom. Then, the mixture turned thick and black. With a scoop of a bottle, she took the poisonous mixture and went into Triglav's room. He was still sleeping soundly. The wrenched place where his heart lay was still open.

Baba Yaga moved closer, and in a hissing sound like a cat, she spoke, "After I have killed you, I wille at you. This poison will kill the feeling from your toes to your head and force your heart to stop slowly. It will feel like you are trapped under the snow shortly before your death, and you will also slowly suffocate. Thankfully for me, when I eat you, I will not succumb to the same fate."

Baba Yaga took a swig from the bottle, and the black substance stained her lips and mouth. The smell of her breath was putrid and acidic. She stood on top of Triglav, eyes red with rage. As soon as the bottle was tipped over Triglav's heart, Triglav took a great arm and grabbed Baba Yaga by the neck. Like a rabbit, the giant god hoisted Baba Yaga and walked out of the ruined alter room. Vesch came swiftly through the blossoming trees. Like fireworks, the trees and plants all bloomed and sprouted fruit, finally being free of their slumber. The animals began to prance happily, stretching their legs.

Vesch made it to the house with chicken legs flat to the ground, no Tallon or claw in sight. Vesch ran to the attic and found the giant Triglav holding what looked like a red-skinned devil with claws longer than branches of a tree and teeth sharper than any sword. Baba Yaga's eyes were wide, black upon black eyes that shined like stars. Triglav was in the attic holding Baba Yaga over the cauldron. The liquid stirred faster as if it were excited.

Triglav looked down at Vesch, "do you think she deserves death?" he asked.

Vesch thought for a moment and then replied, "I don't wish for anyone to die. I just wish that she no longer decided our fates."

Then Baba Yaga bit Triglav's hand and ate off his thumb. She ran out of the house, a blazing fire of anger ran like an animal. On all fours, she raced through the forest. Vesch ran after her, her heart beating faster and harder with every step.

Baba Yaga flew over the treetops as Vesch followed after. Baba Yaga called out in a growling howl, "Death, I beseech you. Come to ME!!" She screamed. In a flash, Death appeared before Vesch as she halted. Vesch saw the black void as it consumed everything. Her breath halted slightly, and her heart fluttered. Death looked at Vesch and then looked at Baba Yaga. Death then, in a deep voice that rumbled the souls of all earth, "You have no power over me, moral witch." Baba Yaga screamed as Death allowed Vesch to drag the witch back to the house. Pon enters the house. Baba Yaga's scream shook the hanging herbs and set off all of the talismans and tokens. They flickered madly as she tried not to move past the doorway.

Finally, Vesch pushed Baba Yaga into the cauldron. A huge cloud of smoke shot out of the house… and then finally stopped. The cauldron was empty.

• • •

Vesch found herself walking through the forest. She rested underneath the Rowan tree. Before she fell asleep, Life came to her.

"Hello, daughter," said Life. He was fully dressed in a robe made of moss, leaves, vines, and flowers. Fruits grew from the tops of his head, and his amber eyes glowed brighter than ever. "Have you chosen a name?"

Vesch remembered the first conversation with Life. She realized that she never really thought about her name or who she was. Never had the chance to think for much.

"I have not decided yet. My life hasn't really begun. So much has happened. I think I will rest here for a while."

"I understand. Then, may I bestow one more gift on you?"

Vesch nodded. Life touched her forehead. Vesch was covered in olive skin, with black hair, hazel eyes, and soft lips. The vines and fur fell away. As she finally fell asleep, she became fully human. Under the Rowan tree, she rested as the house of the Baba Yaga disappeared into the trees.

AMPHIBIOUS TOTALUS

Long ago, as one might expect this story to go, a young King was cursed to become a toad by an evil witch. He would only be able to turn back into a King if he found someone pure of heart who could help him. However, unlike most stories, this one doesn't end how one would expect. The King never becomes human again, and the pure of heart never finds him. Or does it?

Many long years have passed since that day. The day that the King enforced the final tax on his people and how the crops were destroyed by floods. What little people could give was given all for the sake of avoiding extra labor in the debtor's prisons, their homes taken away, or part of their land sold back to the King. A young woman, a healer and sorceress of the village, gave her portion to the King. She gave many herbs, but the King (fattened by delusion) turned up his nose at her and said, "This is not the full payment? Where is the rest?" He picked at a fingernail on a finger the size of a sausage.

The woman said, "This is all I can give. Like many of us, we are not able to give our share because there is no food and no crops."

"Surely, the winter did not take away your ability to find more herbs and healing things than this? You do not have to grow this yourself, so why have you slacked on your portion?!" the voice of the King grew stern as he narrowed his eyes at the woman. The ladies of the court behind him snickered behind their painted faces. His ruffled collar dug ever so slightly into his neck. His feet bulged out of his shoes, and his crown, rusted in some places, slid atop his greasy head.

"I have had to tend to the weak and the worn. There are too many people in this kingdom dying of disease, hunger, and thirst because of the floods."

"Yes, well, no matter. You must give your portion or face the consequences. What else might you give that would benefit the kingdom?" asked the King.

"I can give you my talents, but I cannot give you anything else."

"Your talents! Ha! That must be a joke. In this entire town, you have done nothing but help little old ladies with bunions or old men with their head colds!"

"I help those who need me most. You work these people to the bone so your fat, loathsome buttocks can lounge around all day!" the people behind the woman were whispering and urging her to stop. Some even said they would give her their portion in order for her to leave freely. Children held on to the skirts of their mothers and eyed the guards that were at attention in the throne room. Fathers clutched their taxes and gritted their teeth.

"How dare you insult your King!" he cried, standing now. His face was covered in grease, and his body was plump like a ripe peach, "I am the appointed ruler of this kingdom! You besmirch me. You besmirch my father who bled and died for all of your sake! Do you wish to insult him and your country?" A common tactic. The citizens of this kingdom adored the King's Father, King Raymond. King Raymond was kind, brave, and forthright. He would have died for any of them, and they all believed him. However, when the King died, there was no one who could take care of his son except for the King's advisors. One can imagine how effective their tutelage was. This King became nothing like his father. As he spoke, his voice rose into a shrill like a pig. His eyes were bloody and rageful. But the woman didn't stop.

"I would rather cut out my tongue than besmirch your father. As for you, I would cut out my tongue if I didn't besmirch a meddling, cheating, slovenly, fat ogre of a man like you! You greedy pig!" she pointed a finger at him now and cried out in a voice that shook the bones of all who heard, "May you become what you truly are. May no one save you except those with a pure soul!" In a swirl of light and color, a toad plopped from a height and landed on the throne of the slovenly king. The guards were astonished, and the ladies of the court screamed. The people behind the woman backed away in shock and waited for *their* doom.

She turned around. Her eyes were wide with shock and surprise. She looked at her hands and at the slimy toad as it croaked and hopped miserably on the cushioned seat. In a rage, she picked up the toad, picked up her skirts and marched out of the castle. All of the villagers, taking their food and wilting crops with them, followed her and excitedly chatted about what she might do. She marched through fields. She marched through forests. Little children jumped and played around her feet as with unyielding focus, she clenched the toad in her hand. The toad, or formerly the slovenly king, was croaking and squirming. His yellow eyes bulged, his back legs flapped, and with what little control he had with his front legs, he was trying to push himself out of her grasp. He did not budge, but he did not give up.

Finally, the woman came to the edge of a swamp. The crowd behind her, a little thinner now than in the beginning, huffed as they stopped. Some sat, and some were bent over, trying to take in gulps of air. She, however, was standing straight as an arrow. Her face was scrunched up, her brow furrowed, and her eyes bulging. She brought the toad up to her face. The toad, formerly slovenly ogre king, was weak and breathing heavily, too. He did not have the strength to fight her grip, and his body was like water in her hands.

She spat in his face and mocked, "This is your kingdom, pig!" and with all her might (and a little magic), she hurled the prince high into the sky, and he crashed down into the briny waters. The people cheered as he sailed and landed in the bog. The woman and the rest of the villagers finally went home. As for the castle and the guards and the ladies, the small kingdom disbanded and the castle housed weeds and dust from that point on. The fat, ogre-sih, and slovenly king sank beneath the waters, but that is not the end of our story.

• • •

Sinking slowly, the toad opened his eyes. All around him, the murky color of swamp water, caked in algae and covered in lily pads, filled his vision. He stopped and stared around him, and as soon as he realized he was in the water, he gasped and flailed around until he finally swam to the surface. He broke into the air and continued to paddle aimlessly until he found a lily pad sturdy enough. He spread himself onto the lily pad and wept. He had lost everything he loved, and now he was truly a miserable oaf. He was green, covered in warts, with yellow eyes. He smelled putrid and hated the fact that the only thing he craved was a dragonfly and not roasted pork or bread like any normal person would. He stayed like this for some time. Wallowing in misery and asking the Almighty God what he had done wrong, until he heard a voice that twinkled like bells.

"Hello, are you alright, Mr. Toad?" said the voice.

The King did not look up from his wallowing. The owner of the voice took a delicate hand and raised up the frog to her face, "Poor thing. You must be under some sort of spell."

The king wiped away his slimy tears and looked into the face of the one holding him. She was a beautiful princess. Golden locks and startling blue eyes. Her lips were soft and pink, her skin was perfect, and her cloak marked her in every aspect as a princess. Her cloak was a soft pink with gold embroidery and jewels that looked like blossoming flowers. The King was speechless but quickly gathered himself. Finally, he said, "My name is King Peter of Paduah. I have come under a terrible curse, and only one pure of heart can save me."

He gestured a webbed hand and bowed slightly. He waited. Eventually, he raised his head to look into the eyes of the princess. Her head was cocked to one side, and one eyebrow was raised. She was utterly confused, and now King Peter was sweating (if, in fact, toads can sweat). He tried to speak again, saying the exact same phrase, but again nothing.

The princess shook her head and said, "I am sorry, I don't understand what you're saying."

The King realized something. Though he spoke plain english to his ears, to hers, it was a hoarse and croaky language. His throat even expanded as he warbled and grackled. Embarrassed, he squatted into her hands and thought hard about what to do next.

God in heaven, do I have to do charades?!" he thought. Yet, thinking longer on the idea he decided that it was his only choice. Finally, the games began. King Peter stood again and held up the number two with one webbed hand.

"Oh! How clever! A game of charades. You must truly be noble, sir Toad", giggled the pretty princess.

The King's chest puffed up a little (literally), and he began his sorry acting. He flung himself in the arm, he failed his arms, he made impressions, and eventually, the princess half understood what he was saying.

"To be clear: you are a prince cursed to be a toad until someone saves you? Am I correct, Sir Toad?"

After all the flailing and dancing around in the palm of the pretty princess, King Peter nodded excitedly.

"Well, how exactly must I save you?" asked the princess, bringing King Peter closer.

King Peter gestured to his heart, for that was all he could do. What happened next would be part of recorded history forever, even if the records are wrong on almost all accounts.

"I must fall in love with you? Is that it?" asked the princess, now slowly becoming disturbed by her circumstances. She traveled for miles in hopes of a gallant king. She and many other maidens heard of the rich, handsome, talented, and brave king who lived beyond the swamp, the forest, and the fields. And just like many other maidens like her, she would have been granted a much ruder awakening upon arrival at King

Peter's castle. Thankfully, however, the current circumstances are not as bleak.

"Yes! I have heard of tales like this from my nursemaid. I know how I must save you!" cried the princess. She pursed her lips, and in one swift motion, she kissed the toad. Granted, King Peter was not opposed to the experiment. But, the longer their kiss remained, the more that both fell into an awkward silence. The pretty princess had enough and threw King Peter back into the water. She spat and wiped her face a thousand times with her handkerchief. She squealed in disgust and stared down at the bobbing head of the devastated toad.

"I am sorry that I wasn't able to save you and that I threw you." she brought out a small parcel of sweets to eat to take away the swampy taste of toad, "I did try my best, Sir Toad. I suppose I am not the one to save you." She shrugged. Eventually, she walked back towards her gilded carriage.

King Peter hopped towards the fringe of her dress and began to climb his way back towards her lips. She screamed and swiped at him as those guarding the carriage grabbed the King and flew him back into the swamp. Big tears fell down her face. She (artfully) fainted and was brought back to her carriage, where her nursemaid brought her back to health. The carriage whisked away to King Peter's kingdom and abandoned castle.

Peter once again found himself on a lily pad and stared out as he watched the carriage go by. Eventually, the familiar sounds of buzzing and whirring of insects filled the air. He was without a castle, creed, or kingdom, and the humid air weighed down his thoughts. The summer air was putrid, and so was destiny.

Months passed, and Peter lived an ordinary life as a toad with contempt. The only thing he could be happy about was the plentiful bugs and the fact that he could sing. In another life, Peter was able to construct songs and ballads, which were not so bad for a fat, ogre king. Now, he hummed the tunes he created. Unlike most frogs who sang one note, Peter was able to construct melodies even with the voice of a toad.

The rest of the toads would sing their droning, one-note songs he would try to harmonize with. Besides avoiding most frogs, he made one friend who he named Happy. Happy was a young frog who talked with him often, however, in frog-speak, the vocabulary of Happy was woefully limited.

"Hello friend, come and sit?" gleefully asked, happy most mornings.

"No Happy, no sit," said Peter, which was his usual answer, and he began to sing his song again.

"Why?" asked Happy.

"I am not well Happy as I have not been well for the past 210 days."

'What is day?" at this Happy hopped closer to Peter with a confused expression.

Peter groaned inwardly, and his eyes narrowed. His mouth dropped into a scowl as he resigned himself to his fate. For the 173rd time, Peter recounted to Happy what a day was: "Happy, a day is the course that the sun makes. It rises in the east and sets in the west. It is a way of telling the passing of time. Do you understand?"

"What is the sun?"

"The sun is a great big ball of light in the sky that makes everything warm. Do you see? There it is in the big blue sky. Funny how you again miss it entirely," the last part Peter said under his breath.

At this, Happy said, "Sun hurts."

"Yes, it does. Happy, you are very observant." Peter condescendingly nodded and confirmed Happy's realization like he would a child. And in vain, the same answer occurred: Happy stared for a moment longer and said, "Come sit?"

Peter relented and sat with Happy on the same lily pad, both singing songs. Peter never asked any questions of Happy and was satisfied with that. He was determined to never acquaint himself with any frogs until his death. Happy was just another bland character within the bland repetition of existence. However, Happy surprised Peter on the 174th day of their acquaintance.

"Peter, am friend?"

Peter looked at Happy more seriously, eager to hear something other than the usual dribble, "Of course, Happy, you are my friend."

"Don't think so," said Happy, who looked out into the distance with seemingly vacant eyes.

"Of course we are friends! We sing together and then leave our separate ways. You are the best friend I ever had. We know loads about each other," Peter repositioned himself and moved closer to the vacant-eyed creature beside him.

"No," said Happy matter-of-factly.

"Happy, you are speaking nonsense!" cried Peter who settled himself back into the ballad he had been perfecting for a month now.

"Come, I show you home," and Happy leaped from pad to pad, heading towards the thicker part of the swamp with hanging limbs and drooping moss. Peter followed, narrowly missing a lily pad or two. Happy stopped abruptly on a lily pad. Deep within the shades of a tree, there was a colony of frogs singing and eating together. Some of them were sunbathing. Others were sitting on top of one another. In one small little enclave, small tadpoles swarmed together and were carefully watched over by their father as their mother hunted. The air was thick and humid but perfect for a colony of frogs.

Peter was disgusted. He wanted nothing to do with any of these creatures. Oftentimes, he made many journeys back to the castle but with no success. The group of frogs mindlessly went about their usual habits until they noticed Peter. Flashes of conscious thought showed through their eyes momentarily as they recognized Peter, a bug, a friend, and then Peter again.

Peter missed hot food. Peter missed having a soft bed to lie in. He wanted to have a young girl to kiss or a peasant to scream at. Even the coldest nights with very little fire were better than the swamp. Peter followed Happy, looking around at the slimy, blank faces. Several frogs attempted to sit next to him or even sit on top tranquilly, but Peter hopped and flipped frantically. He tried to remember what it was to be human, what it meant to be warm-blooded and with hair on top of his head. He started to swim away from it all and decided that maybe one last-ditch effort towards the castle. Maybe someone will recognize him. Maybe it he could do the same with the princess, he would be able to tell someone the truth.

Happy stopped, "What? Why run?"

"I am human for goodness sake, HUMAN!" and Peter began to swim fast, paddling like a dog. Happy swam beside him and poked his head above the waters.

"You are frog. You like me. What is human?" said Happy. He thought very hard about what a human was but couldn't form the idea in his mind.

"I am NOT a frog!" screamed Peter. He continued trying to escape, but swimming seemed to only make things worse. He began to go to dry land, the banks of the pond. There, he met more frogs like him, green with large, black eyes and wide mouths. They were poised at the edge of the bank, singing their droning calls all in harmony. Peter stopped, breathing frantically. Happy caught up to him and sat next to him. Peter directed his attention to the singing chorus and listened, feeling the vibrations of the chorus.

Something about the alien choir reminded him of when he was a child. The droning hum of the frogs reminded him of the coronation of his father in the cathedral. He remembers the deep singing as his father approached his throne, his song following behind. Peter began to sing in his own frog voice the Latin verse that was sung along with the deep Gregorian tone that echoed through the stone walls.

"The King has come to take his throne

The sword in one hand and the olive branch in another

He will rule over his land in the name of God

As the appointed Lord and rightful ruler

May he reign in justice and peace.

And may God rule over him forever."

The words were simple. Peter sang with the choir of frogs this verse over and over recalling when his father was alive. Peter remembers his father playing music for him when he was a child, but those memories were few. He remembered when his father died and how quiet everything became. The advisors mildly tolerated him as they taught him and raised him. Peter realized how angry he was and looked around at the choir. This was his life, and it infuriated him. He raced towards the castle once again, hopping madly. Happy followed him again, saying nothing but trying to keep up.

"Wait, Peter. Be Slow!" cried Happy. But it was too late. Turning around, Peter heard and saw splashes of water rise as frogs scurried into the pond. A crane had flown into the waters and was making its fill of the frogs who were not so lucky. Peter began heading towards the castle until he heard the flapping of wings close by. He scrambled while Happy followed behind, also trying to make an escape. Peter found a small opening in a tree and climbed in. Looking out, Happy was being swallowed by the crane, and then the crane flew back into the air without a second thought.

Peter felt alone, vulnerable, and scared. His body shook as he recalled the image of poor Happy being snatched from thin air. Peter realized then that he would no longer have Happy for the company and that Happy was never truly his friend. Peter was not anyone's friend or confidant anymore. The furious splashing and flapping of wings ceased, and Peter came out of the tree. All was quiet, deathly still. Peter hopped closer to the edge of the pond and began to sing- alone.

• • •

Many years passed, and Peter fell more into the ways of the wild. He hunted, sang, and swam in the shaded waters of the swamp. He did not meet any frogs like Happy. There were none he grew close to, either because of things he could not control or because of his own lack of interest. He was used to being alone for the first time in his life, and there was a part of him that didn't want to let go of some of that control.

On a beautiful summer day, Peter sang his song in the early morning light and heard the familiar sounds of a horse and the clinking of armor. It had been so long since he heard those sounds, but he knew exactly their purpose and who would be wearing them. A gleaming, plate-armored foot rested at the edge of the wamp as a handsome prince and his noble steed rested from their journey. The prince wore more ceremonial garb, anticipating a kingdom to marry into and rule. Yet, he did not know that there was no kingdom beyond the swamp.

Peter grew silent as he stared at the imposing figure. The prince must have known he was being watched because as he looked down, he saw Peter. Peter's gaze was no ordinary gaze of a frog, blank and numb. It was a knowing gaze, and this Prince saw opportunity like in all the tales his mother told him who in turn was told by her nurse-maid before her. He leaned further into the gaze of Peter, who saw his own reflection. It was the first time that Peter saw what he looked like as a frog. He was a small, green thing. His wide-eyed face showed no fear but also showed no significant sign of expression. Regardless of what his very soul told him, he was far from human and wondered if he would ever walk upright or eat from a knife and fork ever again. He forgot what it was like to not have webbed fingers or to not have a retractable tongue.

The Prince finally spoke to Peter after a long pause, "You have quite a mind about you. I can tell. A mind of a man within the body of a frog. What a shame." said the prince. The prince's voice was a sturdy, well-practiced tone. Peter looked more directly at the prince and moved in closer. He squatted, brought his legs further in, and nodded.

The Prince stood back a little, shocked to even have a response. His eyes changed expressions rapidly as his mind was working on what to say next. He had never encountered such a thing in his life. Remembering his mother's stories, he decided that he was destined to save this poor soul and with his sword drawn and lifted to the sky, he shouted with a mighty voice, "I vow to save you from your plight. Tell me, how have you come upon this curse?"

Peter was unsure of how well this would work. Despite being a frog, his eyes narrowed, and his mouth curled down in the most annoyed expression a frog could make. Peter didn't know how best to communicate with the prince, but before he could even think of what to say, the prince spoke again.

"I know what I must do. I will give you the horn of a unicorn to purify you entirely, and that way, you will be able to return to your human form." He said gallantly.

Peter was surprised. He hadn't thought of that and figured that it wouldn't have worked. However, he thought that maybe if he could be turned into a frog, then maybe the horn of a unicorn could possibly heal him.

The Prince mounted his beautiful white stead and rode off into the wild to find the elusive unicorn. Peter sat and looked out. He knew that it might take many days and many nights in order to find the creature, fight it to the death for its horn and then bring it back. So Peter waited, more curious than hopeful if it would even be possible. Then, a ripple in the water moved its way towards him. There was no wind.

From the waters, an alligator reared its ugly head. Bright yellow eyes peeked out from a dark green mass. The alligator growled from somewhere deep within himself. Slowly, he swam up to Peter and looked at him curiously.

"You are different. Too smart to be eaten, yes?" said the alligator. He dropped deeper into the waters and swam around Peter. Peter breathed fast and kept his eyes solidly on the alligator.

"What do you want with me? I have no quarrel with you!" said Peter. The alligator kept spinning in slow circles. Peter stepped over the edge of the lily pad and saw the great monster churning. He went into the water and saw it. The monster was almost as wide as a tree and almost as long. Peter swam beside it and landed on top of its head as it rose above the waters once again.

"Do you have a name, little one? You do not seem like a normal frog." as the alligator.

"How can you tell?"

'All predators can tell the difference between true prey and true predator. It is a way that you looked at me- with intelligence. You are not something to be eaten, but to eat those who are smaller than you."

"Do all predators think like this?"

"Yes, we must make decisions. Weigh the outcomes and think about the future. It is necessary for us and our offspring to be alive." Peter noticed that as they swam, they were going deeper into the swamp to the point where the sun was no longer visible.

"What other predators do you know personally? Are they mostly those who dwell in the water?"

"No, little one, I know the fox, the bear, the wolf, the crane, and many others. They are all simultaneously my friends and my enemies. I fight with them for survival like your webbed-fingered friends as well as talk to them like any other. That is life for us in this world."

Peter pondered for a moment. Peter thought again about his old life, but instead, he remembered the people he ruled. They were the mice bent under his will while he was the cat that played with them. Now, he does not feel so strong. He thought carefully of the faces of his people but could not think of one. Peter knew now what it meant to be weak in the face of a stronger opponent and then thought that this conversation with this beast was him toying with Peter. He kept his body under control as best as he could as he continued to talk. *Better to know your enemy than not, better to be close with advantage than far away with disadvantage*, thought Peter, who recalled that saying from an advisor.

"Yet, there is one creature that puzzles me, the unicorn," said the Alligator with a hint of scorn in his voice.

"The Unicorn! So it's real?" whispered Peter.

"As real as either of us. It eats, sleeps, and dies like any other animal, but it is tougher than anything I have ever seen. Many men have tried to capture it or kill it, but the Unicorn always has the upper hand."

"Tell me, why do men search for the Unicorn?"

"Men believe that the Unicorn possesses great power to heal or to bring fortune. All of this is true, but no man has lived to succeed in capturing the Unicorn."

Peter was stunned. He was surprised to learn that such a creature was capable of violence... or was it the unicorn itself he should be worried about? The prince that left to find the unicorn may never come back alive. And for what? For him? Why was Peter needing to be saved in the first place? He missed being human but slowly got used to being a frog, seeing how he had no choice. How would that benefit the prince? Then Peter felt a rumble deep within the alligator as it slowed slightly. The trees were closing in around them, and the water grew colder.

The alligator spoke again, "If you are not a frog, what are you?"

"Well, I once was human."

'Ah, yes. The truly most dangerous animal, but also can be the most stupid. Did you hunt former humans?"

Peter began to shake and then answered, "Yes, when I was human, I used to hunt a stag or a fox."

"Ah! I knew it. You did smell of blood, but more than foxes", said the alligator.

Peter noticed that he was more disturbed by the comment than the person saying it. He cautiously probed, feeling a lump in his throat, "What do you mean?"

"I have smelt and tasted the blood of man before. You reek of it! You must have been a formidable hunter. You have the heir of thousands on your hands. I see quick deaths and slow deaths- agony is all the same. Did you eat your kill, or was it for sport? Personally, I find killing for sport wasteful."

"W-why are you asking me this all of a sudden? Am I really a killer to you?"

"Yes. You smell rich with it", chided the Alligator. Peer looked and saw many yellow eyes around him. Some were from within the water, and some were on the edges of the bank. Some were in pockets of trees, and some were hiding behind branches. The eyes stared intently at Peter, probing and testing his every move. Peter began to weigh his options. He could not outswim the alligator, and he could not hop away. He could not dig his way out or fly. He knew he would die- or worse, be part of the council or yellow-glowing eyes that only thought of blood. Peter's eyes adjusted more to the darkness of his surroundings, and he could see clearly a fox, a snake, a vulture, a bear. All were looking at him with blank expressions. Or at least Peter could not identify what they thought of him. The alligator finally stopped towards the edge of the banks and began to crawl his way onto shore. Peter grasped onto the beast and waited with bated breath to see what would happen next.

"Former-human. Frog. Doesn't matter; you once killed, and now you are prey. You have nothing to save you now," the great chasm of the alligator's mouth opened. The rows of teeth shown and the laughing voices of the animals surrounding Peter echoed to the point it was almost deafening. Without warning, a blinding bright light crashed through the dark swamp and there in front of Peter was the dazzling Unicorn. All of the predators scattered like shadows as the Unicorn leaped through the air and landed on the other side of the bank. The Unicorn then looked down at Peter. Peter noticed that the horn of the Unicorn looked like it was cut at the base of the horn, but the cut did not go through but merely scathed the horn. The tip of the horn had a rosy tinge to it, but it did not seem natural- more like a stain.

Finally, the Unicorn spoke to Peter, "Are you the one who sent the Prince to find and kill me?"

Peter was stunned beyond words and merely stared at the shining creature before him, but the Unicorn grew impatient. Leaning down, it asked again, but with a force of power behind it, "Are you the one who sent that *Prince* to kill me?!"

Peter felt prostrate before the Unicorn, "Yes, it was me. Well, you see, he actually offered that that was the only solution for my curse, but I never really wanted him to kill you just to find a way to cure me. He was the only one doing all of the talking and making assumptions, but I really didn't want him to have to kill you or attempt to kill you." Peter's words fell out of him like water from a cup. They tumbled and fell before the Unicorn.

The Unicorn replied, "However, you made no effort to stop him. Despite your noble feelings, you had every intention of letting him try. Is that it?"

Unmoving, Peter stayed in his position and did not respond. The Unicorn let out a huff from his nostrils and pawed the ground. He said, "Even so, his blood is truly on your hands. The poor fellow never had a chance before I attacked him. You are the one responsible. And the curse you are under would not have been cured by me. He cannot save you, and I cannot. So, you must find a solution on your own." Immediately, the Unicorn ran into the swamp, a glittering blur.

Peter got up. He was alone once again. Going back to where he originally was, he saw the Prince's horse eating grass not too far away, but there was no rider. The second attempt of becoming human didn't work, and it caused the death of someone more worthy than he was. Peter felt the gravity of the death weigh on his mind. He also remembered what the Alligator said. The blood of thousands on his hands. The monster was right, after all. Peter allowed so many to die and for what? After having to live through several summers, he learned what it was to be hungry.

Peter sat in silence for a long time, taking in the events of the day and knowing there was nothing he could do to make things right.

• • •

Years passed. Peter had lost all but his mind and was truly an amphibian. He no longer sang. He no longer spoke but duly passed days and nights as the animal he feared becoming. Then, one day, a woman arrived at the swamp.

Peter sat on a lily pad. Small, dull thoughts raced through his mind-thoughts only concerned with survival. A shadow of a human cast over him, but he did nothing. He did not swim away or flinch, nothing.

The woman peered down at him and spoke: "My, bless you, your majesty. I didn't know what my powers could have done, but I never dreamed that they would extend your life."

Peter's mind blew up with memories. He remembered that voice, even as it was caked in age and experience. Turning now, he looked into the eyes of the woman. There was no mistake that they were the eyes of the witch who cursed him and threw him headlong into the forsaken depths of the swamp. He did not know what to think: rage, sadness, pleading, begging, all swam through his mind, but the only thing he could say was, "You are still alive?"

The woman laughed and sat down at the bank of the swamp. She smiled and offered her hand to the Prince. He hesitated and then finally went into her hand as she brought him level to her eyes.

"Your majesty. I will not ask forgiveness for what I did. You enraged a powerful woman, and that is a dangerous thing. But I cannot imagine what life must have been like like this."

"Nature has a different course than the world of humans. Things are cyclical here. I truly am the only constant that worked against nature's design. And thus, I couldn't figure out whether I am alien or deemed useless in nature's world."

The witch nodded.

"I haven't learned anything, you know. I understand what you meant by a pure heart. I haven't changed."

"How do you know?" asked the witch.

Peter laughed, "Old woman, your eyesight must be failing. Do you see *any* human features? Golden locks, blue eyes that face forward, a mouth that isn't as wide as the sea, pale skin that doesn't ooze?" Peter was becoming angry, but fatigue took over quicker.

"No, your Majesty, I don't. I am sorry."

Peter looked at her. Her eyes were filled with compassion- Peter wept.

The witch gently rubbed with her forefinger the back of the small frog. She waited for him to finish. In gasps, Peter finally cried, "I am so sorry. I am so sorry for everything. I starved those people. I besmirched my father's name. I drove them to death. I don't deserve to be human, and I don't deserve to live. What can I do? What can I do to help my heart from sinking so far into this?"

The Witch kissed Peter on top of his head and said, "I forgive you," and tears strolled down her face.

Peter bowed his head before her and raised it, "Thank you. Thank you very much. Thank you for healing me." He put a flipper to his heart as he smiled.

"Now, do you wish to be human?" said the Witch with an upraised eyebrow.

Peter was startled to silence. He hadn't thought of being human for years now. He didn't remember being human. His mind had erased the smell of bread and the softness of clothing for a very long time.

Eventually, Peter spoke, "I don't know if it will solve my problem."

"What problem?" laughed the Witch, "you have already broken the curse, and now you can make a choice."

"Do I deserve it?" asked Peter.

"I won't tell you what you do and do not deserve, but I will ask if there is a change you would want to make in your life. What would it be?"

Peter looked deeply into the Witch's eyes. There was no malice or deceit. Peter nodded and said he wanted to become human.

In the blink of an eye, Peter saw that his height was taller than the Witch. He looked and saw a pink hand inside hers and thin, bony fingers. He looked at his clothing, the same as when he was transformed into a frog, but they were baggy and misshapen. He was sullen and weak, and he realized he was slightly light-headed. Bugs were not enough to fill his diet anymore. His hair was matted and his beard too. He looked at the Witch.

"I have nowhere to go. What should I do?"

She smiled as the wrinkles near her eyes creased and tears cupped the edge of her eyelids, "would you like to come with me?"

Peter nodded and followed her hand in hand to the once-kingdom. Then Peter truly lived contently ever after.

THE BAKU AND THE LOST DREAMS OF A STORYTELLER

Yagi Toshiaki was so named when his mother noticed him making a paper crane while in the marketplace. She saw that one day, he would be highly intelligent and well-favored, and finally, she gave him a name that would tie him further to his destiny. Yagi Toshiaki lived in Edo, Japan, with only his mother. His father died when Yagi was just a baby, and for the longest time, Yagi was only a poor washer woman's son. His mother was also a seamstress, and as Yagi would fall asleep at night, he listened to the sound of his mother's voice as she sewed and told stories. Yagi's mother, Momo, was very imaginative but plagued with bad fortune. She believed she was cursed by a witch when she was born, but when Yagi was born, her fortune changed. She never complained, even on her dying day.

Yagi would often dream of the stories his mother told him. However, instead of the stories as they were, his mind changed them into swirling and miraculous ways. They shifted and transformed into amazing illustrations of life, death, and all matters of the human heart. When Yagi awoke, he would tell the stories to his mother, who grew in shock at every story he would tell. She urged him to keep dreaming and to remember all of his dreams. Eventually, Momo saved enough money in order for Yagi to have a tutor and to learn how to write. Yagi wrote all of his dreams. He wrote so much that the floor of his small room was filled with his pages. Then Yagi thought of an idea to share his stories.

When Yagi was fifteen, he set out into a busy area filled with people. It was an early morning in the market where the fresh fish were being sold and where vendors cooked various dishes with squid, octopus, salmon, and tuna. He stood on a box and looked over the crowd. The crowd was so thick with people, all hurrying to and from different vendors that it seemed like a sea of faces. The rumbling sound of voices was like the chattering of birds in trees or the rushing of water. Yagi smelled the oily scent of fish and the putrid smell of humans. He saw the smoke stacks and the flying signs and the great house of the Tokugawa Ieyasu himself, and with exhilaration, Yagi yelled in a loud voice, "Hear me! I come to tell a tale you will never believe!" As he said that, several faces perked up and set eyes on Yagi, waiting to be impressed or even disgusted. Yagi froze as his arms were high in the air with outstretched fingers to heaven. He was terrified of himself, and sweat dripped down his forehead. The passersby were just about to continue walking when Yagi began his story. Again, in a loud voice, he recalled a dream in detail. The onlookers came closer to him as he told the story.

Suddenly, more came to him and Yagi noticed that he had almost a dozen people within his bubble. Yagi's heart raced. He wove a pattern of color, sound, taste, and touch. He encaptured his characters as if they were real, and in the settings he would describe, the people could see perfectly in their mind's eye. Some children sat closest to Yagi as they watched him performing and telling the dream he had. Yagi's mouth was dry as he spoke, but he continued despite the creaking box and his failing voice. His excitement was so much so that it made his story even more intense. At the base of the box, there was a small bowl meant for change. Some people brought change to him, but they never took their eyes away from Yagi, and some, as they backed away from the bowl, bumped into others within the group who only half noticed the disturbance.

Yagi acquired enough money to buy his mother some fish, noodles, vegetables, and broth. He even thought of getting her a small vase of flowers. He calculated that much within the bowl when he was almost finished with his story. With bated breath, the people waited as Yagi was about to finish. They all knew the story was about to end by the way that Yagi spoke, yet their hearts broke knowing that the euphoria would end. Yagi eventually finished, and silence crashed upon the crowd, which quickly became two dozen. They all seemed as if they themselves had awoken from a dream. Some had stopped breathing for a long time as Yagi spoke and had to catch their breath. Yagi was exhausted and was bent over taking in gulps of air and trying to maintain his composure. He was sweating to the point that his clothes were almost wet, and his throat ached from the strain of his voice. A man walked towards him with a gourd and gave it to Yagi, who eagerly drank from the gourd. Yagi wiped his mouth and bowed a deep bow. Then, the crowd erupted into a roar of cheer for Yagi. It was so surprising that the vendors stopped their barking, and all those walking in the marketplace stopped in their tracks and looked. The little boys at Yagi's feet danced and cheered his name.

Yagi was still bowing. Tears welled in his eyes as he looked down and saw that the bowl of change was overflowing. He decided that he would dedicate his life to stories and tell all people his dreams. He looked up at the crowd, gave the gourd back to the man who was still waiting and smiled at Yagi. Yagi thanked the man and then got his things as he walked away. People still cheered after him as he went away, and when he was just out of sight, groups of three or four discussed with glee the events of the story as they bought their wares.

Yagi went home to his mother. He presented the goods he bought to his mother and recalled the events of the day. His mother grabbed him and kissed him, and both were holding each other together as they finally found a way to live. Yagi promised his mother to continue this new vocation and that, eventually, she would never have to work again. They ate and slept soundly. That night, Yagi dreamt again and the real story of his life began as well.

• • •

A servant girl opens the paper-lined door that opens to a beautiful garden. Fresh-faced spring had come and was in full bloom. Cherry blossoms and bonsai trees circled a small pond filled with sparkling koi fish, swimming to and fro into intricate circles of color. Birds sang trilling songs, and Yagi awoke from a dream. Upon waking, he was dressed, ate his breakfast, and then sat on the floor at a small table. The table was lavishly polished and decorated with small engravings of demons, dragons, maidens, and animals of various legends. Yagi began to write his dream in intricate detail. Every dream was crisp, even towards the end of the day, as the sun was just beginning to set below the horizon. When Yagi finished, he allowed the ink to dry as he looked upon the garden and looked at a small grave that was covered by flower petals. He bowed to the grave and then began to call two servants to find him a rickshaw and to gather his things for the day. The great Tokugawa Ieyasu was waiting as he craved to hear a story. Any story would do as long as it came from Yagi Toshiaki.

Yagi dawned a kimono that marked him as an artisan. Although the garment was a soft gray on the outside, on the inside, there was a flash of intricate embroidery that showed flying cranes over mountains. Yagi traveled through the streets of Edo towards the castle with his dream written on paper and rolled into a scroll. In all his years living in Edo, the city seemed to change and yet stay exactly the same every year. The faces he saw in the marketplace when he was fifteen had gone, but their descendants, children and grandchildren, play out the same actions and mannerisms as he knew before. He sometimes spoke with these people and offered his services if they were in need. However, no one truly grew hungry these days. The world slowly molded around him with higher buildings and newer inventions. But every day, he still noticed a man who had given him a fish cake when he was starving working at the same stand in the marketplace; although the man had acquired several new wrinkles and failing eyesight.

Yagi approached the palace walls. He got out of the rickshaw, paid the man more than the usual fare, bowed and entered. The palace was a maze of sensual delights. Every courtyard was handsomely adorned with every beautiful plant or flower. Ladies with sleek black hair and bright kimonos darted glances behind their fans like the sun hitting the ocean with glittering light. The samurai lords were rough sculptures of war but graced with poise as they slowly walked and discussed matters of state. Yagi was lower in status, but some were quick to bow their heads slightly as he passed.

Yagi would not enter the throne room. The throne room was much too official for his purposes, and instead, he would enter a separate way further south of the palace into a large room with many wooden ukiyo-e picturing grand battles as well as serene pictures of nature or romance. Tokugawa Ieyasu would be lounging in a small chair, his head resting in his hand as he leaned and discussed with various friends and artisans about new and old things.

Yagi Toshiaki entered the small room, kneeling on the floor and bowing deeply to the shogun emperor. The emperor greeted Yagi and Yagi positioned himself among the various artisans who were discussing the changing philosophies of the new world approaching. Many of the artisans discussed writing poetry or plays about the subject. However Yagi noticed all of the conversations in silence as he merely listened. He concentrated on this new thinking of the youth that so many were either fascinated or afraid of. Before Yagi could listen further, the emperor called his name and requested a story. Some of the older artisans hushed their conversation and listened carefully to every word that Yagi spoke. Some narrowed their eyes in jealousy, while others consumed his tales with rapturous hunger. Yagi bowed once more and began a story, beginning with the same words he always used, "Deep in sleep, I dreamt a dream…" Yagi spoke for what seemed like an eternity. None of the fellow masters at his side, older and wiser than he, interrupted and eventually, all were coaxed once again into his bubble.

The sun touched the horizon as the cooler air of spring blew into the room. The door never closed as the emperor liked seeing nature at his reach, just a small breath away from something truly divine. Yagi's mouth became dry, and his voice cracked, but he did not ask for water, and he did not ask for rest. None of the masters in their fine silks and official garb noticed themselves as they slumped wide-eyed with every changing tone of the story. Their kimonos developed wrinkles that embarrassed them as they left the private room of the emperor. Despite all of this, the men were entranced. When Yagi had finished, the room filled with a sigh of relief. Some of the masters congratulated Yagi on another story and deeply enjoyed remembering certain scenes. Some discussed with him and others how they would adapt his story into a play, adding color, sight, and sound to his dream- working furiously in their mind how to create scenes that matched what Yagi had designed. Some discussed certain characters and what they symbolized within the world as a whole.

Uchida Akihiro, a kabuki playwright, spoke first among the crowd of voices, "Yagi, you must allow me to create something akin to this. All I have are love stories, but I must create a place of dreams!"

Yagi smiled and nodded. He did not keep his stories in cages, for they truly were not his own to begin with. He was given a gift, and any gift given should be spread.

Yagi responded, "I would be deeply honored to see what you create, and I would be glad to see your masterpiece when it is fully realized."

Uchida chuckled and promised a free seat in any theater of Yagi's choosing for such a blessing, and both men smiled and laughed.

Kuno Satoshi, a writer of stories himself, although more scandalous, teased Yagi a little for his lack of slimy characters or raunchy plots, "You are conveniently without such sin, Toshiaki, what a shame. There is more money in such stories."

"I create what god has given me. Nothing else is necessary."

"You are close to god? Then you are better than most of us!" said Satoshi, which made several artisans laugh.

Tokugawa Ieyasu motioned for Yagi to come closer to him. Yagi did so and bowed his head lower than the emperors. The emperor asked the question he always asked after every story: "From where do you receive your inspiration? From heaven or from hell?" and Yagi always answered, "I receive them as I receive them. The simplest answers are sometimes the hardest to believe." The emperor nodded and smiled. The evening concluded with all of the artisans bidding the emperor goodnight and leaving the castle walls in a parade of rickshaws and lanterns. They seemed like a trail of fireflies dancing in the night. Yagi was the last to leave.

Upon entering his home, he was greeted by his servants, had his story stored safely among the many others, ate and then finally slept. Another dream came to him that night.

• • •

The dream began like any other, with Yagi stepping into a blank space- a void without breath height or depth. Nothingness. Then Yagi took another step and found himself in a peasant garb on a raging sea. The waves grew into monsters of water that reached the sky and crashed headlong, tossing and turning the small sailboat. On the very edge of the boat, a boat only fit for menial fishing in small rivers, was an old man with only a white headband and loin cloth. At the end of the pole was a talisman which read *'bless this fisherman in order to catch a furious sea dragon'*. Yagi called out to the old man, shouting at the top of his lungs. The wind carried his voice away and seemed to push him further towards the end of the boat. He crashed into netting and crab cages, and finally, the old man noticed him.

"You lazy, worthless wretch! Help me catch this creature!" shouted the old man. Yagi noticed his mouth only had what seemed like nine teeth and scars all over the man's head and face.

Yagi blinked past rain and wind, desperately trying to gulp in the air as the storm kept pushing him toward the bottom of the boat. He screamed at the old man, "It is impossible to catch a dragon with that thing!" and Yagi motioned towards the miserable bamboo pole sitting on the edge of the boat as if tranquil. Yagi was taken aback at how the fishing pole was not affected.

The old man took a large oar from the boat and threatened to hit Yagi with it. Cursing and flailing wildly as Yagi blocked his face. The old man raised the oar above his head with one arm and threw it over the side into the dark waters.

With a great cry, the old man shouted over the storm, "I will catch this beast, and I will eat its heart, and you will die from the sight or live to tell the tale by helping me!"

Yagi sprang from his place and began tightening rigging and hoisted a small white sail that shone like a feather in a dark sky. Yagi wrapped a rope around the waist of the man and attached it to either side of the boat so as to give the man leverage as he threw the endless stream of line into the sea. Yagi noticed his garments matching the man, his hands rough from the work on the sea and his face hardened with a grizzled beard. His arms were stringy and taught with the strength of a fisherman, but the pain in his body made him push harder. The old man cast his line and drew it back to him. The line flew and danced with the waves, bringing nothing back each time. Lightning etched and scattered across the clouds as well as met the waters in a great clash of fire. The thunder was so loud that Yagi prayed to any god who could hear him even though he hadn't prayed in what seemed like ages.

The old man motioned for Yagi to look, and in front of them, an ominous wall of water loomed. The old man shouted orders to Yagi. He hoisted the small sail and braced the ship to follow the steep curve of the wave. The old man reeled his line back in, put his pole in between his legs and braced his body against the ship. As they climbed the steep wave, the old man stared head-first into the rushed waters that threatened to kill them. Then, he got into the water of the wave, and they swam through to the other side. Fish piled into the ship and quickly dissipated as they came to what seemed like rolling hills cascading and moving into coiling shapes.

Once again, the old man let out his reel and the line went flying as the wind carried it. The coiling waves and bounding thunder carried them. Yagi never broke from his ritual of rigging, hoisting, rigging, bracing, and waiting. Then, the earth seemed to growl beneath them. Clamping their hands over their ears, the men in the boat felt a vibration of sound in their cores and looked. There in front of them was a deep jade dragon, furious and shining with the light of the clashing lightning and blazing like icy fire. It sprang from the sea, and its body slithered and twisted in the air and it spotted the tiny speck of the boat on the ocean as it dived back into the water.

The old man screeched with glee as Yagi stared into the sky. Then he realized, looking around them, that the dragon surrounded them, and its giant body encircled them in a swirling mass. The old man reeled in his line and let it out with fury and passion. His eyes were wide and bloodshot, and he screamed to every god and demon he could think of. The talisman finally ripped by the wind flew into the air and the line grew taught as the pole bent. The head of the massive dragon appeared, and the boat was flung into the air. Yet, the boat wasn't there anymore as the old man and Yagi jumped onto the back of the dragon's head and rode it into hell and high water. The dragon roared past the thunder and the rain. The old man held onto his pole, feeling the rain pierce his skin as the dragon swam faster and faster. Yagi closed his eyes and prayed for a miracle of safety, holding onto the horns of the dragon as they swam. They reached the heart of the storm.

The storm's heart held tornadoes that spiraled and disappeared and then reappeared again. From the sea, two other dragons, one in the mouth of the other, struck through the water and then fell again, their bodies entangled in a battle that ordered the earth itself to respond in kind.

"YES, I HAVE CAUGHT THE SEA DRAGON, AND I HAVE FOUND ITS LAIR." The old man let out a yelp of victory as his bridled dragon furiously swam towards the battle. Yagi stared in disbelief and felt his hands give way from the horn of the dragon. He slipped and fell hundreds of feet, faster than a sparrow, towards the crashing waters. His heart beat out of his chest, and just before he hit the water… he awoke.

• • •

Yagi Toshiaki awoke from his dream with pain all over his body. His head spun, and his face was pale. He mumbled to his servant to send for a doctor, who did promptly. Shortly after, the doctor arrived and examined Yagi thoroughly. With a narrow look, the doctor gazed at him for a long while.

"You are perfectly healthy, and yet I cannot deny that you are deeply afflicted. Have you cleansed this house recently? Discussed with any spiritualists of any spirits or demons?" asked the doctor, packing away his things.

A raspy "No" was all Yagi could manage.

"Then I suggest that you do so. Rest for now, but I will have someone come to your house tomorrow to clean it. You will not need to pay. Everything will be taken care of."

The next day, a Buddhist monk came and blessed the house while all of Yagi's servants and himself stood outside. As Yaga looked at the ritual, his brows were knitted. His eyes stared into the distance. In his mind, he wondered to himself, *This dream did not end. Why did it not end?'* He searched every detail of the story as best he could. The more he searched, the more that the dream faded or details were blurry. In his mind, he raced after the dream with searching hands. Then it was gone. He maintained calm as the Buddhist monk finished and left. The servants were asked to leave him in privacy for a while. Yaga frantically wrote all he could, but it was not finished. In fact, there truly was no story. There were only vague patches of visions.

Yagi's eyes grew wide as he sat back from his desk. His hands shook as he looked out towards the grave at the end of the garden, shaded by the cherry trees. He remembered the fish bones, his mother's pinpricks from sewing, seeing her arms grow thin with work, the stealing, the hiding. A hand unconsciously clamped at his heart. He looked down at the page and crumbled it, the wet ink staining his hands. Yagi walked further west of the house into a tidy storage room filled with parchments and scrolls neatly labeled and preserved. Lining his finger along each tag with the story titles, he picked one and cracked open the wax seal that bound it. Yagi briskly read over the story, and suddenly, he was transported. As his eyes darted across the page, his vision was taken over by a war of samurai fighting a horse made of fire. Reading and consuming every detail, Yagi finally finished the story. He decided that this would be one that he would tell the emperor the next day.

The events of the day were as usual, and Yagi told his story: the samurai was commissioned by the lord reigning over the province that there was a stallion made of blazing fire that was destroying the homes of the townsfolk and that there must be someone to kill the stallion before the entire province is burned to the ground. The samurai, young and newly trained, requested this task as he saw it as an opportunity to prove himself. Although his master objected, the lord gave the young samurai the task and so the samurai decided that during the night, he would trap the stallion. The stallion came on a cloud from the heavens and whisked through trees and forest, creating a great fire. The samurai got onto his horse and tempted the stallion all the way to the sea. Eventually the stallion touching the water felt its sting and flew back into the clouds. The raging fires stopped at that instant and the forest, as well as the people, were saved.

The artisans around Yagi were engrossed. Yet, the emperor, although still intrigued, gave away a look of familiarity as he listened. Yagi noticed this even in the midst of showing how the samurai raced on his stead towards the ocean, and the smallest bead of sweat formed on his brow. Anyone who didn't know the truth behind the moment could have sworn they saw Yagi Toshiaki sweat from the strain of the story and beheld his passion- that was not the case. When the story finished, the group of artisans again marveled at Yagi's creation. When the evening was over and the rickshaws were gone, Yagi remained to have an audience with the emperor. The emperor was now in his office, signing laws to be enacted and reviewing documents over the various provinces within all of Japan. Yagi sat patiently, slowing his breathing and controlling his emotions. He did not want a stitch to be out of place, or the emperor might pierce Yagi's side for insubordination. The emperor finished the work for the evening and ushered his advisors away.

"That was a beautiful story, as always, Toshiaki. You must be proud of your creations", said the emperor in a serene voice.

Yagi bowed his head, "You honor me with this compliment, my emperor. It is a gift that I was blessed with early in life. I have no other explanation."

"Yes, you have a gift. However, that story was told once before."

Yagi did not lift his head but instead bent further into a deep bow to the point that his forehead touched the pristine floor.

"I beg your forgiveness, emperor, for this. I have recently experienced a spiritual affliction that caused my latest dream to vanish from me. I will not deny as soon as it was born, it died."

The emperor's expression did not change as he listened to Yagi. Eventually, the emperor spoke again, "You did not disappoint me, Yagi. Hearing any of your stories is a blessing. I advise you, if you are to remain successful and maintain these dreams, you must speak to a spiritual advisor."

"I will, and I thank you deeply." Yagi got off the floor and backed out of the room, never lifting his head. Once he had left the room, he turned, quickly sent a messenger to find a wise spiritual advisor to be at home or Yagi Toshiaki as soon as possible, and went home. Shortly after Yagi's arrival, an old monk was sitting at the door of Yagi's home and was meditating, letting incense trail into the night air. Lamps were posted around the home, so an eerie light clung to the dark house. Yagi bowed to the monk, and the old man looked at Yagi and then spoke in a voice that sounded like wind rustling through trees.

"Your face says that you are intelligent, but there is also no denying that you are touched with something from the gods. Why have my services been requested?"

Yagi Toshiaki explained his abilities and recent events. The monk did not move, and there seemed to be no change in his expression. Instead, he rose slowly from his spot and requested that he go into the bedroom of Yagi Toshiaki.

"A jealous spirit wishes to take your dreams. It is hungry for it, and until you have this spirit banished from your home, all of your visions will be lost forever. I will stay with you as you sleep, and I will banish the spirit. I must also have paper and ink. We must make shide to cleanse the room."

And thus, servants worked to create what seemed like hundreds of shide talismans and attached them to the rope. They lined the walls of Yagi's bedroom. The monk also had a shide on a pole, which he waved over Yagi's head and around the room, praying under his breath several prayers as he walked. Yagi was instructed to continue his normal routine. As he lay down, he instantly fell into a deep sleep. The monk continued his ritual as Yagi dreamed.

The smell of sweaty men, as they shouted towards a sumo ring, filled Yagi's senses, and he awoke with a jerk in one of the stadium seats. He was wearing peasant attire (however, this time, he was fully clothed) and then sharply looked in all directions to take in the dream. Men drinking heavily behind him yelled and laughed, making lewd jokes and reminiscing about when they had a mistress or two. Smoke filled the room as several men had kiseru being held in one hand as they smoked and chatted from the corners of their mouths. All sorts of men, young and old, rich and innocent and infamous, were present to watch two warriors fight out of a ring.

The first sumo wrestlers were tall walls of flesh that seemed to be more poised than any geisha Yagi had ever seen. Both wrestlers stalked the ring and threw salt in preparation for the ceremony. They never locked eyes but displayed their strength simply by striding in wide steps and showing off their tsuna and kesho-mawashi. Yagi knew instantly who these men were by their differing garb and symbols. The man who had the embroidered blue dragon of his kesho-mawashi was named Arima Raiden. He was known as the son of thunder. The sumo wrestler with the blazing tiger was Nii Toru, also known as the Tiger Warrior.

Truly, seeing the two men was like seeing the distant descendants of giants. They towered over the crowd with broad shoulders and arms that almost reached past their hips. Their legs were the size of tree trunks. The crowd cheered their respective wrestler, and the wrestlers began to remove their ceremonial garb and only the regular mawashi loincloth. The standoff began with both wrestlers opposite each other, staring into each other and through each other. They squatted and assumed their positions. The Gyoji, an older man who looked more like a child in the midst of the two beasts, waited as the arena hushed to silence. The drunken, the old, the poor, the wealthy, and the true believers in sumo all gazed and waited.

The gyoji shouted for the match to begin, and like tectonic plates, the two sumo crashed into each other. The whole platform vibrated, and the crows shouted into a screeching roar. Men shouted and flung their arms as they watched Nii Toru and Arima Raiden crash into each other and fall away like a tide against a cliff face. They grabbed each other's belts and almost hoisted one another in the air. They pushed and pulled. They both expertly evaded the other's attempts until, finally, Arima Raiden was pushed outside the ring and slipped under his ankles. That was only the first round.

Arima Raiden got up from his place while Nii Toru went to his corner, soaked in sweat. Yagi finally wondered why these two were the only ones fighting in the ring and nudged a man next to him.

He shouted above the crowd and asked, "Why are only these two men fighting?"

The man next to him looked surprised and shouted, "Other sumo who were selected to fight refused because they knew these two would be present. There will be more than one round, and they will fight until the other gives up or dies!" Yagi gravely turned his attention back to the two sumo who were still fighting. They scuffed dirt into the air as they continued to fight. Both sumo looked furious with hatred. The sweat seemed to drift into the air like steam. Nii Toru finally pushed Arima Raiden off of his balance and Arima went flying away.

The crowd's elation and excitement of the match seemed to grow more rampant and wild. Yagi watched quietly in his seat, staring intently at the two sumo. He noticed, even with the obstruction of the smoke, that Nii Toru's veins seemed to pop out. His nails turned into claws, and his mouth foamed in anger. His perfect appearance waned a little into something more monstrous. Arima Raiden also seemed out of sorts. Only Yagi could see, but under Arima's skin, ripples of something moving scattered and then vanished. The breath from Arima's mouth wafted in great clouds- almost like he were in the coldest winter.

Yagi was on the edge of his seat, looking over flailing arms and concentrating as best that he could, watching the two men. Nii Toru was about to leave the ring when Arima leaped from where he was and crashed Nii to the ground. The gyoji completely left the ring in fear (he wasn't very useful to benign with), and both Nii and Arima began to wrestle and pin each other down. Hoisting, scratching, biting, clawing, throwing, tumbling, and punching. The crowd saw the two giants do away with the ceremonies of the fight and begin to almost kill each other. Blood poured from orifices, and scratches went deep into the skin. The sumo did not weaken. In fact, they grew stronger.

Many men began to run out of the building. They ran over each other and pushed each other away to escape from the giants and their wrath. All but Yagi. Yagi watched intently. The scratches from the sumo went deep into the skin, and blood spilled like water from fountains. Their eyes were wild, and their teeth were jagged. Horns, claws, fur, and roars cashed into a whirl of color and lightning. From the shells of the two men, ripped away like cloth, came the true tiger and dragon. Both flew into the sky and continued in a twirling mass of orange and blue.

Yagi ran, keeping his eye on the two. The blue dragon curled into whipping and circling forms while the tiger hung on and bit into the dragon's throat. Thousands of people saw and ran away in terror. The hurling mass of power began to fall rapidly toward the ground as the tiger's weight pulled the dragon. The dirt was dug up by the impact, and the tiger began to rip away flesh from bone. The tiger: a giant beast bigger than a house with raging fire around its paws. The dragon: a snake-like creature, but with deep sapphire scales and cresting white fins along its back. The broken samurai stadium, torn in shatters from its belly, thousands fled. Yagi, however, ran towards the scene. He dodged people and animals, fleeing in panic. The dragon was attempting to fly back into the air, but the tiger put its full weight on top of the beast and was tearing away flesh from bone.

The dragon eventually broke free from the tiger and lifted into the air faster than anything. The blood poured from its right eye, and half of its jaw was gone. The tiger, bleeding as well, kept running. And Yagi ran after. All three were in flight. The tiger leaped and bound over roofs, its muscles pushing past the limit. The dragon, swirling and diving, did everything that it could to keep to the sky. Both creatures were almost past the point of return.

Yagi ran through the streets, feeling his lungs burn. The dragon's flight became a hover as it barely touched the rooftops, and the tiger began to gain speed. Eventually, the dragon crashed into a series of taller buildings, and its body lay in the rubble. The tiger slowed its pursuit, blood pouring from its mouth. The dragon breathed rapid breaths, and steam began to rise from its wounds. Yagi finally stopped, catching his breath. The beasts were oblivious to the tiny spectator who still felt as if he were watching the ritual of the sumo. The tiger paced around the dragon as if still in the ring and growled a deep growl from within its stomach. Yagi stood several yards away, standing behind what was left of a torn building. Not a soul was left to witness.

The tiger finally approached the dragon and put a paw on its neck. It lifted its head and roared like thunder. Buildings shook, and some crumbled around it. The dragon with its left eye looked up at the tiger, not able to scream or bite. The dragon breathed faster which made the blood spill into gushing pools. The tiger lowered its head and wrapped its jaws around the neck of the dragon. The crunching of bone and the tearing of flesh nauseated Yagi to the point that he fell to his knees and held his hand over his mouth.

Yet, before he could see if the tiger ate the head or severed it, Yagi's vision began to fade. The world around him started to melt like watercolor, and everything darkened. Yagi looked around him, and his world vanished… And he awakened.

• • •

In the cool of the spring morning air, the servants heard their master scream. His voice rang through the whole house. One servant crashed through the sliding door to find Yagi standing in a destroyed writing room. Paper was strewn all over the floor, and ink was splattered all over the floor and walls. Yagi, barely dressed, looked rabid. The servant lowered his face to the floor in a bow, shielding their fear and asked, "My lord, do whatever you ask of me. I am here in your time of need."

Yagi turned his head. Words were smeared onto his skin. He walked slowly to the kneeling servant and said in a hiss, "If the gods will not help me, then maybe devils will. Send for a witch, and do not return until you have found one that can cure me of this curse!"

The servant rushed from the home. Yagi sat in the middle of the floor, surrounded by half-finished thoughts. He crushed them all into his hands and wrung his hair. It wasn't long after this that he learned he was no longer invited to the emperor's house.

The witch, covered in a cloak, entered the house of Yagi Toshiaki three months after the dream of the sumo (although Yagi did not remember what he dreamed). The majority of the stories were sold at that point, which was enough to keep a handful of servants. However, the grand house was mostly closed. Yagi limited himself to small meals and sold most of his more expensive belongings. He did not leave the house and would not relinquish it despite the well-meaning suggestions of many who knew him.

The witch approached Yagi and, with a bony hand, reached for his face. Yagi did not move but allowed the woman to inspect him. A crone, old and decrepit, had a fading tattoo of a snake that slithered down her right arm and rested its head into the palm of her hand. From the ghastly black cloak, a whispered voice spoke out, "A spirit ales you in this place. It takes away a gift you have been given without a trace. I know this creature well. Allow me to stay within your sleeping chambers tonight as I capture the beast for you. There is nothing you need to prepare or give me. I have everything that I need."

Yagi nodded. He was skeptical and tired. He had spent too much time selling his work, which did not sell as highly as he hoped. Since his rejection from the emperor, his reputation slowly dwindled. The majority of his buyers adapted his previous stories into plays or works of art, but his name was slowly being erased from history. He was becoming obscure and this frightened him most of all. Yagi bowed, and the witch left, returning as soon as the sun left the horizon.

A veil was cast between Yagi and the witch. A couple of attendants of the witch had prepared his sitting area where she would concentrate her magic. This time, the witch was dressed in a pure white kimono and a white veil cast over her head. The sheer fabric showed her face. She was old, but she was not comely. Wrinkles cascaded down her face, and her hair was white as milk, but her eyes were still sharp- black pools of ink in the center of the parchment. She held a bowl of incense in her hand that gave off a slim trail of smoke reaching toward the ceiling. The smoke was intoxicating. The witch inhaled in deep breaths the vapors as Yagi fell asleep. Her eyes grew a darker color the more that the vapors entered her lungs. Candles flickered lightly around her.

Yagi could faintly smell the earthy incense. He fell suddenly into sleep as his body grew lifeless into dreams.

• • •

Yagi was faintly aware of the coldness in the air and the fact that he was slowly moving forward. Upon opening his eyes, he realized that he was in a forest. Snow covered the earth is soft rolling mounds that glistened in the light of the sun. Tall larch trees were speckled throughout. It was utterly silent. Yagi noticed his garments. He wore peasant garb that was clumsily sewn and large straw boots that were lined with fur and fabric. He wore a mask that covered everything but his eyes and a large reed basket was on his back. He kept walking. There was nothing within him that told him to stop. He took in everything around him and on him with sparse notes of wonder, but his only inclination was to keep moving, or else something terrible might happen.

Slowly, as Yagi began to get used to his dream, he realized that he was growing faint. His vision gradually grew blurrier. He shook his head slightly and blinked hard to try and keep his focus. His legs were growing weaker. The effort to move them was almost too much. From his side, he felt a warm sensation of liquid and noticed that he had a large gash on the left of his abdomen, steadily pouring blood. His heart began to race as he realized why his body kept moving- it was trying to save him.

Yagi put down his basket and looked within it, trying to find anything that would help him. The only things he saw were small roots covered in snow. He did not know what they would be good for, and he knew he did not have the time to find out. Resting felt more like a luxury he couldn't afford. The forest grew thicker, with black trees blocking out the glimmering light of the sun. Yagi ate some of the fresh snow for moisture but knew that sooner or later, he would fall and wouldn't have the strength to get back up again.

Yagi's steps grew sluggish, and eventually, he tripped over a tree root, which caught his foot. He went tumbling down a hill, a basket flying over him into the snow. He crashed at the bottom. Yagi's ears began to ring and his vision was white as the snow. He didn't have anything to save him. Yagi closed his eyes and resigned himself.

"At least, if this dream ends quickly, it has an ending. But not a story. Not a story worth hearing", he thought this as he closed his eyes.

Yagi awoke slowly once again, thinking that he had awakened from the dream unscathed. Yet, Yagi found himself in a bed in a small house next to a fire. His vision cleared to find a peasant woman dressed in a winter jacket, dressing his wound with an earthy paste. He did not move but studied the small interior of the house. An ordinary room with a grass roof that looked like it had been repaired. The bed that Yagi slept on was made, of course material but stuffed with goose feathers and wool. The floor was wooden, and so were the walls. One sliding door was on the far left of Yagi. It was the only entrance and exit. Towards a far corner was a small table and a shrine that was modestly decorated with fresh burning incense.

Yagi could hear a muffled voice. To him, it sounded soft and mewing like a cat. A small hand touched his forehead and he could feel the calluses on the palms and fingertips. Although his vision was blurry, he could see a face framed by messy black hair that was once tied up in a bun. The hair dripped down the shoulders of the woman who seemed to calmly speak to him. He didn't understand and was content with sleeping for much longer as she continued to dress his wounds. Eventually, he did sleep deeply and with no dreams.

Days passed. Yagi awoke dressed in clean clothes and covered in a clean blanket on the makeshift bed. The clothes he wore were soft from use but were too big for him. They almost engulfed him, hanging loosely on his small frame. He sat up and saw more clearly the small house. It was neat and orderly; there was the smell of something cooking on top of the stove that Yagi slept by, and there was incense at the shrine. Beside the shrine sat the woman. She was kneeling down, head lowered quietly praying under her breath. The words seemed almost earnest and frantic but hopeful. He took away the blanket and saw her as she turned around, startled. Her face was round and pale. She had small lips which seemed to turn up like the petals of a flower. Her hair was completely covered in a handkerchief. Her eyes were a deep dark color, and freckles were spotted under her eyes- the slightest touch of imperfection in a milky white face.

She was dressed warmly in fur-lined boots, rough pants, and a thick layered jacket that was tied by a small bit of string in the center. She looked at Yagi with anticipation, waiting for him to speak. Yagi's voice was crackly and hoarse, but he managed to say, "May I have something to drink?"

The woman nodded and swiftly went to a small cupboard opposite the shrine. A tiny alcove was made within the house that kept dry goods and preserves. The woman meekly went beside Yagi. She cupped a small saucer of water and gave it to Yagi who gently took it from her and drank heartily. It was colder than anything he ever felt, but he drank greedily and asked for more. He had his fill and nodded to the woman, who nodded back and put away the saucer. She sat at a distance from him and watched him closely. Yagi could sense she was weary of him. Her hands were clenched around the bottom of her jacket. Her face was calm, but her eyes watched every move he made. With effort, Yagi kneeled as well and bowed before her. Without lifting his head, he greeted the woman and thanked her for her hospitality and for saving his life.

"I thank you deeply for your kindness. It must have been difficult to spare a part of your home with a stranger, especially during this season when food is so scarce."

The woman fixed her gaze on her hands and said nothing. Yagi continued to speak, "My name is Yagi Toshiaki. I am a…" Before Yagi could speak further, his mouth forced out another word: carpenter. As that word left his lips, something within him slipped like a feather. A gap was formed, but effortlessly, it was filled again.

"I am a humble carpenter traveling to find work elsewhere. I have no bearings and no direction. I heard of farmers needing talents like mine near this place and so I came. The storm had come as I was traveling."

The woman continued to say nothing and was still as stone. Yagi did not raise his head from the floor. They both stayed like that for what seemed like forever. Finally, the woman spoke in a small voice, "You may stay here until you are well. When the snow lessens, then you can travel further north. There are many farmers who need work and repairs." She bowed and left the small room out into the snow.

Yagi did not move but listened as she soundlessly walked away. He arose finally and thought. Memories slowly slipped without him noticing, and a new man grew within his mind's eye. He grew up in a village not unlike the one who would find himself in and he was a carpenter. Images of a peasant's life started to blossom into color. The palace of the emperor was a dream that died as the new images were conceived. Yagi laid down again to sleep. The storyteller died in his dreams.

• • •

Time passed, and the snow lessened. Yagi left the small woman's house and started north towards a small village that indeed needed his services, but Yagi could not have expected the dire situation he was in. There were farmers with broken homes and burned barns. A band of raiders had come and there were little that were left to pick up the pieces. As Yagi came into the center of the village, there were some that were scavenging what little could be found and the majority of the injured were being treated in a shrine that had been abandoned a long time ago. Many offerings were made outside the doors of the shrine as well as incense, and people bowed and said quick prayers before entering with blankets and water. The woman was there tirelessly tending to the injured.

Yagi was overwhelmed with people who saw his calloused hands and pack. They knew a carpenter by the nature of the calluses and flooded him with requests. A village elder hushed them away. He was a taller man, well built, but his hair was graying slightly at the sides of his temples.

"Thank you for being here. We understand that you did not expect a broken village with needy people, and we understand if you wish to leave." He bowed.

Yagi was struck with grief, but he was no savior. There were very few able-bodied people left and those that were the strongest were far from capable. They had lost much of their strength when the raiders had left. What was left were women, elderly and children. Some of the children were still clinging to their mother's bosom.

Yagi bowed, "I will accept the task at hand."

The elder bowed, "thank you," he said. He slowly rose and left, organizing several things about the ravaged village. Ash tinged the homes, and farms were uprooted from the hooves of flying horses. Cattle lay dead in the fields with their throats cut. Yagi's stomach churned, and his throat closed as he looked around. He saw death, and no words could paint or capture what he saw. He wanted to run and find somewhere beautiful and unburdened instead. He kicked himself for agreeing to help, but it was too late.

Yagi could do little now but gather what was left of the village and put together the pieces. What cattle was left was cooked or dried. Those who were injured in the shrine had small makeshift fires to keep them warm. The crops that were growing in the ground were burned. Many women started to gather herbs from the forest and count what dried goods were left in storage. Yagi began to gather a record of all of the homes that needed repair, how long it would take, what supplies were available, and what was necessary to start from scratch. Many homes were torn down and burned. Bonfires lit the darkening sky. Who was left was made to stay within homes that were not destroyed.

Yagi looked into the forest that flanked the outskirts of the village. There were strong trees, but now was not the time to begin. The woman, who Yagi learned later was named Koharu, looked at him through the peak between the shrine doors. He never noticed until that moment that her eyes were laced with gold towards the center, like a candle flame in utter darkness.

The next day, as the sun rose, Yagi continued with the rest of those he gathered to burn the charred remains. He talked with many of the farmers, listening to them as they recounted the raid.

"I saw a dozen of scroungy men riding horses. It was in broad daylight. They ran through the village screaming like they were mad with red eyes. They cut down men and women. They sliced through our livestock out in the fields. There were some that had torches and burned down their homes. They pillaged and stole what little we had," said one elderly farmer.

"Our men are not fighters. They took their pitchforks and shovels and defended what they could. The men tried to keep the fires contained to stop them from spreading. There are some men in the shrine that may not walk again," said another.

Yagi did not dare enter the shrine. Many women came in and out with herbs and boiled water. There were sometimes soft cries or screams that could be heard. Yagi could not stand to see what was inside and was perfectly content with his ignorance.

The sun came out at that moment and warmed the faces of the men. They looked at the clouds, which seemed to quickly depart. The sky was a deep red as the sun began to rise. Spring was close to approaching, the farmers said. Some fields were untouched, but many wondered if it would be enough. The oldest encouraged some that they had dealt with famines before and they would do it again. The gods of the earth would provide even in the most difficult times.

The snow was stubborn to leave, but finally, the days began to get warmer. Fruit trees within the forest produced a heavy bounty, and many of the elders smiled as they knew that their predictions had grown true. Yagi, along with the men who were injured, now healed, began to build more houses. Some of the men had lost limbs or fingers (some did not survive) but continued to cut down sturdy trees. Many of the women had begun hunting for fruits and started planting vegetables within their home gardens. The rice fields that grew for miles started late. The harvest would not be as plentiful, but many were thankful to eat despite this.

Yagi had finished his work on a home near one of the fields and was sitting on the edge of the front door threshold. He looked around at the green trees. The wind blew warm from the east and Koharu appeared seemingly out of nowhere near him. She was dressed in a plain kimono, a soft green color with pink flowers embroidered on the color. She wore a wide-brimmed tengai that hid part of her face.

Koharu approached Yagi as he sat and placed a small handkerchief on the ground. Koharu grabbed a fresh peach and presented it to Yagi, who nodded and accepted it.

"I wanted to thank you personally for helping this village. Without your help, most would not survive", said Koharu, silk not looking at Yagi.

"I am not the one who saved these people. I am not a wise man. Do not give me the praise that many others deserve. You were more necessary than me. You healed too many who believed they were at death's door. You should be the one who is thanked," said Yagi softly.

Koharu sank her head further down and contemplated. Yagi merely held the peach in his hands and stared at the ground.

"My name is Koharu."

"Hello Koharu. It is a pleasure to speak with you. Where is your family within this village?"

"I have none," she said, "They all passed a long time ago."

Yagi's brow furrowed as he said, "You live alone?"

"Yes," Koharu nodded and began to eat her peach.

"Are you a healer?" asked Yagi, who kept looking at Koharu.

"Yes. My father and mother were healers and gatherers of herbs. They knew the forests well, and they taught me. I am the sole survivor of their legacy", she smiled slightly, "sometimes I wonder if I should take on an apprentice, but many times I have decided against it."

"Why?" asked Yagi.

"The training for my knowledge is difficult, and there are not many young people within this village," she sat a little further onto her heels and ate the sweet fruit.

Yagi stared off into silence and contemplation. The air was warm and sweet, full of the smell of damp earth and growing things. He watched the slow circle of life around him.

Then, he looked again at Yagi, "You should not be so discouraged. You must pass on your knowledge. These people do not have the strength to live without your talents. Think of them as you find an apprentice."

Koharu looked at Yagi for the first time since their meeting. Again, he saw her soft, round face and the bright eyes that looked back at him in earnest. There was earnestness, fear, and deep thoughts about the future that welled up within the pools of her eyes. She got up from her place, bowed, and said, "Thank you. I will consider what you have said." And left. The rest of the peaches stacked high were still sitting next to Yagi. He finally bit into the fruit in his hands and relished the sweet taste.

Summer came with the humidity and the plentiful rice. Many men and women harvested the small grains. Some men who had lost a leg from the raid worked by laying out the rice and beginning to let it dry. The shrine was once again empty, but many small headstones with names engraved in them were decorated with offerings. Yagi passed by the shrine on a wooden cart carrying dried rice leaves to pastures for cows and oxen to eat. He would read the names of the people who passed only seven months prior. Then, something in his heart would cry out and fade. He felt he had forgotten someone. Someone he knew from his past that never seemed to come to mind. He felt the pain subside and would continue again, guiding the horse that pulled the cart.

Yagi would often visit Koharu. She had taken on three apprentices, all young girls, who were learning how to identify different herbs and mushrooms local to the region. She also taught them how to create meticulous teas and potions. Yagi often brought fruit or various herbs he knew Koharu would live. Even if, for just a moment, he longed to see her golden eyes. Koharu would give him food or a liniment to help his joints and hands and then continue with her teaching. She sometimes would linger in the doorway, allowing Yagi to speak to her about his day and the lives of the farmers. She would smile and nod, listening intently. She rarely spoke.

Some of the wives of the farmers would catch Yagi as he approached, stopping their work to say, "You need to marry that woman soon. She is all alone, and it is dangerous to be a woman alone these days. Who knows when lurking men will come" or "she is too sweet to be without a lover. Take her as your wife and have children. I know they will be the strongest and prettiest of the village."

Many of the villagers were still touched by the raid and the fear of it still clung to the outer reaches of their minds. It wasn't long after the raid that they recovered, but it wasn't long ago that they saw many of their family members die in a rundown shrine. Yagi knew this, and even in the most pleasant conversation, in some moments, he could see the fear pass through their minds and disappear just as quickly and quietly. Yagi also thought of Koharu. He thought more and more about her. His mind went over her face as she gave Yagi the peach. Remembered the sweetness of the peach and the gentleness of her touch.

One night, Yagi came to the door of Koharu, who was wrapped in a pale kimono. He stepped through the threshold and kissed her. Her small frame was taken over by his rough outline, and along they stood there until the moon reached its peak.

• • •

Three small children were playing in front of a peasant home with the doors open to a glorious sunset falling behind mountains and trees. A woman held a small baby to her breast as she nursed her newest child. Five years previously, Yagi and Koharu were married in sight of the whole village and the village elders. The elders finalized the marriage by giving Yagi and Koharu land of their own a few miles away from the village. Koharu still was a medicine woman, giving away her various mixtures to the fellow villagers in exchange for food, cloth, tools, etc. Yagi was still a carpenter but recently specialized in making wooden bowls or cups. Sometimes, Yagi even made small toys for his children who would occasionally lose them in the forests. There were two girls and one boy, and the youngest was a little boy who was only a few months old. Many of the women came to each birth that Koharu had, and even then, Koharu bore most of the knowledge that brought her through each pregnancy.

Yagi was content in every way. Sometimes, he would run with his children if he had the chance or allowed the little boy to come with him as he traded his wares to the villagers. Often, Yagi would hold his youngest boy and whisper stories that poured out from him. Stories of things he often never knew were carefully tucked away into his mind. He thought that it was a blessing from a spirit of the wind and paid no more mind to it than a bear to a flea.

Over time, Koharu and Yagi watched the days wax and wane. Their children grew a little older, and so did their parents. One night, Yagi awoke from a dream he couldn't remember. He looked toward Koharu, who was still as stone. His hand was close to her arm which to him seemed cold. He brushed her hair out of her face and felt no breath from her nostrils. He got up now, hovering gently over her. He placed his hands on her chest and gently tried to coax her awake. He brought her closer in his arms and shook her now, almost strangling her. She was dead. Yagi tried and tried some more. He placed two fingers on her wrist and did not feel her heart. He placed an ear to her chest and heard nothing. She was dead.

Yagi, looking down at his wife in his arms, buried his face in her hair. He adjusted her to where she laid in his lap, almost like she was asleep. He wept silently, biting his lip so as not to wake his children, who were sleeping only a few feet away from him. Yagi gingerly placed his wife back in her sleeping place and sat beside her for a while. Thoughts strung together like tangled yarn in waves of fear and hopelessness. The light that came in through the panes of the door were shards of piercing glow from the rising sun.

Yagi looked towards the door that opened to the sun. He hated the sun, he hated the room, the bed, the thing that took his wife. He hated his uncertainty, he hated his lack of knowledge, he hated. He burned, and the world kept turning. He held his head in his hands, brushing his fingers through his hair. He stayed there, not wanting to move from his spot because he felt that in that stillness, there was comfort. Comfort in what he could control, which was his wife still laying beside him and his children sleeping soundly in their beds.

What he would do next was to take Koharu's body and wrap it in a shroud. He would use her sheets and neatly tuck her into the blankets. Second, he would place her in her small room where she kept her herbs. There was no time for advice or thinking; he simply did not want his children to see their dead mother's body. He stepped out of the room and did what he planned. Then he stood in front of the door. The sun's glow was amber and red. A thought sat in the back of his mind. It slithered its way through his throat and past his tongue, and slowly, he said, "Why is the sun rising and setting in the same place?"

He opened the door, and the blinding covered him in a warm glow that was hot and all-consuming. His nostrils inhaled smoke, and Yagi awoke surrounded by fire. The witch in the center of the fire was dead and consumed in flame. Her body lay there, a flickering mound of flesh and black soot. Yagi watched as the flaming paper doors burst and crackled in front of him; Yagi got up and ran. He ran through the winding halls of the burning house, holding the edge of his sleeve to his face. He ran to find the rest of the servants running away from the house, some saving what was left. Some were surprised to see Yagi running towards them, his kimono trailing with fire behind him. Many of his servants beat out the flames as he fell to the ground.

So the house burned to the ground. The witch's body was turned into ash, and the smoke rose high into the morning sky. In little time, many came with buckets and with help, but Yagi simply sat in front of the ruins and watched. Some papers flickered through the air with half-written thoughts and promptly crumbled as they fell. Yagi allowed the world to turn around him, and in silence, he waited for the flames to dwindle into nothing.

• • •

In the rain, Yagi found shelter underneath a small shrine on the side of a country road. His dress was much simpler now as he waited for the downpour to stop. Wrinkles creased his eyes as he held a bundle of papers under his arm. Every time that he stays underneath that particular shrine, he remembers the day that he first came to it.

He kept walking until his feet bled.

After the burning of the house, Yagi walked out of Edo. He left the gate and kept walking until the small scattering of houses and people left him. Eventually, rain began to fall and Yagi was drenched, dragging the weight of the water in his clothing and hair. He looked to his left and saw a small shrine with a tiny stone, a faceless figure meditating under a wooden awning. Yagi sat beside the figure and stared into the distance, listening to the sound. It was the first time since he gained his wealth and prominence that he faced silence. And he hated it.

He hated every inch of the rain, the blood under his toes, the wind, the shrine, his clothes. He loathed it all. Thrashing in the rain, he screamed at the gods.

"YOU GAVE ME THIS GIFT, AND NOW YOU TAKE IT AWAY?! WHAT WAS THE POINT? TO SEE ME SUFFER?!" he screamed and threw rocks and tore at his clothes.

He slipped and crashed into the mud. He brought himself up carefully and sat again in the shrine. Looking over he noticed an apple at the bottom of the shrine and was about to eat it when a child with a large leaf over its head stopped and stared at him. The child smiled and pointed at Yagi.

"You have mud on your face!" it said. The child said that as if it had discovered a profound mystery and giggled with glee.

Yagi simply stared back. After a long pause, he started to laugh. It was like a gush from a volcano. It burst out of him, and the child jumped back from him. The child went further into himself and curled his body underneath the leaf. Yagi stopped laughing, holding his stomach. His face was red, and snot trailed down his face.

"I am sorry. I am so sorry," he said through tears, "Do you live close to here?"

The child nodded hesitantly.

"Would there be anyone who would be willing to give me food and drink? I am a traveler. I can work however I need to."

With that, the child ran away.

Yagi, thinking about that time, smiled. He teaches that young boy. The child prefers more numbers and his abacus rather than writing. The rain finally stopped, and Yagi continued down the road back home.

He no longer dreamed. For years, he had forgotten that life or willfully allowed himself to become a new person. He engulfed himself in the new village along with its people and his teachings to the small village children. It was odd to have such a learned man dwell in a village. It was a privilege for him to teach their children. Some of the people were skeptical but warmed up to him quickly as time went on. They taught him how to tend the fields and he taught them to read and write.

He never married. In a way, he felt that he was still married to Koharu and found himself mourning her loss from time to time. He wondered if the last dream he had was a nightmare or a paradise for him. Of all that time, it was the only dream that he remembered vividly, but the memory stung him deep in his chest. He would sometimes have to choke back tears and forget once again.

One day, a friend of Yagi's had called upon him for advice. The friend was a man his age, but since the man believed Yagi to be wise as well as learned, he went to Yagi with a question.

"I have had the strangest dream. I dreamt that a crane as big as a tree with sprawling wings swooped over the village and blotted out the sun. Then it laid an egg…" the man continued with a sprawling tale that lasted for a while.

Finally, when he had finished, the man asked, "What all could this mean? What should I make of these things?"

Yagi was surprised. The friend produced quite a tale. Yagi, however, knew the crane's significance.

"I believe you might have encountered the great crane Tsuru. The egg he laid must have been a blessing upon you. Luck, marriage, or a good harvest, I am not sure. But we shall see what will come to fruition and if this dream has any merit. I suggest that you watch the world around you in the days to come."

The man left Yagi's home grateful and left Yagi fresh bamboo shoots to eat. It wasn't long after the man had talked to Yagi that he and his wife had their first child. It was known that the couple had struggled for years, and now a healthy baby boy came into their lives.

A week later, a young girl (one of Yagi's pupils) had a dream: "I dreamt that a snake tried to choke me in my sleep, but that a spider bit it and the snake died. I am afraid. What should I do?"

Yagi advised the young girl to take care of herself and to beware of any literal snakes that might come into her home. Suddenly, she was afflicted with asthma and couldn't breathe in the middle of the night. A medicine woman had given her some herbs to open her airways in the event of an attack (medicine the girl had asked for), and the medicine worked.

Yagi had several people who came to him in the following days over dreams or visions. Some were waking, and some were sleeping. Yagi advised them as best he could, noticing the symbols and themes that commonly were found within each. Being a master of dreams, it was easy for him to understand what each meant. Yet, in his heart, he hated the mention of every dream, and he jealously coveted the visions of the people, who majority of which were frightened and shocked by the dreams and their presence.

An old woman who had visited Yagi for a dream consultation had not only suggested that Yagi charge for his interpretations but that there was an answer to their current predicament, "there is a creature called the Baku. He is a consumer of dreams. His presence may be sparking the imagination of all the village people, and his appetite might encourage their minds to grow fruit for his hunger. We may simply be his ground and our dreams his crop." She said this matter of fact after leaving Yagi homemade noodles and spices.

Yagi did not wish to charge a soul, considering how they always left food or clothing. Their reception of him and their kindness was payment enough. However, something within Yagi's brain greedily captured the thought of Baku. He had never heard of the thing, and before the old woman could walk down the road any further (though she hadn't gone far), he stopped her.

"What is the Baku?" he asked her, and like a child she had him sit with her as she told him of the Baku.

The Baku. An aloof creature. An amalgamation of different animals: a bear's body, an elephant's trunk, a tiger's paws, an oxen tail, and rhinoceros ears or eyes. He could be as small of a dog or as large as an elephant, but still, his body, like a mist, would appear at night and consume your dreams with its trunk. If it was not satisfied, then it would consume your hopes and desires. The creature was never spotted or found. Those who would dream would forget their dreams as the images would be consumed. Some say it is a menace to the minds of men, and some say that it is a spirit that brings blessings and inspiration.

Yagi took in every word. He looked back on his past life, a life he abandoned, and saw how the sequence of events had led him to this. He realized why nothing could contain or name the creature because it was a spirit without binds and power beyond his dreams. He thanked the woman and gave her a golden hairpin (one he had in his hair the day he left Edo). She left, and Yagi developed a plan to meet the Baku that very night.

• • •

Yagi sat in the middle of his bedroom. He breathed in slow, deep breaths and allowed his body to relax. Beside him was a contraption of his own making. He put nails in the side of a large candle and left the candle. As the wax melted, the nail would fall onto a metal chime, and he would awake. He set the nails a half inch apart from each other so he would have ample chances to spot the Baku between sleep and awake. He opened his mind and allowed his thoughts to slow from the flight of a hummingbird to the smooth trickle of a brook. His body slowly became limp, and his mind grew heavy with sleep. At almost the same time as sleep would have completely taken him over, the nail dropped, and the sound awoke him with a start. Nothing. The room was absent of any vapor or presence except for the small candlelight that flickered. Yagi was conscious of the candle, making sure to keep it in a safe place so the house would not burn down.

Yagi repeated the process. He would fall slowly into sleep, and then the nail would crash. Nothing. Sleep, crash, nothing. Sleep, crash, nothing. His body was becoming weary with the constant change. Yagi was becoming weary. He feared he would find nothing and the theories of the old woman would have only been just that. After all that time, he was simply robbed of his gift. There would be no explanation. It was ordained so.

Yagi refused to change his course, and he repeated the actions seven more times. On the eighth try, the nail no longer worked, and Yagi fell into a deep sleep. Yagi did not dream, but in the dark of the night, when the candle was snuffed, he felt a cool air come in. No doors or windows were open. No cracks were in the sturdy house made for him. His body felt the air shift around him. He was enveloped in a thick cloud.

The padding of feet circling him brought him further towards consciousness. His body was still. He could not move, but his mind was awakened. He could sense everything around him but could not make any movement. In a way, he felt that movement was not necessary. In his mind's eye, he could see the room from his perspective. He saw the vague outline of a large body with large paws and a drooping trunk. The creature continued to circle and its form continued to become clearer.

Yagi did not feel afraid. His mind echoed a sense of calm. He felt the figure probing and searching his mind. Leaning in and out of thought and memory. Yagi did not feel afraid. The creature was not invasive, wishing to control. The Baku, its presence fully formed, was curious. Like a dog sniffing the air or a foreign object, the Baku sniffed around in Yagi's mind without malice or favor towards him. It merely searched.

Yagi felt fear under the induced calm. He was curious as well. He wished to be able to see and touch the creature, but he knew that that would not be allowed- or possible. The Baku sent waves of recognition, hunger, interest, discovery, and disinterest through Yagi's brain. There were no words but vague feelings that came like the tide. Yagi allowed his body to completely consume the calm. He allowed himself to be opened like the petals of a flower.

The Baku opened Yagi's mind completely, and Yagi could see the giant figure before him. It was everything the old woman had described: a bear, an elephant, a tiger, an oxen, and rhinoceros ears and eyes together. The fur of the creature was a blue hue that was transparent and yet opaque. The creature's eyes were a dazzling jade that pierced intently at Yagi. The trunk was dexterous, probing Yagi's scalp and forehead. Yagi felt a wave of emotions within himself as he realized the trunk was moving and grasping.

To his surprise, the Baku responded with feelings of reassurance as well as passive, matter-of-fact feelings that this is how things have always been done- he is simply another point in a long line. Yagi and the Baku communicated this way with small flashes of feeling, like twinkling stars in a night sky. Eventually, Baku found what it was looking for. Yagi could simultaneously see a small spark in the center of his mind as well as Baku reaching for it with its trunk. The tiny firefly of light floated towards the trunk, and the Baku took in the light. The jade eyes closed as the Baku consumed the spark.

Yagi could see vision after vision after vision. Like a rushing wave, his past dream flooded his mind. In what seemed like seconds, his vast treasures came to him again. He traced over every scene, attempting to remember it all. He could not. It was like losing a limb, the tearing of flesh and bone leaving only a wretched stump.

He tried to fight back the Baku. He threatened and gave visions of death and destruction, but they seemed to be consumed like the rest of the small spark that was hiding within him. Finally, the spark died, and the Baku disappeared.

• • •

Yagi awoke the next morning. He saw the melted wax and nails on the floor. He felt light. It was not a relief- only the sensation of an opening that would forever be vacant. He sat in silence for a long time, allowing the events of his life to culminate in the current moment. It was a deafening blow to realize what was taken and how. He felt as if he died a needless death while the world around him continued to live. It almost took him entirely until he realized one thing: he understood what each dream meant, their truer essence. Yagi got up from where he sat. He brought out ink and paper, something that was largely untouched, and began to write his thoughts. He recorded his previous interpretations as well as new ones that swirled in his mind.

Eventually, Yagi had a large plethora of symbols and meanings. Yagi continued to teach but began to interpret the villagers' dreams. Soon, outsiders came to find meaning in their dreams, and his reputation grew. From that night until his death, he took each vision and dream into his speculating hands and searched them- probing them. He still felt the presence of Baku who also still searched for dreams still unknown.

The Funnel of the Universe

In the midst of the unfettered chaos, without form or purpose or soul, sat 12 gods. In a void, contemplating the words their Father had given them. They looked like a constellation. Some were many millions of light years away from each other. If humans were alive at this time, they might be able to see the spectral lights as they sat within the void.

Their Father, a greater light that encompassed everything, had previously given his twelve children a task:

"You must create a world unique to our own, filled with everything we are and can be."

The spirit that was most talented with creating things that flow and change (much like their brother) spoke up, "What must this world look like? What should we create, destroy, invent?"

The Father looked at the spirit with his gleaming omnipotence and said, "You must allow yourself freedom within this task and allow your brothers and sisters freedom as well."

Each of the children looked at each other without their eyes meeting. Eventually, the blinding light of the father left them in a flash, barely enough time for human eyelids to touch before the light vanished, and the inky black was all that remained. None of them moved at first. Some grew closer to the other, folding the inky pools of nothing around them to stand together. Some swayed or stirred slightly, thinking deeply of endless possibilities.

Without warning, two darting lights crashing through space collided in blinding heat. Sparks flew in all directions. Two of the brothers, creating a foundation of stone and ash, set fire to the void. Swirling clouds of fuming and mounting color extended to the whole of the universe. Twinkling stars grew and inflamed themselves. In the middle of the crying sky sat a flaming orb. The birth of a world. Watching in curiosity, the rest of the siblings huddled closer to each other. They saw raw matter mold and contort, stretching and aching for shape, for an answer.

At last, three other brothers darted towards the orb. Closer to its surface, the craggy mountains and cracks of the earth were swimming with molten lava and flame. The first two brothers decided on their new names, Erde and Rauroha. Erde himself, as he crashed into his brother, hardened into a giant being. His legs were permanently sent into the ground, but from his waist up, he was free-moving and cold. Below, his brother moved slowly, changing shape and seeping his fingers into the rocky surface. Climbing higher and higher by the will of Erde, mountains rose with sharp faces. Rauroha crawled steadily. He swam through the open cracks and filled them. He melted with his deliberate hands and shaped things around him. He created his home in the center of the orb. His form would always be a living and dying being, forever trapped within the center until provoked.

Hrom, Reka, and Samudra . Samudra, landing on the surface of the planet still a spectral light quivering in the heat, spread himself thin across the surface of the orb. He grew in size, and water covered everything. Erde's head was consumed, and Rauroha's form finally froze in an uneasy stillness. Samudra, a giant wave that flung itself with abandon, stretched to the furthest reaches until everything was consumed.

Reka looked on. He knew that his brother would take away territory. Reka then flew down from the universe and found his brother. Rising like a tsunami, Samudra met Reka.

"You and I are the same. We have the same soul, but we cannot be the same soul in one form. You *must* give me a place to fulfill my purpose for our Father." Hearing this, Samudra brought back the tide, and land began to surface. Erde, softened by water, called his brother Rauroha to stretch out his hands once more. Rauroha cut through the land, and Reka made his home like a snake. He lengthened his body and coursed through the bare earth. Reka and Samudra would change their course or their shape many times before they were satisfied. Even then, as the world began to lean on its access as a star warmed its surface, Reka and Rauroha would never be satisfied.

Testing the boundaries, the four brothers pushed and pulled each other's abilities. Erde continued to create and shape the mountains as they rose high in the air. Rauroha, however, kept taking parts of the mountain to melt within his grasp and bring it further into the core of his home.

Erde and Rauroha would stay like this for a time until Erde finally spoke, "I create the stone that must reach towards heaven. You are taking more than I can create. Why must you do this?!" Erde was exasperated. Rauroha called deep within the planet and said, "I must do the same as you: create. I must have something to form and grow."

Samudra, the raging waters that he was in, slowly began to chip away from Rauroha's land. The mountains also began to smooth under the weight of Samudra's force. Erde and Rauroha also called out to Samudra, "You also chip away and destroy what we must create. Why do this? We all must do as our Father commands!"

Samudra, rising to meet Erde, exclaimed, "Do you think I do not know this? My brother and I must share our twin purpose. We must flow. You must allow this to happen as Father wishes. What do you suggest that must be done? We cannot cease our course for yours." Eventually, Rauroha spoke, an echo from the abyss, "We all must share this new creation. Erde, as you create the mountains, I must take them. Samudra and Reka, as you create water, you must also extinguish me. Let us continue this way, but only take what is needed. For change to happen, let it happen when necessity rises. We will all perish by the other's hand if this does not happen."

They all agreed to these terms. The natural currents of the ocean settled slightly, the rivers flowed with a gentle trickle. The mountains stopped their constant growth, and the molten rock deep within the earth cooled. Things stayed this way for a while. Patterns began to show within the new world. The star that was closest to the planet showed brightly while its sister gleamed with a pearlescent glow. The brothers saw that this was good.

Two more of the glowing siblings came- sisters. Sagah and Zver. Sagah landed on a cliffside, peering over her brother Samudra. Swirling in light, she contemplated this new world. She traveled to every inch, finding her brothers hard at work in their slow-paced cycle of creation and destruction. One mountain rising to a peak opened up to a passage to Rauroha. Deep in the heart of the mountain, the fiery furnace of Rauroha's home beat like a heart. Sagah lept deep within to speak with her brother.

The swirling mass at the center formed a face so as to speak with his sister. The cinders bloomed and dyed over and over. Rauroha addressed his sister, "What, little sister, do you wish from me?"

"I have a new creation of my own. I wish to begin this on your land. I will not destroy what you have made, but your creation and mine could exist together. Will you allow me this?" she said, peering down at the changing face.

"I give you my land, but do not take from me, or I will consume you." he gave his final warning, and the face within the lava disappeared. Rumbles could be heard and then dissipated.

So Sagah left back into the air. The day was just beginning, and the star in the east cast its warm light over everything. Sagah darted across Rauroha's land. Beneath her feet, green foliage began to sprout. Vines, trees, flowers, fruits- wild things began to cover the whole of the land. Sagah's darting feet continued, spreading to the ocean once more. She called out to her brother Samudra, who rocked and swayed in constant motion.

"Samudra, I wish to give you a part of my creation. Will you keep it?"

"Yes, sister," he called out like the changing tide, "I will keep it as long as you allow my dominion to be mine." A giant wave crashed over her and as it drew back, coral reefs, seaweed, and fish began to burst like a dying star. The swimming and growing things transcended even to the very bottom. The ocean was now their home.

Sagah continued. Digging deep within the dirt, she bowed her power till trees began to crash through. Racing towards the sky, they reached great heights. The girth of the tree spread for miles, and its branches held sweet-smelling fruit. Insects whirled through the skies, finding homes in the flora across the entire world. Sagah's powers sprouted from her hands as she touched the earth. In light and color, everything drew breath. Her legs planted themselves in the earth. She reached her hands towards heaven and grew into a flowering tree that would never die and would never be bitten back by heat or cold. Seasons began. The birth and death of every season covered everything. The currents of Reka also teemed with life. Fish jumped and leaped over rocks and towering waterfalls. Reka journeyed like his sister Sagah, and for a while, her growing trees that lived near his banks were well-fed.

However, much of the earth died out as soon as it was born. In the distance, coming from the warmer south, Hrom barreled through the sky. With a bolt of lightning in his hand and the growing clouds billowing in rage, he let go of his deluge. Sagah looked up. She thanked her brother wordlessly. The water that came down gave life to her creation and fed her children.

Hrom, in his ambition, created the thunder and the lightning. He flashed the striking lights everywhere, and great storms began to blow. The winds kicked up. Samudra felt the passion. He swam through the whole of the earth and stirred the great currents of the sea. The roaring waters crashed violently against the rock face. Erde enjoyed the crash of the water and the spray of the salt. Rauroha could feel the movements that brought him and his mountain to rumble violently. Reka's streams did not change, but his rivers rose and flooded the land. The planet and everything in it roared a deep grumble. All of the creation cried in victory.

The raging fires of the mountain burst, and everything stopped. The flood of lava and ash covered all of Sagah's work. Her branches thrashed in pain as the fire struck her and her creation. Reka's flood stopped the fire, but there was nothing else that could be done.

Sagah's tree was uprooted by the wind, and thus, her spirit flew from its home towards her brother Hrom. She climbed further into the clouds, meeting the giant. He shot his lightning bolts with a bow made of starlight. He was a swirling mass of cloud and wind. His face only had two slits that beamed impossibly bright.

"YOU HAVE DESTROYED EVERYTHING I HAVE DONE!" her voice cried out amidst the thunder that burst violently.

Hrom looked at his sister, "Why can I not crash and burn like the rest of my brothers?"

Then, Erde, with his mighty hand, reached into the clouds and captured the spirit of Hrom. The clouds dissipated, and the chaos died. Sagah sat on the shoulders of Erde, who peered down at the flickering light of his brother Hrom.

With a mighty voice that shook the foundations of the entire planet, Erde declared, "You must bring balance like us all, or you will not be needed or wanted. You will stay in the void of space, never to join your kin, and Father will no longer find you useful in his or our kingdom."

Hrom's light seemed to quiver at the words, knowing that each of them was true. Erde's hand closed further in as he lowered his head, looking straight to the heart of Hrom.

"Do not make a storm such as that again unless the very trees demand it themselves', 'Erde released Hrom like a dove catching to flight, and Hrom scattered himself into soft white clouds that crested the sky. The sky also grew to be a blue color that would melt into magenta, lavender, and gold as the sun rose and set. Sagah went back to growing her trees, fruits, and flowers, and Reka helped her by allowing the roots to seep into his rivers. All the brothers and Sagah obeyed their brother Erde, who they revered as their master from then on, for he was the root of everything, and nothing could take him. Except for his brother Rauroha.

Harmony was found again. Hrom let the rain fall when the world needed it, and the turning of the planet brought winter, spring, summer and fall. The world seemed to rest for a moment. Sagah's tree was once inhabited, and her children spoke to her constantly, telling her what they see every day and what fruits they are growing in her honor.

Zver crashed into the planet when the moon was full. The impact burned her completely. Her light died soon after as the earth around her buried her. Encrusted in stone, her heart faintly beat like the flutter of butterfly wings. Rauroha and Sagah saw their sister crash into the ground. They both came to her and felt her pulse waning quickly. Rauroha warmed the earth beneath her, and Sagah fed her different roots to revive her. Slowly, Sagah stripped away the crusted earth. Emerging from the cracks was vibrant fur, claws, a mane, an elongated face, darting eyes, a forked tongue, giant hearts, and a massive tail that was the same length as the body. Sver stretched and yawned. It was as if she were merely asleep. She sniffed at the air, and her ears twitched violently as she listened to the sound of crickets and frogs chirping in the night.

Sagah thanked her brother, who descended once more into his home, and Sagah led her reborn sister to her tree. Zver pounced and lept through the growing grass and climbed up the towering trees. With glee, she raced around as Sagah made her way to her home. Zver pounced and lept through the growing grass and climbed up the towering trees. With glee, she raced around as Sagah made her way to her home.

Zver, however, did not stay long. All of Sagah's efforts at caring for her little sister stopped as she realized that Sver didn't want to be coddled. She growled whenever touched, and it would be many days between visits. Sagah sat Zver upon a mossy patch one day and finally said, "Little sister, I will no longer hold you here. You are not destined to stay with me, and your purpose has not been found. So go, find your purpose in this new world." With that, and without blinking, Zver dashed like the wind and was never seen again.

Along the open fields of gold wheat, Zver raced the sun, trying to catch it in her teeth. With that, the horse was born. Zver climbed the trees and scaled Erde's mountains- bounding over the rocks and borrowing in the caverns. With that, the ram, the bird, and the lizard were born. Zver slept in caves and hunted the small insects that buzzed and chirped. She rolled her back in the dirt, grabbed fish with her paws, sang to the moon like it was her lover, and crashed headlong into the snow.

With that, her children were born. Everything that crawled, flew, slithered, and ran. Every talon, claw, and hoof. Beasts of burden and prey. She was their mother who guided them and taught them to roam.

Finally, the planet that was so hot and unruly fixed itself in a rhythm of life. The seven gods that sacrificed themselves needed nothing. They created everything and built for themselves and each other. Rauroha's volcanic mountains heated the deep. Hrom's rain turned into ice and snow that rested on Erde's mountains. Reka's rivers gave Sagah and Zver water to drink, and Samudra's wide, expansive sea cooled the forming land from Rauroha's hands.

As the world took its course, settling and content, the gods slept deeply. The world did not need them- their work was finished.

• • •

Myslel, a god of pure thought and idea, found himself walking and then running in a jungle. He was the first visitor in millions of years, and he prided himself on being so clever. He was a child. His face had nothing but two glowing eyes that, unblinking, consumed everything. Every leaf and stone was his new discovery, and he held its secret knowledge close.

To himself (and to his brothers and sister slumbering), he said, "I hope my escape will make the other curious. Atmina must be here to see and answer my questions." The child was a blue colored boy in a tunic that was the same color. He looked as if he were ten or eleven years old, although his existence extends far beyond. Gold runes were embroidered into his garment. His skiing gleamed in the sun, changing color as he turned or heard a noise. His ears were pointed up to listen.

Myslel traveled to every corner he could. Once, he came to a sandy beach speckled with palm trees. He held a shell in his hand and handed it to the water.

"What is this?" he waited to hear his brother's voice in the water.

Samudra, his spirit lapping against the bank, whispered, "It is a shell." Then, he promptly went back to sleep.

Myslel pursued and followed the retreating tide, "why did you call it this? What is it made of? What is it for?"

Samudra lunged toward Myslel until Myslel's knees were underwater. Floating towards him was a shell of the exact color and size as the one that was in the sand. Myslel picked it up, and underneath, spindly legs and two claws emerged. They tentatively flayed in the air until Myslel walked out of the water and sat the creature on the sand. The beady eyes looked up, and the claws snapped as if they were testing an idea or notion.

"I still do not know what this is!" Myslel called out to Samudra, impatient. Samudra did not answer, and the crab continued to stare.

Myslel looked down at the creature, "I shall call it crab," he gleefully proclaimed and ran across the sandy beach, leaping and bounding with his new name. Samudra beckoned for the creature, and it crawled back into the water.

Atmina, a goddess of memory, inspection, and study, arrives alone in a dense forest. She herself was the opposite of her brother. She was taller with dark purple skin that was matte. Her face was void of everything but a mouth, and her ears were slanted downward. She was clothed in a dress that was folded and draped on itself, and a shawl covered her head. The shawl was a dark purple as well, covered in detailed embroidery that seemed to slowly morph as she walked. The ground beneath her crackled as she carefully walked. Without sight, she had to depend on her sense of hearing and touch. Without smell, she could not identify fire or rain. She was walking downhill and could hear a small stream flowing. The black rocks were beginning to smooth out after millions of years.

Touching the water, Atmina whispered to her brother, "Help me find our brother Myslel. I have tried to sense his whereabouts for many days now, but this world is too big, and I cannot be without him. Do you know where he is?", as she finished, her voice cracked slightly, but she tried to control.

The water continued to flow as if to give no answer. Beside Atmina's ear, she felt a hot breath brush against her face. She quickly scrambled away and ran wildly, curving and swaying around trunks of trees she barely brushed. Hooves bounded after her, and the wind blew against her, which tumbled her to the ground. The creature, a male elk, gently walked toward her, nosing her gently as she lay on the ground. He nuzzled her face. Atmina began to trace her hands across his flank, and nimbly, she mounted the elk. The elk bounded towards the ocean, and there Atmina would finally call out to her brother, who would hear her amidst the blaring creation.

Myslel was watching a group of monkeys as they groomed each other. They had small faces with large eyes that appeared blankly and long arms that swung expertly from branch to branch. Myslel hid carefully from a distance. He learned not to make noise as he encountered more of this island. He learned that some things had teeth that did not hesitate despite him being a god. He could not die, but he did not wish solely to be chased.

So he sat, watching the mothers pick fleas from their babies clinging to their chests and the younger teenagers swing and play and crash in the trees. They whimpered or hooted or yowled in such varied ways that Myslel couldn't help but stay frozen for hours on end. At night, the creatures would sleep soundly, and then Myslel would find a place to rest. Myslel thought to himself, "monkey. Monkey is a good name. I wonder if there are more of them than just these?"

Myslel began to wander further into the island. Birds flew in all directions as they traded spaces for better vantage points. At this time, no birds had the gift of song, so only the insects' gentle whirring and the falling of rain made any noise. The monkeys would be heard in the distance, but still, the world was relatively silent. Myslel was getting closer to the other edge of the island when he heard a voice calling out from the west. Myslel thundered against the ground as hard as he could and raced with joy towards the voice. Atmina had finally made it towards the edge of the ocean. The craggy rocks towered over her as she stood on the wet sand. Her feet sank a little, and she picked up her skirts.

Myslel came to the beach of his island and continued to hear the echoing call of his sister's voice. Myslel swam with the assistance of dolphins through the water while Atmina waited patiently, letting the cool air of the ocean brush her skin. Samudra stretched the tide further towards her feet. Atmina started a little but got used to the feeling of surprise. She calmed quickly. The water felt cool, and she reveled in her brother's gift.

Myslel came running up to her, sloshing sand back as he emerged pristine from the water. Without the need to open mouths or use words, they both called for each other, and Atmina scooped Myslel up into her arms. While still in the comfort of his sister's arms, Myslel relayed everything that he had seen and learned. He gave out different names, places, images, sensations, and feelings. Atmina took in everything.

"You found so much, little brother! I am impressed. And you have found so many creatures that live there." She easily leaped to the top of the cliff, where the grass waved in the wind. Gray clouds covered the sky, and the air smelled like iron.

"I still have so many questions," protested Myslel, "I wanted to know what some of these creatures eat, why they must groom each other, and what they do at night. Why are there 'crabs' and why the earth beneath me must be so gritty." He dangled his feet, which were still covered in sand.

"Well," Atmina put her brother down, "I see that the creatures you call 'monkeys' groom as a way to show affection. The 'crab' used his shell as his home. He grows it himself. I see that the birds must reach the fruits and seeds that the trees create. I see that the seeds left from the fruit fall to the ground and birth more tall trees, fruits, and flowers. The thing you call a 'snake' lies in wait for easy prey. The 'ants' work together to feed themselves and each other. You have found a great deal."

Then, mostly to herself, she said, "Our older brothers and sisters have worked diligently to create this world so that it may feed and resolve itself. They have truly finished their work. We are just beginning. I wonder how long we will take for our final creation?"

Myslel held Atmina's hand and said, "Come on! Do you wish to see more things?"

"I know a place that I think you would like very much!" they walked together back into the forest with the redwood trees, the elks, the bears, and the squirrels.

• • •

The sun was hottest towards the desert sands. Rolling hills of thousands of colors seemed to swirl infinitely behind the goddess Utsaha. Utsaha, a goddess of passion, love, creativity, and heart, walked along the sands and dyed the grains into deep blood reds, golds, blue, turquoise and green. She herself was a vibrant feminine body, voluptuous and naked. She had golden eyes, full lips, a small nose, and giant wings with soft white feathers. Her skin was as pink as roses, but her eyes blazed with a fiery white flame.

Walking along the dunes, she smelled the pungent air. Not too far away, the mountains with their hot sulfur burst into light, and ash began to fall. The top of the mountain showed a great hole where hot magma spewed and gushed- a gaping wound. Rauroha climbed out of the mountain, clawing his way down towards the sands. Mounds of lava reached high and settled upon itself. Erde awoke. He saw the river of lava slowly moving towards him and began to mold and shape. Rauroha spread his fire in every direction. New mountains formed. Wordlessly, Erde smoothed the mountains (like clay in the hands of a potter) and carved crags and caverns within. A canyon, deep and wide, broke apart as Erde spread his hands and parted the sides of the canyon while the lands parted.

Utsaha just watched, sitting on the warm sand with her knees tucked up to her chest. In a moment of inspiration, she leaped into the air and flew towards Erde and Rauroha. In the walls of the canyon, she traced her fingers over the surface and created layers of color and texture. Then she gave every mouse and snake a name according to their color, size, habits, and shape. Floating over the clouds, where her brother Hrom slept soundly, she saw the sunrise. The pale light casts over the clouds. Utsaha touched each cloud and saturated the skies with purple, rose, gold, and blue. In a field of flowers, she gave each a name and a scent. She painted each petal lovingly and bathed in the soft winds of the trees.

She gave the animals voices as well. Every squawk, roar, gurgle, and cry came from her lips, and she gave them to the animals that dwelled in the land. She made water droplets stay on the tiny strands of spider webs and taught birds how to fly together in giant flocks moving and swaying in the wind. She taught animals to mate and to breed. She taught birds to dance and to sing. She taught the flowers to spread their seed. She taught the bees to make honey. She embowed herbs to heal. She gave butterflies their designs. She taught cicadas to hum. Everywhere that Utsaha went, the world burst into life with song and color.

Utsaha began to pick flowers and created a crown for herself. Her wings were laced with sunlight, and her skin glowed from the dew of the morning. As she walked among the trees on a fresh spring morning, she saw one of her brothers walking in the woods. Tall and stark white, the figure moved slowly with a staff as pale as bone. Clad in a white robe embroidered with gold, Eleos walked carrying a fawn in the crook of his right arm. Eleos, the god of mercy, compassion, patience, and peace, walked gingerly over the ground, trying not to wake the sleeping creature in his arms. Eleos, for being so frail-looking, was strong in his presence. His staff was a slender stick with a floating orb that rotated ever so slightly that it was untraceable at times. Only when you saw the orb out of the corner of your eye did you notice it was moving.

Eleos's head was covered in a bright halo. The halo was twice the size of his head and was so bright that one could only see the outline of his head. He made no sound as he walked and watched the world around him as it breathed and lived in its natural course. Utsaha watched him from afar. She loved Eleos most out of all the others because, like her, he craved the same things- although his course was slower and more gentle than hers.

Utsaha leaped and bounded excitedly toward her brother, who scared the fawn. The creature leaped from Eleos's arms and plopped to the ground. It was thin, and its legs were wobbly as it attempted to walk. Utsaha relaxed her pace. Eleos picked up the creature again, leaned his staff against a tree and began to comfort the fawn.

Eleos looked at Utsaha and, in a voice that was like a soft symphony of hums, said, "This one was abandoned after its mother was killed. There are not many of them left."

"What do you mean, brother?" Utsaha came closer and began to stroke the ears of the fawn.

"There were many of these beings when I first came, grazing in a field. However, now there is a new creature unlike anything I have seen." Eleos's voice grew more urgent.

Utsaha's heart began to beat faster in fear and curiosity, "what did the creature look like? You must tell me!"

Eleos described a two-legged creature with a broad face and two front-facing eyes. The creature clothed itself and its mate in the hide of a deer and began to hunt with sticks and stones. Sometimes, the creature would capture smaller animals in its bare hands and kill them with its teeth. Its mate would gather herbs but also catch fish from the rivers and streams. Utsaha listened transfixed, raging against the death of one creature but longing to know about the life of another. Eleos continued speaking about the stones carved to points and the fires that blazed in caves at night.

Finally, when Eleos stopped, he walked further into the woods. He held the fawn in both arms and covered it with one of his long flowing sleeves. In the distance, a female deer appeared, and both it and the fawn joined together- as if death were only a dream.

Eleos turned towards Utsaha and linked his arm to hers, "what have you created since you entered this world?"

"I have created color, sound, taste, and touch. I have created sex and birth. I have created song. There are many other things that I wish to do, but I do not know how I might spread these things. What, dear brother, have you been able to create?"

Eleos shook his head, "I have not found anywhere where my creations would be best. I see this world. I see the natural order that has been created by our eldest brothers and sisters. Everything is designed to fulfill itself without interference or correction. I have no need to insert myself."

"What would you wish to do? Surely, you will not hide forever."

"I do not intend to be useless, I promise. I wish to create a sense of being where the gentleness of this world may be preserved and kindly sought. I wish for there to be many generations that live and die together, caring for one another. I wish for there to be bravery in the face of heartache- using love and compassion as the weapons against destruction that so easily shatters all good. Like you, I am also searching for a place where these things can be fulfilled."

"Brother! Your answer has been fulfilled, and mine has been. This new creature you speak of, the one who seems to rampage against this land, can be influenced by both of us. We must seek out its creator and convince them that our ways are beneficial!" She darted around him excitedly.

Eleos hesitated, lowering his head slightly, "I know the creator of this creature. He is currently speaking with our sister Sagah, trying to find a home for the creature, considering how it is destroying half a population of animals other than deer in such a short time. Come, we will discuss these things with him."

Utsaha knew exactly who Eleos was speaking of, and both hurried towards Sagah, who sat underneath her tree.

• • •

Myslel squatted down and stared at a frog as it buzzed its song. Atmina listened carefully and dragged her brother towards the conversation so his ears could pick up every little thing that could be said. They will communicate later, and she will take time to examine new things and ideas while the moon is high in the sky. There are not many nights where she can rest easily. Both because of the world around her and its endless possibilities and because of her lack of time to think during the day. Myslel scurries across the face of the world in reckless abandon. Sometimes, he is lost for days, and Atmina has nothing left but the same cycle of thoughts: race and race and race.

A tall, crimson-skinned figure, muscular with four arms, stood tall and foreboding against the peaceful Sagah, whose hair was covered in every growing thing that one could imagine. It was so heavy that it looked like a blanket cradled her, and only her face was visible. Atmina and Myslel sat opposite the interaction, listening intently. The tall figure's head was a floating pyramid with a point resting between the shoulders. In one of the right arms, the figure held a golden spear. The tip of the spear was so narrow and sharp that it seemed to disappear when turned in a certain way. The figure was naked except for pants and a long sash that hung from the pelvis to the ground. Iustitia, the god of justice, order, truth, righteousness, and control, stood unmoving as the group had been speaking for almost three days straight.

"My creation is just as animal as the rest of your creation. Zver, however, will not have to teach it how to run, hunt, sleep, or survive. It is something with thought. It has the capacity to reason- create and destroy with intent rather than on instinct. It is wholly unique, and I cannot allow it to be sheltered away from the rest of the world", the figure boomed.

"I also wish for this creation to be able to thrive, but it will not have a world to thrive within if it does not have restraint. My creation, every living thing, along with Zver's work, has a balance and intent. It does not kill for pleasure and does not burn for spite. You have created something with no fear or sense to feel content. You must curb these desires, or this world will not exist as long as it lives. I will be tempted to destroy your work if you wish to destroy mine!" Sagah rose to her full height. She was winnowy and thin, but she grew to meet the face of Iustitia and her long hair cascaded behind her. Shivering, the trees seemed to echo her sentiment.

Eleos approached Iustitia and bowed, "Brother, you have always been innovative in your work, but Sagah's work is imperative in that it brings life to everything you see, touch, taste, and smell. Sagah's creation feeds yours, and to dismiss her means death to everything you hope for. Please, I give you this offer."

At this, Utsaha also approached Iustitia alongside Eleos as he continued, "I give you the opportunity for my work to be finished, which will greatly benefit your work as well. I wish to teach your creature contentment, patience, kindness, mercy, and hope."

Utsaha stepped in as well and offered her gifts, "I also wish to bring an offer of love, joy, pleasure, and creativity. From both of us, these things will help your creature to not only live but thrive. What things can it create in response to the new ideas that it has been given?" Utsaha's voice grew strong, and her skin deepened in color. Her eyes gleamed bright. Eleos looked at Atmina and Myslel. Atmina carried Myslel on her hip and, despite her godhood, looked weary.

Iustitia sat for the first time in three days, leaning his large head on both left fists while his spear laid on the ground. He contemplated, looking over every possibility.

Utsaha leaned down and peered into his face. And in a voice like fire, she whispered, "You must consider what we are saying, brother. This world is a gift from our elder siblings. They worked tirelessly, and seemingly, with no effort, they understood the balance that must be kept. I understand it, too. Bask in this world's glory and tell me you do not see it!"

"I see a world that will remain stagnant and lost in mediocrity if change is not found. The blossoms of this world will not change along with its beauty, and there will be nothing special except what we force ourselves to believe. Why cannot change, rapid change, come along with the tides and the moving of the earth? Are we to settle forever?" said Iustitia emphatically.

Atmina finally spoke, gently letting down Myslel, who was wide-eyed and intent, "I see all sides of this. I wish for Sagah to thrive. I wish for the creature- you named it 'human,' yes?- to thrive. I see the need for Eleos and Utsaha to touch the human heart, but I also see the possibility of radical change and its marvelousness. Brother, you must think of what this could mean for your creation. Its longevity will increase if its restrain increases."

Iustitia looked at Atmina, "You have always seen to reason. You have made it plain." Iustitia stood and addressed Eleos and Utsaha, "You may touch the heart of this creature. However, do not change them. They are mine, and I am not so merciful."

Eleos stood then to meet his brother, "We are not so cruel, and you will not be so bold."

Eleos left them along with Utsaha, who looked back at her siblings once and then scampered away, meeting with her brother Eleos.

• • •

Eleos and Utsaha found the humans, male and female, sleeping in a small cave, curled in each other's arms. Utsaha found them first, and something within her blazed. She found her purpose and her catalyst. Whispering in their ears, she began to dispel her gifts, "I gift you with the gifts of love, joy, passion, strength, laughter, romance, sex, and soul. I give you to your mind creativity, color, music, voice, language, and art. Use these to spread your lineage and tribe."

She whisked away into the night, letting the currents of the wind carry her to its delight. She landed in Hrom's domain, choosing a soft cloud to sleep in. Eleos finally came at the approach of the dawn and awoke the two humans as they saw the mounting sun.

Both humans were frightened and made their way further into the dark cave, but Eleos calmed their spirits and kneeled before them, "Do not be afraid or discouraged. Listen to me and know more about this world and yourselves. I give you gifts: I give you hope, patience, kindness, mercy, forgiveness, family, gentleness. I gift you peace, democracy, truth, and reason. Use these things wisely and never forget that you are both each other's gift as you create a home and a life."

The human's minds churned with thought. They looked at each other as if never before had they known that the other existed. Eleos led the humans out of the dark and gloomy cave- they were simultaneously excited, anxious, and curious. The man held his spear in his right hand, but looking back, he gestured for the woman with his left. Gently, they walked together. Hand in hand, they traveled for a home.

Iustitia kept watch, looking over their progress in the years to come. Soon, the man had built a suitable home, and the woman gave birth to their first child. Sagah and Reka kept the humans nourished. Zver sent many animals to investigate the new creatures. Some were welcome, the horse, dog, cow, chickens, mule, and bull, and some were not welcome.

The soft ground underneath the human feet was tilled. The seeds of fruiting things were sewn. The waters of Reka were used for irrigation. The metal of Erde's caverns was heated and beaten to shape. The towers grew taller. The earth became populated. Threads were sewn into garments. Bone was carved into instruments. The wine was fermented. Paintings on cave walls were made. Language is united and divided at the same time.

Humanity started to grow in number and lived in a temperate harmony with nature. Humans on the distant island revered and feared the volcanoes that destroyed but brought anew. The humans of the mountains found freedom in the pastures below but feared the winters as they blanketed them with snow. The desert somehow made the humans resilient and strong. Dark skinned and fierce.

Iustitia watched closely as humanity tamed the wild. However, he was not happy. Atmina and Myslel also observed the humans. Myslel grew in stature and age, consuming what was found within the minds and hearts of humans. He saw their curiosity as food for his own pursuits, which turned into geometry, chemistry, geology, mathematics, philosophy, and the written word.

He planted all of these things in those he found the most worthy and brought them back to his sister, who helped him to elaborate and extend all of his findings. Atmina grew older in his ways as well. She stayed within the tall forests that Sagah dwelled in the most. Sagah grew quieter, but it could be felt everywhere.

Myslel came to his sister one day, holding tomes and scrolls. Many were etched in maps and flags. He stole them from a leader of a nation who was sleeping, leaning over a table filled with small miniatures and plans. He was clad in the richest garments and jewels, but his face was smothered in wine and spit.

Myslel approached his sister and laid out all of the things he had found. Atmina, with wrinkles and thinning hands, slowly came closer with a twisted cane. She looked over the maps but only saw blank scraps of deer skin.

"I do not know these things. What is it you have brought for me?" asked Atmina.

"These things the humans have made for war. They wish to destroy each other in conflict over lack of resources and no compromise on tribe boundaries. Over time, one tribe has tried to sabotage another. Eventually, both tribes' leaders have decided to wage war. They see *death* as their only option."

"I see", said Atmina. She looked over the documents. The flags and lines that indicated mountain ranges and populations wrote themselves as they spread across the pages. Atmina's mind darted, piecing things together. Pointing to the map, she located a group with the tip of her cane.

"These people wish to invade during the night and raid their opposing enemy in the east. No one is meant to be left alive." Atmina's mind raced a little faster, "from where did these humans get this idea? They will destroy themselves before they destroy each other!"

"I know. They are already destroying themselves. There is already a threat of famine and drought on the horizon. They do not know, but the wind and the rain have been telling them for many weeks now. They do not *wish* to listen anymore."

"They cannot be blamed for what they do not know. If they wish to make these decisions, it is not our…"

"But they will be doing something ridiculous. And over what?! A few handfuls of grain and whether this pond is over here or over there? Why can they not see beyond their own noses?!"

"Again, we cannot blame them for something they do not know and have not learned. You and I must take the chance to be able to teach them", said Atmina.

"Yes, I agree, but sister, you have not been well for a long time. What shall we teach them and when?"

Atmina sat for a while in thought. Finally, the truth resigned itself within her, "You must do what I would do and teach them. You understand what they must know, do and believe… it is time that you do this task yourself."

Myslel, as if awoken from a fever, looked at his sister. He tried to hide his eagerness in his eyes, "Are you sure, sister? Are you sure I can do this? I only receive information, but you are the one who truly understands."

"You understand as well as I, if not better." Atmina stood slowly and turned towards the depths of the forest, "go, Myslel and teach them truly who they need to be." She left into the forest, and the trees cradled her, helping her walk.

That night, Myslel looked over the humans. Like planting seeds, he left small thoughts within their minds. He prompted their dreams and visions that Utsaha had gifted them not long ago. He made some dreams of their wives in their beds, their children, their soft-hearted mothers. He made them think of a brighter future where they continued to eat, drink, sleep, and cultivate their farms. He made them think of peace. He made some dreams of revolution and victory. Not a victory of blood but a victory of the spirit that so easily quivered from one direction to the other. Myslel's hopes were high, but he did not know if the dreams would hold.

The next morning, the troops of either side continued their toiling for war and, in fact, had grown in vigor. Their hesitancy grew into a fever. Myslel watched from a distance. His wide eyes grew dark in fear and regret. The next night, Myslel tried again, with dreams of rage and torture. The soldiers continued their work, but within their eyes, the fear of death lingered.

Myslel saw that his efforts would not work. He found Iustitia observing the humans and their preparations from one of the mountains of Erde. Iustitia balanced his head in one hand and pondered. He found every heart within his creation and saw a multitude of questions lay before him. All the questions humanity would have to answer somehow.

Myslel bowed before his brother and spoke clearly. He straightened himself slightly and lifted his chin to attention, "Iustitia, I assume you are aware of the current events."

"Yes, little brother, I am. Sit", Iustitia spoke plainly. Myslel sat cross-legged beside his brother and listened. His eyes were attuned to every word as well as every tone within Iustitia's voice. Iustitia could feel the paring eyes.

"You see here," Iustitia opened his palms, and beside each other were separate visions of kings discussing or arguing with commanders of legions. Both seemed similar in stature and face.

"They are brothers, Myslel. Brothers who have inherited a profitable kingdom. They do not want anything, and their people thrive. Their people are ignorant, but they have no need to read if they must gather corn. They live full lives and die when their bodies deem it necessary. What type of life would you call that?"

Myslel looked at his brother, "I would say that that is a full life… but empty."

Iustitia said nothing but watched his brother.

"I see that life can only lead to one place. There are no new roads to tread, and such a life can become pointless. Why would anyone wish to live solely in one place and in one way for so long?"

"They make that decision themselves." Iustitia stood, "I have given them the gift of free will. They make their own decisions."

Myslel processed the word slowly.

"But they have no knowledge. What will they do?"

"What you see here?" Iustitia motioned towards the vision. Slowly, battle plans were confirmed, and motions of attack were made for the next dawn.

Myslel peered over, "We must stop them! They cannot kill each other!"

"Why not? Death will happen to any creature in any case. What is the difference between dying in one's sleep and killing them? What matters is that there is order found in everything, whether good or bad."

"I do not think that life must only be confined to kill or be killed." Myslel stood up and turned himself towards his brother. Iustitia continued to pour into the vision.

"You cannot let them live without a purpose. Sagah gave all of her children purpose, but you leave them to slaughter and ruin. They cannot have free will without knowledge. They *must* not be without knowledge!"

The giant, strong Iustitia turned and faced Myslel. His bottom left arm gripped the golden staff tightly as the rest of the arms swayed gently beside his body.

"I will do what I please," said Iusitia. His voice was stern.

Myslel responded with effort, trying not to let his voice shake, "and I will do what is right." Myslel left and began plans to create new gifts for mankind.

• • •

Three days had passed. Atmina walked in a forest scorched to ash. Sahah wailed in agony in the distance. Zver ate the remains of fallen soldiers with the carrion birds while Utsaha and Eleos wandered the burnt battlefield, seeing the faces of every man under their feet.

Myslel curled into a ball. Only his eyes peered over his knees as tears streamed in rivers down his face. The rivers carried the bodies of the dead to sea, and Myslel watched them as they floated downstream.

A voice called out, "Myslel, Myslel!"

Atmina, older in shape and spirit, walked with Eleos's assistance towards Myslel. When she grew closer, Myslel leaped into her arms and wept. Atmina cradled him and rocked him, whispering in his ear. Eleos watched from a distance. Utsaha met with him, and they stood together, looking over the carnage. Utsaha pointed in the distance. The two brothers who ruled their kingdoms were facing headlong unto the other's spears as blood poured out of their mouths. They killed each other and died on their weapons.

Myslel spoke through sobs, "I tried everything. I gave them all I had. I wanted to save them. I did not want them to die."

"Hush now. Hush. You did everything you could. You did well. Your gifts did well."

"But they are dead! I did nothing!"

"NO! Do not believe that!" said Atmina, "You gave them things to discover and to learn. Those who survive this battle will teach the children the things they learned, and their children will carry the gifts you gave to the ends of the earth."

Myslel laid there. Atmina drew him closer.

Eleos and Utsaha walked back to Atmina and Myslel. Eleos gently placed a hand on Myslel, "We must leave. The humans will take care of their dead."

Myslel looked at Eleos. His eyes were sharp and indignant.

"Where were you when the humans decided to kill each other?"

Eleos was taken aback. Utsaha drew closer.

"What do you mean?" asked Eleos.

Myslel stood up, "where were you when the humans decided to slit each other's throats over a few extra blades of grass? Where were you with your gifts of 'kindness,' 'humility,' 'grace,' and 'charity'? You were nowhere to be found!" at this, Myslel threw ash in their faces.

"You are a hypocrite and a sloth! You did nothing to stop this! You speak of peace and are nothing by a liar!"

Utsaha spread her wings and came between them both, raging in fire and wrath, "You are ignorant of your true purpose. We create, but we do not intervene."

"And you. You reveled in their fury. You snuck into their camps when they took whores. You sat in their debauchery. You encouraged their hate and ate from their soul's malice! You speak of love but are a glutton!"

Myslel lunged himself forward and started to run after both of them, but Eleos caught him in his grasp and held him tightly.

"Calm yourself! You will be no better than us if you start a quarrel!" Eleos bellowed, and his body brightened like a star.

Myslel, smaller and faster than Eleos, slipped from Eleos's grasp and continued, "And you. You speak of peace, joy, kindness, and forgiveness. But you did *nothing* to stop Iustitia! You stood there and watched as they killed each other!"

"That is enough!" cried Eleos. Thunder could be heard from a distance. Eleos's stature lessened. Myslel picked up Atmina but still faced his brother and sister. Utsaha was shocked and waited behind Eleos, who finally gained his composure and usual radiance.

"You have no idea what our role in this world is for. You are also not in charge of the humans, considering how you have not made them. As for the many gifts you have given them, they may help them to learn from their mistakes. They have been given free will. Let them learn on their own."

"And if they don't learn, whose fault will that be?"

Eleos grew silent, and both he and Utsaha left. The rain finally fell. Sagah, in vain, planted new seeds, and Zver gnawed the bones of the fallen soldiers.

• • •

A thousand years transpired. Cities spread slowly through their vast buildings and towers across the face of the earth. Languages filled the air, and papyrus recorded the passing of the days. Philosophers grew in popularity along with the ideas of mathematics, astronomy, physics, and literature. The first plays were made. Add so were the first gods.

Myslel walked among the humans in their cities and marveled. He looked over the intricate architecture, the sculptures, the music, the clothing, the colors, the smells. He traced his fingers over the written scrolls in a library in one of the most successful cities- and one of his favorites. He listened to their speech, letting his mind consume every meaning and creating new forms and methods of translation.

Atmina had transpired long ago. He gained her knowledge, and she faded into dust among the stars. Iustitia focused his time on one particular nation. He helped them create an order and system of government that would last for eons and strengthen their government. So far, their power has increased over the earth. Eleos and Utsaha found themselves intrigued by the humans' attempt at spirituality. Some gods were created, and some died with the humans' forgetfulness and disbelief. In the end, the gods that the humans worshiped were only stone and smoke.

Erde, Rauroha, Sagah, Samudra, Zver, and Reka had all noticed change within their worlds. Erde saw the humans digging into his tunnels and finding precious jewels. Rauroha found the humans using his hot springs to bathe and nourish themselves. Samudra found a fisherman dragging his creations into their nets. Zver often ran away from the bows and arrows of those who hunted. And Sagah watched from afar as the humans tore up the land and began to grow their own food rather than taking from her trees and bushes. The wild boar were now bred as domesticated pigs, along with cows, sheep, horses, and bulls. The yoke infuriated Zver so much that she attempted to destroy it, but she was mistaken for a wolf and was almost killed by a shepherd.

Erde grumbled in anger. Deep within his chest, he began to growl. Rauroha noticed the humans coming closer to one of his mountains, and he seethed in anger because of their arrogance. Reka haunted the boats that the humans created, using them to catch his fish and water their crops. Hrom often did not have much conflict with the humans except for their abuse of the world below. He craved to see the lush world once more, but now the humans grew and spread like maggots. For a while, the world experienced a drought or other extremes: tornadoes, tsunamis (with the help of Samudra), and hurricanes.

Sagah, fatigued of having to feed a growing and ungrateful race, decided that all of the siblings come together to discuss a solution. She called for her brethren at the edges of the earth. All of them gathered at the snowy tops of the highest mountain and created a plateau where everyone could sit. Sagah climbed the mountain on the back of a Zver whose fur was white like the snow. Eleos and Utsaha sat together, whispering and quietly discussing many things. Rekah, Hrom, Samudra, and Rauroha did not take a more manageable form, but their voices could still be heard from where they stayed.

Sagah, with her cascading hair, approached the circle as everyone stood and bowed in reverence. Iustitia kept his eyes on her and waited for her testimony. Zver cradled herself at Sagah's feet and smelled the air. Utsaha smelled of spices, sweat, and musk. Her cheeks were flushed. Eleos was stoic and silent, his light icy. Myslel had grown taller and stronger. His pursuits in giving the humans knowledge had stretched his abilities further than the rest of his siblings, and thus, his form became grander. His skin was still teal blue; his garb had not changed. However, in the center of his forehead, there was a third eye, the same size and color as his two original ones.

He held tomes of scrolls in his hands and was prepared for his arguments in defense of humanity. He already knew why Sagah wished to meet. He was determined not to let his hard work fade nor give up humans in their pursuits.

Sagah stood and addressed her siblings, "Thank you all for meeting me here. I know that some of you are aware of why we are here, but I will be frank and state my business: your eldest siblings of the earth who created the waters, the trees, the skies, and the animals are unhappy with humanity's dealings. They take from our creation and use it to destroy, rebuild, and destroy again. They take without asking and are unaware of the delicate balance that has been maintained since before you, my younger siblings, came. Humanity believes that they own this world, but in fact, they are only allowed to live."

"What solutions do you propose?" spoke Iustitia.

"I wish for humans to learn how to be thankful. To only take what they need. Once before, they understood this concept, but now they have become haughty and ambitious."

"Do you believe that their ambition is wrong?" asked Myslel.

"I believe that their ambition comes with little limit."

"What limits do you suggest be implemented?" asked Iustitia.

"I believe the humans should truly know our presence and our intentions. They already created gods for themselves and invented ways for this world to begin without any knowledge of our influence. Would it truly be wrong to announce our presence?"

"It would give away a secret we were sent to create, not to overtake our father who enlisted us to one simple task," spoke Eleos.

"If it was never said, then why must it become a rule?"

"You of all people should know Sagah our Father's intentions even without a single breath breaking from his nostrils," said Utsaha, "I would be careful, Sagah, with your own ambition."

"And become slothful like you, Utsaha? What have you created since the beginning? What have you done except stew within the lust and wrath of mankind? You even smell like them." Said Sagah, sneering.

"But that *is my* work." Utsaha got from her place and approached Sagah. Her hips took on an exaggerated sway that emphasized her shape, "I may not grow corn, but I certainly grow passion and help your world be filled with animals. As for war, I may be the spark, but it is up to the humans as to where they direct their flame."

"And so far, they have directed it to destroy each other. You must be so proud of being the harbinger of death as well as sex!"

"Sisters, I implore you to sit!" said Iustitia. He stamped his spear, which gave out a sound like the banging of a gong.

"My elder brothers, what do you say about Sagah's remarks?"

The growing, howlings, rushing, and crackings of the earth seem to come out all at once.

"I believe that Sagah is right. These humans have been ill lead and trained to take more than they have right," said Samudra.

"They believe they can control the weather and the deep," said Hrom and Rauroha.

"They believe they can build into the mountains and carve the stone I have created for myself," said Erde.

"They cut their way through my rivers and pass over my waters as if I were only a passageway," said Reka

From Zver's foaming and hissing mouth, he could manage four words. With effort, in a gravelly voice, she said, "I am no slave." From a hidden rock, Zver brought out a bridle she stole from a farmer. The bridle had a bit that was bent from many years of use. She threw it at Iustitia's feet and hissed again, going to back Sagah's feet.

Sagah slowly stroked Zver as Zver calmed herself. Iustitia stood and put all of his arms behind his back. He looked towards his siblings and felt the presence of his eldest brothers, who waited to hear what he would say.

"I believe that Sagah has a point. There is a definite need for balance within the world as humans continue to dwell within it. They must learn how to take only what is needed. Excess in anything is dangerous. There has been a surge in population south of here in one particular nation after they overthrew their neighboring enemies and took their wives. Now, they are trying to maintain resources and feed the new mouths of a still weak nation. They have had to make compromises and find new resources."

"I propose that we satiate the ambition of mankind. We must teach them forgetfulness, fear, and doubt. They must have these things before they become gods themselves," said Iustitia, and most of the siblings agreed.

Myslel, however, was staunchly against the new proposal, "My dear brother, I have a retort to this idea," said Myslel, standing.

"What is your retort, Myslel?" asked Iustitia, tightening the grip on his spear ever so slightly.

Myslel unfolded a scroll and lifted it midair, so it floated delicately before him, "Hear, I have a scroll containing an estimate of how many cows, sheep, grains, etc. were sold within the last year of this nation. This is not something I created on my own accord; and this was created by the King's head treasury, who meticulously calculated the export and import of goods within this nation. This man was especially considerate since there has been a drought."

In the distance, lightning struck with a flash, and the gurgle of thunder could be heard not far. Myslel continued.

"If you will observe," the gods came closer, looking at the scratches of ink within the papyrus, "this treasurer calculated a decrease in vegetables and an increase in meat. However, rations were still enforced, as you can see within the drop in numbers and by Thai ordinance made by the king", Myslel produced a written ordinance sealed with the king's seal.

"What does this mean to us?" asked Sagah.

"This means that the concerns for your land are not as severe as you think. Humanity is very capable of learning from their mistakes as well as adapting to their environment. They are not breeding and taking and enslaving animals to an extent that is cruel, but they are using innovations that were given to them by us. We made the cow, goat, and sheep produce milk, and thus, they created cheese with it as well. We made the ox and the horse strong, and they used that to their advantage. The boar with its tusks are allowed to till the earth, but humans should not?"

He could hear murmurs among the siblings, but Sagah was enraged.

"Little brother, I do not believe you see the entirety of this world. You are blindsided by the progress of your favorite nation, your pet. The world is not as virtuous as them, and their progression does not reflect all of humanity's hearts. Look", Sagah waved her hand and opened a vision towards the deserts. A tribe of men were chasing down a lion. In killing it, they simply left the carcass and only took the hide and the mane. The carcass sat there for the carrion birds, but no human touched it.

Sagah continued, "They are still capable of waste. And torture." Again, she waved her hand and brought forth a vision of an elephant being whipped by several men as it pulled with all its might a giant marble pillar. Zver whimpered as if she were in pain as well, "humanity must learn to cease its zeal and bring peace. I ardently believe that showing our presence to them will help them see reason, as you believe they can."

"Humanity is as much as Iustitia's creation as the earth is."

"Then free will must be revoked from them!"

"I will be in charge of my creation!" shouted Iustitia, and his spear crashed between them, sending them back to their original places.

"If you step in front of my creation and its natural progress, then you will step in the way of the command our father gave us. I will not revoke free will from my creation, and I will not stop their ambition. It is their instinct, and that instinct must be upheld like any other creature. If wolves are made to run in packs, then humans are made to make cities.

Yet, I will not deny that humanity has become too selfish. Utsaha and Eleos, you must now speak for yourselves."

For the first time, the siblings saw the perfect posture and pose of their siblings pale, and somehow, both of them seemed like twins. Their lights harmonized to the point that maybe, in some way, they were always meant to be twins, held together in the same womb, but never announced as such. That being said, both of their roles within human hearts could not be any more different than they are now.

Iustitia faced Utsaha, "You are now a mother of war and lust. You breed more bastards than legitimate sons, and whore houses distract the progress of strategy. You sit within their filth. Do you believe that this is your purpose?"

"'Progress of strategy.' What an interesting concept. You have no understanding of anything else. So, I can understand why your vision is so limited. I heighten passion. That is my purpose. Whether it is love or war, I have no bias."

"Why should there be war? Why should humanity have war?" asked Myslel, who became increasingly agitated.

"They are allowed to make their own decisions, and I respond to their needs and cravings. I am a flame to dry grass, and you are surprised?!"

"You are nothing but a pig that festers in filth!" cried Myslel.

A crash from the heavens came down, loud enough that if humans were around, their ears would bleed, and their hearts would burst from their chests. Hrom thrusted his lightning, and it stretched across the mountain, and his clouds began to block the sun.

"We are not here to discuss our purposes when that was already given to us by our father. We are here to discuss balance within the world we have created."

The brothers and sisters sat back in their places, and Iustitia stood again and addressed his siblings, "There is one solution. Humanity must be obliterated, and a better race to take their place. We must learn from our mistakes and make room for better opportunities."

The silence that came over the council was heavy. Then, as if noticing the calamity would fall anyway, Eleos stood.

"I will not let this happen."

The rest of the council's words were caught in their throat. They all thought the same thing. They were all going to scream, shout, or cry the same thing, but Eleos took their voices into his own and spoke for them all. Eleos's body shone brightly as he approached his brother. In truth, they were almost like twins standing in front of each other.

"These humans, your creation, are your obligation. However, the work that all of us have put into maintaining and creating a life not only for us to survive but to live is indisputable. To destroy them is not just destroying them but also destroying the work that all of us have contributed. This is *not* what father intended," his voice grew low and growled in his chest.

"And I will not let the conversation continue any longer. It is obvious that none of you are willing to discuss what we have brought, and thus, we will make our own decisions", said Sagah, and she whisked away along with the rest of her earthly siblings.

Iustitia and Eleos were stuck in the middle of the now stagnant mountaintop along with their other siblings, who still sat on the edge of a knife. Iustitia drew back and sat in his seat; Eleos followed suit.

"We must protect humanity, for better or for worse," said Iustitia, and he ran down the mountain. Myslel, Utsaha, and Eleos followed after him. It was not long until they discovered the havoc that their earthly siblings were creating.

• • •

It began with the cracking of the earth.

Steam broke from the giant of cases, and oozing like blood came hot magma spreading across forests and glades. Erde grabbed deep within the earth and broke every mountain he made. He threw the giant boulders, larger than houses or castles, and cast them to the farthest reaches of the planet.

Sagah killed the trees, flowers, insects, fruits, and grain. She stole the soul of the earth and crushed it within her Han. Zver invaded small villages and snatched children from their mothers. She ran with the wolves and the wild carrion, picking off the weak. Hrom brought tsunamis and hurricanes. Samudra hurled fishing boats and ships back to land, letting the wooden vesicles crash against the cliff faces. Reka dried up his streams and allowed all of the river creatures to die. He receded into the oceans and flooded the neighboring villages.

In a matter of moments, the earth was ripping itself apart. Strong kingdoms were reduced to ash. Thousands scrambled to find freedom but were crushed. Some tried to find retreat in caves and caverns, but their jagged roofs came tumbling down. Some tried to escape into the forests, but wolves bit into their heels. Some tried to take their animals off the burden, but the cows and oxen reared back and bloodied their horns. Humanities gods, the ones they invented and gave power to, were silent and burning.

Utsaha flew across the sky and traced across the whole earth. The pain in her chest deepened into it felt as if a knife pierced through her chest. Suddenly, an arrow shot into her ribs, and she lost control. Tumbling down, she crashed through the desert sands and felt at the feet of Sagah. Sagah came forward with a sharp dagger in hand.

Eleos sped behind Sagah and, with his staff, cut her feet from under her. Sagah fell and scrambled; Utsaha slowly moved backward, trailing dark red blood. Eleos grabbed Sagah from behind and raised his staff. Sagah stabbed Eleos in his left leg and cut through the muscle. He cried in pain. He drew his staff down and hit Sagah across her face. She cried and blood-spattered to the ground. Sagah, however, still furious, came crawling towards Utsaha.

"You made the humans destroy my forests and my land. You made them kill my creation. I will kill you and water the earth with your blood." Her eyes were wide, and the knife came crashing down and stabbed Utsaha below her hips.

Iustitia, fashioning his spear, raced towards Erde. Erde roared and threw his boulders. He crushed temples and colosseums, castles and grand towers. He ripped parts of his own body, hewn in stone, and created a club. He ripped his legs from the earth and began to walk, throwing the club over his shoulder. He walks towards the nearest volcano and summons his brother.

"Rauroha!" he cried, pointing towards the east.

The sun was a red festering wound in the sky, and Iustitia came flying over them both. Iustitia aimed his spear toward Rauroha's flaming heart. Erde came in the spear's path with his hand. The spear broke through, shattering the fist. Erde roared and picked up part of his hand. He hired it towards Iustitia, who dodged and picked up his spear.

Rauroha slithered towards Iustitia. Rauroha trapped Iustitia's leg, and the flesh of his leg began to sizzle. Iustitia shouted in pain and stabbed the melting stone. Rauroha roared but kept his hold on the leg. Rauroha began to crawl up towards Iustitia's body while Erde continued to walk the face of the earth, crushing, breaking, burning, and upturning.

Myslel began to harvest what was left of humanity, taking them to safety in various places. He disguised himself as generals and soldiers, as wayward wild men who knew the forests. He fended families from wolves and tamed unruly livestock. He guided ships out of storms.

He cast his soul in thousands upon thousands of directions. He melted his body, throwing his consciousness towards distant lands.

Zver sniffed the air. She smelled Myslel's stench and began to race toward him. She gathered lions, wolves, falcons, and bears. Myslel, disguised as a soldier on a horse, called throughout the city and guided fearful people out. His stead navigated the narrow roads and alleyways.

Myslel then saw the world turn upside down and teeth piercing into his neck. Zver clenched her jaw and dragged Myslel out of his stead. The horse ran out from under him and turned towards Myslel, who struggled to grasp Zver's jaw. The horse was surrounded by wolves nipping at its heels and clawing at its flank.

Myslel managed to get his fingers within Zver's mouth. He pried them open and flung her back. With his sword, he slashed at the wolves and drove them off. Zver got up, and both Myslel on his stead and Zver were racing through the once prosperous town that built itself at the heels of a volcano.

Out in the distance, farther towards the outer reaches of the universe, the Father looked on, watching. He was a column of light in the middle of a pool of darkness. Walking out, sending ripples of energy like ripples in a pond, he began to tread lightly toward the wayward planet. Getting closer, the planet itself seemed as if it had broken and separated. Like an egg cracked and its contents spilling out from the edges. Upon reaching it, the Father landed within the ocean that tithed and churned, reaching unimaginable heights and breaking the delicate, feathery clouds. The Father walked and said, "Samudra, calm your temper." The oceans subsided.

Hrom, striking down lightning rods and creating a whirlpool of clouds that churned, heard the Father's voice say, "Cease your lightning and thunder." The clouds turned dove white, and the sky turned blue.

Sagah, still trying to strike after Utsaha, who crawled away in misery and pain, heard the footsteps of the Father behind her. In the desert, Sagan's skin blended into the color of the sand.

She turned and addressed him, "They have taken everything from me. They have destroyed everything I have worked for. They have disobeyed You!"

"Cease this and sleep," said the Father. Her body melted into the earth, and then the world became green.

Utsaha crawled to her Father's feet, "Please heal me, Father! I have done what you asked in this world!"

"Have you?" he replied. Utsaha's body dissipated, and a faint pink light was cupped in the Father's hand.

Eleos followed after the Father silently, "You must also join your sister. You know this?"

Eleos nodded, "I also know that my efforts were in vain."

The father turned toward Eleos, "actions and words are two different things. Forsaking one and then the other means that all you are worth is wind." Then, a golden light appeared in the father's hand.

Myslel, still racing through the crumbling city with Zver at his heels, could see the mountains firing rocks and soot. He crashed his way through the gates of the city, and the lava crumbled afterward. Zver leaped over him. Then, the mountain was asleep. The city was still in ruins, but the fires of Rauroha stopped.

The Father stood at the edge of the city gate. Myslel got off of his stead, which was panting furiously. He scratched its flank and encouraged it to breathe. The father drew closer to Zver first.

"You have grown wild but have not met a true purpose. Sleep now." And she disappeared. The animals lost their fury and started to go back to their natural ways.

Myslel looked at his Father, "Will I become like her? I have done everything you have asked!" He tried to prevent his voice from sounding like a scream.

"You have done well, but you will meet the same fate," a blue light formed in the Father's hand.

Iustitia speared the heart of his brother Erde. The glowing silver light flickered softly as Iustitia held it captive. The Father appeared before Iustitia as he planned to find Sagah.

Iustitia kneeled and gave his Father the soul of Erde, "I have vanquished those who would attempt to disobey you."

"They were not the only ones. You have done as they have." Before Iustitia could respond, he joined his siblings.

The rest of the earth slowly came back to order as the Father traveled across its surface. Humanity, however, was not restored. Those who died were bid to return to the earth, and their souls were given peace.

The Father set his first command, "This earth will hold no souls to command its natural course. It will be as it is," and so it was.

As for the gods in his hand, he molded them together. He took some dirt in his hands and molded humanity with the spirits of passion, justice, thought, memory, and mercy. And so it was.

THE RISE AND FALL
OF THE MONKEY KING

Mustafa was born in the tallest tree in the jungle. The thunder and lightning were so close that he could almost touch the jagged brilliance with his tiny paw. The rain came down, pouring furiously, and Mustafa's parents huddled together, grumbling to themselves.

"He should not be named Mustafa," said Mustafa's father, "this storm is an omen to his future!"

"And what future is that? Since when did any of your hunches come true?" She was already irritated with her husband, who was determining doom for their child, whose eyes were not even open yet.

"This time, I feel I am right. He will have a lot of trouble in his life, all because of his own stupidity. He should not be Mustafa!"

Mustafa's mother grabbed her husband's ear. He shrieked, but the thunder drowned out his complaints.

"You are a stupid fool! Let your child alone!" but they both continued bickering through the night, and this would be Mustafa's first and only lullaby in his small life.

It wasn't long after that night that Mustafa did, in fact, get himself in plenty of trouble for multiple reasons. Some accredited his father for predicting the unlucky circumstances that Mustafa would find himself in. Some agreed with his mother, who fervently believed that Mustafa had a nose for trouble. Mustafa believed that both were delusional and would create trouble (even if nothing really happened).

He was a master storyteller. He would weave together strange things and heroic tales for smaller or dumber monkeys to believe in. Sometimes, when he would come back from venturing too far into the jungle to the point that the rest of his family members would have to call other tribes of monkeys to help search for him, he would appear at the proper time, sometimes looking ragged just to make the state of shock more real on the faces of his family members. His father would begin raving, his mother would begin arguing, and the whole tribe would shower him with sympathy. Some young females competed with one another over who would be their first mate the next spring. He never noticed them, despite their efforts.

On one particularly hot summer day, when the moisture of the earth seemed to rise like lazy clouds, Mustafa came running through the trees covered in pomegranate juice (his favorite cosmetic to use to create fake blood), shrieking so loud that the birds began to crash through the canopy and flit away in anxiety. Their voices squeaked and yelped in tandem with him. The rest of the tribe of monkeys were picking at each other's fur and tearing open mangos, eating the fruit. Until they finally heard Mustafa's cries.

"Everyone, I was almost killed! I was almost killed!" cried Mustafa, panting heavily and then collapsing on one of the strong limbs within his birth tree. The rest of the monkeys jumped, leaped, and swung their way through the canopy, meeting Mustafa. His mother was the first to break through the feverish round of grooming females and excited smaller males who wanted to hear of his heroic escape. His father, still munching on a mango, came at last and heard the story as well.

"What happened? Where are you hurt?" asked his mother. Mustafa motioned towards his side, where the thickest part of the pomegranate juice had congealed. The smell of his sweat and the sweetness of the pomegranate juice was just enough that it had a faint whiff of blood. Mustafa told the story with perfect timing. He knew what his family liked best, and over time, he knew exactly what to say and how to say it.

"I was swinging through the trees, minding my own business. I was looking for a particular flower that bloomed on the farthest part of the tree line."

"Your first mistake; you went past the point of no return," snickered his father, his mouth filled with mango.

Mustafa gave him a sideways look and then continued looking towards the females who gazed at him lovingly, "This flower would have been perfect for you, mother," and just like that, the females swooned.

"Yet, I realized that in this particular tree, a snake likes to sleep. I wanted to find the tallest vantage point that I could in order to try and find the flower. Then I heard something behind me," his eyes grew wide, and his fur stuck up on end, 'I heard- a hissing sound."

The males then came closer, ignoring the obvious flirtation he made and his ability to almost alienate all the females for himself.

"I looked behind me, and then the snake grabbed onto my side. It thrashed about. I tried to scratch its eyes out."

"Was this snake a cobra, perhaps?" Slyly asked his father, who threw away the stone of the mango.

"Yes, Father," said Mustafa with a hint of sarcasm, 'It just so happened it was."

"Then any fool would know that cobras try to suffocate their prey. They don't 'thrash' about as you say."

"I agree, and all of us know this fact," the rest of the monkeys nodded in tandem, "but because I was also trying to get free, the snake couldn't help but thrash about."

The crowd murmured in agreement and scratched their sides as if they could also feel that bite.

"So, I continued and finally scratched out the eyes of the snakes to the point that the blood poured onto my side. That's why there isn't any wound, Mother; it's not my blood." At this, everyone sighed a sigh of relief, and some of the monkeys even yelped and jumped in delight.

"Yet again, you act like an idiot. Why can't you have some sense and settle down already? You know one day you will get yourself in so much trouble that you won't be able to get out of it!"

"Quiet old man," said Mustafa's mother, "just be glad he is alive!"

"I am finished with this group of ignoramuses. If our son wants to die so badly, he might as well let an elephant sit on him and turn him into monkey jam." Some of the older monkeys who congregated next to Mustafa's father chuckled. Their broad, wrinkled faces pulled up into toothy grins.

Mustafa only smirked and went back to flirting mildly and with the utmost humility his adoring fans.

• • •

Many days later, Mustafa was hopelessly bored. All that was available to do at the moment was to maintain a leaf midair with his breath. Every time that the leaf would slowly fall to earth, he would let out a great gust of air, and it would flitter up again. Mustafa wanted to look for trouble, but his mother had strictly forbidden him from leaving since the last time he went out. Although there were no serious injuries, she knew that he was internally bleeding and his body needed time to heal properly. So he was bound to solitude while his mother doted on him. She even made sure that he didn't leave, and so her ears were unusually tuned to his whereabouts.

The last time he tried to escape, she pounced on him like a jaguar and pinched his cheeks, screeching at him at the dangers of leaving so soon. It was as if her wrestling with him wasn't enough to dislocate something within him, and he told her as much. She began to wail violently and accused him of not treating her with the love and respect that she deserved. Mustafa apologized profusely and promised never to leave the spot that she mandated him to stay in. His father was nowhere to be found.

Mustafa tried to brew a plan in his head, but the heat was scorching, so thoughts would not so easily come together as they had before. Once he began, it seemed that they all would fade and turn into dust. Then, an idea finally popped into his head. He would have one of his siblings take his place. He would make sure that the sibling smelled, acted and spoke like Mustafa so that it would be seamless. This plan would work because all of the rest of the tribe looked almost exactly alike, and so the only way to differentiate between one and the other was by smell, sound, and actions. Mustafa hooted and howled for his brother, Maasoom.

Maasoom, gangly and more scraggly than the rest of the tribe (some believe that his mother fell in love with a spider monkey, which explains his long limbs and stature), came flying through the forest. Maasoom grabbed his little brother and started to chatter happily. Mustafa had to quiet his brother and pull him to the side.

"I have something very important that I need you to do. I need you to lay on your side. I will then trade scents with you. Then, I will train you in how to walk, talk, act, and even think like me. I must be off. There is something very important that I must do, and so you need to take my place. My mother wouldn't understand, but I hope you do."

Maasoom nodded and gathered himself in order to receive instruction. First, Mustafa laid Maasoom down and rubbed a leaf all over him, wiping away any residual stench that he might have had. Then Mustafa took another leaf and rubbed it all over himself. Mustafa took that leaf and rubbed Maasoom down in all the important places. After a few adjustments and testing sniffs, Maasoom was indiscernible! Mustafa was actually impressed with himself. Then, Maasoom and Mustafa began working on acting, walking, and talking. Maasoom took his usual lazy drawl and learned how to be charming and chipper. Maasoom learned to slow down his gate and even raise his head slightly with a prideful look. Finally, Maasoom made sure that his chest was slightly puffed out and applied a haughty gate, trying to mold his eyebrows to be uneven.

Maasoom and Mustafa were completely identical. Mustafa hugged Maasoom, licked a small finger, and ruffled Maasoom's hair a little bit. Then, he pranced and danced his way through the trees. Maasoom resumed the last position that Mustafa was in: absolute boredom and desperation.

• • •

Mustafa ventured further than ever before. He found his way to a clear opening, the sun finally peeking through the trees and shining light on a soft patch. In the air, Mustafa smelt something strange. Once his nose identified the scent, he immediately went further into the leaves to hide. A tiger was coming through the brush.

Rumbling somewhere in the dark, the slinking animal came through the brush. The giant paws softly crush the grass, and yet the haunches and shoulders of the animal show the powerful muscles underneath. The tiger's golden fur gleamed. The giant, once coming into the light, decided to lie down for a while, basking in the sun. Mustafa started, holding his breath. He believed somehow that the tiger could even hear his thoughts and thus made efforts to clear his mind entirely.

The tiger slinked into the sun, letting his fur catch the warmth and spreading his body across the grass. The air stirred slightly, letting the trees grow further apart, almost as if they were allowing more of the light to catch the tiger's pelt. A rapid shiver of the tiger's left ear caught something not far from him. He pounced into action and lowered himself, crouching among the leaves. Mustafa slowly transferred himself to another part of the canopy and saw that there was another beast.

This beast stood on two legs. Its bronze skin was horrifically uncovered by any fur or scales, but a long protruding instrument seemed to be clutched in his upper paws. The tip was sharply made and frightening. Mustafa watched the tiger, only a few yards away, creep soundlessly. It was used to hunt and knew how to stop its own heartbeat if necessary in order for even the most perceptive of ears to be deaf to it. The furless, scaleless creature locked eyes with the tiger and did not move. The only thing covering the beast was a white wrapping, almost like strung leaves around its groin and waist. Upon closer inspection, Mustafa realized that the beast did have fur, but it was only on its head and face.

The furless beast, with the sharply pointed claw, began to gradually step forward with a gate that you would have to squint in order to tell. The tiger came closer, its eyes almost glowing. A flash, a thrust, a roar of pain, then blood.

Mustafa watched as the two-legged, furless beast took his mighty claw and thrust it straight through the head of the tiger, right between its golden eyes. Mustafa rushed toward the scene, and just before he could be caught, he stopped. The beast looked into the canopy, and the wind covered Mustafa's scent. Then, the beast left, only taking the tiger's teeth and striping it of its pelt. What was left was a miserable lump of flesh that opened itself to the elements. The claw broke as the beast tried to retrieve it, and what was left was the sharp edge sprouting out of the raw, red mound.

Mustafa was speechless, and tears gathered but did not fall as he watched the ugly beast with its flying claw leave. He came down the canopy and approached the tiger. The smell of blood and raw meat overwhelmed his senses. Curious, he came toward the jutting thorn and steadily wiggled it out of the tiger's head. Something so beautiful was ravished, and nothing could be said or done about it. His hands were covered in blood, and the sharp thing was heavy. For a moment, Mustafa decided to stay in the tiger's presence a bit longer, but not too long. The buzzards had already smelled the death of the great tiger and decided that his fate, like so many others, would meet the same end.

Mustafa rushed home to a distraught and furious mother who knew her son better than anyone and saw right through Maasoom's attempt at mimicking Mustafa. Mustafa arrived with the spearhead in his hand and his hands covered in blood (this time, it was real). Mustafa's father, staying at a distance, smelled the musky scent of a tiger and the iron tinge of blood. Mustafa's mother rushed toward her son, and once again, she scolded him for running off without considering his condition. However, Mustafa does not have a fantastical story; he is still grieving the loss of beauty.

However, Mustafa's father came forward, even pushing away his terrified wife.

"So, you finally have a worthy story to tell?" he motioned toward the spearhead.

"I-," but Mustafa stopped. He didn't know what to say. He was tongue-tied, and it didn't help that a sea of other faces asked the same question.

"What was it this time, Mustafa? It smells like a tiger!" called out one young monkey.

"And what's that in your hand?!" exclaimed another, which brought many closer as they inspected him from head to foot.

"Your heart is beating so fast. Were you running?"

"Why are you sweaty? You look like you have seen a ghost!"

"Whose blood is that? What happened? What went wrong?!"

The rest of the tribe became more concerned, and their excitement grew into panic. Mustafa hushed them all and put down the spear-head.

"It's all alright. I am fine. A tiger was killed today", was what he could manage.

Mustafa's mother shrieked in a panic, her fur standing on end. "WHAT! And you were there to see this?"

"Not just see." said his father frankly. His eyes gleamed for the first time in a long time, "Mustafa, tell us what happened."

Mustafa saw that look within his father's eyes, and miraculously, a story lay out in front of him in immaculate detail- perfect pacing- original and never before heard.

"Mother, I will admit. I did set up Maasoom to take my place. But the jungle called ot me and I followed. I decided to venture further towards the forest line. Then I came upon a clearing-"

"Is this where you met the tiger?" asked a young female.

"Yes, it is. I met the tiger face to face; his eyes were green and venomous. He claimed that he knew my name."

The group huddled together closer, trying not to move too fast, or they might attract the omnipotent eye of the tiger.

Mustafa continued, "He said that he knew my name and knew where my family was. He vowed he would eat us all in one gulp. I stood in his way." Mustafa glowered over his audience and made claws with his hands, growling from deep within himself. Mustafa's father nodded and concentrated on the story.

"I said, 'You will never take my family! You will have to come through me first!' Then I found this- rock. I dodged and weaved the giant paws of the tiger. Finally, after jumping high above his head, I plunged the rock down. He died right then and there!"

The rest of the monkeys hooted and cheered. They danced around with glee. Mustafa's father smiled, and Mustafa felt a small twinge in his chest, like an ache. Mustafa's mother wept with joy. Then and there, Mustafa's father raised his son's arm with the spear-head and cried, "We must tell this tale across the whole of money tribes and families. They must all hear this!" and thus, the journey through the money tribes, the gibbons, the lutung, macaque, capped langur, Nilgiri and golden langur, and many more heard the story.

So Mustafa and his entire tribe all traveled. They first met the langur family. They were, in fact, cousins and did not live too far away. The Golden Langurs were first. Sitting in the middle was a large matriarch with a dozen children who seemed to cling to her, along with the aunties who were gathered behind, patiently waiting. The matriarch had known

Mustafa's parents for a very long time. She has known the mother to be a bore and the father to be a stick in the mud. But when it came to the food available for the neighboring tribes and the trees there were to occupy, she tolerated them and spoke briefly.

This time, she listened while munching on a bouquet of flowers. Mustafa addressed the matriarch with a deep bow and began his tale. He told it the same way he had before. This time, with his newfound memory after the initial shock of it all, the detail blossomed like flowers after rain. He told of the dashes and darts, the smell of the tiger's breath, the heat of the day, the exact location. He spoke of his efforts to pry the rock out of the ground within inches of the tiger's face and then leaping a great height before plunging the sacred weapon into the tiger's skull. Mustafa performed for an audience he was not accustomed to, so the stakes were high. He added embellishment here and brought himself back there. Finally, when he finished, he brandished the spearhead aloft in the sky. The stain of red blood had now turned a maroon. He handed the weapon to the matriarch on his bent knee like a knight supplicating himself before a monarch.

She inspected the rock. She touched the point with a small finger while also holding back a tiny baby scurrying from behind her left shoulder with her tail. A drop of blood sprouted from her finger, and for the first time, as Mustafa's tribe and the Golden Langur spoke, she changed her expression.

With a single lift of an eyebrow, Mustafa has sold the story. In fact, he did so well that after a hearty meal of papayas and beetles, the matriarch decided that as witnesses for this astounding story, they should also caravan with their cousins. Mustafa's mother and father agreed. The matriarch said that she would have to bring her whole family, who miraculously had a fruitful mating season, and that the few males present would be in charge of scouting. Mustafa's father inspected the males (sniffing them from afar as they listened scattered within the canopy) and approved them as diligent scouts.

Mustafa stood straight, and his tale curled slightly at the tip, "We would be deeply honored to have you as part of our group. Thank you for your patronage." He kissed her paw, and although the matriarch tried her best to hide it, she couldn't help but smile at the brave fool.

Mustafa continued further towards the rest of the langur family and then headed further towards the gibbons, the lutung, and the macaque. Eventually, the group of fifty turned into hundreds as a hoard of chittering and squealing monkeys. The entire troop of monkeys found a large tree that held onto the very peak of a large mountain. The roots wrapped around the money peak crushed parts of the rubble so that the mountain looked like ripples of fabric draped over a chair. The entire troop stood within the canopy of the tree, but Mustafa stood in the center of the crooked trunk where every eye and ear could have full access to his story. Over time, his story grew to like the size of the troop and adopted many details that seemed to change with every telling or retelling. As if someone were trying to recall a distant memory, the details seemed to change with every attempt, and thus, Mustafa's stories grew more into the tales of the old gods in the abandoned temples found throughout the jungle.

Mustafa bowed, and as if the monkeys were at a concert, they cheered for Msutafa. As soon as he raised his head, they fell silent and clung to their neighbors as they heard the miraculous tale of a humble monkey defeating the king of the jungle.

"It was a day like any other," he began, "I found myself, after healing from a serious wound where I was bedridden for many weeks, being called by the wind itself to avenge my fallen brothers and sisters. The wind whirled around me and whispered into my ear the many terrors of lives lost. For the Gibbons tribe, the loss of a patriarch who had guided the tribe through famine. From the Golden langurs who lost many males and were barren. To my very own tribe, when we lost one of our youngest one fateful monsoon."

The respective tribes held back tears and held onto their young, clutching them to their breasts. The matriarch of the golden langurs lifted her head and steadied herself, hiding her trembling bottom lip.

"I know your pain, and by fate, the cycle has been broken. On hearing the wind's call, I traveled for miles, listening over and over to the names of the dead. Then, out in the distance, a light shined upon a sacred clearing. There, in the center, was a stone shrine in the shape of a monkey smiling as it held a bowl. The bowl was filled with fresh spring water, untouched and pure. I will admit I was tempted to drink from the monkey shrine's bowl, although I knew full well that it would be a sin. Yet, I was drawn to the drink and had my fill. The water was sweet, but what was sweeter was the grace that I found at the smiling shrine. Then, a shadow cast itself across the sky and blotted out the sun. There in the distance, the looming head of the tiger hung over me… I was speechless and fell back to the ground. The world around me seemed to darken. The air grew heavy with the smell of iron from the earth itself."

"I heard, like the menacing rumble of thunder, the voice of the tiger speak out to me, 'You are not the first to drink from this shrine, and yet, you will not be the last to feel the piece of my teeth in your flesh,' he said. His voice rattled my bones, and my heart leaped into my throat as I scrambled backward, keeping my eyes trained on the glowing green emeralds of the tiger's eyes. In vain, I believed that if I could just keep looking at him, I would prevent him from surprising me. Maybe I could keep myself sharp enough to where I could run away. Then he laid a giant paw upon my chest. I felt the sharp, needle-like claws dig into me. My ribs were almost split as he extended their full potential."

Mustafa cradled himself, wrapping his long arms around himself as he painted a look of terror; he mustered a look of horror, like a haunted soul trapped within the same loop of death.

"I could hear him taunt me. Over and over again. He said, 'I remember the old gibbon, stringy and tough, she used to track through this jungle. I stomped on his head and ate his heart. I remember the young males, much more supple and sweet, with their golden fur scurrying through the trees. I sprang into the air and tore their limbs from the branches. I also remember that small child you left in the forest as you were told to watch him and how he squealed his last breath when I ate him whole!'"

The taunts repeated. He remembered every name and every face. He started to put weight on his paw, crushing me slowly. Then, the wind picked up again. The clouds grew darker as the force of the gust pushed the tiger off of me. I stood up and tried to run, but the tiger grabbed my tail and reeled me in. Again, the win batted him back. I scrambled towards a tree, but I soon realized he was fast and nimble. He sprinted towards me as I darted from trunk to trunk, trying to find a tree tall enough to escape. He was always close behind. In desperation, I ran through the trees and came upon this."

Mustafa held up the spearhead. Tumbling down, several troops came closer to see the blood-stained weapon. Some swore later that night that they could smell the blood and hear the screams of the tiger emanating from the enchanted object.

"I grabbed it, scaring my own two hands. It was stuck between two other rocks that had tumbled from a landslide long ago before any living creature breathed." Mustafa's eyes beamed as his heart grew faster, "The tiger began to crouch towards the ground. It readied itself to crouch. I pulled harder, but the rock would not move. Finally, the tiger flew through the air and a great roar sprung from his mouth. I kept pulling and watching him as he grew closer. The moment that I could see the whites within his eyes, I pulled out the rock. I jumped into the sky! With one great swing, I plunged the rock into its head, and the very tip I could see went straight through his jaw! I had killed the beast, and the blood of our lost ones was avenged!"

Not a moment after Mustafa had finished part of his tale, the entire troop of monkeys crashed with excitement. The entire great tree shook as if it were in a storm, and the screeching of the monkeys was enough to draw the attention of more or less apathetic animals. Some monkeys' jaws were unhinged, showing their k-nine teeth. Their lungs were about to burst before Mustafa simply held up a hand and calmed their ecstasy. The matriarchs were the ones who were calm, facing the news in their own solemn worlds but holding onto the joy packed away in special places in their hearts.

Mustafa continued, "After the death of the tiger, I took the rock out of its head and decided that I must begin telling all animals of the jungle, starting with my dearest cousins, that these events happened and the jungle will no longer fear!"

The same outcry erupted again. The jumping and shaking of the tree was so erratic that some of the branches were wrenched loose. Mustafa climbed up towards his tribe, and his father put his hand on Mustafa's shoulder. Mustafa felt his Father's warmth for the first time ever since he was little, and the pain inside him grew stronger. But he did not mind.

The consensus was made among the elders that there needed to be a permanent spot for the tribes of monkeys. If they were all to be together, then the monkeys would have to help somewhere with plenty of food, water, and protection from any predators around. Enemies were still a foreign concept to some of the tribes, which were relatively isolated. But Mustafa trained them in the way of dealing with snakes that disguised themselves in the trees, as well as their habitual habit of telling lies to convince other creatures to come along with the snakes. For once, Mustafa was telling the truth. While on his adventures, he had observed the habits of many animals and had come close to some of them.

Mustafa led the group through the jungle, delegating who would be scouting, where, and at what times during the day. He had many of the females take on duties to manage the young ones, and some were older and could not hunt for themselves. Some of those who stayed behind (younger males) were in charge of making sure that food was evenly distributed. Mustafa had proven to be incredibly resourceful and understood the exact response to give everyone. Most times, he made up a response that sounded good, and somehow, he had given the right answer. If things failed, he would say that it was the angry spirit of the tiger presiding over them and to not worry. The spirit will soon leave after they have found the perfect place to settle.

Finally, after three weeks, the tribe found an abandoned temple. The temple was covered in vines, but the intricate designs of many-limbed and many-headed figures still stood in impossible poses. The temple had three separate rooms, all joined together, making the shape of a "T." The temple looked like a tightly layered rock that had been cracked open to expose the many years of pressure and art. The rising soft mounds and the jutting peaks of the temple made it look more like a mountain, except for the stories that it told through the sculptures, all of which had been forgotten and would certainly not be remembered by the monkeys who used them as places to sleep or to swing off of.

Mustafa found a small altar where incense was burned to a mighty forgotten god who had several heads and arms all balanced on one out-turned head. Mustafa decided that this would be the place he would stay, underneath the watchful eyes of a beast stronger than him and yet not as legendary as he assumed.

The monkeys spread out, and waves of the ocean pushed further towards the land. They dominated the forest with their presence as new food was discovered. Mustafa became the new elder of all the tribes, and the older monkeys became his advisors.

One day, the fluttering of wings was heard overhead. A flock of a dozen birds, all various types, flew towards the temple and landed within the lush, overgrown gardens. Several monkeys scrambled after them, enamored by their voluminous plumage. At the head of the flock was a peacock with a tale that seemed to stretch five feet long and five feet wide. The peacock glided across the gardens and entered the temple. Mustafa got up from his makeshift throne (a gnarled branch that was shaped in such a way that it could be considered a throne) and approached the peacock with a new sense of superiority and importance. He stood tall on his hind legs and shook his fur to make the plumage on the sides of his face stand out more.

The peacock bowed, and so did Mustafa. The peacock opened its great plume of feathers. Stepping around the room, the peacock let the sun coming from the ruined roof shine off his luminous colors, hypnotizing all that saw him.

He turned and addressed Mustafa, slowly closing his tail, "Are you the great Mustafa who slayed the tiger?"

"I am", declared Mustafa.

"I bow to you, great warrior. We are representatives of our respective flocks and have come to pledge our allegiance to you and your clans. We have heard of you from many of our own kind and wish to join you in peace. We deeply sympathize with your loss as we, too, were plagued by the ravaging claws of the tiger. A survivor of an attack from the tiger died. The poor creature was plagued by fear to the point that it pulled its feathers from his head." Tears welled in the eyes of the peacock as well as the rose-winged parakeet that was standing on top of the astute head of the ostrich.

Mustafa touched his heart and shook his head in disbelief, "we would be honored to have your flock be part of our tribe. What if your name?"

"My name is Kunal. I am the leader of my flock of peacocks. Here, my associates behind me have heard of your story far and wide." Behind the peacock was an ostrich, a Himalayan Monal Indian Paradise flycatcher, an Asian Fairy-bluebird, a Painted stork, a Rose Winged parakeet, a common kingfisher, a Grey-headed swamphen, a Red (irritable) junglefowl, a Black Kite Hawk, a Great Hornbill Toucan, and an Osprey. The smaller birds rested upon the back of the ostrich; however, the visibly irritable junglefowl stood at a slight distance from the crowd, trying to look official but also more concerned with finding stray ants.

Mustafa welcomed the flock and gave them plenty of bugs and fruit to eat. Those who mainly ate fish were presented with various small fish from ponds as well as frogs that hid in leaves. The dinner was well received, and the animals traded stories and traditions with each other. The junglefowl slept on top of the head of a serene statue, waiting for the sun to rise.

The next morning, the flighted and flightless birds decided to head back to their homes. Mustafa swore to give them his help in times of need, and the same was given to him. Mustafa and the rest of the monkeys spent the rest of the time creating homes within the trees, as well as trading stories of things they possibly might have heard or seen about Mustafa.

"I heard that he was born during a thunderstorm, but Mustafa was able to tame the lightning with just a touch of his finger!"

"I heard that he created a little brother out of his imagination. The little brother was made of clay, and Mustafa taught the clay figure to act just like him!"

These stories circulated and changed depending on who was telling them. Mustafa continued with his duties as leader and had several meetings over food and supplies. He smiled constantly, but on the inside, his mind raced. This would not last for long. Many would start to question or grow bored of the same stories. And stories were not enough. They needed to see something real. To feel fear and love and hope all at the same time.

That night, Mustafa decided to take several leaves and weave them together. Next, he took black mud and the mashed flesh of papaya and painted the woven leaves. He also decided to create a cylinder to catch his voice and to throw it out into the air louder and stronger. That night, he went around the trunks of the home trees. He growled and snarled. He disappeared and reappeared within the brush.

One small monkey, wide away, went down from his home tree and tried to see what was the matter. In a flash, gold and black flashed before his eyes and the guttural roar of a hungry tiger. He screamed up the tree. Waking his parents. They also were assaulted by the vision and leaped with their little one further into the brush, huddling together.

Another group awoke because of the commotion. In the distance, they saw the massive haunches of the tiger hurrying away, growling and snarling. Eventually, groups of monkeys, all from different tribes, conversed together. They snuck towards the brush and gathered rocks. Brandishing their weapons, they waited for the hide of the tiger to rear its ugly head again. The moon is shown on the forest floor. Finally, one of the monkeys saw the tiger's stripes, and with all its might, it threw down the rock and something that grunted and fell. A rain of rocks and twigs came crashing down. Horrible howls and yelping came from the canopy. The monkeys continued, hurling rocks and scurrying away the frightened tiger.

Mustafa ran as fast as he could, using the weave he made as a shield. The first rock that landed hit his left shoulder, which ached beyond reason. Mustafa scurried into the temple, which was exclusively his domain, and stashed away his things. He went into a corner, which was secluded by empty jars, and sat there. His shoulder thumped- fire seemed to pulse through his muscles. He tried to move his shoulder, but every tiny stretch made the pain shoot through his back. He laid his back against the cold stone, holding back tears. But it worked. They saw what they needed to see. Now, vision would have to give birth to belief.

Mustafa woke up the next day. The pain in his shoulder lessened, but movement was still a challenge. After coming out of the temple, one of the elders immediately noticed Mustafa's injury and asked, "Did you see it, too?"

Mustafa nodded gravely, "Yes, I saw the spirit of the tiger."

The elder nodded as well and began to create a sling for Mustafa's arm. Many of the langur family who were gathering dry grass for nests stopped as they watched Mustafa struggle to come out of the temple (he also decided that leaning on the elder was a nice touch of desperation for their injured savior).

The monkeys gathered around him. Mustafa's father was notified by a gibbon monkey that Mustafa was hurt. He and the rest of the elders flung themselves from the trees and ran to Mustafa. Mustafa was attended to by many who gave him water and cold earth to soothe the pain in his shoulder. A hearty macaque monkey rounded his brother, who had organized a patrol around the jungle. Mustafa hushed the worried crowd around him.

"I do not wish for anyone to worry. I am sure that everyone has seen or heard about the spirit of the tiger coming back to haunt us. It is my fault. I have brought him here."

"Mustafa! Do not say such things!" proclaimed his father. He managed to break through the crowd to speak to his son, "You have done a great deed. Some spirits refused to rest knowing that their reign has ended."

"I believe you are right. I ask that the elders please help manage the majority of the organization for today. I wish to think about how we might overcome this battle."

The elder agreed and respectively went to their tribes, creating homes and properly distributing food. The macaques, for the first time in a long time, didn't argue amongst each other and thankfully did not find the fake tiger tucked away within a shrine of the temple.

Mustafa did the same thing again that night, only this time, he was sure to miss the rocks. The next morning, a crowd had gathered outside of Mustafa's temple. They asked themselves questions about whether the tiger was truly dead or if it simply had a brother who was determined to avenge his fallen comrade. Mustafa calmed the crowds. He had healed a little but did not want to diminish his feeble condition just yet. There would be time for that.

Struggling, Mustafa stood tall above the crowd, "My friends, please calm yourselves. After much consideration, I have determined that this spirit will not leave us with just rocks alone. I think that we must consult those who are experienced with spirits", Mustafa motioned towards the stone statues. Some of them had freshly lost their head, and some were crumbled heaps that were completely destroyed upon impact.

"I tirelessly paced and thought, knowing that I was powerless to confront the tiger like this. But I heard voices in the night. I listened as their echoes bounced across the walls of the temple. I realized that the statues, the figures that have stood here despite time's cruel fate, have given me their help. This next night- this next night will be different. But I cannot do all of this alone. I need a friend to call our brother the macaques. They will be necessary in this fight. For now, rest. You have all been plagued, but no longer."

Murmurs went through the crowd. Some were relieved, and some were doubtful. However, all of them clung to hope, which was exactly what Mustafa had intended. The macaques were not far, coming back after all that time, unsuccessful to find any origin of the predicament. Mustafa consoled their hearts and prepared them for that night.

• • •

Mustafa, as well as the rest of the macaque, watched the sun go down below the horizon, and as soon as night had settled heavily over the sky, Mustafa and the macaque went out into the brush. The moon was still full as it had been the past couple of nights. Mustafa told the macaques to first go straight to the edge of the home trees, and he would meet them there. He must consult with the spirits of the statues as they wait for battle. The macaques did just that, running through the grass as they were instructed.

Mustafa watched them. After the last one was gone, he went behind a tree and tugged tightly onto a vine wound around the trunk. He climbed a little further, gently using his right arm and making sure everything was ready. Then, he went for his tiger disguise and walked into the dark forest.

The macaques were quietly inspecting the brush, looking for tracks and smelling the air for the deep, musky smell of a beast they knew all too well. Some had not slept in the past two nights as they scavenged the jungle. Their vision blurred. Some had to shake themselves awake and tried to climb into the trees. The largest of the macaques scolded them not to do so, as they must trust the plan that Mustafa had made.

As soon as they turned, the haunches of the crouching tiger could be seen, as well as the bone-white tip of the tail that gently breached the tall grass. None of them moved. Their eyes locked on the tiger as they watched its strong shoulder blades pierce through its muscles. In the blink of an eye, a figure crashed through the trees and flew through the air. Its many heads and arms could be seen from the shoulders it cast. Then another figure soared through the air, but this one held a staff with a disk on the top. Many more glided back and forth, entwining and then moving past each other. Their grand shadows lengthened as the moon rose. The macaques were so overwhelmed with fear that they started to scream wildly with their eyes fixed on the spirits that ravaged the air. The tiger was also consumed by fear and, thus, ran away from the home's trees.

The macaques watched as the spirits disappeared along with the tiger. The moon was bright and full. They sniffed around and walked slowly, not saying anything. Out of the trees, they heard a rustling noise and prepared once again for the hellish visions to come back, but Mustafa came out of the trees and joined them on the ground.

"My brothers, you look distraught. What has happened?"

All of the macaques could only look at each other until the largest of them said in a hoarse voice, "There were flying figures that crossed the sky and scared away the tiger. We didn't know what to do. Will they also haunt us as the tiger did?"

Mustafa took a deep sigh and put his left hand on the large Macaque's shoulder, "No, they will not. I told you that I needed help. The spirits that have guarded the temple have given us that help. They will always protect us."

The macaques drew a deep sigh of relief and awe, stupefied by what they saw. Mustafa, as well as the macaques, recounted the night in detail, growing the congregation of monkeys stronger towards a belief that destiny had finally favored them.

•••

Over the course of many weeks, several other species pledged their allegiance to Mustafa. The story of the spirits coming to the monkeys' aid spread far and wide. And so, Mustafa gained many different admirers as well as loyal subjects that stayed within the temple as they drew council from Mustafa. Mustafa grew to be quite distinguished, fashioning a piece of torn curtain around his shoulders and a staff that brandished the blood-stained spearhead. The peacock, along with a water buffalo, a deer, a hog, a small tree frog, a mongoose, and the monkey elders, all shared the temple.

Life was harmonious. Everyone knew that large populations in a small area would deplete resources quickly, but having a spattering of representatives and courtiers would be perfect for intercommunication and jurisdiction. Mustafa gave advice on many matters (praying to the spirits, if they could even hear him, that he was successful), but the experience gave him an advantage. He finally settled down and had three wives. All of them were from his own tribe, and all of which had numerous children who grew with the same sense of curiosity and mischief.

One day, the ground trembled. The trees seemed to crack at the roots, and a large roar came from the distance. Many of the followers knew in their bones that it was not the tiger… but was it something worse? Out of the trees came a large female elephant. Her forehead was speckled with dark freckles that trailed down her large nose. She also fashioned a pattern on her forehead that looped and spiraled in concentric circles and spinning notes. Behind her was her herd, seven strong females with their smaller ones tucked underneath their fearsome mother's forms.

The matriarch looked around her at the many different animals that lived together. No one knew for sure, but some swore she smiled.

"Mustafa of the Bengal Sacred Langur tribe. I am Aarushi, the leader of my herd. We have heard of your stories…"

Mustafa stepped forward and interrupted, "I am gracious to receive you and your herd. Please stay great, Aarushi, and we will…"

"But I have a warning for you," continued Aarushi, "I have seen a vision, and you must hear me clearly."

Mustafa's mouth was closed shut, and with every effort, his lips seemed to retract further into his mouth. Aarushi lifted her head and closed her eyes, "a descendent of a great villain will come and destroy you. He will go through your inmost parts and disembowel you. You will fall, but you will not be alone. Head these words."

Mustafa's mouth opened again, "what else may I do for you? You cannot leave so soon. You have traveled all this way!"

The rest of the animals nervously looked at each other, and some even looked at the almost bare trees after harvesting.

Aarushi shook her head. She and her clan left and were never seen again. An eternity passed before another single animal breathed until finally, the peacock screeched, "What on earth does this mean!? That almost seemed pointless!"

A crash of voices like a wave almost knocked Mustafa down as he was berated by worrisome faces. The rest of the clan of animals spoke with one another, wondering why this had to happen. What was the meaning of "villain" and "disembowel"? Who will come to destroy Mustafa? Should we begin to fight or to defend Mustafa?

Mustafa's advisors surrounded him, speaking anxiously to him and to each other.

The peacock, wide-eyed and with the feathers on his neck unfurled, spoke up the most, "What ridiculous bull-dung! How impertinent it was for that lug of an animal to bring her and her **entire** family to this place, which has done nothing wrong and tell us that our leader will die soon!"

A hog spoke up, "Aarushi is a distant cousin of mine and takes her visions seriously…"

"You know of this creature?!" interrogated a mongoose.

"Yes, and she is a deeply respected member of my family. Her visions are reputable but are not always what one expects them to be. That does not mean our way of life will be destroyed."

"You may worry about yourselves, but we worry about Mustafa!" shouted one of Mustafa's wives.

"We must make every effort to barricade the home trees and have posts even towards the furthest edges of the jungle!"

"What about the spirits? They can help us!"

"No one has consulted with them for a long time, and their presence is sporadic at best. We don't know if we can fully rely on them."

"We must fight now!"

"SILENCE!" bellowed Mustafa. The whole of the clans heard his voice ring out. He was breathing heavily, sweat pouring down his face. He climbed to the top step of the temple so everyone could see him, "we **will not** panic at this time! The new growth of the trees has **just** come upon us. We have **just** now been able to eat our fill. There is no solution to fear. This prophecy is about me. It is not about our home or our families. I will take this burden. For now, I will consult the spirits. They will hear us in this time of need as they have in the past. For now, rest. The sun is almost under the earth. I will take this night to consider these words."

The animals still murmured as they went to their resting places, looking over at Mustafa, who sat on the temple steps. Mustafa's father came over. He had grown a few more white hairs around his face, and the wrinkles cut deeper into his skin. Mustafa looked up.

"You will find a way, my son. You have gotten us this far. You will find a way."

Mustafa stood and nodded, "Please have the leader of the macaques meet with me after sundown when all of the rest of our clan has gone to sleep. I wish there was a watch organized for the night, just in case."

Mustafa's father nodded and went back towards his clan. Mustafa stepped into the cool air of the temple and slumped back down into the small space where his right shoulder was first injured. Ever since that day, it was harder to move his right than his left, but he was, for the most part, healed. He crawled up into a ball, dreading what the morning would bring.

Mustafa did not sleep. In his solitude, he traced the words over and over again in his mind. He scoured every piece of memory or evidence that could connect together. But there was nothing. When the sun rose, Mustafa finally slept. He was found by one of his wives alone in the small corner and spoke to the other two wives.

"I heard him mumbling all night, whispering to himself," whispered one.

"He might have been praying. Let us let him sleep. All we have is hope now", whispered another.

They all agreed and took their children with them out of the temple. One of the wives sent a buffalo to guard the entrance so that not a soul (or even the pensive peacock who also did not sleep that night but spent his hours preening his feathers nervously) would disturb Mustafa.

The next morning, while Mustafa was still sleeping, an uproar could be heard from outside of the temple. HE opened his eyes, but his body could not move. Everything within him dreaded the thought of peaking above the debris that protected him from all the woes of the world. However, when one of his children came and grabbed him, he was tugged so tightly that the pain in his shoulder started to ache. Coming out of the temple and into the light, he saw it: large, wild cats. At the head of the group of them was a robust leopard with shiny black spots. His brother was completely black and had jumped onto a fallen statue, licking his paw. Behind them both was a menagerie of cats, which included a Pallas cat, a lynx, and a caracal. They all sat behind the leopards. The black leopard, upon seeing Mustafa, came down from the statue and slinked his way.

His eyes were steady and guarded. His expression was that of a shielded individual. He was not to be subdued, and no one would decipher his innermost thoughts because those were precious. Mustafa stood in front of the leopard as it sat with its tail curled around its large paws.

Looking down, the Leopard spoke in a smooth and deep tone, "Are you the one they call Mustafa?"

Mustafa arched his shoulders back imperceptibly and nodded.

"I, like many others, have heard of your glory, but I and my kin do not come to bow to you. Our brother, the tiger, was killed. We mourn him, and we shun you. However, we come to ask for peace. Let known of your kind disturb us, and we shall not disturb you."

Mustafa, at that moment, felt a twitch in his left eye. Steadily, a burning sensation grew from within his chest and finally made it to his head. It was rage. Mustafa's brow furrowed, and he looked at the leopard as if it had insulted his even most infamous ancestors.

"NO!" shouted Mustafa.

The Leopard only lifted his head slightly, "you refuse peace?"

"Yes!" Mustafa laughed, "Of course I do! Do you think that I will give peace to any pompous fluffy-lynx who waltzes in? I killed the tiger because of its terror upon my tribe as well as the others that you see here! Do you think that I will allow another fanged creature to endure? No! You will not come and demand peace to save yourselves when your fangs catch and eat my kin!"

The rest of the animals, the birds, the hooved beasts, the frogs, the lizards, and all of the monkeys progressed towards the temple, glaring at the leopard. Seeing all of those animals at once made the leopard shiver and his ears fold back. He moved to all fours and kept a careful eye on his comrades, who did the same. Some were looking from on top of the statues, crouching with their tails flicking madly about.

Mustafa continued, "In fact, if I ever see you within my home again. I will make sure that every animal here will claw, bite, stomp, kick, and beat you to death until nothing left of you is fur!"

Without warning or order, the rest of the animals sprang themselves upon the big cats, and a giant tumble of fur and claw flew in every direction. Mustafa took his spear and began to pierce at the cats, who were all desperately trying to get away from the mob and to him. He cut out their eyes and bruised their hides.

Monkeys that were still in the trees hurled down rotten fruit towards the cats that were making their way up the trunks for safety. Flying through the air. They tackled the cats as they plummeted from the trees. Teeth, claws, fangs, and shrieks burst into the air as loud as the cries of thousands upon thousands of birds. Mustafa joined the fight. He took his spear and pierced the soft underbellies of the cats and scratched out their eyes. He had some of the cats held down, and their tails were cut. Some of their large claws were wrung from them.

The more that the rampage continued, the more bloodthirsty the monkeys became. The fight continued until falling from one of the trees tucked tightly within the branches was a slender figure that plopped down right in the middle of the monkeys versus the pride of the cats.

All of the animals jumped back, badly beaten, but still, the adrenaline was pumping forcefully through their veins. There in the center was a long boa constrictor who slithered slowly with aching muscle through the crowd. In a hoarse voice, the snack managed to say, "sssstoop thisss madnessssss!"

No sound or wind interfered with the small voice of the boa constrictor. The snake steadily weaved around the legs of the two-legged beasts, who now had finally changed their expressions from rage to confusion and astonishment.

Mustafa was also astonished but quickly said, "How dare you invade this war! How dare you hide in the trees and spy on my family."

"They are not your family. They are your followersss. They are your ssslavess who believe your every word in order to feed a fantasy", said the snake, who adjusted his long body in order to face Mustafa properly. Mustafa's hands were covered in blood. He was a terror to behold, with nostrils flared.

The snake continued, "You have made thisss world of yoursss, but have stolen theirsss. What do you have to sssay about your deliberate liesss towards your brethren?"

"I have not lied! I have protected these animals from the evil and conniving spirit of the tiger who has stolen the lives of my tribe!"

"I was there," slyly said the snake, "I was there when the two-legged beast took the spearhead and killed the tiger within the clearing of the jungle. The spear once mounted a long stick and was bound by a vine. The two-legged beast was skinny but sharp-witted. The tiger was not used to such a tactical match. But, neither were you when you first pried the spearhead out of the skull of the tiger."

For the first time since his ascension into a leader, Mustafa was stunned to silence. He did not have words that would fill his mouth quickly enough in order to stir the wild rage of his followers. Looking around, however, he saw the faces of the monkeys who fought alongside him start to curl deeper into madness.

Mustafa leaned into the urine-yellow eyes of the snake and spoke in a low voice, "You are one to talk, deceiver. You come from a long line of liars. Especially when the two leggings trusted you and ended up making the wrong decision."

This was true. The snake did not deny his inherited past. He did not deny that his reputation was then tainted by an ancestor whose blood only imitated his design and features. He knew he was blamed for a wrong he did not commit. No matter, he would not be provoked by the charlatan before him.

"Tell me, Mustafa. Were the pomegranates enough for you to fake a dramatic injury, or was it necessary for you to take the blood of an innocent animal to make yourself larger than you are? Or was it the lies? Tell me Mustafa, was it truly the spirits of the gods who guard this temple that helped you?"

As if on cue, the makeshift twigs and branches that became the shadows of the gods tumbled from one of the trees. Another tumbled from one of the hidden ledges of the temple. The monkeys that were around Mustafa gazed lack-jawed at the sight. Those of the macaque immediately recognized the shapes, and they looked toward Msutafa, who suddenly grew small and frail.

"Do you remember the day well? Was it the wind that gave you strength? Your long-dead grandmother? The collective strength you never knew you were born with? Tell me: what story is the correct one?"

Closing in now, the rest of the frogs, birds, and beasts started to listen carefully towards the boa. Mustafa started to trace back in his memory. All of the twisted versions of the truth collided into a mess of far-flung fairy tail or tragedy.

Mustafa darted his eyes toward every face he saw around him, and the eyes of the beasts around him grew narrow. In the distance toward the temple, a sharp cry came out. On the top of the temple, Mustafa's father screeched in ecstasy and delirium, pointing at Mustafa.

"You finally have learned your lesson, my boy! You finally learned your lesson! Everything the snake said is true. He used the juice of a pomegranate to seem like blood, and he never touched the tiger. Everything that comes out of the disgusting liar is false, and all of you fell for it!" holding his stomach, Mustafa's father bent over in outrageous laughter.

"Mustafa, my son, you were destined for trouble, and now you have found it." Like a wave onto the sea, the Father's words broke the stunned silence of the animals (including the remaining cats who were able to fend off the mob) and plunged their way towards Mustafa. Mustafa was completely consumed.

The father danced on the top of the temple, throwing the shambled visages of the temple gods to the ground. The snake slithered away into the darkness of the forest, never seen again.

THE SEVEN EYES
OF WONDER

The void opens itself before me as I open the veil. Stepping out from the candlelit hall behind me, I find myself in absolute darkness. The only thing guiding me to my ultimate goal is the twinkling light in the distance and the resonant pull of the seven eyes of wonder. All of them are stashed in a bag which I hold in my hands. There is no air, no sound. Nothing. My heartbeat is the only indication of life. Cautiously, I walk towards the light. The feeling of the eyes grows heavy in my hands and their pull strengthens, like someone with a rope pulls my very soul towards a single purpose.

At my feet, a whirlpool of the cosmos slowly stirs itself, funneling constantly down into itself and then out of itself. It did not end or begin. All of them are seemingly insignificant, bearing the keys to everything. I remember feeling exhilarated for the first time in a very long time. I remember the numbness in my chest releasing its hold as the whole of the universe opened itself to me.

A brilliant flash of light reached into the boundless black void, and I was transfixed. I felt everything. I heard everything. I knew everything. One by one, the eyes opened the pool, and I could see. I could see and comprehend the universe in all its glory.

• • •

Niccolo Mancini was born on January 1st, 1500. His mother predicted that his coming would be tumultuous, but she never predicted that her son would be born feet first. What came next was 15 hours of arduous labor that required the aid of five maids, three midwives, and a priest who continually prayed over the screaming woman as if she were possessed.

When the baby was finally born, the father immediately ordered that a new set of sheets were to be bought and that his distant family be notified of a new heir. Francesca Mancini, beautiful, voluptuous, was given her baby boy and looked down at him, bathed in sweat, with contempt. She saw the slimy creature screaming out for life and for love as a worm that must be dealt with swiftly. She managed to list three different ways of getting rid of the child, but she was not talented when it came to plotting, so she resigned from her role.

Antonio Mancini held his son in his arms and wept. All the maternal feelings reserved for his wife were transferred to him and he vowed with every fiber of his being that he would be the one to raise the child in a way that his father never could. However, unbeknownst to Antonio, he would fail.

After Niccolo ate from a well-endowed and experienced wet nurse (who would die because of an infected leg), Antonio cradled the baby once more in his chair by the fire. The warmth of the fire and the beating heart of his father calmed Niccolo.

"You are Niccolo Mancini," whispered Antonio, "you will be the inheritor of this estate as well as the future director of my current trade. You will be very rich, and you will never want for anything. My son. My loving, beautiful boy."

Francesca lay in bed sleeping, dreaming of sex. Antonio stayed all that night, whispering the future to his son.

• • •

Niccolo, at age five, walked with his father towards the ports of Vienna. He smelled the salt of the sea as well as the sweat and stench of the men carrying loads of cayenne, salt, sugar, ginger, cloves, and saffron. The small saffron flowers wilting in the wooden crates expelled their aroma which melted both Antonio and Niccolo's hearts. Antonio brought Niccolo upon a trading vessel that had just come back from its current voyage. The vessel was damaged, but the goods within the hull were untouched. Many men died on that voyage.

Antonio opened one of the barrels full and scooped the saffron flowers into his hands. He gave them to his son, who deeply inhaled the smell.

"This, my son, is what makes the world worth living for. Spice. Beauty transforms all things and makes the soul leap for joy." Antonio ruffled his son's brown, cropped hair as he giggled like little boys do.

Niccolo prepared himself to ask the question that he knew would receive the same answer, "Papa, where is Mama today?"

Antonio felt the all too familiar lump in his throat and stabbing pain in his chest (a pain that persisted and increased throughout his life; this also killed him) and replied to his son as he had before, "Your mother is a very busy woman who must see many people. She will be with us again soon."

In reality, Francesca was having an affair with a rich gentleman with no children and with a talent of discretion. Truly, she would not return after three days and then promptly leave for Paris. She took every chance to escape.

Antonio loved Francesca but knew he would never receive the relief he desired from his heart or his chest. Niccolo went to bed that night listening to his father's voice, telling stories of his boyhood or of impossible things. He wondered if any of those stories were true.

The next morning, Niccolo awoke to the smashing of plates within the main hall. His mother had returned. Normally, the maids would lock his door so that Niccolo would not have to see the war that unfolded the mornings his mother was back, but this time, they forgot as they were trying feverishly to prevent the madame of the house from being strangled. Antonio leaped into a rage. He knew full well that his wife had affairs, but not a single one was easy to ignore.

"I am a lady that is capable of doing what she pleases. You knew when you married me that you would not feel affection from me, and you said you understood. Why do you attempt to kill him if you knew what life I would lead."

"I lied to myself, my love, believing that I could ignore the pain. I will not have it! You are my wife. You are my responsibility and my property. You will not be allowed to leave this house under any circumstances unless the dead scream from the mountains!" He slapped her hard across the face. The main hall was covered in broken plates and torn curtains. Little Niccolo looked upon the scene. Through the small crack in his door, he saw his mother struggle to her feet. She conjured tears in her eyes from a fake sense of remorse and swore upon her life that she would never commit such a sin again. Antonio grabbed her neck and shook her hard.

"I would rather see you die than see you leave my side", she left to her chambers, nursing her wounds.

Antonio, feeling eyes watching him, saw his son. Niccolo quickly closed the door and hid. Although he felt in his heart that his father loved him, he was never sure if his father would also strangle his neck or slap him across the face for his own sins.

"There was the time that I accidentally broke an expensive vase. Maybe he would see the stain that I made spilling blueberry jam in the kitchen."

The door creaked open and the defeated figure of his father walked towards his son. Antonio scooped Niccolo into his arms like he had many times before and both of them silently held each other. Niccolo, still in his nightgown, crept to his mother's rooms. She was weeping too, but for a different reason. Niccolo wouldn't understand until much later why.

He knocked on the door and cautiously went in. He walked to his mother who sat on the edge of her large bed with the red silk sheets. She clenched the sheets in her balled fists and stared out the window, looking out towards the ocean.

"Momma, I love you", said Niccolo. She said nothing, only kept her eyes fixed on the craggy rocks that bore the crashing waves.

The next morning, she was gone. She had left for Paris and would stay there for three months. Niccolo felt secretly happy that she was gone. He would be in ecstasy living with his father who loved him. They went back to their routine as father and son, forgetting the past. Niccolo would wish less for his mother as the years went on.

Three years passed and Francesca stayed in Paris. She lived off of the money she would receive from her husband. She invested in expensive clothing, furniture, and men as she stayed in her chateau. Antonio invested himself within his work as well as different studies that mulled the pain. He was a patron for several artists and the new scholars that call themselves "humanists." Niccolo often sat at his father's feet listening to the scholars and artists debate endlessly over everything and nothing at the same time. His father listened as well, finding the passion for knowledge a nourishing venture. Niccolo's heart sped up in excitement with every word. He kept himself awake at night, sometimes thinking over and over in his mind the new discoveries of what they called 'the classics."

Antonio brought his son to the ports of Vienna as well as to various meetings with business owners and partners. Niccolo kept a charcoal pencil and parchment with him, either taking notes or drawing depending on what he felt was important or interesting.

Slowly however, Niccolo became more of a nuisance. Asking questions about what things meant or where things were located became impossible. Glares from his father's business partners stunned him frequently into silence. Eventually, he was left alone in his father's house.

• • •

My first tutor, I never attended any schools within Vienna- I was tutored strictly by private tutors since my father could afford it. I was an austere man with a long beard and beady eyes that never seemed to open any wider than a squink. He looked as if he were always suffering a cold. He taught me Latin and Greek. I learned to read the Bible in both languages until, eventually, we transitioned to Spanish, French, and some ancient languages from Bulgaria.

"Homo unius est creaturarum maximarum quae stultissimus experti sunt. Ignorantia innata seu amor ruinae nostrae est", he said.

I began to write down what I heard, spelling what I understood. My tutor whacked me hard against my right hand. I froze so as to not show any tears.

"You must NOT write. You must listen. You must listen to what I am saying. Listen to my words. What do you recognize?

So I listened. I lifted my head and swallowed the pain running down my hand to my elbow.

"Diligenter debemus ad tollendam ignorantiam et contentionem ambitionem. Humanitas nimis pretiosa est et nimis potens ut mentibus nostris in otio incidat. Ita discendum est ex antiquis nostris. Qui intra Romam magnam scientiam ab ultimis maioribus suis acceperant. Incipiamus discere de ratione regiminis." He finished. ANd stared at me. I sat in my chair staring back at him and wondered. I recognized Roman and I recognized "regiminis." "Antiquis", "humanitas", "ignorantiam." I recognized those words.

"So", boomed my tutor (who I now remember was named signore Piccolo), "what did I just say."

"Signorer", I said meekly, "I believe you said something about humanity and government."

"You have a basic understanding. You are still lacking in much", he said this more to himself as he stroked his long, salt and pepper beard.

I simply nodded. We then delved further into Roman history as well as culture. I learned more of the roman language by exposure than a simple list of words. As much as Signore Piccolo was strange, he was an effective teacher. One of the few men I would remember or care for in my life of tutors and learning.

A year later, I had mastered Greek and Roman. Signore Piccolo and I started to communicate regularly, crossing between both languages as well as translating one from the other.

One day as I was entering the study, Signore Piccolo spoke in a language I had only heard from the sailors that were hired for the spice trips (now he was mostly gone for silk, spice, jewels, and dyes for various paints and textiles).

"Bonjour, Niccolo. Je me demandais si nous pouvions essayer quelque chose de différent", he said proudly. He smiled for the first time in the year that I had known him.

It has been a long time since I have been surprised like this. I was still an anxious child who depended on my father. Again, I stared at him in silence. Yet, there was something within me that changed those words into something comprehensible.

I replied, "you wish to do something different? Maybe speak in French? I have heard more of the language from the sailors my father employs."

"Tre bien!" he cried. He jumped up a little from the leather chair and we began with the same routine.

It was also at this time that my father employed two more tutors, one for philosophy and one for the "sciences" or more so experimentation and understanding the basics of the natural world. I will flatter myself and say that I was an excellent student. I asked questions, I worked in advanced levels.

There was nothing more exciting to me than to discover more about the world that I lived in. There was nothing more exhilarating than to be able to see the strands of truth transcend between everything. All things were connected with each other. All things were intertwined into a fabric that grew larger by the day.

It was at this time that my father's presence began to wane even further. He was very busy with his exports in trade and his expansion of the arts. My mother was obsolete. I took many efforts to forget her as time progressed. My father, however, was a harder burden to bear.

I remember seeing him one night sleeping at his desk. His head was covered in his usual black robes that signified he was going to bed. He never made it to his bed. I was coming in to show him the progress I made within geometry. Instead, I decided to look at him in the candlelight. The candle was melted down to the last ounce of wax. The wick had almost fallen. The flame was so small, that it barely lit his brow. However, I looked. In all the time that I have been separated from my father, I was astounded to see his wrinkled face.

He was an old man. When my mother first left, he looked as if he were in the prime of health. He was light and bright. He exuded a firey passion for life. He never took a mistress. I sometimes would see him go back into Mother's room, looking over the items she left. A comb, a bottle of perfume, a pair of stockings. He would sit on her bed. I refused to remember Francesca. I burned her out of my mind. She was only a useless vessel for me. I did not at that time regret my birth, but I regretted that she would vex me.

I would then lose my father as well. He died when I was thirteen. They said he died of a broken heart.

• • •

The day that Antonio Mancini died, he was looking again at his legers. He was pouring over the shipments, exports, imports, and purchases. He meticulously calculated every penny. His allowance to his wife was his most extensive expense. He sold his fine clothes and silks a long time ago in order to afford Niccolo's tutors. His son's latest tutors are students who need the training. Antonio Mancini rubbed away the sleep within his eyes. He was 43 years old, but felt two decades older. Looking again at the numbers, he gave up worrying.

Antonio first met Francesca when he was twenty. She was only fifteen. At the time, he did not think much about the young girl. She was a duty he had to fulfill and it was her duty to accept the new task of motherhood and wife. The day they met was their wedding day. He looked into her eyes as her soft veil was removed and saw anger. Intelligence as well. She was a burning flame. He was the moth that would be singed. He fell in love and for the first time in his life, he decided to deeply ingrained himself into another's life. He was alone, like his own son, as he grew up. He had very little to depend on.

Francesca grew up within the confines of her mother's training. Her mother was "the snake in the garden" (or so her father would say). Her mother was intelligent, clever and beautiful. She trained her daughter to never settle for less.

"This world is too big, my love, for mediocrity. Find your way to the top of the social hierarchy, and you will be able to see the world for what it truly is", Francesca's mother told her this often.

However, her father depended dearly on security and so Francesca was married to the merchant. Her first encounter with Antonio made a hateful seed to grow in her heart. The world was too big to settle for this little man. He was a fool. She could see from the moment that he swooned for her. She would never allow him to woo her. She was leaving his side constantly in search of the grander things her mother had promised.

Antonio worshiped her. He worshiped her cunning eyes and her ability to be able to subtly shame her enemies, being able to dig into the softer parts and pierce them where it would hurt the most. He allowed himself to be seduced and allowed her affairs to continue. In spite of it all, he loved her. In his heart of hearts, Antonio needed her.

Antonio was a man who allowed himself to bottle his anger. He did not allow his malice to come out often. When it did, it was an explosion of frustration that spread to everything he touched. He was a ravenous wolf. His shame and guilt then brought him down to his most base form, a worm drying in the sun. Francesca could not stand a man who would allow himself to grovel in his own pity. She validated her own anger towards the world as she saw her husband break apart. When it came to Niccolo, however, she knew that Antonio would always be the favorite. Niccolo loved his father. In fact, Niccolo saw Antonio as both father and mother.

Francesca, being a child herself, could not understand raising another child. So when she knew she was pregnant, she made a plan to destroy herself along with the baby. She shortly became a drunk and a fiend. She hosted many parties that would last for days on end, allowing every form of debauchery to take place. None of the servants were allowed to report on the things that would happen within the Mancini household or they would be fired. So naturally, none of the servants disobeyed their mistress and even for them, their realities of living and working for a she-devil became a fact of life.

One day, when Antonio had lost the fight within himself to pull her in, to control Francesca, he asked her, "why do you run?"

Her feline attitude, a haughty and sly heir she carried beneath a soft exterior, quivered slightly. She exposed herself to her husband for the first time and in that moment she was just a little girl, "I will not be confined to a place I did not choose", then she left him. That was the night before she left for Paris.

Antonio then thought of Niccolo. He remembered one day when Niccolo was ten, it had been a long time since Niccolo had been with his father on one of his meetings. Niccolo tried to keep up with his father who was running around Vienna, consulting with various clients as well as those that were working for him. Niccolo grew weary and sat on the steps of a St. Stephens Cathedral. He ate what little snacks he brought with him and took off the dress shoes his father made him wear. His aching feet cried out to him. A priest of the church saw Niccolo sitting on the steps and offered him water. Niccolo obliged as well as went into the cool cathedral to sleep. He cradled himself in one of the back pews of the church while his father, forgetting his son, went about the busy city.

It wasn't until much later that Antonio Mancini and several other men had crashed into the cathedral, almost before nightfall, when they found Niccolo. Niccolo was still asleep. Antonio gently picked up his son, careful to not wake him, and looked at him the way he did when he was first born. Antonio had one of his employees pay for the men who helped in the search. Then, for an hour, he sat before God with his son in his arms.

Thinking on that day, he realized how he had truly failed his son. He allowed his son to be abandoned in the streets. More than that, he allowed himself to push his son away. He had effectively repeated the same mistakes his father had made before him and now his son would carry the same burdens that life had granted him. In that special place where humans dare not look, the magnitude of Antonio's regret started to grow bigger. At the same time, Antonio experienced a numbness in his left arm and his heart began to go into cardiac arrest.

Clutching his chest, Antonio began to struggle to breathe. His body lost control, and he crashed onto the ground, taking the leger with him. He writhed on the floor, eyes bulging out of their sockets. Finally, he groaned his last breath. He was discovered three hours later.

At the funeral, Niccolo's heart had given up. He gave up on the love of his father, he completely disowned his mother, and God Himself was also a worthless venture. He resolved to no longer believe that God had a merciful heart and so threw away any need to believe that there was a god at all. Right up to the time we met, Niccolo would change his relationship with his father in his head, tweaking the saddest moments of his life to be real tragedies. His father was a careless fool who abandoned his own son. Niccolo's sense of hope for his father renewed time and time again and for what? He waited for his father in the most precious years of his life and was given nothing. He was a lost child in a world full of dark corners. He learned quickly that hope was a deceiver of all.

• • •

Looking into my father's tomb, it took everything in me not to spit into the earth. My mother had already made plans to marry a rich Count. I hated my father. I hated his ignorance and his willful attempts at pleasing my mother despite her abandoning him. Now, he had abandoned me. In truth, he abandoned me a long time ago.

He was not moral. He was spineless. I endeavored to make sure that I would not inherit his fatal flaw. Working was my savior. Knowledge was my god. I knelt at its feet countlessly, and it gave me life beyond the pain that I felt. Shortly after Mr. Piccolo, I studied various subjects, including the sciences of nature, architecture, mathematics, and philosophy. The pursuit of knowledge and greatness beyond the physical limitations of time drove me further toward the altar of wisdom.

I began studying at the public university in Vienna. I was still living in my father's house. My uncle inherited what was left and promptly moved in with his wife and three children. All of them were girls under the age of ten. At thirteen, I was an advanced student, but understanding people was not a subject I was interested in. I came out of my room only to eat and bid my aunt good morning and then the rest was to read, write, and reconfigure.

I excelled in mathematics. It was comforting. All of the digits lined up in perfect rows that always gave a reliable answer. I craved more. I fell in love with shapes, lines, and the possibility of structures. I craved even more. I read the works of Konrad Celtis, which inspired me to ask my aunt and uncle If I may study at the University of Erfurt (I had already passed the preliminary courses, and it was becoming harder to find more advanced teachers. I had resorted to teaching myself, but I craved a different environment).

"Why on earth would you go to Erfurt? It is so stifling there!" exclaimed my aunt, who was nursing her newest child, Maria. I was fifteen at this time.

"I wish to be able to pursue architecture as well as mathematics. I have an affinity for it as well as many recommendation letters from my previous tutors." I laid the stack of papers, all signed. It was a unanimous decision by those that I most trusted and now I waited for the approval of strangers within my own household.

My uncle looked over the papers and shrugged, "I do not see why you should not attend. But you will have to live there. You will be away from Vienna."

I feigned surprise and slight disappointment. I then replied, "That is a sacrifice I am willing to make."

It was decided. I traveled to Erfurt. I left the majority of what I had from boyhood. I brought only a few extra clothes, my books, plenty to write with, and a spare amount of change. Of course, my uncle was willing to pay my tuition, but I did not take advantage of his kindness. In fact, I didn't even write.

During my first year there, I was able to be in my own small room, which was more like a monk's cell. I had one small bed, a table, a latrine, and a mirror with a small dresser. The basin of water that I filled every day became frozen during the winter. I would have to take a large rock that I kept underneath my bed to crash through the thick layer of ice and get to the cold water beneath. I invested the majority of my time studying in that cold room. Much of my money went to candles, parchment and soup with crusted bread.

However, I loved every second. I loved being alone for the first time in my life. The pain of yesteryear slipped away as I invested in more time. Many days, I went to the private offices of my professors, who obliged (occasionally begrudgingly) my questions as well as the works that I pondered on.

A teacher that I found to be the most intriguing was Professor Bauman. He was a professor of nature sciences. His class consisted of looking over life specimens and understanding the function of various organs and humors. He refuted the ancients in believing that the heart was the center of human reasoning.

"It is the brain!" he said with a thick German accent, "It is the mind that brings reasoning. And the common man is capable of such reasoning. Looking at the specimens before us", we were given a wide variety of animals, all of them dissected with their organs placed on another side of the table, "all things are connected inwardly with the same basic parts. Man, however, is given the gift of reasoning. So we must not forsake that reasoning at all costs."

He was what they called "a humanist." He believed in the renewal of art, science, literature, and architecture. He was much like my father, who financed and housed humanists for years as I grew up. I wanted to be like them.

Another Professor, Professor Abraham, that I found compelling was a mathematician but also an architect. Often he would say, "anyone who believes that God did not create shapes in nature is looking at the world with their eyes closed. Let us look around us once more and tell me that patterns and shapes do not exist!."

Often during that class, we were brought out into nature in order to identify and document shapes and concentric patterns. That was when I decided to be an architect and master concentricity within my work. The trouble, however, was that my first commission was spent building housing communities towards the Alps. Professor Abraham recommended me to be the head of the architectural design and overseer of the labor. He introduced me to none other than the financier and owner, Fraur Jakob Fugger.

The Fugger family was a wealthy merchant-banker family that had vital connections. Connections a young man like me needed as he traveled back to Vienna one day. I planned to take what I learned and make a name for myself. Jakob Fugger commissioned several units to be built that would house large communities of people coming from farming regions and seeking work within the city.

"We have too much to do and too many people to wait for. We must start now. You have four months to complete this task, or you will be replaced", was the first thing that Herr Fugger said to me. Both Professor Abraham and I bowed politely as he left and then looked at each other like two naughty boys who had just been caught eating sweets from the kitchen.

So I worked. I calculated the amount of men, supplies, time, and resources needed to the most minute number and set the plan in motion. We finished the housing communities, larger buildings divided into fours with the same floor plan for both upstairs and downstairs, that were lined in tight rows. There would be little gardening, but many people would not be worried about that. There was even room for a small community center to be built in order for trade and commerce to be held. We finished the project within three months and 28 days.

Herr Fugger, a clean-shaven man who had a bulging underlip and beady black eyes, looked over the entirety of the buildings after everything was finished. He inspected several of the rooms as well as irrigation systems that were made (an inspired idea from when a child slipped in a mud puddle and almost died because of a severe head injury).

Standing there with him were myself and several other men who I selected as minor overseers over different sections. Then Fraur turned to me, "You were selected by Professor Abraham to be overseer, yes?"

I nodded politely.

"Then who are they?" he asked, waving his hand and motioning to the equally nervous men behind me.

"They are architects that were assigned different sections of the project and would report back to me on their section's progress."

"And you did not decide to oversee those sections yourself?"

"I did, sir," again, I bowed slightly.

"Stop sniveling. The job is done, is it not?" and he walked back up the hill. I noticed in his right leg he had a slight limp, but he refused a horse or carriage.

I motioned for the rest of the men to follow. Their knuckles loosened slightly around their plans and notes that they would use to stake their claims, and their faces became flush as they allowed themselves to breathe again. I walked on and couldn't help but have a rye smile across my face.

• • •

Niccolo Mancini oversaw many works within Germany and Austria. He would surpass his masters and take pride in leaving their shadows. At this time, I had not met him yet. Although I knew much about him, the time had not come. Soon, however, we would know each other well.

Niccolo forgot to mention because of his fake piety that, he slowly worked his way into becoming friends with the old Herr, who longed for a son, but was never given the privilege by God. He apparently had other plans.

Niccolo, however, became a pseudo-son. A young man with a keen eye and sharp wit who saw the prospects of life and took them. Herr Fugger saw much of himself in the scrawny Italian man with no family prospects (at that time, his uncle, aunt and their children would die of smallpox. The house was burnt to the ground in order to scourge the sickness).

One day as Niccolo was at the Fugger house, he met Matilda. Matilda was the lone surviving daughter of Jakob Fugger and would be the inheritor of his estate, although the name would become obsolete once she married. Jakob Fugger would attempt to deliberately put Niccolo and Matilda together often in order for a marriage to come soon after. Niccolo felt uncomfortable most of the time. He stumbled when he talked, and he was always nervous looking at Matilda in the eye.

Matilda was a fair-faced beauty with light blue eyes and porcelain white skin. His hair was a deep blonde color that was covered all except the soft fringes of hair that curled towards the temples. Niccolo was not just uncomfortable but terrified of this creature because he would not dare admit that he was in love.

Matilda was a soft-spoken woman. She was not even a true woman yet- she had only turned fifteen that year. At this time, Niccolo was twenty-five. Yet, she was intelligent. Matilda was taught to read and write at an early age and was given a similar education to her male counterparts. Still, like her mother before her, she was a quiet and calm creature who was content with very little but grateful for much. She was blessed early to have a gentle countenance. The nurse who fed her during her most delicate days would cry tears of joy because Matilda never cried or complained.

Matilda and her mother almost shared a secret language only spoken with the eyes. Matilda would not have to speak, and instantly, her mother knew exactly what she needed. Matilda went on many outings in the garden with her mother where they both would listen to the birds in spring. Her mother died when she was ten, but still, every year, Herr Fugger would see more of his wife than his daughter. Jakob Fugger would never remarry. He believed his wife's spirit dwelled in his daughter and would be vengeful despite her contrite heart.

Niccolo found himself struggling beyond human reasoning to hide his feelings from the quiet, wide-eyed girl.

• • •

I met Matilda during a banquet that her Fugger was holding. It was in celebration of yet another successful architectural project, which turned out better than predicted, considering time and resources. Again, I was the overseer. I found it useful to maintain correspondence with Herr Fugger even though we had little in common. In fact, he did most of the talking as I sat and listened or thought more on other matters.

The banquet was held during the winter solstice and Matilda then was only a young girl.

Matilda wore a blue dress with the typical filigree that a wealthy woman would have. However, it was her eyes. They were a crystalline blue that seemed to look through you and see your innermost thoughts. I was not prepared for what she would see within me.

"You are all alone, sir. You have decided that the company of others makes you uncomfortable?" she had come up to me after being introduced to the rest of the party. This was her first year as a woman, which meant that prospects for marriage would come soon. In all seriousness, this party was also a reason to introduce her to society.

I bowed and introduced myself.

"I know who you are. Niccolo Mancini. My father says that you are the one who has been in charge of several of his projects. You are also someone who values knowledge. Tell me, do you also value wisdom or is there any difference between one or the other?"

I will admit, I was taken aback, "I believe that wisdom and experience are closely related to each other. Knowledge can only bring you so far." I realize that in the future, my belief in this statement will change.

"You speak a partial truth," she said. And then she walked away, mingling with others.

That night, I stayed awake and sat at my desk. I was mostly disturbed. I hadn't expected nor prepared myself for that conversation. I spent hours wondering why on earth she asked such questions and what she could mean. It was difficult to guess from such a short interaction. I tried not to put too much weight into her words, and yet they persisted.

Days after the banquet, Matilda was sitting in the garden. Her father and I were working in his study, which had seven windows all overlooking the garden. That time of year, the courtyard of rose bushes and wildflowers looked more like a graveyard. She simply sat at the very center and allowed the winter sun to warm her face. I stared and wondered at her. Her Fugger watched me and saw how easy it was for the bait to take. He allowed my glancing to continue a moment longer until…

"I believe that in the next six months, we will be able to accomplish this task. I am speaking to several artisans who say that they will be willing to co-manage the project. Are you willing to work with newer employees and clientele?"

"Hmm? Oh! Yes, Herr Fugger, I will be excited to see their work."

He only smiled, "My wife begged me to plant that garden," he motioned towards the frozen courtyard, "and in spite of me never being able to enjoy it, my daughter has full use of it. She goes as far as to oversee what flowers grow in what place. Almost every year, the colors and aromas are different but hypnotizing. Do you know anything of flowers?"

"No Herr Fugger. I only have as much knowledge of flowers as you would of shoemaking."

He laughed, "You are right. Let us retire."

He rose from his chair and walked out of the room. I decided to stay and look over the logistics of the upcoming projects. Then something within me said to look once more into the courtyard. Matilda was looking into one of the shrunken bushes and had both of her hands plunged into the thorns. I ran out of the study and into the courtyard. Within her bloody hands was a small dove who was stuck within the brambles.

"Are you absolutely insane!?" I shouted and grabbed both of her bloody hands in mine. I grabbed a handkerchief, but she hushed me. The bird's wined fluttered, but her grip was strong. She gently set the bird on the sill of the center window, allowing the bird to rest. Apparently, it was struggling to free itself.

"The creature is safe. Trust me, Signore Mancini, I have survived worse things."

I gave her my handkerchief, "Thank you, but this will not do."

"I insist. It is the least I could do."

She tilted her head. She looked at me once again. A shiver of vulnerability coursed through my veins. I guarded my thoughts but to no avail.

"You have a kind heart, Signore. I remember a story that my father told me. You had taken up for a young architect who made a mathematical error on one of the projects, which almost made the entire structure collapse. You put the blame on yourself. You are willing to save the broken or even take the fall for other's mistakes. Why is that?"

I shuddered but simply said, "You must be cold. Let us go inside."

"Yes. I will bring tea to my chamber if you will accompany me. You still have to answer my question."

Arguing was useless. She had lured me in and I allowed myself to be coaxed by the fairy-like countenance of this girl.

She had her own sitting room. It was very much like her father's study. A circular room with shelves and flowers in vases. There were three large windows that overlooked the snowy fields. She sat in a velveteen chair to the right of a small table with tea. I sat across from her at a similar table. A large fireplace separated us both. The snow began to fall again in large sheets. Again, I would have to stay the night in Herr Fugger's home.

For a while, we sat in silence. Both she and I were transfixed by the falling snow. It was a mesmerizing flow of soft snowflakes that clung onto everything. A blanket of white crystals began to crystalize around the window panes. The fire kept us warm.

Eventually, Matilda spoke, "I know so little about you, Signore Mancini."

"You may call me Niccolo, and no, that is not true."

"How so?"

"You so accurately determined my heart and soul during our very first meeting. You should know me quite well."

"Ah," she said, reflecting on the banquet, "I am sorry. It was presumptuous and unkind of me. I apologize for making an assumption."

"In spite of everything, my lady, you were right," I regretted my words immediately.

"I was?"

"Yes. You acutely realized that, in fact, large crowds of people make me uncomfortable. I grew up alone for most of my life, so I am not used to being around people. I work. That is all."

"You are passionate about your work?"

"I believe that to create is a great privilege. If I were to not take advantage of that, then I would be bastardizing the call to create itself."

"You have such strong feelings. Where do you believe they stem from?"

"You have quite the habit of asking personal questions."

"Well, are not relationships personal?"

I stopped myself. I hadn't spoken to someone like this ever in my life. For some reason, speaking with her was natural. I plotted the best way to answer her, but she responded first.

"I am sorry. I realize I am making you uncomfortable. You are not used to speaking this way?" she realized her mistake and then said, "Again, I forget myself. I do not mean to make you feel that you must disclose your inner thoughts to a complete stranger. However, I do not wish us to be strangers. I admit I am curious about you, and I admire your work. What can I do to gain your trust?"

I thought for a moment and then said, "You have asked much of me, and yet you have not given. A relationship is something akin to a transaction. If you ask, then you must give. Tell me something of yourself."

She nodded, "you are correct. I will tell you of a time that my mother taught me a very important lesson."

The snow's descent grew faster in sheets of ice as the world darkened. The only thing that I could hear was her voice and the sparks that crackled in the fire.

• • •

"When I was very young, my mother told me many stories of her grandmother. Her grandmother was a very wise woman who knew many things.

One day, my mother saw a bowl of water in the middle of the kitchen table. In the very center of the bowl was a small black lump of leaves.

She at first was not concerned, but the lump of leaves (which I learned later was a seedling) was so ugly that one day she said to her grandmother, 'Why must you keep this? It is ugly!'

'You must never let appearances fool you. The innermost parts of things tell more truth than we think.'

One day, she finally saw what her grandmother meant: in the center of the bowl was a beautiful flower that filled the room with the sweetest aroma. Somehow, in a country as cold as Germany, my great-grandmother was able to grow a beautiful lotus flower.

I believed from that story the importance of knowing the truth. The full expanse of wisdom."

"I remember you asking me a question about wisdom and knowledge. Your story explains the question's importance to you."

She simply smiled.

• • •

Two more months had passed. The snow continued to fall and I found myself as a permanent resident within Herr Fugger's home. Old clothes of Fuggers were given to me to wear (although they were drastically out of fashion). I and Matilda shared a similar routine as their first night together. We spoke about many subjects. Science, philosophy, music, art, the new ways of the world. We spoke of everything. Yet, I learned more of her than she learned of me.

She never pressed any further into my personal life. She never asked if I was ever in love, ever had a family, who my family was, or what my childhood was like. However, she listened a great deal about my schooling and my passion for learning. I found it painful, like a sharp pain in my mind, to speak about my childhood. I made it so that I never approached it. I denied its existence and lived only in the present, now. There was no future, no afterlife, no God, nothing. I found that living in such a way was comforting and terrifying. Yet, if there is nothing to depend on, there is nothing to lose.

Matilda saw this. In the back of her calm eyes were tears that refused to surface. I feel that she would not stop seeing my pain until her own happiness would cease to exist. Unlike me, she opened herself up like a flower. Her heart was worn on her sleeve, and her compassion was overwhelming- sometimes misguided.

"When it comes to forgiveness, Matilda, I do not believe that you allow yourself to be an individual. You allow the hurt of this world to tax you, and you do nothing!" I said.

"I do more than you think, Niccolo. I forgive to heal my inner self rather than to give grace to those who do not deserve it. I move on from the pain in order to look towards the future. Those who hurt me have no control over me."

We were discussing her mother's death. Due to the fatal error of a doctor more concerned with his sleep rather than saving a dying woman, Matilda's mother died in agony. It took Matilda five years to speak again after her mother's death. At that time, she was sent to a convent where she studied the bible and thrived in learning Hebrew and Latin. She also grew into a love of growing things like her mother as well as reading. As a woman, she was as intelligent as her male peers, but her sex would not afford her the same privileges.

"And where is justice?!" I was on the edge of becoming furious.

Matilda simply laid her hand on my shoulder and said, "Justice is the Lord's. I have no right to inflict justice on those who are my equals." That was the end of that.

I look back now and think of those days fondly. Although they were not so far away, I remember them as a dream. I remember the pain of feeling her closeness and the thought that she would inevitably fail me like so many others. I believed ultimately, she would fail me like my own mother, like my father. I refused to allow that to happen again. I would not allow myself to feel the pain of life without receiving relief or resolution. I would not have an empty bed beside me because that torture took my father's heart.

When the snow lifted, and Spring began to melt away the ice, I promptly left the Fugger household in search of a new profession. Architecture no longer held any value. Or at least, I searched for a profession that would cult Matilda from my life. It would take years to forget her. A soft part of my heart, especially now in this place where I stand to meet my ultimate demise, I still long for her comforting voice and calm demeanor. Yet, we cannot enact the past.

• • •

Niccolo Mancini was in love, but he threw away that love for a deeper romance: alchemy. Whispers of a study that searched for the perfect man had found themselves in the Fugger household when Herr Fugger himself hoisted several Alchemists. The man was simply curious and so allowed the eccentric potion makers to enter his home. In the end, he did not believe a single one of the men, but Niccolo was entranced. The more that he learned, the more that the perfect man felt like an answered prayer. His past nullified into a concrete and orderly sense of self that eliminated the imperfect or undistilled. The purification of the cosmos from within his own mind.

It was salvation at last. It was an inner peace that promised transcendence from pain (or at least, that was what Niccolo believed). Feverishly, Niccolo sought out one particular teacher: Nicolas Flamel. Instantly, he traveled to Italy for the first time in years and found himself wracked with excitement and fear.

The following days were a blur of walking on foot and recommendation letters from several of his past professors and tutors. The young man, now twenty-seven years of age, traveled all over Venice and invaded the offices of his professors. He also discovered that Nicolas Flamel was elusive and deeply private. He walked from the university to the churches, to the common dining houses of the poor, and finally to the countryside in the south of Italy. With all the money he had left, Niccolo traveled to a small village in Calabria. By the looks of the people, it was still a place where the ideas of the new age and humanism had not touched the people. He saw their suspicious faces as they crossed themselves. Surely, a man of science was not a holy thing.

Nicolas Flamel lived in a small house with a mill that served as his laboratory. He was a meticulous, experimental man who pursued the physical and its connection to the metaphysical. Something that the Catholic population of the village saw as a blasphemous thing. Nicolas Flamel kept his works not under lock and key but under code and mystic images that concealed the truth. He knew, by the intuition of his long years within the fabric of the universe, that a student would come to him soon. Surely this student would ask him the same questions that he asked himself and would find his way to his door.

The mill itself helps various instruments for diluting and distilling substances as well as combining them over and over and over again. The man kept his books on shelves that spiraled around the mill's inner walls. A contraption that hoisted him up by a precarious seat (something he meant to get fixed) in order for him to access his many works. The largest book within his collection is a compilation of dissections of various creatures as well as the organs and inner parts of a pregnant woman that Leonardo Davinci had hand drawn and painted. The home of the mysterious scientist was removed from his work. It was a comfortable place with very little furniture but a table, chair, silverware, a cauldron over a hot fire, a larger lounging chair towards a fire, and a side table.

Niccolo Mancini arrived at the house and the mill at dusk, just as the last sliver of the sun was descending. The fields of wheat stretched for miles which opened up the heavens in glorious splendor. His mind then brought up a memory he believed he had forgotten. His father one day opened the windows of Niccolo's bedroom. He cradled his son between his knees and pointed toward the constellations.

"There is Orion on the hunt. There is Ursa Major and Ursa Minor. Ursa Major is always in search of her cub. There is Leo the lion, bravely striding across the night sky..." He would continue this way until Niccolo fell asleep.

Looking now into the sky, he realized how much he looked like his father. He sported a strong jaw but a crooked nose. His hair was curly but was a mousy brown color that often looked dreary. He was tall, but his feet were too clumsy. He was his father in the flesh. What remained for Niccolo to cast aside was his connection to his past. He vowed that whoever he became would be his new identity. So, he discarded his father altogether, along with his mother. He vowed to discard Matilda who would evade his attempts for years during his study.

Now, the real story begins. The dreary history of human life opens itself to a sliver of the ethereal and the strange. The day we finally met.

• • •

Nicolas Flamel was crouching over a small insect that was just taken out of a vial of various chemicals. The delicate creature's long limbs were painstakingly placed in various positions with the gentle movements of the old man. He then stuck the thinnest pin with a canvas cloth that carried the insect. Niccolo didn't breathe as he stayed within the doorway of the mill.

"My boy, you are going to fall over if you don't allow your heart to beat properly. Breathe." On the last word, Niccolo let out a giant breath slowly through his mouth and then gulped in more air. He made sure that he maintained composure in front of the man who would become his teacher. After Niccolo could feel his extremities, he noticed that there was something different. Breathing once again was not of his own volition. His brain did not tell him to do anything. From the very center of his being to the tips of his toes, an energy coaxed him. Like a marionette on a string, he was brought to life again.

Niccolo made a note of this and (more tentatively) approached the alchemist.

"You are the one they call Niccolo? Correct?"

"Yes, but how did you…"

"Within small villages, news travels fast. Regardless as to how reliable it is," Nicolas Flamel looked up from his work. There was a light within the man's eyes. He wore a plain, black robe like that of a friar. His head was shaved clean, and his beard was trimmed. His white whiskers did not go past his shoulders like most of the professors. However, the poor man slumped a little and had a slight limp in his right leg.

"You must know that by coming here, you will be tested. Please stand on the other side of the room."

Towards the end of a long table was a small space that was lit by sunlight. Within the center were several concentric circles ornately intertwined. Standing on the four cardinal signs were the four elements. In the center was a picture of the sun and the moon.

"We are surrounded by the basic elements of our world. Yet, we forget the layers underneath what is physical. The "metaphysical" evades us- or so we think," Signore Flamel began to pace around Niccolo as he spoke.

"Humanity is too comfortable with what they see. So, I will test to see if you can properly lift the veil: create water."

Niccolo's expectations were starting to crumble. Even so, he batted away doubt and decided to trust a little longer, "how do you wish for me to do this?"

"You simply must create water. That is not a hard thing."

"You ask for the impossible, signore," he said, almost flabbergasted

"No," Signore Flamel smiled.

Niccolo thought hard about this task. He did not wish to give up and live as another reason for small-minded people to gossip. Niccolo kneeled on the ground and looked closer at the symbols. He touched the symbol for water and felt something like condensation. Then, it grew to be like he was sticking his hand into a puddle.

"Good. Now, give me fire."

Niccolo looked up. Signore Flamel, the inexorable man, was still smiling. Looking down, the symbol underneath him was like a puddle of water that steadily increased larger and larger. Niccolo turned around. He knelt towards the fire symbol and felt a tingling heat. From the center, there was a warm light like a dying coal. A burst of spark flew into the air and a small fire came to life.

"Excellent. Give me earth."

Again, another symbol. He rubbed the palm of his hand over it several times and, from it, sprung saplings that wretched the cobblestone floor into rubble. Before Signore Flamel could finish, he went to the symbol air. Again, he rubbed the last symbol, and a gust of air burst from an invisible place and shot into the air. Niccolo could barely hide my excitement.

Signore Flamel said, "Now, what have you learned?"

Niccolo, the lost child, now looked at Signore Flamel like he had discovered the greatest treasure known to man and exclaimed, "Anything is possible."

"Yes! You are right. However, I am sorry to say that you did not summon these elements on your own." He waved his hand and the incredible visions disappeared, "what is more important is that you decided to trust the unknown. You persisted. That is what I was hoping for."

Niccolo nodded, "teach me everything you know." His body lept toward the old man.

"You will see great and terrible things. Be prepared."

"I am ready. Teach me everything!"

"It all begins with the soul. Do you believe that you have one?"

• • •

What began as a short hour of revelation turned into seven years of dedicated work to the craft. Niccolo's life consisted of irregular hours, experimentation, failure, setbacks, progress, and enlightenment. He was no longer a boy but someone who held secrets no one dared to dream of.

Signore Flamel divided the body into three parts: the mind, the heat, and the soul. The soul was the hardest, but control over its necessary elements would then open the rest. The soul was a light as brilliant as the stars in the sky but infinitely more fragile and powerful.

The mind was a fiery machine of unpredictable proportions and was more unruly. The solution: a slow, conscious analysis of each thought captured and immediately processed. The beast must be domesticated at all costs.

Finally, the heart. The heart is fickle. Yet, its ability to fuel the body, the mind, and the soul was undeniable. The trick is to concentrate that fuel towards a goal.

Niccolo did not have the power to be able to open the veil of the universe yet. In fact, he had been working on creating the potion for it for five out of the seven years of his study. The elixir of life was composed of pure elements distilled into a potent mixture. Alas, the last ingredient was nowhere to be found.

"My boy, do not be discouraged. You will find it", said Signore Flamel.

"You have said this for five years, and none of your promises have come to fruition. You encourage me to continue, but you give me nothing that will help me find the last ingredient!"

"That is because it is only for you to find! It is an ingredient that is connected to your most inward self and will only appear at the right time! I do not tend to repeat myself, and I refuse to do so now." Signore Fla

mel left.

That night, Niccolo went out into the forest of the village, walking under the full moon. He wanted to aimlessly journey as far as he could to allow his mind to rest. He had gotten out of the practice of meditation recently, which was dangerous. The days were growing colder as the world began to turn from summer to autumn. His heart grew slower as he breathed in the fresh air.

The trees closed in and the light from the moon grew fainter as the forest canopy closed in around him. Niccolo was not afraid. The trees started to meld together in black twisted forms until the world was pitch black. Niccolo found a soft place to sit. He sat and listened to the rustling of leaves and the sound of crickets.

The only thing he heard was the heartbeat of the earth. In his mind, he envisioned the movement of the cosmos along with the constellations that often spoke of man's fate. He could smell the dying leaves, which was his favorite.

A strong waft of petrichor drifted across the wind. Niccolo saw a glowing patch of mushrooms. As if it were fate, the canopy opened just enough to illuminate the soft, pale yellow light.

Niccolo picked the mushrooms and examined them. They were flat-topped, with a hollow inside. They smelled sweet but still had the typical petrichor odor. Seeping from the gills of the mushrooms, however, was an illuminated liquid that stained his hands. Selfishly, Niccolo gathered every last one and took them back with him to the mill.

He ground up the mushrooms into a mush and boiled them to extract the liquid. Then, he filtered out the impurities. What was left was a thick ooze that glowed a pure gold color. Then, he mixed the liquid with a drop of his blood in order to complete the ritual. The deep red color was consumed by the light.

Signore Flamel came into the room as the mixture was complete.

He nodded and smiled, "Well done, Niccolo. We must not waste time. It is time for you to finally unleash the veil."

Niccolo brought the glass vial of golden liquid closer to his face. He peered into it and could see the movement of the liquid. In his mind, it seemed that the elixir was alive. His blood, like a thin trail, swirled in the liquid, mixing without even the slightest movement of his hand. The longer the vial stayed in his hands, the more he could feel a vibration or hear a soft ringing.

The tables were removed from the mill. Large concentric circles with symbols were drawn carefully by both men with chalk. They were careful not to step onto the designs. The mixture was poured in strategic places, as small as a coin.

Finally, the rest of the mixture was poured into the center. The mixture pooled into a perfect circle, still churning leisurely. Signore Flamel took a knife and cut his left palm. Then he cut Niccolo's right palm.

"Now we make the ultimate sacrifice. We make ourselves vulnerable to the universe in order to gain the powers that it holds. You must step into the circle and place yourself within the mixture. Do this quickly."

Niccolo did so. He gently crossed over every line and made his way to the circle. Once stepping into the mixture, the curling liquid hung around his feet, slowly consuming his heels and toes.

Signore Flamel spoke in a loud voice, "I call upon the four corners of the earth and the elements to rise." He raised his left hand, the blood pouring down in streaks, and the winds began to rise. They swirled around them. From the outside of the mill, rain began to pour, and lightning streaked across the opened space within the roof. The light of the elixir pulsed like a heartbeat. Niccolo watched in awe.

"I command the stars to witness and the earth to call forth; let us see beyond the veil!"

The elixir surrounding Niccolo, as well as the smaller portions, started to pulse farther until the pulsing became a constant startling beam of light. Each of the lines was not being traced in that light until they convened. Signore Flamel now stepped toward Niccolo. In contrast with the brilliant light, Signore Flamel looked like a dark figure- a void that sucked in the light. He struck out his left hand, and Niccolo held it. Their blood mingled and dropped onto the floor. The elixir again took the blood, but this time the golden light turned red. The world quaked as the light from the circles on the floor began to lift higher. Niccolo kept his eyes closed but felt nothing. In fact, he felt lighter, almost like he was floating.

Looking down, he realized he was floating. He looked at his hands, and they were fading away into dust. The blood from Niccolo's left hand was streaming into Signore Flamel's. Niccolo realized that he was slowly fading away.

Amidst the crashing winds, the rain, and the deafening thunder, Niccolo managed to scream, "WHAT ARE YOU DOING?"

Signore Flamel, with eyes that shone brightly from underneath weighing sockets, started to walk backward. Niccolo scrambled to catch onto the cobblestone walls to prevent himself from flying away, but his hands were dust, and his body was starting to disappear. Niccolo managed to see Signore Flamel mumbling something under his breath as he pulled the blood from Niccolo's body. His lungs collapsed, and his heart ceased.

Before his soul could be consumed, Niccolo cried out, "SOMEONE HELP ME. I GIVE YOU MY BODY, MY SOUL, MY LIFE, EVERYTHING. HELP ME!"

Niccolo crashed onto the floor with his body intact. Nicolas Flamel was dead, his blood spreading out across the circle. Niccolo opened his eyes and saw the stars. The world was calm. His body ached all over, and he could no longer feel his right arm. The cut within his left palm was gone. Holding his right arm, Niccolo slowly got up and slumped against the wall. He looked at the dead man before him. No thoughts raced through his mind as he expected, only a question of what to do now. He stared at the body for a while. He wondered what the old man was trying to do. No. He knew exactly what he was trying to do.

• • •

The sun rose the next day. The tables were back in place. Signore Flamel's body was burned along with everything associated with the ritual. All Niccolo could do now was stare into space. He managed to put his right arm in a splint and a sling.

For a while, Niccolo wondered what Signore Flamel thought of him as he walked through that door. Unknowingly, Niccolo had stepped into a spider's web and the spider took seven years to finally pierce into its prey. He then began to understand the nature of the ritual: it required a sacrifice. That sacrifice would be the key to opening the universe. Or at least, that was what Niccolo could understand. Of all the things that Niccolo could grasp, the strange rituals and (for lack of a better term) "spells" that Signore Flamel used within his work evaded him. Sometimes, Niccolo could feel a presence hanging around the old man. Something dark and powerful.

Even then, Niccolo paid no attention. He desperately wanted to know more. Nothing else was as important as the consumption of knowledge. The last seven years were the most invigorating. Everything was new, wondrous, spectacular, riveting. Everything was a puzzle waiting to be solved. It took all of his time and energy. It was worth it. Some of it was worth it.

Niccolo heard a knock at the door. He snapped back into reality and looked towards the sound. Again, a rap of three knocks sounded. He got up from his chair and limped toward the door. He was still recovering from the night before. He stopped at the door and waited to hear the knocks again. He wanted to be sure.

But the thing on the other side did not move. He felt a presence like none other, a taunting, daring spirit that almost doubted that he had the nerve. Niccolo turned the lock. Behind the door stood a tall figure dressed in luxurious reds and golds, with a large, wide-brimmed hat trimmed with a white feather. The man held a cane with a lion's head for the handle. The figure had a cape draped across one shoulder and a blood-red ruby ring on the right pointer finger.

The figure was looking down, but as he raised his head, Niccolo saw a dashing man. His face was strong, his mouth was in a permanent smirk, his eyes were bright green, and his voice was lilting, yet somehow jolly, like the purring meow of a charismatic cat.

Niccolo blinked in alarm. "Can I help you signore?"

"Yes, actually. I am looking for a man named Niccolo Mancini. He is said to be here around these parts?" The man gestured toward the wide open space that surrounded the small mill.

Niccolo, his himself a little more behind the door. He wearily stood his ground, although he did not have much strength left, "what do you want with him?"

"I have business with him. My presence was requested!" The man smiled and bowed deeply, his hat in his hand.

Niccolo drew himself back. He remembered when he cried out for anyone to help him, but he did not believe until now that his efforts were successful. He believed that a more natural occurrence had prevented him from vanishing into oblivion.

"If I were to tell you where Niccolo Mancini was, what would you do with him?"

The brilliant man shook his head. He took the head of his cane and pushed the door open into the round laboratory. He looked around. Niccolo hobbled on the other side of the table where Signore Flamel was meticulously pinning into place.

"Niccolo Mancini," said the man in a voice like a roar, "I have been summoned to aid you. You wish to possess the secrets of the universe, I have come to help you in that task."

"I don't know what I want. All I know is that I almost ceased to exist last night. Death would have been a sweeter end."

"Ah, but my friend, I would not give up on this venture. You will possess many powers that Signore Flamel could not even comprehend."

Niccolo was not surprised by this man's knowledge, but he was not so foolish as to assume that the man was harmless.

"Who are you?" Niccolo asked.

"I am a spirit from the great beyond! I fly between the spaces of the spaces between. I dwell within the pockets of time and space. I hang on the end of the crescent moon and eat the stars like they are candy!" at that, the man began to laugh.

Niccolo felt a chill run down his spine, "who are you really?"

"You will know more about me in time. But I must ask you a question. What are you willing to do to gain the knowledge of the universe."

"I no longer want this knowledge. I want to once again become an architect and die like a normal person."

"I do not believe that to be entirely true. If you wanted to, you could have left a long time ago."

"I do not think you understand, signore," Niccolo was beginning to get irritated by this fool, "I was almost consumed by my teacher of seven years. He almost took my entire life essence, and now I sit here with a man dressed for a masquerade ball with a broken arm! I do not wish for anything but peace!" he slammed his fist onto the table.

The man sat in a chair. He propped his feet up on the table, "I do not believe you are telling the truth. I believe that you have been itching to know what happened last night. What was Nicolas Flamel doing? What was his goal? Why were you fading? And how am I, this enchanting spirit before you, connected to it all? Do not lie now, Niccolo. I know more about you than you know yourself."

Niccolo looked away. The man, spirit, was right. He was curious. And for the first time in his life, he regretted that this desire was so strong.

"Could you tell me what spells Signore Flamel was using?" asked Niccolo.

"I will not waste your time with such things. I will show you how to achieve them. Even Signore Flamel did not know the ways that I know. Come! I will bring you to this new path." The man stretched out his hand, "My name is Giovanni Amato. Will you accompany me?"

Niccolo looked at the man, tired, angry, and disappointed that he could be read so easily. He shook the man's hand, and his right arm no longer felt any pain. In fact, Niccolo shortly afterward took off the splint as he got into the lavish carriage of Giovanni Amato.

The grand house of the mysterious and powerful stranger was, in fact, a castle. The estate was surrounded by lush gardens, and the castle itself sported many towers that reached towards the heavens. The man mentioned lightly that he was a humble merchant in several trades, but Niccolo knew that his dealings must be in higher places. Niccolo did not have the care to ask what those dealings were.

Niccolo stepped into the grand palace. The interior was lavish and exotic. There were stuffed peacocks that stood on marble pillars and fruits that filled the air with their foreign aromas. The amount of servants was daunting. Each person was dedicated to their work. Niccolo was simply a shadow.

Eventually, after a brisk tour, Niccolo was escorted to his rooms. A silk bed with fine embroidery, a new set of clothes within a closet, and a balcony view that looked over the valley below. Niccolo moved and did what he was told but did not process a single word spoken to him. He laid in the impossibly soft bed and stared at the ceiling.

• • •

I knew the moment that I shook hands with the strange and charismatic man that I had made a deal with the devil. I also knew that my soul was trapped within a bargain I could not refuse. At that moment, I did not care. I will admit, yes, I was curious about how Signore Flamel was able to do what he did. Yet, at the same time, I was tired. The world had caught put to me, and my efforts to run away from my past had come crashing down. I thought more and more about my father, Matilda, and all those who loved me. I missed them.

The night that I lay in my bed at Giovanni Amato's castle, I could no longer hold up the walls. I cried but made no sound. I ached but did not thrash or shout. I let the tears pour down my face and allowed my body to melt. I had no more determination, just the pain and the question of "why."

Why did my father have to die so young? Why was I born to a mother who did not love me? Why was I afraid of falling in love with Matilda? That night, wrapped in a robe, I entered the rooms of Giovanni.

The room was dark except for the light of a campfire. Sitting next to it, shrouded in darkness, was Giovanni Amato (or so he called himself). His right profile was illuminated. What was left in the dark was still in question. I approached him, and he looked up from the light of the fire. He smiled. His smile was full of mirth, pride, and welcome, all at the same time. His visible eye was full of those same things, too. Even then, I felt that behind his smile, his teeth were sharp.

I sat in a chair opposite him and began, "I know who you are."

He simply raised an eyebrow and narrowed his gaze. His tone was neutral, "you do."

I nodded, "I knew it the moment you healed my arm. I called upon you, but you are not fae, and you are not minor spirit. You have plans beyond my reckoning. But I don't care. If I continue along this path, you must fulfill my wishes. In return, I will do what you ask me."

"What does your heart desire?"

"Take away the pain and give me something worth living for."

He settled further into his chair. From the pitch black darkness, a knife gleamed against the light of the fire. He cut his palm and then cut mine. He dug once again into the palm that Nicolas Flamel had done, only this time, he dug deeper. The pain was like fire had raced against my skin.

"You wish me to do this? There will be consequences."

"You don't care about the consequences. And neither do I."

His grin turned into a toothy smile. I could have sworn that within the light his teeth were pointed, elongated, and scattered in many rows lining even the back of his throat.

"Your wish is my command!" And at that, he clasped my hand and the blood pact was sealed. I had made a deal with the devil, and there was no way that I could erase the choice I had made.

Two days afterward, the hard work began.

I sat once again in the chair opposite of Signore Amato, however this time it was a beautiful sunny day.

"In order for your greatest wishes to come true, you must find seven items. Colloquially, they are called the seven eyes of wonder. They are seven objects that will open the doors of the universe."

"I no longer want knowledge," I said.

"Yes, but you want something worth living for. Do you wish for something different?"

I knew that I didn't really have an option, "No."

"I thought not. You must find these objects. They are not jus things you can buy or find in refuse somewhere. The universe must pull you. You must listen to the currents and the flow the universe brings you to."

"My attempts to understand the universe were treacherous, if you don't remember."

"Yes, well, you didn't have me." He relaxed and beamed like a lion in a pride.

"So these things you must find will come to you in time. Then the locks will open for you and you will be able to be obtain power like none before. Now, the things worth living for, that will come in time." He rose from the chair and walked out of the drawing room.

"I have a business to attend you. I suggest that you begin looking." He nodded and left.

The work of finding those items was a puzzling thing. It wasn't even looking that was the hardest part, it was knowing where to begin and how. I began with meditation, I walked around the emasculate gardens, I confided within the servants without really bothering to know them. I was confused as to what the universe wished. I had gotten to a point where all my attempts were futile until I found a group of children playing with balls. They were rolling them across the grass and the colorful balls were knocking into each other. There didn't seem to be any rules or end goal, just silly fun from young children. They were in their own world and they adored the fun they were having. One of the young boys stopped and picked up his own ball. It was a red and gold ball with a even pointed star painted in blue.

"Would you like to join us?"

"No, little man, I do not."

"You sure? You were looking curiously at the game. I know that adults don't really like games, but why not take a chance?"

The last comment had perked up my ears. I decided to take the boy's offer, being drawn to the possibility that this may be an answer to my problem.

I played the game. I knocked the opposing balls skyward and far across the courtyard. The boys joyously ran after their toys, giggling and waiting to see what I would do next. Eventually, they decided that the game was over. They picked up their toys and ran away in opposite directions. All except the young boy who approached me.

'Curiosity is as vital an organ as the heart. And like all organs, it contains a bile that sustains it: joy within the new. You will do well to remember that as you continue your journey."

In my hand was the ball, but the boy was gone. In the middle of the day, I had met ghosts. Or were they simply messengers of the cosmos?

As I walked along, back to my rooms. I looked closer at the ball. The design had changed, the color of the start had changed to a golden color and the stripes were blue and red. I turned it over and noticed it was a checkered print with green and white. I looked around. The colors and designs of the castle, painting and sculptures, seemed to move in increments that were so small that the naked eye could not detect.

The paintings performed their movements and opened up the stories page by page, motion by motion. The statues slowly moved. A beautiful woman sitting on the edge of a pool scooped water to her mouth. Two strong men wrestling each other pushed and ebbed with the curiosity of their power. The world was full of color and motion. The world was full of curiosity. I felt surging excited. I ran back again towards the courtyard. There was a pulsing energy within every blade of grass. I could see the force of a bird's wings push the air out from under it. I saw the clouds gather their water molecules and turn over their vapors thousands of times before a second had lapsed.

I walked backwards, watching as the more I looked, the more I could see. I bumped into someone behind me and was startled. I tripped over my feet and fell onto the ground. Over me was the face of Giovanni Amato.

"You have found one of the seven eyes of wonder. Good! You must continue to listen to your surroundings. Take in everything. You will know more and see more and do more as time continues."

"What am I seeing?" I asked him.

"Everything. You have found the eye of novelty. Finding all things new."

He left. That day, I walked around until my feet grew numb, looking and documenting every last thing. I saw. I drew the schematics for the cells of plants, and I saw the formation of clouds. I could see the hearts of the servants pumping along with their muscles intricately weaving to help them perform a simple task.

I did not sleep for three days. Eventually, I had to be given a small dose of belladonna to sleep. After that, I had to learn how to control my visions. I simply would blink, and whatever was in front of me, the details of its machinations would be outlined in front of me.

A week later, I went hunting with Signore Amato. He wanted to hunt for wild boar because there was an increase of boar within the area. Several of Signore Amato's comrades and benefactors came to join the hunt. One of them being, King Rudolph II. He was a severe man. His personality dominated the entire party. He flew many of his hawks with his party of hunters in order to catch smaller game while Signore Amato's party and I went through the forest in order to find the boars. Many woodsmen came with us who were experts in finding the tracks. However, I had no interest in hunting and slipped away into another part of the forest.

Suddenly, as I walked, a haggard crow flew into me. Its claws and feathers scratched at my face as it frantically cawed and screeched. I struck my arm as hard as I could against the body of the craw and with a loud whack, it was flung to the ground..

The body of the poor creature was almost emaciated. Looking closer, one of its eyes was almost like a crystal marble, a beautiful collage of blue, green, and yellow. I slowly leaned down and gauged my finger into the socket. The marble popped out of the eye socket, and the bird disintegrated like sand.

I looked over the marble. I held it up to the light (like I once did as a child), and suddenly, a glowing line of light grew before me. Then another. And another. I followed the one that appeared first. I followed it, eventually making it back to the palace.

There were another five paths that opened up to me. I saw that at their end, all of them led to a pavilion. The pavilion was filled with laughter and music. It was the rest of the comrades that had finished with the hunt and were all cooking the fresh game. I made my way to the pavilion. Signore Amato greeted me with a toast.

"To a tremendously talented and intelligent boy. One who has found possibility within his grasp!" he raised his glass along with the others. Then he winked, and I understood what I had found: endless possibility. I pocketed the marble and sat with the party-goers. The next morning, I found myself in an unfamiliar bed.

• • •

For Niccolo, it took a year for all of the eyes of wonder to be found. All except one. As we worked together, we slowly strengthened his skills in capturing the threads of the cosmos. He was an avid learner. He worshiped at the altar of knowledge, and I gladly obliged. Finally, we converged. Finally, our stories seamlessly coalesced. I will amidst, he was a young man with a quiet spark. He did not merely know, but absorbed. He experimented often with his new pieces of knowledge.

I coddled him. I pampered him with the world, and he indulged. He forgot many things, including much of his past. He was my son, after all. That was what he understood. He was the son of Giovanni Amato, the rich and wealthy heir of a large estate. He would want for nothing.

He became quite a devilish child, probably because of my influence. He was fond of women. He wooed them, to his delight. Sometimes, they stayed for a day and sometimes longer. Yet, he was not idle. He created schematics for many devices that would save the world and then some. He found new medicines within bacteria that would cure persistent diseases. He created designs for buildings that could outlast earthquakes. He made new economic systems that could stabilize a country for thousands of years.

Some of these things he hoarded. Some of them, he did not. He sold them for a high price. Then, he allowed his name to slip away from credit. He mostly financially contributed to Italy's growing arts. He even was able to meet with clergy, allowing his sins to be annulled with a solemn monthly fee.

He was my son. I had obtained him utterly and completely. The last challenge was before him. He found the last eye of wonder.

I held a ball in honor of my son's newest discoveries within the natural sciences as well as within what he named chemistry. He grew intensely interested in the natural world as well as the human body, oftentimes studying incongruent with Leonardo DaVinci (too eccentric for my taste).

The ball was magnificent. If I do say so myself. The upper echelon of Venice attended with both their best and worst behavior. Then, entering the ballroom, glittering in gold and amber, was Niccolo. He was dressed in gold and white. Heavily embroidered and kingly. The attendants marveled at him. Some of the ladies blushed. With their eyes, I could see them planning how to seduce him.

Out of the array of strange characters, I spotted the strangest. Her Fugger and his pious daughter, Matilda. They reeked of a righteous abstinence that made my skin crawl. Yet, I could also feel and pull to them. And I knew Niccolo could feel it, too. Within his face, the slightest curl of his lips was brought to his attention. Then, he waltzed his way toward Herr Fugger and his daughter. He bowed more conservatively this time and kissed the hand of the pale dove.

Matilda's eyes were full of pain. She saw how Niccolo had changed and wept inside. Niccolo looked once more into her eyes. He lost much of himself but never forgot Matilda.

"I am glad to see you once again, Herr Fugger. I am also delighted to see you as well, Matilda!"

Matilda curtsied and stood tall, "I am glad to see you are well, Signore Mancini. You have changed much."

"Yes, a final liberation."

Herr Fugger raised an eyebrow.

"Liberation? From what?" It was too late. Matilda had asked the question, and she dreaded to hear the answer.

"The past, the present, future? Everything! A liberation from care, I suppose!" Niccolo had chuckled to himself. He was challenging Matilda. "And you? What has changed within your life?"

"Much. I am to be wed to a cousin of the Weber family. We will be wed within a month."

"Ah! Congratulations. I will toast to your happy marriage!" said Niccolo excitedly.

Niccolo left them and began to flatter the party guests as they whisked their way around him. Matilda was heartbroken. She also sensed something was wrong. Every word from Niccolo's mouth seemed hollow. Her father kept her close. They were only there to be able to make negotiations with other Italian merchants. Yet, Matilda couldn't help but stare at him, watching him. Wondering what had changed. What had gone wrong.

Niccolo fluttered like a peacock around the room and then left through a private alcove. Within the dark corridor hidden away, his face melted. He was cold. His eyes were empty. Like a puppet, he stammered up a flight of stairs and settled into a small sitting room with one window. The moon was full. He summoned up the planets Jupiter, Saturn and Venus, configuring them together and then separating them into a million combinations. He molded them in his hands and then let them shatter to the floor. He watched the broken pieces disappear.

He was not alone. Looking now, he saw the small glint of a candle frame the face of Matilda. Tears were streaming down her face.

"What has happened to you? Your soul has left you", she shivered in the darkness.

"I have done exactly what I intended. Yet, it is not finished. You have something I desire."

A chill came over the stairway. Niccolo, now clad in black, noiselessly stepped further towards Matilda. Matilda tried to run, but the door closed behind her. The wood of the small space began to creak, voicing Matilda's fear where her own voice failed. Niccolas, with a wave of his hand, pulled Matilda towards him. Her body contorted and grew limp like a rag doll. He held her up in the air.

"You have what I need. Give it to me!" His voice was hoarse and deep.

Around Matilda's neck was a pearl necklace. One pearl in particular was a darker color, almost gray. It was not as smooth as the others. She had found a freshwater pearl. She had it fashioned into the necklace her fiancé had gifted her.

Niccolo ripped the necklace off of her neck and flung her back. Her bones cracked, and she was dead.

Niccolo held the small pearl in his hand. He rubbed it gently like it was a baby bird. His eyes were impossibly wide and impossibly bright. He walked back into the ballroom. It was void and dark. The moon was high once more. His chance was finally here.

"Are you ready, son of Man?" I asked.

"Yes. Angel of Light, I am ready." he nodded and bowed.

"What is my name?"

"You are Lucifer. The cursed one!" he cried.

At last, Niccolo sliced open his hand. By now, his body was suffused with magic, and his blood turned almost a blue-black. So dark it was impossible for the human eye to understand it. The boy eagerly smeared his blood on the ground, and the light from the runes began to gleam.

He carefully placed each object carefully. I stretched my hand.

"There was one thing that Signore Flamel forgot. He did not divide his soul. You have achieved what he failed to do."

"I give myself willingly." The child almost sounded on the verge of death

The room burst into a showering glow of gold. The floor beneath opened up. Within seconds, the whole of the universe latched onto Niccolo as it filled his eyes and his mouth. Like a whirlwind, he was caught up in the air.

I could hear his thoughts, his last wishes for death, his last wishes to be reborn.

"This pain, this glory. IT IS TOO MUCH! MAKE IT STOP," his mind ached, "FATHER!"

He screamed his last words, and then he collapsed onto the cold ground. He was dead.

Before his spirit rose, I snatched him from the air. We had a deal, after all.

The ground closed, and the house was empty. The seven eyes of wonder crumbled into dust and the fate of Niccolo Mancini ended with his soul in the Devil's hands.